Masking ENEMIES

A Historical Novel of 1803

Enemies Series v.3

By

Mary Ann Trail

ISBN: 978-1798489260 (paperback)

Contents

Acknowledgments

No novel (or at least none of mine) are completed without the help, expertise and time of others. I want to acknowledge and to deeply express my gratitude to Elaine Ingulli, Elaine is my primary editor who keeps me on track and focused with the right amount of criticism and encouragement. My beta readers spent a lot of time helping me find the glitches and typos. Thank you to Cheryle Eisele, Deb Dagavarian, Carol Nestor, and Camille Sauerwald,

Thank you, again to my daughters who remain steadfast in their encouragement and cheerleading.

Chapter One: Corfe Castle, Dorset England Spring 1803

Clive

C live kicked the rock again. This time, the damn thing actually levitated and flew over a hump of rubble from the old castle wall. He could not see where the stone landed, but he assumed it was not far away since the blasted sheep grazing some hundred yards away kept at it as though nothing had landed in their midst. His shoulders slumped. "What am I doing here?" he wondered despondently. "I should be at University with the fellows. I am missing all the end-of-spring term festivities."

He looked around for something else on which to take his frustration out. As far as he could see, Corfe Castle did not offer much besides rocks. Perched on the top of a rise, it was the highest point in the surrounding Purbeck Hills. Grant had pointed out this obvious fact on the carriage ride from London. Clive was pretty sure Grant had talked more about Corfe's importance in history, but his own interest in history had never been strong and he had not paid a lot of attention, being more taken with his own sense of being unfairly persecuted.

His father had been quite clear: he had to follow Grant around this summer, all over southwest England evidently, looking at mounds of rocks, dirt, and whatever else Grant deemed interesting. If he did, then the old man would pay for him to go back to university. If he did not, he was going to be cut off and would have to return home. At that point, his father had growled about learning something useful like husbandry or accounts, skills his father felt Clive needed to take over the family properties.

Clive's temper rose as he remembered the interview with his father. What had he done to get him so up in the boughs about? Lots of fellows got sent down from university for much worse. He certainly had not done anything others had not done, he thought resentfully. *They* got sent home for a few weeks and then went back to Oxford. He, on the other hand, had an old man who was so straight-laced he could not understand a few friends just having a lark. Now he was forced to give up his whole summer to follow his old tutor around "historic sites." Humiliating, that's what is was – damn humiliating.

Grant, who had been Clive's tutor before he went to university, was a good enough fellow, he had to admit, but he was not very exciting. Certainly not one for drinking and gaming like Clive's Oxford classmates. And he barely knew the rest of the travelling group. He had met Dr. Chadwick a few times, but only briefly. If he remembered rightly, Chadwick was past middle-age. Without a doubt, he would want to spend his time navigating the various monuments and other rubbish they were planning to visit. And the others? Who knew what they would be like?

Clive gave a low snarl of anger as he looked for another rock.

"What are you doing?" demanded an outraged voice. A female voice. Clive looked around with interest.

Striding around some of the rubble from the internal castle walls was a young woman. She fairly vibrated with indignation.

"What gives you the right to lob rocks at harmless sheep?" she continued. "Do you not have anything to do but damage property and try to hurt animals when they have done nothing to you?"

Clive smothered his initial surprise at finding someone else in the castle ruins. He had thought he was alone. But as she continued to harangue him, his sense of injustice rushed back. What right did she have to correct him? Even if she was pretty…

"Do what?" he demanded, picking up on the last thing he heard. "What else is there to do here?" That seemed to shut her up.

But not for long. She turned in a complete circle with her arms outstretched.

"Admire the scenery, the peacefulness, the sense of nature," she retorted. "People travel a long way to admire what is right here, the picturesque!" she ended dramatically.

Clive made a point of looking in all directions. "The picturesque?" he asked sarcastically. "It is a mass of stones on a hill surrounded by sheep. Loud, noisy sheep! Smelly sheep!" he added.

"Well, if you are not here to admire the scenery," she returned, "maybe you could just go back to your hole or pub or whatever you crawled out of and leave those of us who want to admire the views alone."

She gestured towards the main gate and stomped off the way she had come. Clive watched her go. Her backside was almost as worth looking at as her front. He was struck by how good-looking she was – tallish with a lot of blonde hair tied away from her face with a simple ribbon at the nape of her neck. The white dress she wore fitted her closely enough that he could see she was shapely. He was not close enough to see the color of her eyes, but he could see they snapped when she was angry. And she had the temperament of a shrew.

He looked around the ruins, wondering how he could see where she had gone without following her and risk being accused of skulking. He had entered the ruins via the main gate leading from the village and then gone through the outer bailey. Enough of the outer walls were still standing to identify the footprint of the castle; some walls even appeared to be intact. But the keep and the rest of the castle had been reduced to rubble. He imagined a lot of the dressed stone could be found in the houses and buildings of the Dorset. Certainly, where he came from, the rock used in monasteries often ended up as ready-made materials for new construction.

In the middle of the debris, Clive thought there was more rubble that should have been removed. There were stairs going nowhere, parts of internal walls with no roof to hold up, and an archway leading to the main gate. This wreckage kept the visitor from seeing across the complete bailey. A tourist had to follow the outer wall to take in the view from all sides. And, he assumed, the view was the only thing that kept visitors coming here.

But the stairs to nowhere offered height. They also seemed to offer the best vantage point to view the castle grounds. He decided to climb the stairs to see where the young woman had wandered off. Once he reached the top of what turned out to be no more than eight or nine steps, he could see the entire grounds. Sure enough, she had not gone far. She was now seated primly on a blanket on the far side of the bailey, rearranging her sketching materials. She had upset her pencils and paper when she stomped over to speak her mind.

He watched curiously as she turned her back to the bucolic scene before her and raised a looking glass. It took him a minute to realize she had a set of Claude glasses. His sisters had just gotten a set. They were all the rage in London, they had assured him in lofty tones. Everyone was using them to give their drawings a more "picturesque" angle. They had shown him how to use them by turning his back to the subject, holding the small round glass in front of him, and reflecting the image onto the glass from over his shoulder. The shape of each glass made the subject appear as if night had fallen, or a heavy fog had moved in, or white snow had covered everything. Clive had found his sisters' efforts hard to comment on without laughing. He hoped this young woman's sketches were better and easier to flatter.

She was certainly a lot prettier than his sisters. As he started down the steps, he scanned the area for a chaperone. His boredom slipped even farther away as he realized they were alone in the ruins. Then his spirits dropped when he recognized Grant coming through the main gate with a companion – Dr. Chadwick, unless he missed his guess. They seemed deep in conversation. Clive thought he might have just enough time to chat up the young miss before Grant found him. With his eyes on his goal, he made his way down the broken steps and around the freestanding walls.

"You are absolutely right," he started. "I should not be taking out my temper on harmless sheep."

But the sheep...the sheep were everywhere. Clive had grown up surrounded by sheep and he had little love for them and their constant noise. "*Day and night,*" he thought irritably, "*the damn things never shut up.*" Even up here, the hills were filled with flocks of ewes and their lambs.

But to get *her* attention, he would become a shepherd, if necessary.

She ignored him.

He tried again. "Please accept my apologies for interrupting your work."

He paused to see if she was still ignoring him. Her attention was still on the glass, and she was carefully not looking at him. She was a challenge. He loved a challenge. "I see you have some of those new Claude glasses. May I see how you have incorporated them into your work?"

This time, the blond head turned to him. She surveyed him with icy eyes. "Did you decide I was more interesting than the sheep?" she asked frostily.

"Absolutely, you are more interesting than the sheep," he answered earnestly. "I am here with my old tutor and all he wants to do is natter on about battles and historical political maneuvering. I find art much more interesting than sheep and rocks any day." He was not sure what expression would be most effective, so he tried for sincere. "I do not sketch well myself, but my sisters are always at it."

Had her gaze softened slightly?

"What do they sketch?"

"Scenery. Their work is not much different from what you are doing here," Clive said. Although she had not invited him to sit, he plonked himself down on the edge of her blanket. Not too close. Frightening her off would ruin the afternoon and leave him no one with whom to flirt.

He moved from sincere to earnest. "They seem to like producing landscapes – the more rural, the better. Sometimes they work on castles or other ruins. Personally, I think it is because drawing human figures is rather challenging. But I have to say, there seem to be sheep in almost everything they do."

"Sheep?" she asked with what seemed like amusement.

"Sheep," he agreed solemnly. "Big ones – lambs, flocks, in everything."

She gave a low chuckle. "You are incorrigible. I bet you do not even have any sisters and you are making up stories about their sketches to make my acquaintance." She paused and picked up her pencils, obviously planning to continue her sketch.

"Oh no," he said defensively, "I most definitely have sisters. Two, in fact. I am the youngest and they have been the bane of my existence since the day I was born." He decided to ignore the rest of her remarks, as they were partly true. "Do you have any siblings?" he asked.

"Ah, good, there you are." Grant's voice broke in before she could answer. At the same time, the other man spoke. "Frederica, excellent…"

Grant and his companion had arrived faster than Clive had thought possible. Clive looked over his shoulder to where two men stood under an archway formed by one of the walls that no longer connected to anything. Grant was dressed in his usual dark clothes; the other man had on a rather festive vest with yellow and blue stripes, and he leaned on a cane. He remembered meeting Dr. Chadwick a few times when he had visited Grant. Chadwick had joined the family at the dinner table, and Clive remembered with amusement his father's eyes glazing over as the two scholars discussed antiquities. But he also remembered the older scholar as both having a sense of humor and being kind.

As Clive decided to do the polite thing and was forcing himself to his feet, he heard but did not see what happened next. He heard Grant's companion say, "Grant, that is…" when he was interrupted by a loud thump. Frederica gave a dismayed exclamation and struggled to her feet. He followed her appalled glance to the archway, where the two men now lay on the ground. A massive rock sat on the ground between them, the dust still settling.

Grant was already regaining his feet, but the older man just lay there stunned. The young woman had scrambled to her feet and thrown herself at the side of the prostrate man, anxiously patting his shoulders and arms.

"Uncle Festus, are you alright? Are you hurt?"

At the same time, Clive asked, "Grant, are you well? What happened?"

"No, child. We're not hurt."

Uncle Festus seemed remarkably calm for an older gentleman lying on the ground. Before Clive or Grant could help him up, he patted the young woman's shoulder and pointed to a boulder-sized piece of castle wall lying nearby. "These old ruins are sometimes unreliable. As you can see, we barely missed being flattened by that rock. However, no one's hurt."

"Are you sure, Uncle Festus? You are dreadfully pale."

"Well, maybe the rock bounced off my shoulder," the older man admitted. "Quite shocking how heavy it is." He struggled into a sitting position, but it was obvious he was in pain.

Before the gentleman could make another move to get up, Clive moved behind him.

"Let me help you up, sir," he said. "Are you sure nothing is broken or sprained?" When the man shook his head, Clive put his hands under the man's arms. "I will lift you from behind," Clive said. "It will be easier for you to get your balance that way. Try to get your feet under you."

As he hefted the man to his feet, he kept his arms in position to steady him. Grant had moved closer and took the older man's arm as he gained his balance. Clive could see the young woman had already gained her feet and was dusting off the knees of her gown. He felt a moment of regret that he had not been able to help her up and get his arm around her waist. She was quite delectable.

"Thank you, young man." The older man was addressing Clive. "Very lucky for us you happened to be here today."

Clive was about to explain that he was with Grant, when Grant gave him a small gesture to remain silent.

The older man continued, "M'dear, I want you to meet Mr. Thomas Grant. He's my very dear friend, the one I told you we would be meeting here."

Frederica swiveled to look at Grant, who was now replacing his spectacles. Keeping his hand on the old man's arm, Grant shook the young woman's hand, rather formally, Clive thought.

"I am very pleased to meet you, Miss Frederica. I am sorry Jeffrey could not join us. I would enjoy seeing my former student again, but I am sure his charming sister will make a welcome substitute."

Understanding flooded Clive. He knew Dr. Festus Chadwick was one of the people with whom Grant had said they were to travel. The other traveler should have been Jeffrey Chadwick, another one of Grant's former students. But there had been a last-minute substitution. With the lovely Frederica replacing Jeffrey on this trip, the whole adventure had suddenly become much more interesting.

Grant smiled warmly at her, then turned to take Uncle Festus by the arm. "I think I would welcome a cup of tea after all the excitement. It is not every day I get tossed into the dirt by falling debris."

"Were you also hit by the rock?" Clive asked.

"No," Grant responded calmly, "but I did end up in the dirt, and Dr. Chadwick is still rather pale. I believe there is a tea room at the entrance to the castle." His calm and somewhat formal speech did much to quiet the situation and perhaps, Clive thought, minimize the seriousness. He noticed Frederica was studying her uncle anxiously.

Still holding the older man's arm, Grant turned him back to the path by which they had walked in. Clive could hear him saying something about revisiting the castle ruins after they had rested a bit and fortified themselves.

Clive turned to the attractive young artist and found her again pointedly ignoring him. She was packing up her Claude glasses and sketching materials without saying a word to him. Clive followed her meekly and carefully folded her blanket, all the time studying her. What he saw was a slim, young blond.

Her white dress, the skirt now with dusty streaks, had long sleeves and a high neckline. A white ribbon bound her hair keeping it out of her face. Brown eyes that should have been warm, now flashed with indignation instead. Her mouth, though, really caught his attention. Her full red lips curved up into a natural smile, giving her the appearance of smiling even when she was angry. And right now, she looked as furious as any of his sisters when he managed to prank them. But why she was angry, he did not understand. She had been on her way to forgiving him for the stupid rock kick and he had not had time to do anything else. But the set of her shoulders, purposeful stride, flashing eyes, and way she ignored him made it clear she was upset about something.

Still in silence, they started for the main gate. Suddenly, she whirled around and demanded, "Why are you following me?"

Silently, Clive held up the blanket. She snatched it away.

"Go away," she ordered. "You have done enough damage."

Baffled, Clive looked at her blankly. "What…what did I do this time?"

"What difference does it make? I do not know you, and I do not want to know you. You are careless and have total disregard for people. Go away."

Clive realized she did not know he was with Mr. Grant. She must just think him a random visitor to the ruins. He opened his mouth to introduce himself, when again he saw Grant approaching.

"Excellent! Clive, Miss Frederica," Grant hailed them, "Dr. Chadwick just realized he must have dropped his watch when he tumbled. Would you two be good enough to return to that archway and have a look to see if you can find it?"

"Of course," Frederica answered promptly. She whirled around and practically sprinted back up the path.

"Um, Grant…" Clive tried to explain the confusion about identities.

"Go, go," Grant said hurriedly. "I don't want to leave Festus alone. I think he is more hurt than he lets on. Meet us at the Greyhound Hotel. You will recognize it by the pillars at the door." He turned and rushed away before Clive could finish a sentence.

Clive caught up to Frederica with little effort. After all, she was now carrying all her art supplies as well as the blanket. She was back on her knees, intently studying the ground.

"Anything yet?" he asked.

"Why are you still here?" she retorted.

"Grant asked me to come help search," he answered simply.

Now, her bad mood was getting tiresome. He stood in the archway and studied the ground as intently as she, but because he was standing, he had sight of a larger area.

"He was talking to me," she responded shortly.

"Is your name Clive?" he asked with some sarcasm. "I thought it was Frederica Chadwick."

"How did you know that?" she demanded.

"You don't listen much, do you?" Clive said. "Grant mentioned it."

Finally, he saw a glint. "Look over there." He pointed to the rock. "Just off to the side, where the grass starts."

Frederica, still on her knees, leaned forward, giving him another good view of her backside.

"Got it!" she exclaimed, standing with the watch clutched in her fist. "Now, would you explain why Mr. Grant calls you Clive? You are too well-dressed to be a servant, so what is the real story?"

"The simple explanation is that my name is Clive Dering," he sighed. "But the full explanation is going to take some time."

"We have between here and the gate," she snapped, glaring at him.

Frederica was beautiful, but she definitely had a temper. He gave a deep sigh as he picked up her blanket. She snatched her box of pencils and paper and made to stride off.

"At least you can walk at a reasonable rate and give me a chance to explain. I don't think it is fair for you to run off and not listen," he protested.

She slowed, waited for him to catch up, and then resumed a more normal pace.

"I am listening."

"A couple of weeks ago, maybe a little longer, my father sent a note to Grant asking him to tutor me for the summer. Grant was my tutor in the years before I went up to university. However, my grades at Oxford are not what they should be," he admitted. Depending on what Grant had told her Uncle Festus, maybe he could spin the story so he did not look the total ass.

"You got sent down from university," she said flatly.

Not admitting exactly what he had gotten expelled for, Clive nodded. "But I can go back in the fall."

"Hmm."

The main gate was looming before them, so Clive finished the story quickly. "Grant wrote back and suggested I join him and a couple of fellows on a trip around the historic sites of the southwest. There was not time to set the trip up formally; I only had time to meet him in London. In fact, I do not think he had time to fill your uncle in on my participation. I assume he is explaining everything to him right now at the tea room."

"You are coming with us on the trip?" she sounded astonished. "Why?"

"Well, Grant was not free to tutor me at home, so this seemed a reasonable alternative. We travel about while Grant and I do some book work on the side."

Frederica stopped suddenly in the middle of the path and turned to face him. "I doubt very much Uncle Festus would have agreed to your coming with us if he had known about it."

Clive had to agree. It was stretching propriety for her to be travelling with two older men; add one her own age and eyebrows would definitely go up.

"I suspect Grant also did not know about you or he would not have suggested it," he said.

"I think you are probably right that Uncle Festus does not know about you. And I feel sure that when he does, you are going to be sent home to find another way to waste your summer," she retorted.

"Look, I apologized about kicking the rock at the sheep. That was petty of me. Why are you still angry?" he questioned. "Since Dr. Chadwick organized this trip, he certainly is not going to send you home. If anything, he will kick *me* out of the group."

"As he should," she practically snarled. "You are a careless sort with total disregard for others' safety or property."

"What are you talking about?" he asked, confused. "That rock was not even big enough to startle the sheep. They never even noticed."

"Not that pebble, you idiot," she rejoined. "The rock that fell and hit Uncle Festus. *That* rock!"

"I did not have anything to do with that rock," he protested hotly.

"I saw you up those stairs looking around. You must have knocked it loose."

"That is ridiculous," he responded.

"Is it?" she countered. "Rocks that have been in place for centuries do not just tumble down of their own accord. You had to have loosened it somehow."

She must have felt she had the final word, as she turned and marched towards the main entrance.

Clive kept step with her. He was furious. He had gone up those steps, taken a look around, and then come down. He did not even remember seeing a boulder the size of the one that had fallen. He certainly had not intentionally loosened anything that could have fallen down to injure anyone. Yes, he was frustrated about being forced to spend his summer looking at historical sites instead of enjoying himself at school, but no way was he trying to hurt anyone.

"I did not loosen any rocks up there." He tried to speak calmly, but he could hear his voice rise in frustration, as she obviously did not believe him. "I did climb the stairs, but that was only so I could see where you had gone. I came right back down."

"Did you see anyone else around who might have done it?" Frederica tossed over her shoulder.

"No, I saw only you and then Mr. Grant and Dr. Chadwick," he admitted.

"You are careless and thoughtless, and I do not want you ruining my trip," she exploded.

"*Your* trip?" he rejoined. Irrationally, now that there was a possibility he might not be welcome on the tour, he was determined to go. Besides his ambivalence about returning home, she was by far prettier and more interesting that any of his more recent acquaintances. "Thankfully, you are not the only person making decisions about this trip."

"We will see about that!"

Thankfully, Clive spotted The Greyhound. "There is the hotel where we are supposed to meet Grant and Dr. Chadwick." he pointed out, gesturing at the buildings with the columns at the door.

A change in direction was her only response.

Chapter Two: Sparks

Frederica

Frederica stormed into the Greyhound Hotel. Between the main gate to Corfe Castle and the door of the hotel, she had lost track of the number of names she had called him in her head, arrogant, selfish, and thoughtless being the kindest of them. Even as she stretched her brain to devise even more inventive ways to castigate Clive's nature, Mr. Grant came out the door of the dining room looking for them.

"Oh, there you are. Come on in. The tea and cakes are here and Dr. Chadwick is wondering about your absence." He held the door and gestured them into the room.

Before Frederica could explain that they had spent much of the time arguing, her unwanted companion cut in. "It took us a bit to locate the watch. It tucked itself almost under that boulder that caused the ruckus in the first place. Thankfully, it was not crushed and seems to be working normally. That is, if Miss Chadwick has not crushed it in her fist," he added with a smile.

How Dering knew that it was working, Frederica could not tell. He had never handled the thing. She opened her fingers to show Mr. Grant the watch.

"How did you know it was not broken?" she demanded.

"I am sure you would have mentioned it, Miss Chadwick, if it had been broken," Dering responded, "and you would have added it to my list of transgressions. By the way, how is Dr. Chadwick, Tommy?"

The trio moved into the tearoom, where they found Uncle Festus enthroned by the fire and looking much better and with more color in his face. In front of him was a table loaded with sandwiches, small cakes, and pots of tea. There were other small tables scattered around the room, but only a few other patrons who sat nibbling on pastries and talking quietly.

Frederica placed the leather folder containing her sketching materials on an empty chair and gave Uncle Festus another hug. "Are you feeling better?" she asked with concern.

He patted her arm and said, "I may have been a bit more bruised than I first thought, but I am sure some tea and rest will set me to rights. Now sit and have some tea yourself. We have a slight change of plans to discuss."

Clive carefully placed the blanket over the back of another chair and went to greet Uncle Festus. To Frederica's amazement, they not only shook hands but also hugged each other like long-lost relatives.

Mr. Grant held Frederica's chair as he explained. "While Clive was a student of mine, he met and sometimes studied with Dr. Chadwick, usually when Dr. Chadwick was visiting me at Ripon. That is where the Dering home is. Indeed, Clive's presence here comes as a surprise to Dr. Chadwick. Clive's father's request came just a couple of weeks ago, so I had no time to write and tell your uncle of the addition to our party. Ironic, as Dr. Chadwick similarly had no time to write me about you." He smiled ruefully at Frederica. "Please, sit here, Miss Chadwick, and pour for us?"

To Frederica's close scrutiny, Uncle Festus seemed much less ashen. He was certainly animated enough talking to Clive. She poured his tea and added several scoops of sugar. When she leaned forward to hand it to her uncle, Clive jumped up in appropriate fashion to place the tea where Dr. Chadwick could easily reach it and then filled a plate with sandwiches and cakes for him. At least he had some manners, she thought. She softened a bit when she saw that he was treating her uncle respectfully. Frederica turned to the tutor. "How would you like your tea, Mr. Grant?"

"Just one sugar and a little milk," Grant answered in the measured way that Frederica was coming to recognize.

After preparing Grant's tea, Frederica turned her attention to her unexpected travelling companion sitting across the table. Pot held expectantly, she raised her eyebrows questioningly.

Now that she had time to study him, she saw a young man not much taller than she, but solidly built with broad shoulders. His clothing denoted a gentleman without the touch of the dandy or the flashy styles of some of the men she had seen in Tunbridge Wells. His trousers were brown and he wore knee-high boots. A black coat topped a white shirt and loosely tied cravat. He wore his clothes with a studied casualness – or maybe just comfort – she associated with her brother Jeffrey. But it was his hair that caused her a flash of jealousy. It was a deep rich chestnut and fell perfectly straight. Her hair, neither straight nor curly required a lot of time with the curling iron to achieve either style.

Frederica had to admit to herself that his appearance was in direct contrast to her accusation at his having been cavalier about loosening rocks that had caused the accident. In addition, his now-respectful demeanor did not fit the mischief that had twinkled in his blue eyes or the quirky slant to his mouth.

Instead of answering her unspoken question about the tea, he grinned at her and turned to his former tutor. "Grant, I am afraid that with the chaos in the castle, no one formally introduced me to Miss Chadwick. She might still be under the impression I am your valet."

While she sputtered at the thought that he was a valet, Grant immediately put down his tea. "I am so sorry, Miss Chadwick," he said. "Clive is correct, but such an oversight can easily be corrected. May I introduce Clive Dering, a former student of mine? His father asked if he could be added to our little trek, as he is at loose ends this summer and could benefit from some extra tutoring."

Frederica, who had been watching Clive during this explanation, saw him give a sigh of relief. What was it that Grant knew but Dering did not want Uncle Festus or her to find out?

"Clive," Grant continued, "this is Miss Frederica Chadwick, who is, as you now know, Dr. Chadwick's niece and Jeffrey Chadwick's sister."

Clive finally seemed to take pity on her still holding the tea pot and asked, "May I have one sugar and lots of milk?" He smirked but thanked her properly before he turned to Uncle Festus to ask, "Where's Jeffrey, Dr. Chadwick? I thought Grant said he would be joining us."

Uncle Festus answered, "Well, Clive, Jeffrey thought so, too."

Frederica listened with some surprise as Uncle Festus related his version of the events that had led to her joining him on this tour to find the "picturesque." He calmly explained how Jeffrey, Mr. Grant, and he had been planning a trip to various historical sites when Jeffrey's appointment to the Alien Office in Dublin came through and he was ordered to report there as soon as possible.

"One of the vagaries of his position there, you know." Jeffrey had asked his uncle to take Frederica in his place and he, Festus, was very glad to do so. He smiled warmly at Frederica as he finished. "Jeffrey and Frederica are the only relatives I have left. I enjoy spending as much time as possible with them."

Frederica's version was a bit different, but she assumed Uncle Festus was just glossing over family issues. Surely Jeffrey had enlisted his aid in arranging the trip and Frederica's inclusion. As she poured her own tea, her mind drifted back a year to the death of her beloved father.

* * *

After the funeral, she and her step-mother Hermione had been left to live alone in the house in Kent. Although Jeffrey was executor of the estate, they did not see him much. His position with the Home Office kept him in London most of the time. (Frederica was not positive what Jeffrey did there, since it seemed so hush-hush.) He had tried to make up for his absences by sending Frederica books and art supplies. Any day that brought a letter from Jeffrey was cause for happiness.

In some ways, Hermione did not change. Before her husband's death, Mistress Chadwick had generally ignored Frederica's existence and left her to the company of her governess, Elizabeth Black, and of course her father when he had time. However, once she gained charge over the household finances, Hermione tightened the reins on purchases and tried to reduce household expenses.

"We must practice economy," she repeated many times. "Your father did not leave as much as he had hoped."

This caused major changes in the household, most particularly in Frederica's life. The governess was dismissed first. In fairness to her step-mother, Frederica had to admit that this was not an inappropriate change, given that she had turned eighteen and was ready to make her entrance into society. Girls no longer had a governess at that age. Unfortunately for Frederica, Miss Black had become more of a friend and confidante than a teacher, so the loss was especially hard on Frederica, who managed to persuaded Hermione to pay Miss Black's wages for the rest of the year.

Then her pony was sold.

"He is too small for you now."

She missed riding Ginger, but she had to agree with her step-mother that the hard riding she enjoyed was not appropriate behavior for a young woman whose father had recently died. And, she agreed, the pony was actually too small for her. Somehow, though, Frederica had assumed a new horse would arrive after they were out of mourning.

Now that the mourning year had ended, it was acceptable for the young woman to wear quiet colors other than black. Hermione did indeed provide some print muslin, but not much.

"It is not a good time to purchase a lot of new dresses until you finish growing," she explained. "Besides, you will get a new wardrobe when you go to London for your debut."

She rarely won an argument with Hermione, so Frederica did not point out that she had likely finished growing, as she was the same size she had been at fifteen. Instead, she tried to make the best of things. Frederica was not an experienced seamstress, so she had enlisted the help of their housekeeper. The results were certainly wearable but lacked the polish of the dresses made in London, like those her father had bought her. She now regretted dying all her old dresses black, wishing she had kept some to wear once the mourning period was over. The lack of color in her life was almost as depressing as losing her only companion.

After Miss Black had been dispatched, Frederica realized how much she had depended on her and her father for companionship. There had not been many young people in her father's immediate circle, so she had not formed any real friendships with girls her age. For the year following, as dictated by society, she had stayed quietly at home with little but her art to keep her company.

It had been an unexpected relief, though, to find that Miss Black had not moved far when Hermione had let her go. Once her duties as governess ended, she immediately married the local curate, James Randall. The couple lived within walking distance of the Chadwicks' home, in the village near the church.

"We were waiting for you to grow up and not need me anymore," Miss Black had explained. Well, that clarified the curate's frequent visits to the Chadwick house over the years. Frederica laughed to herself, remembering that she had always thought Mr. Randall just liked her father's brandy. She certainly had been blind to that romance! The two kind souls welcomed Frederica's almost daily visits during that long, lonely year after her father's death.

Hermione's social life, however, didn't seem to be as affected by the death of her husband. She continued to go to card parties and musicals as if everything was perfectly normal. "Nothing public, you understand, just close friends. I don't think your father would have wanted me to waste away grieving for him," she explained.

Frederica was sure her father would not have wanted Hermione to waste away, either. In Frederica's experience, he had never denied her step-mother anything. But, in truth, they had not gone about much together. Her father had often traveled and, when he did, Hermione had often entertained local friends both at their home and in Tunbridge Wells. Occasionally, the couple had traveled to London together, but as Frederica usually had been left home with Miss Black, she had no idea how that had gone.

The young orphan had trouble understanding how Hermione even wanted to go about or how Hermione could say the spa at Tunbridge Wells was "not a very public place." When asked, Miss Black (now Mistress Randall) said she thought Mistress Chadwick would only be seeing very close friends, not attending public assemblies or concerts. And, of course, drinking the waters was for health purposes, nothing for which a new widow could be criticized. Frederica had to agree that Hermione was quite different emotionally from herself, as she was satisfied with solitude and visiting the Randalls and did not, she insisted, resent not being included in her step-mother's travels.

Her former governess also delicately tried to explain how having a full-grown step-daughter might make Hermione feel less than young.

"I think she does not take you with her because it might make her look…" Mistress Randall paused for thought. "Um, the comparison?…"

"Oh," said Frederica thoughtfully, "do you mean I make her look old?"

Mistress Randall nodded in agreement.

"But Hermione is not very old, not even forty, I think, and she still looks fine." Truthfully, Frederica had not studied her step-mother's appearance in ages. She was just there, like the furniture, always the same.

"It is not as if you make her look old," Mistress Randall continued. "It is how she thinks it makes her look. She might be worried that people prefer the fresh and young over the more known figures."

Frederica gave a most unladylike snort. "It is not as if I was in competition for male attention. I am not even out in society yet."

Mistress Randall gave a shrug. "Again, my dear," she said, "it is the perception, not the reality, I fear your step-mother worries about."

It was during one of Hermione's stays at Tunbridge Wells that Jeffrey had showed up unexpectedly in Kent. Uncle Festus later told Frederica that Jeffrey had been upset, even furious when he found his sister home alone with the few remaining servants. Frederica had never seen Jeffrey's angry side. To her, he was always her sophisticated, polished brother.

He never wore his uniform anymore, but he was still as tall and fit as when he had served in the King's forces. In the few days before Hermione got home, he was only kindness and consideration. The siblings spent a lot of time together. They went walking over the Kentish countryside, where their conversation drifted from memories of their father to their favorite books. They often spent the evenings reading together. Jeffrey seemed very interested in her art and spent a flattering amount of time studying her sketches.

But one night, Jeffrey started asking questions that seemed odd until Frederica realized he was asking about Hermione.

"Frederica, you seem so alone here. Wouldn't it have been better to keep Miss Black on for a while longer? Or did she leave because she wanted to get married?"

"I would have loved to keep Miss Black on, but Hermione told me we needed to economize. And besides, Mistress Randall, as she is now known, was waiting for me to grow up so she could marry. Did you ever meet James Randall? He is the local curate and probably will get the vicar position soon."

"I've never met him, but I have heard about him from Miss Black. She wrote me that you felt you were too old to have a governess and it was an unnecessary expense. She also reminded me that you would be old enough for your season in London to be introduced to society." Jeffrey frowned into his brandy. Looking up, he asked, "Did you sell Ginger for the same reason?"

"I had gotten too tall for a pony. Hermione did say the upkeep of the horses is expensive. She sold all the saddle horses. You know she rarely rides herself and kept only two for the carriage. That way she could reduce the number of stablemen we need."

"There are no stablemen here right now," Jeffrey said. "I had to stable my own horse."

"The driver went to Tunbridge Wells with Hermione," Frederica explained.

"I've only seen a cook and housemaid here now. Is that all the staff?"

"Hermione took her ladies' maid, Marie; Sally, the housemaid; and Frank, the footman. She left Rose, the other housemaid, here with me and the cook. I guess she hired a cook in Tunbridge Wells. Actually, Jeffrey, with only me to look after, we don't need so much help." Frederica paused a moment, then continued, "The gardeners are still here."

Jeffrey was shaking his head and frowning. "What is the cause of all this economy, do you think?" he asked.

"Well…she said Father had left little money…" Frederica's voice trailed off.

"What else did she say?"

"That you were…a bit tight-fisted."

Jeffrey seemed to change the subject. "Why are you still in mourning? Surely as it has been a year, you should be wearing brighter colors? Gray and navy blue are colors for old women."

Before Frederica could answer, he raised his hand. "Wait, let me guess: another economizing measure?"

"I cannot actually fault her," she responded. "She said it would be wasteful to buy clothes for me as I am still growing and I will be getting a whole new wardrobe when I go up to London for my coming out."

Frederica looked down at her navy gown. She did not want to complain about her clothes, but she could see the dress from Jeffrey's point of view. It was dumpy looking and did nothing to show off her coloring. She had the muslin dress that she and the housekeeper had made, but sewing a complete dress had been a lot more difficult than she had ever imagined. She actually did not want Jeffrey to be angry with Hermione. After all, she had to live with her step-mother and if Jeffrey took Hermione to task, the older woman might somehow take it out on Frederica.

Jeffrey dropped the topic, at least with her.

Frederica decided that evening must have been when Jeffrey got the idea to take her along on the trip. It was, however, some time before he mentioned it aloud in the household. She supposed he had to check first to make sure Uncle Festus was agreeable. Unexpectedly, Hermione was not agreeable. To Frederica's surprise, Hermione said she did not want to lose "her dear companion."

"I did not realize I was 'her dear companion,'" she said to Jeffrey privately.

"No, I suppose you are not. I think she was more afraid I was going to use some of her allowance to pay the expenses of the trip."

"Are you?" Frederica asked curiously.

"No, of course not," Jeffrey answered with a grin. "I let her think that for a bit because I was—am—annoyed that she called me tight-fisted. While we're on this trip, we will make plans for your debut in London. That is coming up quickly. I will need to find someone to sponsor you and take you around."

"Not Hermione?" she asked, surprised.

But Jeffrey never actually answered that question, just smiled and suggested they go visit the Randalls.

* * *

Frederica was brought back to the present by Uncle Festus's voice saying, "Just a bit more, dear," and seeing him holding out his cup. "Then I shall take a little nap before dinner. All the excitement, you know." He smiled genially as Frederica filled all the teacups again.

Then, Uncle Festus addressed Mr. Grant. "Maybe, Thomas, we can delay our departure tomorrow so that we can visit the castle without any boulders ruining our tour?"

Frederica realized with dismay that the older men had already agreed to include the thoughtless twit in their group. She would have to resign herself to his company for the next few weeks. She wanted to see something of the world besides the fields of Kent, however beautiful they might be. She wanted to talk about art and history and not what was for dinner or whether the sheets should be mended or newly purchased. Home was the last place she wanted to be.

Uncle Festus continued speaking. "Young Clive, please share with us why you are not at Oxford, where I thought you were studying, and are instead joining us old men on a tour of southwest England. I am sure it will make an entertaining and erudite tale."

Clive's lighthearted facade seemed to crumble a bit and Mr. Grant cringed as Dr. Chadwick calmly sipped his tea and waited for an answer. Mr. Grant found the sandwich tray to be of utmost interest as he made his next selections. Clive himself seemed struck with muteness. Maybe she would find out sooner rather than later what Mr. Grant knew about Clive's sudden appearance.

As the young man remained strangely inarticulate, seemingly searching for words, Mr. Grant took pity on him. He cleared his throat. "Festus, let me make this a little easier for Clive. I will start the tale, then he can fill in what is missing. Two years ago, when Clive reached the age of eighteen, his father decided he no longer needed a tutor and was ready to go to university. Forgive me, Miss Chadwick, it occurs to me that perhaps you might not know my history with your family." He gave a small bow in Frederica's direction. "When Jeffrey was at Oxford, I served as his tutor. Jeffrey introduced me to his uncle, Dr. Chadwick. Dr. Chadwick also holds the position of lecturer in ancient history at St. Mary's College at Oxford. Much to my gratification, we became friends. After Jeffrey graduated and went into the army, I left Oxford to take a position as tutor to Clive at his family home in Ripon in Yorkshire. When Clive was old enough for Oxford, his father dispensed with my services. With Dr. Chadwick's help and recommendation, for which I am deeply grateful," he gave a small bow in the direction of his mentor, "I applied for and received the position I now hold at Cambridge as lecturer of Greek literature at Christ College. During my tenure in Ripon, Dr. Chadwick would visit us from time to time. Occasionally, Jeffrey accompanied his uncle and, along with Clive, we had several very enjoyable visits together."

Clive sighed, "I can tell the sad tale from here, Tommy."

Having heard the background, Frederica thought Clive's use of Mr. Grant's first name was not impertinent, but rather a term of affection.

"I didn't want to go to Oxford at the time, but rather to join the Navy. However, I am an only son and my father was adamantly against it. Father has never been very clear about what I should do with my life, but any ideas I come up with are never the right ones. The church and the bar are not to my taste, so Tommy suggested I go to Oxford for a while. Father agreed. I actually do not know why. Unfortunately for me, Father would not pay to have Tommy accompany me to Oxford. You may not know, Miss Chadwick, but lots of fellows have their own tutors with them to help them study. On my own, I soon found that while Oxford has many opportunities to expand one's horizons, most of them have nothing to do with studying and learning the classics, but more with how to drink and gamble...."

It was quiet around the tea table as they waited for Clive to continue. Frederica took the last seed cake as she listened avidly.

"You know, I still do not understand Father's aversion to the Navy. We are at war and I thought there would be room for advancement." He shook his head. "Oxford seems to have two kinds of students. A small group of serious ones, probably like Jeffrey, and a much larger group of fellows who have no interest in learning, only drinking and..."

Mr. Grant cut in with an admonishing "Clive, there is a lady present."

"I know that." Clive seemed grateful for the interruption. "And a talented one at that. Say, Tommy, have you seen her sketches?"

Uncle Festus laughed. "Do not try to change the topic," he said genially.

Clive nodded and added, "I was only going to add that, unlike Jeffrey, I am not a good student. At least, I am not a good student of the classics. I don't find learning how to conjugate verbs in Greek and Latin relevant to my life. Obviously," he explained to Frederica, "I was not in the small studious group who are set to be ministers and dons. I realized pretty early on that learning to become a gentleman does not have much to do with studying. It is almost a relief to be sent down; maybe I can get my stomach back in order."

To Frederica, he seemed surprised, as if he had just discovered a truth he had been unaware of. "I still feel my temperament would have been better suited to the Navy. We have been at war for so long, surely there would have been a position in which I could have succeeded." His whole body sagged dispiritedly.

Dr. Chadwick said thoughtfully, "The Navy is a hard and difficult life, Clive. Much boredom and sometimes near-starvation attend the few moments of glory. I understand the appeal of some of our victories at sea, but perhaps you can ask Jeffrey about some of the grimmer aspects of military life. I can understand that your father would not want to put his only son in such a perilous position. Surely, he must want you to take over the management of the family properties. Has he instructed you at all in running the estates? The family holdings seemed quite extensive to me the times I visited Thomas Grant."

"Well, no." Clive's voice kept getting lower. "That is actually why I am here. After I was sent down, of course I went home. Father and I had a terrible row. He was furious that I had been tossed out of Oxford, although it is not forever," he added hastily. "Only a few months. We called each other awful names and I stormed out. I have been staying with my mother's parents since then. I think it was my mother who finally talked Father into sending me to stay with Tommy. I got a letter from him only last week inviting me to join this trip."

"Yes, it was short notice. I myself received your lady mother's letter only last week, asking if you could just stay with me for a visit. This trip seemed to be just the thing." He seemed to want to say more, but some inner caution restrained him.

Frederica had been studying Clive closely during the story. Oxford! He had actually been to Oxford and thrown it away. She had been forced to try to educate herself and he had not grasped the education handed to him. Her disgust knew no bounds. Still, she wondered, would he be angry enough at the world to resort to throwing rocks at people? She started to demand an explanation of his presence on the rocks when she realized Mr. Grant was speaking again.

"The purpose of our little trip, Clive, as I tried to explain to you earlier, is to view some of the noble ruins of our age. Places, Festus and I have read about but either have never seen for ourselves or have not visited in some time."

Festus drained his cup and picked up the strands of conversation from Thomas. "Our plan is to go from here to Dorchester to see some of the Roman sites, including Maumsbury Rings, Maiden Castle, and the giant at Cerne Abbas, then to Glastonbury to view the cathedral ruins and the Tor. After that, we head to Avebury and Stonehenge and end up at the cathedral in Salisbury. There has been some new research about the stone circles at Salisbury and Avebury that I am most interested in and I wish to see the sources for their ideas. For Frederica's education, we are including some places that will give her an opportunity to improve her drawing and her grasp of history."

"Jeffrey is interested in Roman ruins and old rocks?" Clive seemed astonished. Clearly Clive admired Jeffrey, but the man's intellectual side was new to him.

"Clive...." Mr. Grant started to admonish Clive's blunt speaking when Dr. Chadwick cut in.

"Clive, my nephew Jeffrey is an educated man, a 'man of taste,' and well-conversant with Roman writers and Roman history. He also enjoys expanding his knowledge of the world and learning by pursuing serious inquiry. While he has been waiting for this transfer for some time, he was quite put out that it came along just now. My point is that a sophisticated gentleman has many interests, and Roman ruins and old rocks may well be among them. When I met you as a young man, you, too, had an interest in learning about the world. Have you lost that curiosity?"

Again, Frederica could sense Clive's palpable discomfort. Clive was saved from immediate response as Uncle Festus continued. "Whatever the reason for your being here, Clive, I am glad of it. I am afraid Mr. Grant and I might bore my dear niece to tears with our historical discourses and you will be able to better entertain her, being somewhat closer in age."

Frederica protested, "Uncle Festus, no. You never bore me. I love listening to you talk. You know so much."

Frederica saw Clive studying her quizzically. He seemed to be questioning her age being similar to his. She feared that with her hair falling out of its ribbon and her new white dress grimy about the knees, she probably looked younger than she was. "I am older than I look right now. I am being presented next season." She had no idea if that was true or not with Jeffrey now in Ireland, but at least it would let the annoying Mr. Dering know she was no babe in arms. "More to the point, Uncle Festus has promised to help continue my education and that is my purpose in coming on this trip."

"Well, child, I think you are being polite when you say you do not find us boring. Come give me your arm and we'll go back to the inn. I think I am more tired than I realized. Thomas, I took the liberty of ordering dinner to be served at eight o'clock. We can discuss our travel plans for tomorrow over a nice game pie."

Chapter Three: Dorchester and Surrounds

Clive

The next day, Dr. Chadwick had them up fairly early, certainly earlier than Clive had ever risen when he was at university.

"We do not want to waste the day. It will take a bit to reach Dorchester," the older scholar explained. "It is a good place to find the remains of the Romans. There are a number of ruins that are well worth seeing, but even more exciting is the news I just received from a friend. While doing some renovations, a local merchant uncovered a complete floor of Roman mosaics. My friend is providing us with an introduction and we are going to be among the first to see it." His excitement was so apparent that even Clive managed to find some enthusiasm.

* * *

It was midmorning when they arrived at their first destination.

"The Maumbury Rings," announced Dr. Chadwick triumphantly.

Clive studied the low hills before them. To his surprise, the Rings were not rings at all, but two long hills facing each other with a large flat area between them. The hills were concave and would have formed an oval except for the openings at either end.

Miss Chadwick did not seem too impressed, either. "Excuse me, Mr. Grant," she said, "what were these hills used for?"

Clive suspected if he had asked the question, Grant would not be as calm in his answer. Grant would probably accuse him of "never listening."

"The Maumbury Rings are the largest known amphitheater built by the Romans in England. And there were quite a number constructed, as we've found amphitheaters in almost every town where the Romans lived."

The four of them gathered in the opening nearest the street and stood gazing at the vast green slopes.

"Mr. Grant, where did the people sit?" Frederica probed. "I have seen a picture of an amphitheater in Greece, but it was made of stone and the seats were terraced upwards from the stage. This does not look anything like that picture."

Dr. Chadwick answered, "Think in terms of the Coliseum. The action, fighting, games, and so forth happened down here," he gestured to the flat plane in front of them. "The audience sat on those hills. I think there were seats carved into them then. They have worn down, of course, being made of dirt and not stone. Let us walk through to the other side."

But Clive had another idea. "Miss Chadwick, do you want to see the view from the top? We can just follow the crest and meet Dr. Chadwick and Tommy at the other side."

Frederica nodded. "I am hoping the view will make a good subject for my sketchbook," she said.

Clive led the way up the crest of the hill. Even though Frederica was burdened with the bag containing her art supplies, she managed to keep up, denying him any opportunity to offer her assistance and perhaps to hold her hand. Reaching the top of the easternmost hill, Dr. Chadwick and Tommy now appeared to be only inches high.

"These mounds are much higher than they appeared from down there." Frederica gasped.

Clive chuckled and replied, "I assume these were the cheap seats. Pretty hard to throw orange peels from this distance."

"Orange peels? Why would I want to do that?" Frederica seemed confused.

"Haven't you ever been to the theater when the audience does not like the presentation? They will throw almost anything."

"No, I have not been to a real theater. We had some tableaus at church, but of course no one threw anything. Such behavior must be humiliating for the actors, but I suppose it could be fun for the audience," she admitted.

They were walking now along a path worn into the crest, where they paused to study the scene.

"Yes, it is," Clive agreed. He looked down at her face as she studied the ancient amphitheater. She seemed so serious. "What are you thinking?" he asked.

"I am trying to imagine what this place would look like when it was filled with people," she said. "Do you suppose they only used it for those awful gladiator fights Uncle Festus mentioned?"

Clive nodded absently but he was really thinking how different she was from her brother Jeffrey, a sophisticated man seemingly comfortable in most social settings. She was quite attractive but seemed socially naive. And, shockingly to him, she had never even been to the theater! He dragged his mind back to her question.

"Oh, I suppose they must have enjoyed some plays also. Even Romans could not spend all their time killing people. Would not that become rather boring? Besides they would probably run out of victims, no?" he responded.

"Are you suggesting Romans were just like audiences today?"

"Doubtful," Clive responded. "I do not know of very many modern-day spectacles where they fight to the death."

"But you speak as though you have firsthand knowledge of the way some audiences act today?" Frederica asked slyly.

Clive just grinned without admitting to any such rude behavior as tossing rotten tomatoes at unimpressive performers.

When they reached the end of the crest and were about to start downhill, Frederica asked her companion to wait a few minutes while she made a quick sketch. Clive watched admiringly as she rapidly outlined the hills and the open area between them.

Frederica started to put away her materials.

"Are you not going to finish it?" he asked.

"No, not here. I can fill in the colors and details later. I just need an outline from which to work."

Getting down the hill was not as easy as getting up and now Frederica seemed quite willing to have him take her hand to help her over the steeper spots. She even let him carry her satchel.

"The view up there is tremendous, Dr. Chadwick. And those old Romans could really build, couldn't they? I bet this place could hold thousands of people."

"It is huge," Frederica said in agreement. "And I loved the view. Did you see the sheep over on the other side? From the top, they looked like toys."

After a brief stop for bread and soup, washed down by beer and cider, they were again back in the carriage, to the next site.

* * *

The carriage rolled to another stop a few miles outside of town. Exiting the carriage, the two young people stared up at a grassy hill dotted with black-faced sheep similar to the ones gracing the fields at Corfe. Given the flatness of the surrounding area, the hill looked shockingly out of place.

"What are we looking at?" Clive asked. He saw a fairly straight path disappearing over the lip of the hill but to his annoyance, the blasted sheep were everywhere.

Chadwick emerged from the carriage with his walking stick. He pointed upwards like an officer leading a cavalry in a charge. "Maiden Castle!" he exclaimed.

Clive laughed out loud. He found it impossible to keep up the bored façade of a sophisticated man about town when surrounded by the good doctor's infectious humor. He grinned at Frederica. "Well, Miss Chadwick, shall we see what mysteries Maiden Castle has for us at the top?"

Frederica studied the long path upward.

"Do you want your sketching materials?" he asked.

But Grant emerged from the carriage already holding her art materials. Clive shouldered the bag and gestured to Frederica to start up the path before him. He studied her dress as they went uphill. Today she was wearing a printed muslin that was too light for the weather. The white dress she had worn yesterday was obviously new and without blemish, at least until she had landed on her knees besides Dr. Chadwick. Today's dress was not new. He was not completely up on styles, but it looked like what his sisters had been wearing before he went off to university. If that was the case, he was sure either of his sisters would have refused to wear the dress and instead handed it off to a maid. Her cloak also looked well-worn. Odd – he had been under the impression that Jeffrey Chadwick's family had plenty of blunt. Also, how was she going to sketch if she had to keep adjusting her clothing?

"It looks pretty breezy up top, Miss Chadwick," he said. "That wrap is going to be a liability. Do you have one of those spencer jackets or a pelisse that will free up your hands for sketching?"

From her stricken look, the answer was obvious. Instead of responding to his question, she asked, "How is it you know so much about ladies' fashions, Mr. Dering?"

Clive laughed out loud. She really should meet his sisters. "I told you yesterday, Miss Chadwick, I have sisters who have tormented me all my life. I know more about ladies' fashions than any of the fellows I know."

She did not comment and kept striding up the path with her face forward and shoulders stiff. Any man worth his salt could read her body language. Fashion was a sore point, although why was a mystery. Art was a better subject.

"I have an idea about how to manage sketching in a wind," he said hurriedly to change the subject. "If you do not have a brooch to hold your cloak closed, we can use my cravat pin. Then I can hold your sketch pad and your hands will be relatively free. Do you think that will work?"

"That is quite thoughtful of you, Mr. Dering," she said gratefully. "I think that will do nicely."

"Then we are agreed; I will act as your easel," he said easily.

She smiled in agreement and they reached the top in good spirits with each other and the breezy but beautiful day. Mr. Grant and Dr. Chadwick followed somewhat more slowly, but Clive noticed they always remained in sight.

They soon realized the path did not lead straight to the top. Instead, it started to zigzag down and around the lower hills. Although grass covered all the slopes and numerous sheep covered much of the grass, it was obvious there were several ditches they would have to cross before they would reach the main promontory.

Studying the slopes covered only with grass, Frederica mused, "I don't see a castle or ruins, only grass and hills. Has it been covered up, do you think?"

"I do not know. I thought there would be ruins too, like at Corfe Castle." Clive called over his shoulder, "Where are the ruins? How far do we have to climb?" They stopped to let the older men catch up.

When they did, Uncle Festus was smiling. There was nothing he liked better than instructing young people about their own history. "Maiden Castle is not really a castle in the sense of brick walls, gates, baileys, and moats. It is much older than any of the castles built in England after William the Conqueror. It was here when the Romans invaded. I think the confusion comes from the name. Maiden comes from the Celtic, *Mai Dun*, meaning a great hill. We are not really sure how old it is, but at least 2,000 years, wouldn't you say, Mr. Grant?"

Clive knew well that Tommy Grant could lecture as well as Dr. Chadwick. He smiled to himself as Grant elaborated about how the Romans wrote about it and how recent historians thought the only tools available to dig the moats were deer antlers. "A truly amazing feat!"

"Let me understand you," Clive spoke to Mr. Grant and Dr. Chadwick. "This was a fortress with large moats, trenches, or what have you, dug around it for protection, and it is believed this was built before even the Romans?" He sounded incredulous even to himself. "But this place is enormous! Tommy, can you draw a basic outline?"

Using Frederica's sketching materials, Grant quickly sketched an oval. "Now I have only been here once before," he said. "From what I remember, the center part is larger than the average farm, maybe 40 or so acres." He added three rings around the oval. "There are outer rings – ditches or moats we might call them. To get to the main entrance, the ancients made the trail wind around several ditches. We just crossed that part." He gestured behind him with the pencil. The he added an X to the map and an arrow pointing off to the top right of the page. "We are here, I think, and Dorchester is in this direction. I believe I read that about here," he made another X on the map, "they found some Roman ruins."

Fergus Chadwick nodded in agreement. "You can see this hill is not natural. Dorset has many other hills, but they are more rolling. Nothing else is as big or as molded; it has to be manmade."

Clive shook his head in amazement. "It is hard to believe it was built by people with deer antlers and baskets; it is enormous! Come on, Miss Chadwick, let's see if we can find the Roman encampment from Grant's map." He gestured towards the middle of the plain.

"I really like being around Uncle Festus and Mr. Grant. I enjoy their explanations, even their everyday conversations, so much. My governess was lovely but nowhere near as knowledgeable. But surely you must be bored with such academics, having heard so much at university."

"Do you really enjoy them?" Clive asked with interest. "I would have thought the stuff would bore *you* silly."

Clive was looking off in the distance, trying to spot anything to guide them to the ruins Grant had mentioned.

"I know it would bore my sisters," he added absently. "I have not met many females who were interested in much besides fashion and the latest novels. Certainly no bluestockings."

He cringed when he noticed her frown at his unintended insult. "I do not mean you…" he tried to correct himself. "I just mean my sisters are really not interested in historical studies…" he ended lamely.

"My father let me read anything I could find in his library," she responded stiffly. "It is not his fault he died and I have no one to discuss these topics with."

Clive stopped in the path, forcing her to do likewise. "Miss Chadwick, I am sorry, I did not mean to insult you or your interests," he said sincerely.

She nodded an acceptance of his apology and resumed walking. "I thought these historical subjects would be something you would have studied a lot at Oxford."

"The curriculum at Oxford concentrates on classical literature. That means Roman and Greek literature. When I went there, I did think I would be studying subjects that would help me in the Navy, such as mathematics, geography, or astronomy. Then I thought I probably should study natural history if I was just going to be a farmer," he said ruefully.

"No history?"

"Damn little," he groused. "Oh, sorry for the language, Miss Chadwick. And what one studies is not even the history of England," he continued. "I am just not really interested in Greek history. I want to study subjects pertaining to today."

"I do not understand how you cannot be interested in all history," Frederica said. "To me, history means getting to hear stories of the past all the time. But I can sympathize with having to study subjects one is not interested in. For me, that would be mathematics or grammar. Miss Black did her best, but I still shudder when I think of what she tried to instill in me."

They continued following the path into the center of Maiden Castle. *I don't think I am making much headway in getting into her good graces. This is going to be a long trip if we cannot find some subjects in common. She seems to disapprove of everything. What can I do to make her friendlier? I have already apologized.* Clive had to admit to himself that he was not used to a young female that waffled between disapproval and cool friendliness. With the exception of his sisters, he found his charm, his smile and his dimples, had the fair sex of all ages vying for his attention. Frederica was a challenge. *Maybe a change of subject.*

A lush plain lay before them. It was indeed enormous. For the next two hours, they wandered the fields. Clive sacrificed his cravat pin to tie Frederica's cloak closed and acted as a human easel so she could make sketches. Their conversation skipped over a number of subjects, as Clive worked to find common ground with his traveling companion. They talked about the many shades of green they could see and wondered who owned the sheep that were everywhere. They speculated as to how many people had lived up here, what they had eaten, and where they had gotten their water.

At some point, Clive realized, their traveling companions had disappeared. He appreciated they did not feel they needed to act as chaperones all the time and that he could be trusted with Miss Chadwick.

They kept returning to food, whether Romans ate food found in England or had had it imported. They decided that at least wine had to come from Italy. During the discussion, Clive realized lunch had been sometime in the past. Miss Chadwick admitted to being peckish as well. They abandoned their search for the Roman ruins and made their way back to the carriage.

Their companions had obviously arrived back earlier and were already dining al fresco. Dr. Chadwick had thoughtfully ordered a picnic basket to be brought along. They had laid out several blankets to the side of the carriage and must have loaded plates with chicken and various side dishes. Clive was glad to see several bottles of wine were open.

"Sit down, sit down. Tell us what you found!" Dr. Chadwick seemed in fine humor.

Frederica sat on the blanket next to her uncle and helped herself to bread and cheese.

"May I help you to some boiled eggs or a piece of chicken, Miss Chadwick?" Mr. Grant asked in his kindly way.

No one needed to help Clive, who had dived into the food with one hand and was pouring himself wine with the other.

"Yes, thanks so much, Mr. Grant. Is there anything besides wine to drink?"

"Should be some lemonade in the basket. Clive, look alive and find a bottle of lemonade for Miss Chadwick." Dr. Chadwick waved a chicken bone at Clive.

"We didn't find any Roman ruins." Frederica opened her sketchpad to show her work. "But I did a sketch of Dorchester in the distance and another of the moats from the main gateway. This place is so beautiful, Uncle Festus. Thank you for bringing me here."

Clive grinned impishly as he handed her the lemonade. "Your stepmother wouldn't be so happy if she could see your face right now. Even with your bonnet on, you managed to get your nose sunburned," he teased.

"Oh no!" Frederica clapped her hands on her cheeks in dismay.

"Clive, don't tease her." Dr. Chadwick patted Frederica's hand. "Hermione is not a woman to joke about. Don't worry, m'dear, tomorrow we'll get you some cream to put on your face; but by the time we return, I am sure your face will be its normal lovely pale hue."

"Besides," Mr. Grant said kindly, "I do not think it unattractive to see some color in a young woman's face. Personally, I do not find the current fashion for white skin all that charming. A little color makes a woman look healthy."

"Thank you, Mr. Grant. I know you are just trying to make me feel better. Hermione would be happier if I never went outside. She, of course, has perfect skin. But don't worry, I have some cream with me. Our cook is quite clever with potions and such." Frederica piled her plate with food and began eating with a good appetite.

"While you young people finish eating, I am going to tell the driver to put the horses to the carriage. I think we should make our way back to Dorchester and our lodgings for the night. Tomorrow we will see the Roman mosaics before we leave for Cerne Abbey. Here, Grant, give me a hand up. Sitting on the ground is a bit much for an old man like me."

Clive made sure he beat Grant to his feet so he could be the one to help Dr. Chadwick.

* * *

"I sent a messenger ahead to order a late luncheon in the village of Cerne Abbas. That will make a nice break in our journey to Glastonbury. We should get there around dusk. We have rooms waiting for us at The Pilgrim."

Before Frederica could ask Mr. Grant what was in his travel book about the village of Cerne Abbas, Clive spoke. "Say, isn't this where the Giant is? You know, the big chalk figure cut into the hill?"

Mr. Grant answered. "Fancy you knowing that! Yes, this is where the Cerne Giant resides. Well, not in the village – a little way outside. We will be stopping there later as it is further along the road to Glastonbury."

Frederica was all questions. "What is the Cerne Giant? What do you mean 'cut into a hill'?"

Again, Mr. Grant answered. "In various places around England, there are giant chalk figures carved into the sides of a mountain or hill. Usually they are so old no one has any idea who carved them or why. There is a horse figure cut into a mountain that we will see when we go to Avebury."

"But this one is a figure of a man?"

This time Uncle Festus answered. "Yes, a great big one, over forty feet high. I personally think the Giant was carved as a warning. Maybe the ancients put him there so any invading armies would be frightened off, thinking every-one in the district was a giant."

Clive asked, "And he is just part of a hill? One of the fellows at school came from around here and he mentioned the Giant. Wasn't real clear about anything but the size of him."

"The figure was carved right into the side of the hill. The ancients scraped away all the material above the chalk. There is no doubt he is male."

"Yes, that is what my friend said," Dering paused. "He said…."

But before he could continue, Grant interrupted, "Well, seems we have arrived. Where do you want the driver to set us down, Festus? At the inn over there?" Grant gestured to an inn on the right side of the village square.

"Is that The New Inn?" asked Uncle Festus.

"Yes. I can see the sign now."

"Then tell him to stop here."

While Mr. Grant gave the driver directions, Dr. Chadwick told Frederica and Clive the parish church was well worth viewing as well as the Abbey ruins nearby. "I can't remember the name of the church – named after a saint, of course. But I know I read there were some beautiful stained-glass windows and the altar screen is from the fifteenth century." Then, to Frederica's dismay, he added, "Unfortunately, I am having another headache, so I think I will have some tea and a rest at the inn."

Mr. Dering was the first to alight and he turned back to help Frederica descend. As she was balancing on the step, the young artist could hear Mr. Grant questioning her uncle. "Are you really meaning to take her to see the Giant? I mean, it is quite graphic. She is – excuse me, I do not want to appear critical – she seems somewhat naive."

Uncle Festus seemed amused. "Well, Tommy, the Cerne Giant is a great historical figure."

Clive chuckled as he took her arm and drew her along the sidewalk. "They never really want us to grow up, do they?" he said.

Frederica, who had been embarrassed by Mr. Grant's description of her as naïve, felt better with Dering's casual dismissal of the comment. Of course, all Mr. Grant's questions served to do was pique Frederica's curiosity about this mysterious chalk figure.

"Mr. Dering, what is the problem with the Giant?" she asked him. "Why shouldn't I see him?"

"He is dressed, or undressed, as I imagine our ancestors presented them-selves and might be considered somewhat shocking for a genteel young woman," he answered with a shrug. "Obviously, your uncle does not seem to think there is a problem, so I am sure there is not one. Now, shall we look at the church first? I know Tommy finds these small parish churches to be places of beauty and peace. Not sure I agree, but we have to do something until luncheon."

"Is Mr. Grant coming with us?"

"I'm sure he will catch up. It is hard to get lost in such a small village."

But they did not see him again until they emerged from the church, ready to explore the ruins.

"Hallo! I've been settling Dr. Chadwick at the inn. Poor old thing is really done up. Anyway, he is tucked up taking a nap and says he will be ready to go in about an hour. I think we should just take our good old time and then have tea or chocolate before we even think of leaving."

"Oh dear, I hope he isn't taking too much on," Frederica worried aloud.

"He probably needs to rest more than he has been doing," Mr. Grant responded.

"Why don't we slow down the trip and stay here longer than we had planned? We outvote him, right?" Dering chimed in. "Maybe when we arrive in Bath, we can just stay put for a few days. Give Dr. Chadwick time to rest up. What do you think? He could even drink the waters. Have you ever drunk those waters, Miss Chadwick? My dear mother made me when I was still in skirts. I still remember how bad it tasted. Thought she was trying to kill me."

Frederica had to laugh at the way Dering's face twisted at the memory.

"You know, I think I will go back and see how Festus is doing. Clive, would you take our young artist to see this well the fellow in the church was telling us about?" With a nod, Mr. Grant headed off in the direction of The New Inn.

"Of course, I would be delighted to escort you to view the local sights, Miss Chadwick." Clive's voice took on the nasal tone of a town swell. He mimicked an elegant bow and offered her his arm. "Got your sketchbook? By the way, in which direction are we going?" The last was in a normal voice.

Frederica laughed and pointed him to an overgrown path at the back of the cemetery that led into some shrubbery.

Clive raised an eyebrow. "Do you think your reputation is safe with me, Miss Chadwick?" He grinned at her.

"Oh Mr. Dering," she replied archly, playing the society miss, "I feel sure I will be safe with you. After all, this is a 'holy well,' St. Augustine's Well, I believe it is called. Surely even so sophisticated a gentleman as yourself wouldn't take advantage of a young miss in such a holy place? Besides, there are lots of people about," she ended on a laugh.

Perfectly content with one another, they started towards the well. Tall arching tree limbs met over the path, forming a green tunnel mottled with sunlight. The well itself was a small pool-like area. They stood admiring the quiet and calm of the little grotto.

"This looks like an ideal area for one of your sketches of the picturesque," Clive said. "Why don't you get out your pad and do whatever it is you do? I will sit over here," he said, indicating a tree a short distance away. "That way, we will be very proper and still give our companions time to rest. I imagine rattling about in a carriage all day can be draining on someone of Dr. Chadwick's age."

So intent was Frederica on her sketch, she was quite startled when Clive announced they should be pushing off. Although her sketch had gone better than usual, the rumbling of her stomach reminded her also of the passage of time.

"Yes, we should get back before Mr. Grant has to come look for us."

Later, over tea at the inn, Frederica produced the result of her day's work.

"Oh Uncle Festus, let me show you the sketch I made at the well. It was such a lovely place, we found it hard to leave." She began to flip pages.

"So that is what kept you so long. I am beginning to wonder if we will make Glastonbury by nightfall."

Frederica glanced at Clive, who gave her a conspiratorial wink. The rest must have been a good thing; Uncle Festus looked much improved.

"Well done, m'dear! A lovely quiet place. Look, Tommy, she's put Clive in the sketch." The last brought Clive around the table to look at Frederica's drawing.

"I say, I thought you were just doing the well."

But Mr. Grant and Uncle Festus both agreed she had caught Clive's likeness well, including the lock of dark hair that often fell over his eyes.

"This is just a bit of fun. I haven't drawn very many portraits. My father used to sit for me, but he was the only one. I rather like the challenge."

"Well, I say, if you are going to put a chap into the picture, you should have given him some warning. Is my cravat really so bad? And I spent quite some time on it this morning!" Clive declared. "Besides, I really am better looking than that, don't you think, Tommy? My nose is not so long." He appealed to the older man for his opinion.

Thomas Grant laughed. "What? Agree with you and swell your head more?"

"If you are going to get me in all my youthful glory, Miss Chadwick, I had better model for you again. Practice, practice, practice." Dering grinned at her impishly.

Uncle Festus laughed out loud at Clive's joking.

"Come on, I see our coachman signaling from the door; he is ready. If you all have had enough tea, let's go see the Giant and be on our way to Glastonbury."

A bare ten minutes later, Uncle Festus was telling the driver to pull the barouche to the side of the road so they could admire the clay figure on the hill opposite. A small valley between them and the Giant placed the travelers on the same level as the Giant, although there was probably a quarter-mile distance between them as the crow flies. Nothing interfered with the panorama as all the trees and brush had been removed. They could not have asked for a more perfect view.

Frederica leaned forward to look around Uncle Festus and gaze at the hillside. Scraped into the side of the hill was the clear outline of a figure with a raised club. It was enormous, filling most of the hillside. Only two eyes had been given to the figure and he possessed two clubs – one in a raised hand and another attached to his waist. Frederica frowned. But before she could speak, Mr. Grant opened the door and stepped out. Clive practically leapt out behind him, then turned to help Frederica descend.

He grinned at her. "Do you have your sketchpad?" he asked. "How are you going to make a melancholy drawing of this?"

Frederica smiled at his teasing but did not respond as she studied the Cerne Giant. She had spent all her life in rural areas. She knew there were differences in the male and female anatomies. But while she knew about sheep and dogs and cats, she had never been quite sure what the difference was between men and women. She glanced back at Uncle Festus who, unlike the others, was still in the carriage.

"Is this part of my education?"

He raised an eyebrow at her. "Well m'dear, the Cerne Giant is a historical monument." He smiled benignly at her. "I still believe he was put here as a warning to other tribes to beware. The fact that his club and…other parts are enormous is for intimidation purposes. Not necessarily anatomically accurate."

Frederica opened her sketchpad.

"Oh, I say!" Clive jostled her elbow. "You are not really going to draw that, are you? Not very proper, is it, Tommy?"

The last was addressed to Mr. Grant, but he had wandered off to view the Giant from another angle.

Frederica laughed at Clive as she roughed in the outline. "Uncle Festus says he is a historical monument and you know I am recording all the places we visit."

"This will give your stepmother something to think about," he remarked.

Frederica laughed at him. "Well, she is not really interested in my efforts, so maybe I just will not show her." So many questions had been answered for her, she felt almost giddy. "Look, Mr. Dering." She showed him the drawing. "I am only outlining the scene for now. Later I'll add melancholy clouds in the appropriate spots, or maybe some snow."

Frederica finished her rough sketch, with Mr. Dering offering suggestions, most of which were ridiculous. The good mood of the afternoon continued as she outlined the Giant with the intention of filling in his second "club" later.

Frederica was grateful for Uncle Festus' complacency and even the rather open anatomy lesson. Now Frederica could at least fill in one of the blank spaces of her rather vivid imagination. If she could just figure out the how…

As she returned to the carriage, Frederica glanced around to see if there were other visitors. She and her companions appeared to be the only tourists. Other people passed by, barely acknowledging the Giant with as much as a glance. They must be locals. Only one other figure caught her eye, a lone horseman who soon vanished into the Dorchester road.

They probably had dawdled too long at Cerne Abby, Frederica decided. The sun was setting and the light was dimming. When asked, the driver assured them they would still reach Glastonbury tonight. He was experienced with the route, but he admitted it would not be until after dark.

Chapter Four: Wolverton

Frederica

When Clive started to moan about being hungry again, Mr. Grant laughingly pointed out the picnic basket under the seat. Before Clive had time to pull it out, the rear of the coach hit a great bump and slipped sharply to the right side. While it slowed, it did not completely stop.

Frederica was thrown against the side of the carriage; the other passengers all slid to the right, crushing her against the side of the vehicle. The coach bounced and continued to drag along, while its inhabitants were helpless to separate themselves from one another. Frederica struggled unsuccessfully to find something to hang onto until, with a particularly hard bounce, the coach slid into a ditch and finally came to a stop.

It had never occurred to Frederica that a carriage accident could be so quiet. No one screamed. There were a few grunts from the men. Then Mr. Grant and Clive both spoke at once, asking how everyone was.

"I think I am fine, but it is hard to breathe with everyone on top of me," Frederica huffed. Uncle Festus remained silent. Clive and Mr. Grant must be at the top, she thought, as they had been seated next to the left side of the coach. Dering seemed to have landed on top of the pile. She could feel movement as he tried to disentangle himself from the others.

"I can reach the door," he gasped. He began to shove open the left-hand door. In the gloom of the near sunset, Frederica could just see him hauling himself out the door. The pressure on her legs eased, but Mr. Grant was still between her and the door.

Dering's head reappeared again almost instantly. "Miss Chadwick, give me your hands. You're the lightest, and if I can lift you out, then we'll more easily see about the others."

Frederica and Mr. Grant spoke at the same time. "I can't move yet."

"Wait, Clive, she is at the bottom of the heap. Miss Chadwick, are you hurt? Festus, how about you?" Tommy Grant was breathing heavily. Although he did not say anything about his own condition, Frederica thought Mr. Grant must be injured, as his movements were also labored. There was still no answer from Uncle Festus.

"Clive," Mr. Grant said with something like a groan. "I think I may have broken my arm. I can't help get anyone up to you. Where is the coachman?"

"No idea," was the response.

"Let me see if I can move enough for Miss Chadwick to get out from under me," Grant said. It sounded as though just moving a little hurt him, but he managed to twist enough to free Frederica.

"I am afraid I will have to stand on someone if I am to reach up," she said.

"Don't worry; it is just my legs and you are light. Just try to reach Clive and get out," Grant answered.

Frederica stretched her arms to Clive, who was standing on the road. He was able to lean into the carriage and grab her by the wrists. Frederica quailed at the thought that she was standing on Mr. Grant. "I am so sorry, Mr. Grant," she gasped.

Clive leaned in further and grasped Frederica under the arms, lifting her high enough to enable her to swing her legs up and through the door opening. Although she heard him grunt a few times, Mr. Grant never complained.

Once out of the carriage box, Frederica scrambled to the ground and surveyed the disaster.

The coach was leaning at an angle with its right wheels in the ditch. Getting out the left door was a scramble but obviously possible. She watched while Dering manipulated Mr. Grant out of the coach through the door. The tutor slumped to the ground, clutching his arm.

"Mr. Dering, where's the coachman?" She could see that the poor horses were struggling in their harnesses and making awful noises, but there was no one to be seen.

Clive didn't answer. He had climbed back into the coach to free Uncle Festus from the wreckage. By then, Mr. Grant had staggered to his feet and was trying to help, but with one arm obviously broken he could be of little assistance. Frederica joined them, not knowing how she might help but wanting to do so.

"Is he still unconscious, Clive?" Grant asked.

"Yes," Dering responded. "Seems to have knocked his head. It is hard to see, but I think there is a bleeding cut on his scalp. I am going to try to get him out of this coach; I really can't see much in here."

Frederica and Grant waited anxiously as Clive rearranged Dr. Chadwick so that his feet touched the door.

"Miss Chadwick, Frederica, come help me!" Clive called from inside, not realizing she was standing in the door watching. "He is not able to help us. Can you lean in and grasp his legs? I will try to support his head." Relieved to be asked to do something, Frederica responded immediately. Awkwardly and very slowly, with a number of pauses to catch their breath, they finally succeeded in freeing Uncle Festus from the wreckage. Panting and exhausted, Clive and Frederica dragged him as gently as they could to the side of the ditch.

Frederica sat next to Festus and gently rolled his head onto her lap. She pulled out her handkerchief and pressed it against her uncle's forehead. Dering was correct; he had a long gash along the hairline. Blood was everywhere. She knew scalp wounds bled profusely and tried not to panic but her handkerchief was immediately useless. Frederica looked around for something else to use as a bandage.

Out of the dark, a gunshot sounded remarkably close by. Then there was a second shot. Frederica froze.

"Clive, Mr. Dering, Mr. Grant! What's happening?" She practically screamed at the top of her voice. Had highwaymen come back to finish them off?

"I'm sorry! I'm sorry! I should have warned you." Clive rushed around the carriage carrying a gun. "It was the horses. Broken legs, both of them. I had to put them down. I found the coachman had loaded weapons in the box. The two lead horses seem to be fine; Tommy is checking them out." Clive's shoulders slumped as he sat beside her.

"What a mess! It is dark, Dr. Chadwick is hurt, and the coachman is nowhere to be found."

Mr. Grant rejoined them. Frederica noticed he was walking with a limp, as well as cradling his left arm. He did not mention his own injuries.

"Is everyone all right?" he asked.

"It's Uncle Festus. He hasn't come to yet; he's bleeding and I don't know what to do." Frederica was on the verge of tears. "Do you have anything else I can use as a bandage?" Both Mr. Grant and Clive offered their cravats and pocket linens.

"Clive, I think we should start some kind of fire. Then we can at least keep warm. Dr. Chadwick is probably in shock and a fire will help us attract the attention of anyone going by." Mr. Grant started to gather firewood.

"Tommy, stop," Dering ordered. "You are looking pretty wobbly. Sit with Dr. Chadwick and see if you can help Miss Chadwick tie up that cut better. First, I am going to look for the picnic basket before it gets too dark. I hope there is some wine." Mr. Grant nodded approvingly. "Then Miss Chadwick and I will get the fire going." Clive started patting down his pockets, obviously looking for his flint box.

"I think Uncle Festus has a box in his pocket – you know, for his pipe." Frederica could just see Clive now in the dark. "I'll find it and then help collect some kindling."

She carefully laid Uncle Festus on the grass next to Mr. Grant. Grant was close enough to the older gentleman that he could use his good hand to apply pressure on Chadwick's wound. Frederica sorted through her uncle's pockets until she found the flint.

True to his word, Dering had also gone back into the carriage and retrieved the food basket, their cloaks, and a carriage blanket. It took him some time and several sheets of Frederica's sketchpad, but Clive eventually got a fire going, then moved Uncle Festus and Mr. Grant closer. He laid a small pile of wood nearby.

Frederica covered her uncle with the blankets and cloaks and persuaded him to drink some wine. He seemed to be coming around somewhat, but now he was shivering. Mr. Grant sat with him, hunched over, silent and withdrawn. When the young woman put another cloak around Grant's shoulders, he tried to smile his appreciation, but she could see how much of an effort it was for him.

She took Clive aside. "I am worried about them, especially if we have to stay out here all night. I think Mr. Grant is hurt worse than he will admit, and Uncle Festus is still bleeding, although not as badly as he was."

Clive nodded in agreement. "I think Tommy got a good knock on the head, too. I was just getting to the rest of my plan. Now that the fire is going, I think I should take one of the horses to find some help. I will simply follow the road backwards until I find an inn or something. I don't like leaving you here, especially as I cannot find any powder to reload the gun, but I don't know what else to do."

Frederica shrugged. "Powder wouldn't make any difference. I don't know how to fire a revolver. But before you go, let me thank you for all you've done. Without you, we would still be in the carriage and in much worse condition." She held out her hand to shake. Clive not only shook it but raised her hand and kissed her knuckles before he reluctantly let her hand go.

"You have been pretty astounding yourself," he said. "I feel terrible about leaving you here. Keep safe. If anyone comes near who seems threatening, I think you could hide in the hedges. I am so sorry; I don't know what more I can do." Frederica could see that he was deeply torn between his impulse to get help and his concern about leaving his companions alone and vulnerable in the dark.

"Don't worry, we'll be fine. Well, maybe not *really* fine, but with the fire and the food, we should do until you return." Frederica tried to sound confident. Nothing would be gained by delay – they needed help soon. "Just be as quick as you can."

Clive scanned her face trying to assess how strong she really was. Suddenly he nodded as if satisfied and headed off to where the horses had been tied. Within minutes, Frederica heard hoof beats moving down the road. She headed back to the fire and wondered again about the curious absence of the coachman.

* * *

Clive

Clive tethered his horse and moved first to stir up the fire. It was hellishly dark out here and hard to see. As a result, he almost trod on Frederica as she lay sleeping on the ground.

"Miss Chadwick! Frederica! Wake up!" She was so deeply asleep, he had to shake her shoulder to get her to respond.

She came awake startled with a gasp, her eyes opening in fright. "Oh Mr. Dering, thank heavens you're back! What news?" Frederica struggled to her feet and shook out her skirts, looking around with dismay. "Oh no, I fell asleep and let the fire die down."

"Easily fixed," he responded. He glanced around and found the remaining brush Frederica had been using to keep the fire going. Help was now following close behind him, so they no longer needed to be conservative with the wood. As Clive added the rest of the brush, the fire gave a burst of light, allowing him to see the people gathered around. Festus Chadwick was slumped against a tree with his eyes closed. He was either asleep or unconscious, Dering couldn't tell which. The bandage around Chadwick's head had slipped and Clive could see where the blood from his head wound had dripped onto his shirt, making it appear as though he had another wound in the chest. Thomas Grant sat near Dr. Chadwick, leaning against the other side of the same tree. His eyes were also closed, clearly with pain. He was holding his left arm as he looked up.

"Oh Clive, good to see you! I am afraid we are in a bad way here."

"Not to worry, old fellow! I have the local squire coming right behind me with a carriage. We are going to stay with him tonight and he has sent one of his men off for the doctor. I expect the doctor will meet us at the house. Ah, here is the squire now."

As Clive spoke, an open carriage pulled up out of the darkness. A figure stiffly climbed out with the aid of a cane and approached the huddled figures around the fire.

"Ah, lad. 'Tis a nasty bit of work, this." He leaned on his cane and shook his head as he surveyed the overturned carriage and dead horses. "You folks are all welcome at the gatehouse. We've plenty of room and the missus will be glad of the company. We should get these gentlemen inside as soon as may be."

Clive had gotten Thomas Grant to his feet and was maneuvering him to the carriage.

"Miss Chadwick, this is Mr. Chettle, owner of the property we are on. Mr. Chettle, Miss Chadwick." He spoke rapidly, making the introductions over his shoulder as he concentrated on slowly leading Grant to the carriage and helping him inside, all the time trying not to bump or disturb his broken arm. He could feel Grant holding his breath and trying not to make a sound. Despite his effort, there was the occasional grunt when, Grant's arm came into contact with the carriage door.

When he returned to the fire, Clive saw Frederica kneeling beside Festus Chadwick, trying to wake him. "Uncle Festus! Uncle Festus! Wake up!" To him, she sounded very anxious. He moved closer to study Dr. Chadwick, ready to help him to the carriage when he regained consciousness. Frederica stroked his face with her hand. Slowly, the old man's eyes opened. He did not speak, and from the way he gazed about, Clive assumed he was confused and did not know where he was.

"Don't try to move by yourself," Clive told him. "I am right here, and I will help." He moved to stand behind the older gentleman, remembering a similar scenario just a few days before. How many blows to the head could one sustain before permanent damage was done? Dering wondered.

As they worked to get Dr. Chadwick to his feet, Frederica briefly acknowledged their elderly Good Samaritan and nodded at him. "We are very grateful for your help, Mr. Chettle."

"Not at all, not at all, missy. Where would we be if we did not help each other?" Mr. Chettle seemed embarrassed by her thanks. "Daniel, can ye' tie them horses up and help the lad here?" he gestured at Dering "This poor gentleman seems to have taken a hard knock and could use some help." Again, he gestured, but this time at Dr. Chadwick.

Clive had not really noticed the driver of Chettle's carriage, who now appeared to be a huge dark shadow. But once he had climbed down and tied the horses to the wheel of the wrecked carriage, Clive could see that the driver was only average in height and it was his caped greatcoat that gave him bulk. He appeared to be much younger than his employer, who sported a bushy gray beard and spectacles.

Silently, he moved to Chadwick's side and hooked his arm over his shoulder. Between Daniel and Clive, they half-led and half-dragged the injured man to the carriage. Once in the carriage, Festus slumped across the rear seat.

Clive stopped Frederica from joining her uncle, saying, "I will sit in the back with Dr. Chadwick. I can hold him steadier." She nodded and quickly climbed in to join Thomas Grant on the seat behind the driver.

"All good there?" their Good Samaritan asked. "I'll sit up top with Daniel. After we get to the house, Daniel will come back for the horses and some of your baggage."

Getting Chettle up into the driver's box took some doing on the silent Daniel's part, but finally he got the squire settled into the box.

The drive to Wolverton Gatehouse seemed overly long—nay, endless—to Clive. And the rocking did not help anyone's comfort. Although Daniel had a lantern on a pole above the horses, the inside of the carriage was so dark that no physical features were discernable. However, Mr. Grant's stifled groans were easily heard over the sound of the horses.

"Can you sit close to him and try to keep him from being thrown about?" he finally asked Frederica.

"Mr. Dering, I am already doing that, but this bouncing is horrible," she gasped. "Where are we going?"

Squire Chettle's voice broke the silence. "I am sorry about the roughness of the ride, but we are taking the shortest route to the house, through the fields. If we had gone the smoother way, it would have taken much longer, and your men look to need help as soon as possible."

Dr. Chadwick seemed to be unconscious again. Clive used his own body to keep Festus propped in the corner and to absorb as much of the rocking as possible. Grant's smothered groans were very upsetting to everyone. The gentle lowing of the cows seemed an odd contrast.

"Not much longer now," Chettle said. "I can see some lights from the house."

Finally, Daniel turned the team left. The road improved so noticeably that Clive assumed they were travelling on the drive leading to a house.

"Oh," said Frederica. "I can see a building. Oh look, there are two turrets. It looks like a real castle."

When Clive peered out of the carriage he could see a dark mass against the night sky. Then everything darkened as the carriage drove under the tunnel running between the turrets.

"Here we are at last, and Mistress Chettle is waiting for us. Good, good!"

The carriage pulled to a stop in a small courtyard, where several torches cast a light on people waiting for them. What must have been the entire household surged forward to assist the injured down out of the carriage.

Mistress Chettle proved to be a round bustling sort of person who emitted sympathetic noises but proved extremely efficient in giving orders and organizing the staff. Clive could see his hurt companions being taken to the gatehouse. When Clive and Frederica began to follow, Mistress Chettle stopped them, putting her arm around the distressed young woman.

"Oh you poor lass!" Her voice was warm and motherly. Clive noticed Frederica's shoulders relax somewhat as the older woman hugged her.

"Now don't you worry. Dr. Bagies is here and he will see those gentlemen are set right. However, watching while he sets bones and stitches up heads is not a place for a young lady like you. We have a place upstairs where you can rest and have some tea while they go about their business. Anyway, you look all done in." Then she gave a started exclamation, "Oh my, you're covered in blood!"

In the excitement and the dark, Dering had not noticed Frederica's dress. "Have you been hurt?" he asked sharply.

"No, no," Frederica explained. "The blood is all his. His head kept bleeding. I finally had to rip up part of my petticoat to tie a bandage on. I am afraid I am quite a mess," Frederica added ruefully.

"Oh, thank the good Lord you are not hurt," Mistress Chettle said. "Gave me a bit of a fright to see you in the light just now. I thought you must have been injured, too."

"No, thankfully I am not hurt. I seem to have landed on top of everyone when the carriage went over."

"You go with Polly upstairs and she will see to you," Mistress said briskly. "I will have a tea tray sent up. Go on now! Don't worry about the gentlemen; they'll be taken care of." And, so saying, she gently turned Frederica from the door of the sick room to the stairwell.

With a sigh of relief that Frederica had not been hurt, Clive Dering turned to enter the makeshift hospital. He gave the young woman's hand a reassuring squeeze and said, "You go along, Miss Chadwick. You did really well out there, but I will keep watch now."

***

Clive

Clive woke the next morning to bright sunlight pouring in the window and directly into his face. He studied the offending window, noticing with annoyance that he had forgotten to pull the drapes. In truth, he remembered little of anything that had happened after Tommy's arm and Dr. Chadwick's head were seen to. Besides the obvious injuries, both men had numerous bruises and contusions. Finally, the doctor had dosed both with enough laudanum to help them sleep. Clive hoped it kept them sleeping well into the morning. Considering the shape of the older men, he thought he and Miss Chadwick had fared remarkably well.

Dressed, Clive started down the circular stairwell to check on the patients. In the daylight, he could see what had not been obvious in the darkness of the previous night. The stairs must have been ancient. The treads were no longer even, but well-worn in the middle, as if many thousands of feet had used them. There was only a rope on the wall side instead of a railing. They went up as well as down, indicating there must be at least one level above. He assumed Miss Chadwick had been installed upstairs.

Below, the patients were still asleep. He carefully drew their drapes so the sunlight would not wake them. Grant had more color in his face than last night, and Dr. Chadwick also seemed in much better condition, as he was breathing easier. Now, to find Miss Chadwick?

He went up the stairs, passing his room to the level above. This floor was still another surprise: not a sleeping chamber, but a large sitting room. Frederica, wrapped in a blanket, her feet tucked under her, sat in one of the overstuffed chairs in front of an enormous fireplace. A tea tray was positioned on a table by the wall.

"Good morning, Mr. Dering," she said hesitantly.

"Good morning to you, Miss Chadwick," he responded. "Am I disturbing you?"

"Not at all, but…" she seemed somewhat flustered.

"What is wrong?" he asked.

"Um, we probably should not be here alone," she said.

"Miss Chadwick, do you think I would take advantage of you, really?" he asked rather incredulously. "I do not do those kinds of things. Besides, you are Dr. Chadwick's niece and he is just downstairs."

"How is my uncle? And Mr. Grant?" she asked, anxious to change the subject. "No one seems to be around to ask."

"It is quite early. People might not be up and about yet. But someone left a tea tray?" he asked, gesturing to the table.

"That was here when I awoke," she replied.

"Must be from last night." Clive moved to the tray. How bad could luke-warm tea be? He poured a cup and sat in the other chair.

"I just checked on the gentlemen and both of them are sleeping. I admit last night was rough, but the doctor gave them laudanum and I think they passed a reasonable night." He took a sip and found just how bad tea left out could be. "The tea is pretty bad, but there is also bread and cheese. Can I get you some?"

"I can get it," she answered. Draped in the blanket, she busied herself at the tray. She brought back a plate with bread and cheese to her chair, but to his surprise, she also placed one at Clive's elbow.

He studied her carefully. "You seem better than last night. Were you able to sleep?"

She nodded, finished swallowing, and added, "I am very relieved Uncle Festus and Mr. Grant are going to be fine. I think it is remarkable you and I were not injured."

Clive made a noise of agreement in his throat. His mouth was full of bread, not too stale, and cheese, warm and sharp.

"I was just thinking the same thing," he said. "You ended up mostly pro-tected by Mr. Grant's body, and I was on the top. Unfortunately for your uncle, he was on the bottom." He did not want to worry her unduly, but even the doctor had remarked on it last night, so he continued, "I am a little con-cerned about him. This is the second accident in a short time. It may take him some time to recover."

He half expected her to burst into tears upon hearing his words. But, to his surprise, she nodded solemnly. "I agree; he is too old for such events not to take a toll. While I hope we do not have to abandon our adventure, I guess I must prepare myself for such an eventuality. He may need to go back home to recover."

"Now, why are you wrapped in a blanket?" he asked, although he had a good idea of the problem.

"I cannot find my luggage," she confirmed his thought. "Not even a brush." She finger- combed her hair but to his delight was unable to tame it.

"Daniel put your luggage in my room."

"You probably could have brought a herd of horses into the room and I would not have noticed. You are right, I was that tired." She sighed deeply and continued, "Mr. Dering, what is this place? No one seems to be here but us! Where's the family? I remember meeting Master Chettle and Mistress Chettle last night. But what happened to them?"

"The family lives in the main house. If you look through the back window, you can see the courtyard and the main entrance to the house." Clive gestured to the window. "We are in the original gatehouse for the castle. The real castle part—walls and such—were torn down long ago. Just this bit remains, maybe partially destroyed during the same war that blew up Corfe Castle. This room forms the arch over the drive."

"How do you know all this? Have you been here before?"

"No, but Squire Chettle gave quite a detailed lecture last night, trying to distract Mr. Grant while the doctor set his arm. He even claimed that Sir Walter Raleigh stayed here in the gatehouse. It took some time to set poor Tommy's arm. It was a bad break." He gave a shudder as he remembered the pain his former tutor had to undergo when the doctor wiggled the arm into place and then bound it with splints. He left out the detail of Grant finally fainting from the pain.

"I hope he is going to recover easily," she said. Her voice seemed calm enough, but her hands were twisting in her lap.

"What else is concerning you?" he asked.

"I think my dress is ruined and I only have two others."

"And one has dirt stains from the accident at Corfe, if I remember rightly," he tried a lighter tone to raise her spirits.

Even as Frederica groaned in agreement, there was a light tap at the door.

"Pardon me," said a quiet voice. A middle-aged woman dressed in standard housemaid's black stood in the doorway holding a tray. "Mistress thought you might use some coffee." She set the tray on the larger table in the corner. "Shall I pour?"

"Quite alright," said Clive. "But I can do the honors." He took the pot from the woman and poured two cups of thick coffee. "But we do need your help."

"Yes, sir, of course."

"What is your name?" Frederica stood and approached the table also. "Oh, this coffee smells so good." She held out her hand for a cup.

"Polly, Miss."

"Miss Chadwick, here," Clive gestured to Frederica with his cup, "is very hard on her wardrobe."

"Hard?" Frederica laughed. "I am a disaster."

"I already took the dress you had on yesterday, miss, and put it to soak last night," Polly stated. "But that was a lot of blood and when I checked this morning, not much was coming out."

At Frederica's dejected look, Clive asked, "Maybe you could look at another dress with has grass stains on it?"

"Of course, sir. Where is it? I didn't see miss's luggage last night."

"It is downstairs in the room I used," Dering responded.

"I will get the dress on my way out, miss," the maid turned to go. "Oh, mistress said breakfast would be served shortly and she wants to make sure you both come to the main house."

"Of course," he responded. "We will be along as soon as Miss Chadwick is ready."

After the maid departed, Clive and Frederica remained in the room drinking their coffee.

"We, or rather you, were really lucky to find these people," she said quietly. "We could have been in a very bad way if we had not gotten help when we did." She drank some coffee and continued, "But where did you sleep last night? Have you slept at all?"

"I ended up sleeping in the first room down the stairs. I thought I was going to stay with Tommy and Dr. Chadwick, but after the doctor set Tommy's arm and then dosed them for the night, I was not needed anymore. Master Chettle had a stable lad sleep on the floor so he could get me if they needed anything. I heard nothing after my head hit the pillow."

"How did you find Mr. Chettle last night? You seemed to be gone forever, although I expect it wasn't as long as it seemed. But you never would have found this place by yourself."

"I started back the way we came, or the way I thought we had come. Turns out the blasted coachman, whom I may add is still missing, took us on a little-used side road. I suppose he thought it was a shortcut. Once I got on the main road to Dorchester, I found a tavern where, lucky for us, Mr. Chettle was having a late dinner. He had Daniel and the carriage with him, so he offered to come back with me. The landlord of the tavern sent messages ahead to Mistress Chettle and the doctor."

Frederica placed her coffee cup on the tray. "I will go find my luggage. When do you think my uncle and Mr. Grant will awaken so I can visit them?"

"I really can't tell you. I am hoping the doctor gave them both enough laudanum to make them sleep all day. I fear they are both going to be in a lot of pain when they do wake."

Chapter Five: Samaritans

Clive

As Dering led Frederica to the main house, he thought she seemed a bundle of nerves. Last night, she had been a stalwart figure after the accident. She had found firewood and bandaged her uncle without any breakdown. But today, as she clung to his arm, she seemed less so. And, the dark dress she wore was hideous. His sisters would have burned it.

The two greeted the Chettles and Clive led Frederica to a seat near their hostess. Breakfast in the main house proved to be similar to breakfast at his home in Yorkshire. Food—the usual eggs, meats, and potatoes—was organized on the sideboard so latecomers could help themselves. The master of the house sat at the head of the table, drinking coffee and reading the paper, with Mistress Chettle at the foot, pouring tea and keeping a sharp eye on the servants while uttering a running commentary that her husband occasionally acknowledged with a grunt or "Yes, dear." Their hosts had obviously eaten before Dering and Chadwick arrived. He assumed they were still at the table, waiting so they could grill their healthy guests and find out who they had let into their home. After all their hospitality, Clive felt the Chettles were owed some answers.

Frederica seemed too shaky to handle a plate safely, so he asked her what she wanted and shook his head at the answer of "Just toast, please." He filled his plate, added a bit of everything to hers, and returned to the table. Once the tea was poured, the inquisition started. Not, as he had anticipated, about the condition of their companions.

"Where, Miss Chadwick, is your chaperone?" Mistress fired the first shot.

Startled, Frederica froze with toast partway to her mouth and looked at Clive in desperation. Clive thought it a perfectly legitimate question. It was odd that a young woman was traveling with three males. When the silence grew too long, he answered for her.

"Mistress Chettle, Miss Chadwick is the niece of Dr. Chadwick, the gentleman with the head wound. She is traveling under his protection for the educational experience. He is a learned scholar of antiquities and often lectures at Oxford. Mr. Grant, the unfortunate man with the broken arm, is also a scholar of some renown and a close friend of Dr. Chadwick's. We are journeying to various ancient places in England. We have just come from Dorchester, where we spent a few days visiting Roman sites, and are making our way to Glastonbury." He stopped, hoping his explanation was enough for the Chettles to see that he and his companions were merely upright citizens who had had an accident.

Grumbling from the head of the table proved to be Master Chettle just clearing his throat. "And how do you fit into this group, young man?" he asked.

Clive swallowed some tea. "Honestly, I am a late addition to the group," he admitted. "Mr. Grant is my former tutor and when my father wanted to get rid of me for the summer, he asked Mr. Grant to take me on." This was not exactly what had happened, but it was close enough.

"What did you do?" Chettle chuckled.

"Got sent down from university," Clive said shortly.

Chettle laughed out loud. "And your father punished you by making you go on a tour with two old scholars? That is just brilliant. I would like to meet your father."

Internally, Clive agreed that his father and Chettle had a lot in common.

"Just so I am sure I understand all this," Mistress Chettle interjected, "you and Miss Chadwick here are not related?"

"No, madam."

"In that case, missy, while you are under my roof, Polly will act as your chaperone, at least while your uncle is indisposed," their hostess said firmly.

Frederica looked relieved. "Thank you, mistress," she said quietly. "You are very generous."

Clive now appreciated that Frederica had probably been uncomfortable being alone with him, even more than he had realized.

"The doctor stopped by before he left this morning," Mistress Chettle continued. "He thinks it will be some time before your friends can travel, especially Dr. Chadwick. Given his age and the severity of the gash, he wants him to stay in bed and rest. He is worried there is a brain injury behind the gash."

"Yes, he said pretty much the same to me last night," Clive admitted.

"Why did you not tell me?" Frederica demanded.

"I was hoping he was wrong and we would be on our way without disrupting our hosts too much more," Clive sighed. "My friends seemed so peaceful when I checked on them this morning."

"Laudanum," Mistress Chettle said shortly. Then she leaned over and re-filled their cups. "You two are not to worry, though. You are all welcome here for as long as it takes to get the gentlemen on their feet. Things are pretty quiet around here, so some guests, even if they are injured, are welcome."

"I agree," their host added. "Besides, the young lady will be company for my missus. Our daughter got married last year and it has been lonesome for her." He smiled the length of the table at their hostess in her cap and old-fashioned gown. He obviously thought the world of her.

Miss Chadwick still seemed tongue-tied, so Clive decided to ask for help on her behalf, in case she could not bring herself to.

"Mistress Chettle, may we impose even more on your generosity?" he began. "Miss Chadwick finds herself in something of a clothing dilemma."

Over Frederica's protest of "Oh Mr. Dering, don't…" he continued. "Polly tells us her dress is not coming clean. I was hoping you might help Miss Chadwick either fix the garment or find a suitable replacement?"

Frederica's face was red with embarrassment. She stared at her plate silently.

"Of course, there is nothing I would like more than to help you repair the damage. Nothing to blush about, Miss Chadwick," Mistress Chettle said encouragingly. "You ruined that dress while trying to help your dear uncle. And you stayed in the dark with the two hurt gentlemen. You must have been frightened to death. I know I would have been."

"I *was* pretty scared," the young woman admitted quietly. "But I cannot impose further on you. You have done so much already."

"Not at all, dear. I am happy to do so. Polly is the seamstress around here.

We will ask her to help." Mistress reached out and patted Frederica's hand encouragingly. "We will have you fitted out in no time."

Satisfied with his intervention and the fact that Frederica Chadwick's face was now its normal color, Clive turned to his host.

"After breakfast, sir, I would like to go back to the wreck. Maybe in the daytime, I will be able to tell more about what caused it. Also, the coachman never turned up and I have been wondering what happened to him."

"Yes, we need to talk to that man about that accident," Squire Chettle agreed. "Take Daniel with you."

"Oh Mr. Dering, may I go also?" Frederica asked. "My satchel with my art supplies and Claude glasses is still in the carriage. Jeffrey just gave me those glasses! Oh, I hope they didn't get broken."

"Take Polly with you," came the firm reminder.

* * *

Frederica

The trip to the accident site was postponed. Mistress Chettle had insisted on seeing the dresses Mr. Dering had mentioned.

"So, I can start work while you are gone," she had asserted.

Clive and Frederica followed Mistress Chettle to her parlor, where Polly had laid out the offending dresses. Frederica cringed as they studied the yards of print muslin spread before them. Large stains disfigured the front of the dress. The white dress was not much better with grass and dirt stains where she had knelt in the dirt.

"I am so sorry, miss. I tried my best to get them stains out, but blood is terrible once it's dry." Polly's defiant stance with hands on her hips was belied by her voice, which sounded upset at her failure with the bloodstains. Their very existence seemed to offend her deeply.

Frederica sighed. She needed to say something; obviously the maid had put in a great deal of work trying to clean her dress. But she only had the three dresses and this one was ruined. "It is not your fault, Polly. I know you did your best. I am sure I would have been even less successful. There just wasn't anything else at the time to use on Uncle Festus's head."

Mistress Chettle patted Frederica on the shoulder. "Don't you worry; we will contrive something. It seems such a shame to dispose of such a pretty dress, especially when there is so much wear left in it."

At that statement, Frederica groaned inwardly. She knew the style of the muslin was rather childish, with its high collar and ruffle around the hem. In her opinion, the extra lengthening flounce necessitated by her recent growth spurt only labeled her as still in the schoolroom. However, there had only been time to make one new dress for the trip. What had she been thinking getting the dress done up in white, especially for traveling? Now her best dress was decorated with dirt stains at the knees and second best covered in blood.

"Perhaps, Miss Chadwick, we could sew an apron over the front; that would hide most of the stain." Mistress Chettle sounded rather dubious, if willing.

Frederica saw Dering moving closer to take a detailed look at the dress. She felt sure he could not understand why she was upset about a silly dress. She waited for him to make some sardonic comment or joke. She was totally surprised when he finally spoke.

"Ladies, may I make a humble suggestion?" She noticed that both maid and mistress glanced at him with the same suspicion she felt. After all, what did a man know about cleaning stains? "The top part – what is that called? – and the skirt are separate pieces, right?"

Three nods.

"Bodice," Polly said. "It is called the bodice."

"And the skirt is completely gathered where it is attached to the top. Again, do we agree?" he continued.

Three more nods.

"So, do you think we can detach the skirt?"

Again, the nods.

"Then I suggest we cut the stains out of the fabric and reattach the skirt. That will make the front of the dress flatter with fewer gathers. Keep the gathers in the back. Less skirt, but I understand that is quite fashionable these days." Clive grinned at the women. To Frederica, he seemed enormously pleased by the surprise on their faces and by his own cleverness.

"Why, young man, I think you have a very good idea. And where did you learn about ladies' dresses, may I ask?" Mistress Chettle asked sharply.

"Why, madam, I have sisters. Both are mad for the latest fashions and quite handy with the needle. I expect they could set up opposite Madame Fregeau's in London and do quite well for themselves."

"What do you know about Madame Fregeau's, Mr. Dering? I understand from my own sister, who goes to London quite often, that she makes clothes for all the stage women," Mistress Chettle said primly.

"Well," the young man responded, "I suppose stage people might be part of her clientele, but I am sure I went there with Mother on some trip or other. So, she has to be the accepted thing." Clive was quite offhand in his answer. "Spiffing clothes, Miss Chadwick; you would love them. Now, if that is settled, are you ready for our walk?"

Mistress Chettle was still surveying the dress. "I think, Mr. Dering, your suggestion will work very well. I do so love a challenge!" She looked at Frederica. "You go along and look for your art things. I will take the dress apart and cut the skirt. Don't worry; there will be long boring seams to sew tonight after dinner." She smiled at Frederica and made shooing motions with her hands.

Polly was still studying the dress. "Aye, Mistress, that young man has a real good idea. We can turn the skirt completely about and put the seam in the back. No one will know it didn't start life looking like that." Polly sounded much happier as she started to turn the dress inside out looking for seams to cut.

"I will do this," the mistress said. "You go with the young people to see the carriage."

"Oh thank you, Mistress Chettle, and you, too, Polly. You are so good to us. I am so grateful." When Frederica began to run out of expressions of gratitude, Dering took her arm and escorted her to the stairs.

"I think you should bring a pelisse or a shawl. It might get cool while we are on our walk."

"I already have one with me. I left it on the table by the door when I came in. That was a wonderful idea about the dress. I don't have too many and that was my best walking dress. But do you think I should leave Mistress Chettle working on it? They have already done so much for us." Frederica sounded doubtful as she draped her shawl about her shoulders and preceded him to the door.

Polly surprised them by chuckling out loud. "Didn't you see the look on mistress's face?" she said. "She loves the idea of remodeling the dress. But I am the one who should stay to help. Mistress loves to sew, but she is not…" Polly paused to think of her words. "…She is not as comfortable with styling. We usually work together."

Obviously, Polly was as interested in fashion as Mistress Chettle. She was probably even better, so she should be the one to stay. "Is there anyone else who could go with us?" she asked.

Polly thought a moment, and with a "Please wait a moment," she hurried back inside.

"You would ruin their good time if you stayed to help," Dering said. "And Polly wants in on it. You will see; she will find some poor sod to take her place so she can go back and play with your dress. Also, remember, Mistress Chettle was kind enough to leave you the boring long seams to sew while she and Polly are doing the redesign. Don't worry; we made them very happy today!"

In moments, Polly returned with a young housemaid. After stern directions not to leave Miss Chadwick alone, she returned inside and left the two travelers with their chaperone to their walk.

"Which way are we going? I am totally lost," Frederica admitted.

"Back through the field we came through last night. Through the tunnel and to the right. I know this seemed like the back of beyond when we arrived here, but we are only a couple of miles from Dorchester." Clive took Frederica's arm again as they strode along the path. "Master Chettle tells me it is not far if we cross this pasture. It was the potholes that made it seem so endless last night. That and our anxiety about our friends. When I stopped in to get my coat just now," Dering continued, "both our companions were going back to sleep. We can stop in to visit when we get back. Depending on how long it takes for him to recover, we may have to adjust the itinerary, but there was no talk of just ending it."

"Do you think they will be up to it?" Frederica was still concerned.

Clive shrugged and replied, "I may have to help Tommy tie his cravat, but he certainly seemed game. But they will be the judges."

At the end of the drive, Clive took a right turn. Frederica could see a mud track disappearing into a spring green field sprinkled with grazing cows and sheep.

"Do you have your boots on?" He looked at her feet, even as she assured him she was well-shod. "I also asked Daniel for directions, so we should not get lost. His directions were more detailed than Master Chettle's. He said for us to turn right out of the drive and walk through several fields until we come to a tall hedge. There should be a small house where the track meets the road. At that point, we should see our carriage off to the right. He also said he thought he had picked up all the baggage, but in the dark he may have missed something."

Frederica glanced behind to make sure their little chaperone was keeping up. Then she surveyed the neat fields laid out with hedgerows covered by the bright blue sky and felt the sun on her cheeks. Her fingers almost itched to get the scene on paper. She smiled at Dering. "Sounds like Daniel was downright talkative this morning."

Clive returned the smile and then laughed. "You really seem to avoid wearing your bonnet as much as possible."

Frederica had pulled her long hair loosely into a braid, but already she could feel bits and pieces were escaping. "Bonnets get in my way," she said. "The sides of my bonnet come out like blinders on a horse and restrict my vision. And in case you did not notice, I also do not have any patience for the fashionable draping of shawls. I want to have my hands free." She readjusted the faded paisley cloth, slinging the end over her left shoulder. She strode along without any of the prancing steps young debutantes were using now in London. She seemed to him quite fresh and unspoiled.

A tug on his sleeve brought Clive back to the present.

"Look, that cow is coming towards us. Should we run?

"She's just curious. She probably will not come much closer."

Clive proved correct. The cow that had caught Frederica's attention stood on the side of the path and watched them in the distance without making an aggressive move.

"Mr. Dering, how do you know so much? Like about women's fashions and what cows will do?" Frederica asked him curiously.

Clive grinned at her. "Just experience, Miss Chadwick, just experience. Look, we are almost at the end of the track. I think I can see another road intersecting. There, by that small house."

The little cottage at the intersection of the track and the road seemed deserted. No smoke issued from its chimney and no dogs greeted them. From the top of the sty by the fence gate, they could both see the road veering off to the right and see the where the carriage rested. It lay almost on its right side, half in and half out of the ditch. They continued closer, then stood surveying the damage.

"Mr. Chettle has promised me some men and horses to get it out of the ditch. We will also need help fixing whatever caused the coach to go into the ditch in the first place. Damn that blasted coachman anyway! Whatever possessed him to take off? He did not even stay to see if we were hurt!"

"Do you think he might have been the one to cause the accident and took off before we could blame him?" She looked around the area. The body of the dead horses were still there, and the remains of last night's fire were clearly visible.

"I'll come out here tomorrow with Daniel and Mr. Chettle and get the carriage upright. Then we'll know what the damage is." Clive walked up to the coach.

"Do you remember where your sketchbook and pencils were?" he asked. He rocked the carriage a bit to test its sturdiness as he spoke.

"Why do you need to fix the carriage?" Frederica asked. "Did not Uncle Festus hire the rig? Would they not come and reclaim their property?"

"Mr. Chettle asked me the same thing," Clive answered. "Dr. Chadwick hired it back in London for the complete trip. I am afraid it would take too long to send to London and wait for them to come out here and get it fixed for us. And, of course, we will need something to take us on the rest of the trip."

"We will need a driver, too."

He nodded in agreement. "However, I can handle two horses, at least until we get to Glastonbury or Bath and can hire another driver."

"You are a man of many talents!" she said teasingly.

Dering laughed in response. "It must be obvious by now that I grew up on in the country. The grooms let me try anything I wanted to."

"That sounds like an exciting childhood. I can only imagine the things you might have wanted to try."

"There were quite a lot, and most involved horses," Dering agreed companionably.

Frederica followed him to the side of the carriage. The young maid found a spot near a tree and leaned back, closing her eyes in the sun.

"Do you think it is safe? My sketchbook can wait. I don't want you to get hurt, too."

Clive pushed on the carriage again. It seemed securely wedged into the ditch.

"I am afraid it is stuck. I think we are going to have trouble getting it out. But I want to look inside anyway, so where…?"

"I had them on my lap as we traveled. The sketchbook was separate, but my pencils and Claude glasses were in my satchel. Everything must now be on the bottom, unless it fell out the window into the ditch."

"Well, let me take a look." Using passenger handholds on the roof, Clive pulled himself to the left side of the carriage. Holding the frame to break his descent, he dropped feet first into the passenger compartment through the window. Almost immediately, he came back up through the same window. His face was ashen.

"Mr. Dering, what's wrong?"

There was no answer. Clive pulled himself out of the carriage and scrambled down the roof to the ground. Still without uttering a word, he ran into the nearest bushes. Frederica could hear him vomiting. After a few minutes, he emerged wiping his face. He walked quietly to where Frederica was standing and collapsed on the grass. Frederica knelt next to him, offering him her handkerchief to wipe his face.

"Mr. Dering?" she said quietly. "Did you find the coachman?"

He nodded, keeping his eyes closed.

"Under the carriage?"

He gave another silent nod.

Frederica thought out loud. "He must have died last night. We never heard a sound from there and after you left, believe me, it was very quiet. You must not blame yourself; it was so dark no one could have seen anything even if we had thought to look."

Frederica put a hand on Dering's shoulder. She had never seen someone look so shocked. Clive's face was still white and his hands shook.

He put his hand on top of hers. He spoke very quietly, "Yes, he must have died instantly. Oh Miss Chadwick, there are parts of him everywhere and his face is looking up into the window. We probably stood on him last night to get out!" He involuntarily gagged again, but there was nothing left in his stomach to come up. He struggled to his feet, pulling Frederica up with him.

"Come on, let's go and get help. We need Mr. Chettle to deal with these matters. It is beyond me."

The trio retraced their steps much more quickly than their outward trip had taken.

"Mr. Dering, did you notice that all the time we were at the carriage, no one went by us? We are only a few miles from Dorchester and Wolverton Manor is certainly well-populated," Frederica stood on top of the stile and looked backwards towards the road. "But isn't it strange no one is out on the road?" Shaking her head, she stepped carefully down to the field.

Clive seemed to pull himself back from the horror that was inside the carriage.

"Mr. Chettle told me last night I was just lucky that I found him at the tavern because this road is not used much anymore. There is evidently a new road on the other side of Wolverton Manor leading from Dorchester to Cerne Abbas and beyond that is more heavily traveled."

Frederica frowned. "Then why were we using this road if there was another better one? I am going to ask Uncle Festus if he knows anything about this. I wonder if he discussed it with the coachman."

"Well, let's worry about it later. Those clouds look like rain and I need to find Mr. Chettle."

After they returned to the manor, Frederica did not see Clive again until dinner. It was a rather late meal, having been delayed so the men could retrieve the coachman's body. There were only five around the table: Master and Mistress Chettle; Thomas Grant, still looking pale with his arm in a sling; Mr. Dering, also still pale; and Frederica. Festus Chadwick was still confined to bed with headaches that were at times quite severe, making him dizzy and nauseous.

Mrs. Chettle had directed Frederica to a seat next to Thomas Grant.

"Now, dear, I want you to make sure that Mr. Grant's beef is cut up for him, what with his arm being broken and all." So Frederica sat next to Mr. Grant, cutting up his meat for him and buttering his bread. The scholar was quite appreciative of her efforts, thanking her profusely and repeatedly apologizing for being a burden.

"Stop thanking me, Mr. Grant," she protested. "I am very glad to be able to offer this small service. After all, maybe the reason your arm is broken is because you softened my fall and kept me from being hurt!" Secretly Frederica worried that Grant, in spite of his protestations, would not be able to continue the journey. He seemed to be in pain still and shortly after the main course, he took his leave and went off to bed.

"That damn—oh excuse me, my dear!—that laudanum makes you awful sleepy." Mr. Chettle could see Frederica was concerned about Thomas Grant. "He'll be fine. Part of his problem is the laudanum, which you need for the pain but puts you to sleep. After the bone starts to knit, he'll need less and will be more himself. Broken a few bones in my time, too. Ain't that right, mistress?"

His wife surveyed him fondly. "Yes, you have, Mr. Chettle. And a right poor patient you were, too. Not like these two gentlemen. But don't you worry, Miss Chadwick, they'll both be right as rain in a few days."

"A few days! Oh Mrs. Chettle, we can't impose on you that long." Frederica was aghast. Unexpected guests in her stepmother's household were given short shrift and sent on their way. The generous hospitality of the Chettles was overwhelming and she did not want to take advantage of it.

Clive Dering had been unexpectedly quiet up to now. "The doctor says they will both be fine, Miss Chadwick. I spoke to him just before dinner. He says it will take a few days for them to come around. Dr. Chadwick especially got quite a knock on the head. We could move to the inn in Cerne Abbas to allow for a more leisurely recovery. We are imposing on your generosity, Mr. Chettle, and I hesitate to burden you for an unspecified period of time."

Mr. Chettle cut off Dering, sounding to Frederica rather angry. "Now, young man, I would be real upset if you were to move that good man with his head so hurt. He and you will stay right here!"

The mistress now interrupted, but more gently. "You two young people are quite right not to wish to burden us, but Mr. Chettle and I really want you to stay." Obviously, Mistress Chettle had a lot of experience deflecting her husband's somewhat rough manner. "It gets kind of lonesome here this time of year and I am enjoying having you around. I know Mr. Chettle has had several chats with the learned gentlemen. We are pleased to be able to show our Christian duty and help out other human beings; you are really doing us a favor by staying and being comfortable with us."

And so saying, she smiled sweetly at them all and the question was settled with her convoluted logic.

Of course, the crash and today's grim discovery needed to be discussed, but Mr. Chettle waited until the cheese and fruit had been served to turn the conversation to those subjects.

"So, young Clive, this is where we stand with the carriage. I learned the name of the company where Dr. Chadwick hired the vehicle. Before you came back this afternoon with that nasty news, I sent them a letter telling them their carriage was in my ditch and two of their horses had been killed. I'll send another tomorrow telling them about the driver."

"I appreciate that, sir. I guess I should have thought to do that, but I must admit that this afternoon really shook me up."

"No, no, my boy, not a problem whatsoever. Entirely my pleasure. There's no problem with leaving the damn thing in the field we dragged it to, but we can't be leaving that poor driver, or what remains of him, in my barn for long. So I figure that if we don't hear from them tomorrow, we had best just pop him in the ground over in the churchyard."

"That is so sad. We don't even know his name," Frederica said.

"True enough. But the carriage hire will know and then we can put up a stone of some kind. Or perhaps his people will want to take him home. But this is what I thought you might consider for the next stage of your journey, if it is alright by you and the other gentlemen, and that is to arrange for a man I know from the village to take you to Glastonbury. He has a carriage that he hires out and as he would be driving, he would know all the local roads. Of course, this would not be for at least a few days until Dr. Chadwick is more himself."

Clive nodded in agreement. "That sounds just fine, sir. Once in Glastonbury, we can hire another carriage to take us to Bath. I believe that was our next stop."

"As there are only the four of us, shall we all move into the drawing room? We can have tea in there while the servants clear up. Also, Miss Chadwick, Mr. Dering, I want to show you something."

Mistress Chettle bustled them into the drawing room where pieces of Frederica's dress were displayed on several chairs. Mrs. Chettle gestured to it triumphantly. "What do you say to that?"

Frederica looked at the dress in astonishment. There were no blood stains on any of the pieces laid out; the top parts of the front and back panels of the skirt were already gathered and ready to be resewn to the bodice. But the bodice really caught her attention. The ladies had totally restructured the neckline. The offending, and she thought childish, collar had been removed. The neckline now dipped down gracefully in front with a matching ribbon threaded around the décolletage. That ribbon would allow her to raise or lower the amount of her neck that showed, depending on her whim and perhaps the weather.

They had even redesigned the sleeves, pinning ribbons down the lengths. All that remained to be done were those "long boring seams." She had never looked forward to tackling a sewing project before.

Dering also seemed impressed. He immediately asked, "How ever did you change that neckline, Mistress Chettle? This is wonderful! You and Polly are brilliant at fashion design."

To Frederica's amazement, Mistress Chettle looked rather coy. "Do you think it might be good enough for that Madam Fregeau you mentioned?"

Clive grinned. "Oh my, yes. This certainly could come from her shop. Except for the material, I would not even recognize this as being the same dress. You did all this in one afternoon? And the style is quite up to date."

"Well, we have you to thank for the suggestions." The mistress of the house turned to Frederica. "How do you like it?"

"Oh Mistress Chettle, it is lovely. I also cannot believe it is the same dress. Look, Mr. Dering, the skirt has such a gentle fullness in the back, just as you suggested. Oh, and the ribbon down the sleeves now match the flounce around the bottom. It is a completely new dress. How can I ever thank you!" Frederica held the bodice in front of her. Indeed, the dress had been so completely made over that it no longer reminded one of the dress of a schoolroom miss. It looked just like some of the pictures she had seen in Godey's fashion book. She could hardly wait to finish the seams so she could wear it.

"Tomorrow, before you start on those seams, I want you to try on the bodice – just to make sure it will fit properly."

"As it looks like we will be staying for a few more days, Miss Chadwick, you will have plenty of time to work on those seams." Clive laughed as he took his teacup from Mistress Chettle. "Do you have any of that ribbon left?" he asked.

"Yes, but do you really think the dress needs more ribbon?"

"No, I thought maybe for her hair."

"Of course, that will look real sweet. You sure do have an eye for fashion, Mr. Dering."

"Oh, it is one of the few good things I learned from those sisters of mine."

Frederica went to sit by Mr. Chettle near the fire. "You and Mistress Chettle have been so kind to us."

Frederica carefully laid the bodice on a chair nearby. She studied it closely as she tried to get control of her emotions. She did not want to burst into tears in front of her host and hostess. Dering pushed a cup of tea into her hands. She buried her nose in her teacup.

Mr. Chettle seemed to have noticed, too, and cleared his throat.

"Well, to be sure, with our own girl gone, mistress doesn't have any girls to dress up, so I am sure she had a good time fixing your dress. Are you looking forward to Glastonbury? What is it Dr. Chadwick is taking you there for?"

"Uncle Festus and Mr. Grant are really interested in old historic sites, but we never really talked about Glastonbury. I'm guessing there must be some Roman ruins there."

"Not that I know of. Old ruins of the cathedral and the Tor. But naught else."

Frederica took a sip of her tea and decided to bring up the subject that had been bothering her all day.

"Mr. Chettle, I wanted to ask you about the roads. Mr. Dering says we were on a little-used road the other night. If the coachman was really a local, don't you think he would have known that road was not the proper route?"

"I agree it is strange. Maybe he wasn't a local if your uncle hired him in London. Could it be he thought he knew the way but did not know about the new road?"

"If so, his ignorance cost him dearly."

Breakfast Room: Chelsea

"**D**o you remember a fellow named Thomas Grant?" Nathan asked. His wife, sitting across the table, paused while pouring herself more tea. "A quiet gentleman, came with Jeffrey and his uncle to dinner during the winter?" Marion asked.

"Yes, that chap." Nathan pushed his cup across the table so Marion could refill his also.

"What about him?" she asked absently. He noticed he did not have her total attention. She had several letters laid out in front of her plate and another one of her continuous lists was at her elbow, ready for another note. As he had learned after their wedding, it was how she kept her life – and now his—organized. He was not great at reading upside down but he thought he saw a menu list, a food list, and was that a calendar? Others probably lay underneath. He was pretty sure the note he had in his hand would get her total attention.

"I just received a note from him," he began. "He and Festus Chadwick are in Dorset doing some travelling."

"Why is he writing you about it?" she asked distractedly, still involved with adding to her lists.

"Seems that before Jeffrey was reassigned, he was supposed to go on a trip with them to visit various places with antiquities. When he could not go, he asked Chadwick and Grant to take Frederica with them instead."

She finally looked up and gave him her full attention. "That is unusual but I bet Frederica is happy to be out from under her step-mother's watchful eye." She put down her pen and looked across the table at him. Yes, he had her attention now. "You remember, Jeffrey took me to meet them. I was not impressed with Mistress Chadwick. But I liked Frederica a lot. She has some real artistic talent."

"Jeffrey suggested Grant come to me if he had any concerns," he said answering her original question.

"Concerns?" Marion asked. "What kind of concerns? Did they run out of funds?"

"No, nothing like that. But there has been a carriage accident and Dr. Chadwick took a bad knock on the head. He, Chadwick I mean, is concerned that they will need to cancel the rest of the trip and he would hate to disappoint Frederica. Grant is asking if she can visit us for the summer instead of being sent home."

"Of course she can," Marion said immediately. "I would welcome the company. I cannot imagine what her life is like stuck down in Kent with that self-absorbed... words fail me," she tailed off.

"That bad?" he joked. He was rather surprised. Marion did not usually vent such negative feelings about people. Jeffrey's step-mother had made an impression and not a good one.

"Grant adds another bit of news that might interest you. Evidently another person was added to their little group, one of his former students, a chap named Clive Dering. He comes from Ripon in York. Grant says he was sent down from Oxford and, as punishment, his parents asked Grant if he could tutor him this summer," Nathan gave a full bodied laugh. "That is rich. Get expelled and your punishment is to spend your summer wandering around Dorset with two antiquities scholars and a young girl."

"Nathan," Marion was smiling even as she interjected. "Frederica is not a young girl. She is old enough for her presentation. Jeffrey was asking me about it not so long ago. In fact, I fully expect to sponsor her next year."

"I do not think I have seen her for some years," Nathan mused. "How old is she?"

"At least seventeen if not older, I believe," Marion responded. "She did not go about much before their father died, and then there was a mourning period. But that year is just now over. Going about with Festus and Grant will be good for her."

"I personally cannot think of anything more likely to bore a young woman than those two old scholars."

"Although I did only meet her once, she struck me as a thoughtful young woman," Marion said. "It was a full afternoon. Jeffrey took us to see the Elgin marbles and an art gallery that had some lovely Turners. Then we went to tea at Gunthiers'. Frederica and I talked a lot about books. As I recall, we had read a lot of the same titles. But it was art that actually makes her come alive. I enjoyed her very much."

"How many times have you met the step-mother?" Nathan asked curiously. His usually proper wife was proving she could hold some grudges.

"Almost every season that I have been in London. Jeffrey's father often brought her to London. He and my father were both old military veterans so of course, we would entertain them and see them at various functions. She is one of those women who try too hard, want to be the center of attention but do not know quite how to accomplish it except by overdressing and gossiping. But I admit it was the flirting with other men that really put me off."

Nathan started to butter more toast while he listened, entranced by Marion's attitude, one that was unusual for her.

"I believe I am getting the impression you did not like the second Mistress Chadwick," he teased.

"No, I did not," she said firmly. "I was, however, very relieved to find Frederica not ruined by her. I believe that is because her father spent a lot of time with her and because she had a sensible governess. What he saw in Hermione is beyond me."

Nathan, who had a very good idea what he saw in Hermione, decided to remain mum. He pushed the toast rack to her as an invitation. Marion shook her head, starting to rise.

"Wait, there is one other item."

Marion reseated herself and reached for the toast.

"He says, almost as an afterthought, that he is concerned about the accident. The driver was found dead at the bottom of the carriage, which by the way, ended up in a ditch. Grant simply says he can't stop wondering about the incident as it occurred on a lane not traveled often. Then he ends with 'if anything else happens that he is concerned about, he will write.'"

"Odd," his wife agreed. "Nathan, how do I write them and let them know Frederica is welcome to spend as much time as she likes here?"

"Oh, he lists their next stops as Bath and Avebury. Avebury," Nathan wondered. "What is there but some rocks?"

"There must be something or Dr. Chadwick would not be taking them there. Maybe you should listen to him sometime." She rose, kissed him on the forehead and moved to the door.

From his seated position Donnay could see with satisfaction the small bump in his wife's stomach just making its' presence known.

"Feeling well today?" he asked.

"After last night, how could I not?" she answered with a satisfied smile of her own. "Back massages help a lot with the aches." Before she got to the door, a brisk tap announced the arrival of General Ambrose Coxe.

"Good morning, Papa," Marion stopped to press a kiss to his cheek and then left.

Chapter Six: Glastonbury

Clive

The appearance of threatening rain clouds compelled the travelers to raise the top of the barouche shortly after leaving Wolverton. But, true to his word, their new driver, Sturdy, made Yeovil in three hours. There they stopped for luncheon and a hot drink, but not finding anything of historic interest to keep them, they decided to push on.

"Sturdy felt we could make Glastonbury by dark, but if we do not, I see there are inns at Ilchester or Somerton we can lay up at." Festus Chadwick had been consulting his *Paterson's Roads* again. "Sturdy could have written this part of the book. He is following the recommended route perfectly. I remember our other driver saying something about going to Shepton Mallet and then to Glastonbury. But this route is much quicker and far more direct."

Clive, from his seat next to Chadwick, had been studying the guidebook and accompanying map over the scholar's arm. "That direction would have taken us out of the way and then we would have to backtrack. I wonder why he suggested it."

"I don't know; I can only think he thought the roads were better. We only discussed the route to Cerne Abbas, which was not covered in *Paterson's,* so I had to rely on his supposed knowledge of local roads."

"This book is excellent, Dr. Chadwick." Clive had now taken over the tome and was studying it intently. "Look, it lists inns and where you can get fresh horses and at what price."

"Yes, it is actually of incalculable worth when planning a trip of this type. It is one thing to read Gilpin's work on some picturesque place in the countryside, but it is another to figure out how to get there. I am still mystified as to how we got on that lane near Wolverton." Festus Chadwick shook his head sadly. "Although in the end everything worked out fine, I shall be less trusting in the future."

"I don't know that I agree about 'fine.' After all, Uncle Festus, you still have headaches and Mr. Grant's arm must still pain him. It is a great mystery to us all as to what that man thought he was doing. When the carriage rolled on him, he definitely paid the price." Frederica shook her head.

"How far is Glastonbury from Wolverton according to *Paterson's*?" Thomas Grant seemed determine to change the subject.

Dering studied the pages more closely. "This column gives the mileage between possible stops and this column gives the total." He turned the book about and laid it on Mr. Grant's knee. Tracing the columns with his finger, he said, "From Dorchester, it is thirty-nine miles, but we started a bit after that, maybe eight miles closer, so let's say it would have been thirty-one miles to Wolverton. We were already at Ilchester, so we have about twenty-seven more to go." Clive leaned out the window. "Mr. Sturdy, what is your best guess as to when we shall get to Glastonbury?" he called.

The coach inhabitants could clearly hear the coachman's bellow in reply. "We're doin' pretty well right now, and God willin' all goes well, you should be sittin' down to eat at The Pilgrim 'fore sunset. Of course, we gets a lot of rain in these parts, and we're crossin' some marshy bits up near Street. Whole area floods a lot, especially in winter. You jest never knows what will slow you down."

Clive yelled his thanks and drew back inside.

"As you heard," he said to his companions, "if it does not rain and the roads do not flood, we should reach Glastonbury in good time. I figure sundown to be about six hours from now. Now, let me have that book again, Dr. Chadwick. I want to see how we are getting from Glastonbury to Bath."

The road they were travelling on now did not have the high yew hedges the travelers had seen around Dorchester. Today Clive could clearly see the lush farmland of Dorset. It was still too early in the spring for most fields to be fully planted, but the acreage was laid out in neat rectangles and bordered with low, well-trimmed hedges. Many had a large oak in the middle for the farmer to rest under after plowing. Other meadows had flocks of sheep; most were white with black faces. There were many baby lambs gamboling around with their perky tails up and stiff legs.

Full from the midday meal and lulled by the rocking of the coach, Clive drifted off. He woke to find his companions' conversation had turned from ancient Romans to, for some reason, King Arthur and the knights of the Roundtable.

"I read Malory's *Le Morte d'Arthur*," Frederica offered.

Mr. Grant looked at her in surprise. "How did you do that?" he asked. *"Le Morte d'Arthur* has not been printed in almost two hundred years."

"My father had a copy. It was very old and the language was difficult, but he helped me with it. So I guess you could say we read it together."

"My brother had an extensive library," Dr. Chadwick commented. "He was, if I may say so even though he was my brother, quite well read for a military man. Interested in almost anything." He turned to Frederica. "He did a lot of your tutoring himself from what he told me."

"Yes, we read a lot of books together. I had a regular governess for drawing, French, dancing, and that sort of thing. But I could always discuss interesting subjects with Father."

"Well, I am embarrassed. I have not read Arthur's Death or whatever title you were using," Clive interjected. "I know of the legend of King Arthur, of course. Everyone does, I imagine. But I thought he was like Robin Hood, sort of a mythical character." Clive sat back. He knew just such a statement would send Mr. Grant and Dr. Chadwick fighting over each other to explain the subject. He gave Frederica a small conspiratorial grin. Sure enough, an hour later, they were both still at it. By then, however, they were onto the history of Glastonbury and its famous cathedral.

"Well, who do you think the monks dug up then?" Mr. Grant asked.

"According to the abbot at the time, the burial vaults were of stone, so the bodies must have been of someone important," Dr. Chadwick responded. "There also was a cross saying something about this being Arthur and his wife Guinevere. The cross could have been placed there, but the stone vault surely signifies if it was not Arthur then it must have been some other king or nobleman."

"It certainly was the remaking of Glastonbury Abbey. Pilgrims started coming again in droves."

"What happened to the bodies?" Frederica wanted to know.

"They were reburied with great pomp and, until the time the abbey was dissolved, were right by the altar. Then when the abbey was torn down under Henry the Eighth, the bodies disappeared."

"Are you saying we are going to Glastonbury just to see two graves which have gone missing for a couple hundred years?"

"Clive, don't be so cynical. Glastonbury has some nice geological features Miss Chadwick could sketch. The town, even before the Romans, was a center of spiritual activity and there are some lovely old churches to visit. Then there is the Tor."

Clive interrupted Grant, "The Tor?"

"Yes, that hill there is called the Tor." Dr. Chadwick gestured to a hill in the distance. Both Clive and Frederica leaned forward to peer out the carriage window in the direction he indicated. They saw an unusual mound rise suddenly from the fairly flat plain around it. They could not miss it. It certainly was the tallest mound in the area.

"The ancients probably used it as a lookout. Tradition has it Arthur did as well. In fact, tradition says Glastonbury is Arthur's Avalon and this is where he came to die."

"Can we climb the Tor? I imagine the view is spectacular." Clive could see Frederica was already planning possible sketches.

"Yes, but let's save it for tomorrow. It is getting late and I for one could do with some food," Dr. Chadwick responded.

There was a general agreement that food would be very welcome, so the next stop for the carriage was The Pilgrim's Inn, where a friendly host was waiting for them.

After dinner, everyone opted for an early night.

* * *

Clive was drinking good coffee and reading a day-old London newspaper when Frederica entered the breakfast room. Their older companions were discussing plans for the day.

"I must admit I am not feeling energetic enough to face climbing the Tor," Festus Chadwick was saying. "Oh good morning, my dear. Did you sleep well?" The three men made to rise at her entrance.

Seated again, Clive waved the coffee pot at her and asked, "Coffee or tea?" He noticed she was wearing the truly horrid blue dress. At least she had her cloak to cover it up. His sisters would have burned the dress and gone about in their shifts before being seen in public in it. It was not to her brother's credit that she even owned such a garment.

She pointed at the coffee pot even as she asked her uncle, "Can't we take a carriage up there?"

"No, I asked our host and he says the road only goes part of the way up. After it ends, you have to walk and it is rather steep. Frankly, I would rather not make the effort; my head still reminds me it has been damaged. I will spend the morning here reading the papers and join you this afternoon at the abbey ruins."

"I did not get much of an understanding of the layout of the town last night," Clive said. "Where are we in relation to the Tor and the abbey? Do we need to take the carriage?"

"No, everything is within walking distance. It is just the steepness of the Tor that I am not willing to venture. Thomas has not been here before, so I took the liberty of drawing a little map."

Frederica turned to Mr. Grant, asking, "Are you going to feel up to climbing a steep hill?" She said to the others, "We shouldn't forget Mr. Grant also sustained injuries."

"It's kind of you to be concerned, Miss Chadwick, but I will be fine. If I find the climb too difficult, I will simply stop and wait for you two to come back."

"Say, Tommy, do you have a walking stick? I bet with a broken wing, you are a bit off balance and a stick would help out."

"Young Clive, what a good idea! Let us ask the host if he has one we can borrow."

Frederica had also been thinking ahead. "Let's also ask him for some sandwiches to take along. I doubt there are any tea shops on the top of the Tor and we may get hungry."

"Excellent idea, Miss Chadwick. I will go and consult our host." Clive left the room but soon returned bearing a thick, gnarled walking stick. He presented this to Mr. Grant with a flourish.

"Our host's compliments, Tommy. Our sandwiches and apples will be ready shortly and he is lending me a leather sack to carry them in. We shall be well-prepared."

"I do not suppose there is any way we can carry tea with us, is there?" Frederica asked wistfully.

"Your every wish will be satisfied, Miss Chadwick," Dering answered gaily. "Our host tells me we are going to be walking by the Chalice Well and we can get fresh water there. He also offered some stone bottles that will hold tea, but it will probably cool off by the time we drink it."

So after setting a time to meet Dr. Chadwick in the abbey ruins, the three hikers set out to conquer the Tor, well-equipped with a map, a food bag, sketching materials, and a walking stick.

Their path first took them through the central part of Glastonbury. Magdalene Street led them past the open-air market with its lively business in produce, chickens, and other sundry articles. At the end of High Street, they turned right onto Lambrook, where the town ended suddenly at a small sign that indicated the way to the Chalice Well.

"Say, Tommy, what is so important about this well?" Clive asked his former tutor.

"There is a legend that Joseph of Arimathea originally founded Glastonbury back in the first century. They also say he hid the Holy Grail in the well. Consequently, people have believed the well has healing properties."

"Joseph of Arimathea came here?" Dering was incredulous. "Wasn't he the chap who buried Christ?"

"It's good to hear you remember some of your religious lessons, Clive. Yes, and he brought the flowering thorn also."

Both Clive and Frederica found the promised well to be disappointing. She said, "It is just a hole in the ground. I thought the well at Cerne Abbas to be much more attractive. It had a nice shaded walk leading up to it. This well is just there; a hole in the ground."

"I agree. I thought it would be something special."

Thomas Grant hid a smile at their youthful disappointment and pointed out the path to the Tor. "Well, I don't think the view from the Tor will disappoint. Dr. Chadwick assures me that it is incomparable and we have been blessed with a clear day. Nothing to hinder the view and we should be able to see for miles."

The lower path to the Tor went first through some treed property, then several fields. Frederica was concentrating on where she placed her feet, as the path was somewhat uneven, when a large bovine head suddenly came over the hedge on her left and bellowed at her. The cow was about a foot from her ear and startled her considerably. She screamed at the top of her lungs.

Clive immediately started laughing uncontrollably and even Thomas Grant couldn't hide his smile. Frederica was so embarrassed she turned bright red and started to apologize. "Oh, excuse me. I just wasn't paying attention."

Clive was wiping his eyes. "Forgive me, Miss Chadwick, but your face was such a study. I could see Old Bossy coming as I was behind you." He started laughing again.

Mr. Grant was more sensitive to Frederica's embarrassment. "Clive, it is not proper to laugh at a lady. Miss Chadwick was quite startled."

As Clive continued to laugh, Frederica stopped being embarrassed and got angry. "Mr. Grant, maybe we could continue while Mr. Dering indulges in his amusement." Frederica picked up her skirts and stomped off, followed by Thomas Grant shaking his head and the still-chuckling Clive.

Although they had been climbing steadily, at the next pasture they could see they had only just arrived at the foot of the Tor. The next part would be almost vertical.

"Clive, I think you should go first. Miss Chadwick and I are somewhat hampered and you will be able to warn us of any problems that might lie ahead," Mr. Grant suggested.

The path was well-beaten by many thousands of pilgrims' shoes. At some of the steeper places, steps had even been built into the side of the hill. However, there were no handholds and Frederica found herself wishing she, too, had a walking stick. It was hard to keep her balance, her sketching materials, and her skirts all under control. Clive seemed to sense this and reached back quite often to give her a hand up.

"Let me carry that sketchpad for you," he offered.

"I'm fine." Frederica was still miffed at his laughter.

"Oh, do not be mad. I did not mean to hurt your feelings, but the look on both your faces was pretty funny. I am not sure which of you was more startled, but it might have been the cow." He grinned cheerfully at her and stayed to help Grant over the same spot.

After about half an hour of hard walking, the three hikers came to the level top of the Tor. Frederica could feel her heart pounding in her chest from the exercise. Thomas Grant looked quite exhausted and immediately chose a place to sit. Clive threw himself on the grass beside him.

"What a climb! That last bit was rather tough. I was surprised – I didn't think it would be so hard." Clive started to rustle around in his knapsack and pulled out the stone bottles. "Here, Tommy, you look like you could use a drink."

Grant uncorked the bottle and drank gratefully. "Yes, I also found it a bit harder than I had expected. It did not look so steep from the bottom. I am so glad we brought food. I do not want to start down too soon." He sat cradling his arm while Frederica and Clive exchanged glances of concern. Noting the exchange, Grant said, "Don't worry, I'll be fine, I just need to rest a bit. Clive, would you help me over to the tower? I will rest against it."

Clive Dering and Thomas Grant sat with their backs to the tower of St. Michael and admired the view. There were no other visitors that Clive could see. With satisfaction, he noticed Tommy had dozed off. Probably the need for a chaperone was the only reason Grant had made the effort to climb the Tor. It had been an obvious labor for him. The younger man watched Frederica sketch for a while. She had moved closer to the edge, focusing on the Levels around Glastonbury laid out before them.

Clive thought back to the previous day's conversation with the driver about how the Levels often flooded. That would frequently make the Tor the only dry spot for miles. It was easy to see how it had become important.

After watching Frederica lose herself in her work, Clive realized he was hungry again. It seemed to him he was always hungry. Now that he had stopped growing, he had hoped his appetite would stop demanding constant attention. Not to be. He sighed as he dove into the picnic bag to see what the landlord had packed.

"Mr. Dering, how about us? We're hungry, too." Frederica announced and came over, ready to stake a claim for herself and Mr. Grant, only to find Clive had already portioned everything into thirds. "Oh thanks," she said ruefully to his amused expression.

After eating, they decided it was time to start back for their meeting with Chadwick. By common agreement, Clive led the way, with Grant in the middle and Frederica bringing up the rear. At a steep drop in the path, Grant paused.

"Clive, let me have your arm for this part. One doesn't realize how off-balance one is without two arms, and going down is actually more challenging than going up."

"Of course!" Clive paused to let him grip his shoulder while climbing down some stone steps gouged out of the hill. "Watch these rocks. They do not seem particularly steady." With Clive on one side and his walking stick in the other, Grant made the descent successfully.

Frederica, however, had started down before Clive could offer her help or take her sack with the Claude glasses and other art equipment. When he turned back, she was already teetering on the steps that had given Grant trouble. He could see she was off-balance with several of the stone steps pulling away from the hill. To his horror, disaster happened before he could say or do anything.

Frederica pitched headfirst down the hill. She had enough sense to throw up her arms to protect her face and they seemed to take the brunt of the first thump. As he raced after her, he could see her trying to grab wildly at anything that might stop her descent but saw only tufts of grass coming away in her hands. She did not make a sound, but he knew she must have felt every small rock and tree branch she rolled over. Finally, with a thump, she came up against a tree, which stopped her fall abruptly.

"Miss Chadwick, Frederica…" Clive was still rushing down the hill, sliding on his heels. "Are you hurt? Don't move! Just lay there. Can you talk?" His words came out in a frenzy, almost tumbling over each other. He knelt by her side looking her over for injuries.

Frederica groaned in a most ungentle-like fashion.

"Oh my! I can't believe what just happened! I am so embarrassed."

Clive put a hand on her shoulder and held her down gently. "Just stay there until we are sure you are not hurt. You could have damaged something and moving will make it worse."

"Stop pushing me! I am not hurt. Lots of bruises, I suspect, and some scratches, but I can't see anything if my face is in the dirt, now can I?"

"How about your side?" he asked. "You smacked into that tree pretty hard."

She seemed to realize the situation was a bit more serious than a slip on wet grass.

"Help me sit up?" she asked.

Together, they surveyed the disaster that was now her dress. Pages from her sketching pad were flying about. Frederica put her hand to her head and found her bonnet had disappeared also. A rip in her skirt showed some scratched legs and, even worse, the total ruin of her stockings. Moving her left arm, she could feel her sleeve had separated from the dress in the back.

"Look at this mess," she said to him. "How can I walk back to the inn in this dress?"

"First let's see if you can walk," Clive said practically. He stood and offered her a hand, pulling Frederica to her feet. He did not let her go immediately, but stood holding her, waiting for her to get her balance. "How do you feel?"

"Not too bad. My ankles seem to work fine." Frederica shook each foot to prove they did in fact work. "What did you do with Mr. Grant?" she asked.

"Oh Tommy!" Clive looked startled and immediately glanced up the hill. "I left him on top when you went over the side. Oh, I see him over there. He's made his way down almost to our level. We can walk over that way to meet him."

"How is she, Clive?" Mr. Grant called anxiously.

"Not too bad. Nothing broken, it would seem," Clive called back. "Wait there. We will join you."

"My dress is broken," Frederica said despondently. "My bonnet is gone and my stockings ruined. I know ladies do not mention stockings but I am so discouraged. Uncle Festus is going to think I am still a child, being so hard on clothes." Her hair ribbon was also gone and her hair now tumbled onto her shoulders and down her back in thick blonde waves. He could see her eyes start to well up.

Clive was stunned. He had rarely found himself in such an intimate situation. He took several deep breaths, trying to keep his eyes from staring at Frederica's leg through the rip in her dress and to keep his hands from losing themselves in the golden mass of her hair. Up to now, he had thought Frederica pretty and talented but something of a spoiled bluestocking. Now he could see she was definitely more woman than child.

He patted her shoulder awkwardly, trying for a light note.

"Oh cheer up, old thing! That was quite a tumble and I am surprised you have not broken something. You were very lucky. I suppose the dress can be fixed, but actually, Miss Chadwick, don't you think it ripped so easily because it is sort of old?" From the look on her face and the sudden flush on her cheeks, he knew that was not the right direction to take.

"Mr. Dering, how many dresses do you think I own?" she managed to blurt out. Clive decided it was time to beat a retreat and started to rapidly gather up the scattered pages of her sketchbook and his own scattered wits. Finally, he returned holding the papers and the ruin that was her bonnet. From the flattened look of it, she must have rolled right over it several times. He put all the found items in her art bag before he took Frederica's hand to lead her off to meet Mr. Grant. For once, even Clive found himself speechless.

Clive was hard put to get both Thomas Grant and Frederica off the Tor. Although Frederica did not seem to have any sprained joints and she claimed no other injuries to make note of, he thought she was not telling him the full extent of her hurts. Her skirt was badly ripped and although she seemed to have moved her petticoat to cover the damages, he thought he could see some blood stains on either her stockings or shift. She seemed most embarrassed by what she called her clumsiness, as she tried to make a joke of the sight she must have made rolling down the hill. Clive was not so sure it was an incident to make light of. Her body must have hit every rock possible on the way down!

As they picked their way down the Tor in silence, Clive tried to think about the conditions the rock steps had been in on the way up. Had they been so loose when they climbed? He could not quite remember.

He tried to offer his assistance to Frederica, but she just brushed him off and insisted she was fine. He disliked watching her struggle down the rest of the path clutching her dress, but Tommy Grant was also laboring and needed his help.

Ironically, Dering's original thought about having to help his companions on this trip had come true, but not in the way he had expected. When they reached the top of the road leading to Glastonbury, he insisted both Tommy and Frederica rest on a convenient log while he searched out some kind of transportation to take them the rest of the way. Neither gave him much argument over his plan. Luck ran in his favor and he soon returned with a farmer and his cart with relatively clean straw in the back to take the bruised and tired hikers into town.

Once Clive and Frederica had arranged themselves in the back and Grant up front with the farmer, they lurched off.

"Clive, I think we had better go straight to the abbey. Dr. Chadwick will be waiting there and will start to worry if we are late," Mr. Grant suggested.

As soon as Clive agreed to this plan, Frederica touched his arm. "What about my dress?" she whispered.

"I will carry everything," he responded. "You just walk naturally, keep your hand down, and hold the rip together. Let me help you arrange your shawl so the sleeve is hidden, as well as most of the grass stains." He paused and removed his cravat pin.

"Here, take this and see if you can pin the skirt together. Just be careful when you sit down that you don't stick yourself."

She took the long straight needle with a small jewel at the end that he offered, and with a quick glance to make sure Mr. Grant and the farmer were still chatting, pinned her skirt together.

"Don't lose it; my father would be most distressed as the pin was my grandfather's."

"I'll be careful," she promised.

"After we meet up with your uncle, we'll go back to the inn," he promised. "We don't want him worrying that we have not appeared."

"Do you still have my sketching sack?"

"All here, safe and sound."

As soon as Dering produced the bag, Frederica started to pull items out, obviously looking for something. Clive picked up the sketchpad and started to flip through the pages.

"You know, Miss Chadwick, these are quite nice. I think you have some talent in the landscape line. Look, Tommy, she's done a study of one of the fields around Wolverton Gatehouse that is very charming." Clive held the pad up for Tommy Grant to peer at, but the rocking of the cart made it difficult for the older man to see.

"No, Mr. Dering, don't look at those," Frederica protested, although her attention was still on her sack. "They are not finished and are only sketches." For some reason, Frederica seemed embarrassed by Clive's praise. He was confused: his sisters loved praise, however unwarranted.

"Oh no," she gasped.

Evidently, she had found what she was looking for and was not happy.

"What is wrong?"

"My Claude glasses are broken," she moaned. "Well, not all of them, but two are. And Jeffrey just gave them to me." Her voice broke, as if she was close to tears.

Clive put aside the sketch pad and took Frederica's hand. "That was a rough tumble," he said. "We are so lucky something did not get broken. I thought for sure the way you hit that tree would break some bones. Are you sure you can breathe normally?" He was not sure how he was supposed to ask a lady if she had any broken ribs.

"No, no, I am fine. You are right, I should be grateful. But these are from Jeffrey." The emphasis on her brother's name showed the importance of the gift.

"Perhaps we can find someone to fix them," he offered.

"Do you think that would even be possible?" she asked doubtfully.

"Someone made them in the first place, so I imagine they can be repaired. We will ask Dr. Chadwick. If anyone knows, he will."

Frederica seemed less upset but remained quiet for the rest of the ride down the Tor.

The cart finally creaked to a halt.

"This looks like the center of town," Clive said to Frederica as he lifted her out of the cart. The market was still open, although not as busy as when they had gone through earlier.

"So it is," the farmer agreed. "The abbey is just through that alley. Town grew up around the abbey and now it is smack in the middle. Thank ye,' sir. Very kind of ye.'" This last was to Grant, who had handed him some shillings.

"Very kind of you to give us the ride. We were in sore need of it," Thomas Grant answered as he struggled to get down from the front perch. "You were the first person we saw up there."

"That's funny, sir. I saw a couple of gents walking down just before your young sir came along. Thought for a while you were together."

"Well, if they were up there, we never saw them. Thank you again for your help." Grant waved as the farmer drove off.

"Well, that was an adventure! Let us go see what Festus has been up to." Leaning heavily on his walking stick, Mr. Grant led Frederica and Clive down the alley to the abbey.

Chapter Seven: Bath

Frederica

The road from Glastonbury to Bath was much smoother and had fewer potholes than other parts of the trip so far. This enabled her uncle to look at Frederica's sketch pad and give her some pointers on how to draw human faces. Until now, most of Frederica's artwork had been devoted to landscapes and subjects of nature. After seeing her one attempt at drawing a person, her uncle had suggested some instruction.

"I have no aspirations to be an artist myself, but I have spent a lot of time looking at great works of art and discussing painting with artist friends, so I have an idea of what makes a successful portrait. I could, perhaps, give you some pointers."

Not having many people with whom to discuss her passion, Frederica now excitedly sat with pad open and pencil ready. She glanced at Dering on the opposite seat with his head back, seemingly half asleep.

"Well, he does look like he is going to stay put for a while…" she mused.

One baleful eye opened. "This better be an improvement on the last one or I won't pose for you anymore. I can't have you ruining my good looks for posterity. Mother wouldn't approve."

"Not to worry. I am sure Uncle Festus will only let me reproduce the most realistic representation."

Dr. Chadwick chuckled and said, "As we can't improve on God's creation, let's see what we can do about replicating it."

Frederica turned so her uncle could see her sketchpad. She concentrated on his suggestions.

"Do a rough outline in circles."

"Start with the nose."

"A three-quarter representation is easier than a full face."

"Shade around the chin to give it depth."

"Avoid the ears. You don't want to give him a jug-handle effect." That suggestion made Clive open his eyes and glare at them.

"Try to emphasize a unique characteristic so that if you don't get the rest right, the viewer will concentrate on something they can recognize."

"And what would that unique characteristic be in Mr. Dering's case?" Frederica asked impishly.

"How about his strong, manly chin?" Uncle Festus grinned back at her.

The sun was casting long shadows by the time Mr. Grant woke up and announced they were close to their destination. He leaned over to nudge Clive.

"Come on, old boy. Aren't you getting a bit stiff there?"

"Don't move me, Tommy. Can't you see I am modeling?"

Mr. Grant looked over at Uncle Festus and noted that Frederica was packing up her pencils, ready to leave.

"I think your time is up; the artist seems to be packing up her tools."

Dering's eyes snapped open. "Let me see," he demanded.

"Not yet," Frederica replied. "I need to finish it first."

"Please, Miss Chadwick," he pleaded, his eyes glinting with amusement. "I want to see what my manly chin looks like."

"Not just yet, Clive." Uncle Festus was smiling as he spoke. "She is still learning, although she shows some talent. Your manly chin needs a little work."

"Festus," Mr. Grant said thoughtfully, "I want to bring up a subject just between the four of us." At his serious tone, his travelling companions broke off their teasing and looked at him with concern.

"Yes, Thomas?" Dr. Chadwick asked. "You seem quite concerned about something. What bothers you?"

"I find the three accidents, the rock at Corfe, the carriage accident and yesterday's mishap on the Tor, to be more than just happenstance. I have been trying to find some commonality or some reason, for the events but I admit I am stymied. But, I believe, there is more than just coincidence in action here and it worries me."

Dr. Chadwick nodded thoughtfully. "I have given these incidents some thought also but I cannot fathom what was behind them so I disregarded them. Tell me your reasoning."

"When Clive and I got to Corfe Castle, I did not go in but waited for you at the gate. I never saw anyone else go onto the grounds through the main gate. Yet, somehow, Miss Chadwick managed to get onto the grounds."

"I needed to buy some sketching pencils, so we stopped to make purchases on the way to the ruins," Frederica offered. "When I got to the ruins, I could see Mr. Dering, although of course I did not know who he was, so I picked the opposite side to sketch from. I did not see any other people in the area."

Mr. Grant nodded at her explanation. "What I was wondering if someone else could have gotten onto the grounds without any of us noticing."

"As I explained, I never actually made it to the top of the rocks in the middle of the ruins," Clive said. "The stairs stop short and you have to be a mountain goat to get up higher. I was able to quickly satisfy my curiosity by going halfway. As Miss Chadwick knows, I joined her shortly after."

"If you never even went to the top, Clive, do you think someone else have been up there?" Mr. Grant continued.

"I suppose so," Dering responded. "Once I joined Miss Chadwick, it is possible someone snuck in behind us and climbed those rocks. We were facing you and the archway."

Festus Chadwick peered at his colleague over his glasses. "What Tommy are you inferring?"

"That rock could have done some damage. Why would it pick that instant to fall when it has been there for over a hundred and fifty years? And now we have had a major carriage accident on a road we should not have been on. Yesterday, Miss Chadwick slipped on some loose stones that were not loose when we went up the Tor. She could have been hurt badly. I think the incidents are connected. Too much going on to be just a coincidence.

Grant added thoughtfully, "Because none of us saw another person at Corfe or on the Tor, does not mean there others were not there. But, of course, there is also motive to consider and I cannot come up with one."

"We could have asked the gatekeeper if anyone else was at the ruins in Corfe," Dr. Chadwick responded. "As the whole castle is open to the public, if there was another person, he might have entered the ruins even before Clive. He might have been so ashamed of pushing over the rock, he hid until we left."

Thomas Grant paused as he mulled over some idea. "But there might be another possibility. In fact, I am reasonably sure there is another path up to the Castle from the wooded side of the hill."

"That farmer did say he saw some other walkers on the Tor although we never saw them. But, even if you believe the three accidents are related, what is the reason?" Clive asked. "It is not like we are rich nabobs to be robbed."

"Quite right, Clive, and I have no answer. But something to think about and be aware of," Mr. Grant answered somberly.

The conversations had kept Frederica from focusing on the bruises and scrapes from her tumble at the Tor. She was surprised at how tender she felt, especially her ribs, which had come against the tree. Her heavily bandaged knees were hard to flex. She tried to forget her aches as she leaned forward for her first glimpse of Bath.

* * *

After her tumble down the Tor, Mr. Dering had proven to be surprisingly helpful. After an afternoon of sketching the Glastonbury Abbey ruins, Frederica found getting up from the picnic blanket very painful. He had been quick to notice and appeared at her side. He had grabbed her by both elbows and stood her on her feet.

"Did you sit too long in one position?" Dering had asked.

Frederica had not wanted their older companions to worry about her, so she spoke to him quietly. "I thought I was moving around enough to keep from getting stiff, but I think the fall has given me a few unwelcome bruises that are suddenly quite painful. Please help me walk them out a bit; I do not want Uncle Festus to worry."

"Of course." Dering had collected her pencil box and sketchpad. Taking Frederica's arm, he had slowly begun to lead her through the ruins to the alley beyond. "I didn't realize you were hurt. I thought it was just your dress that was ripped." He frowned and added, "We should not have been lounging around here all afternoon if you are hurt."

Frederica had waved off his concern. "I wasn't actually hurting, or at least I did not think I was until I tried to get up." She did not want any of her companions to think her missish and unable to keep up or, worse yet, a whiner. What Clive Dering thought of her suddenly mattered more than she realized. She did not want him to think her as self-indulgent as so many society misses were.

"I am not going to argue with you if you insist you are alright," he had said. "Looks like Tommy might have overdone it today, too," nodding towards their companions, who were only then turning right onto Magdalene Street.

"Going to show me your sketches at dinner?" he had prodded, changing the subject.

To her relief, Clive had kept her talking about art on their walk back to the George and Pilgrim Inn. But he had kept hold of her arm even after they entered the front door and headed past the public rooms to the stairs at the back of the inn. He had even walked her to her room on the second floor. The room he shared with Thomas Grant, she knew, was another flight up.

"What is the name of your room?" he asked. "Ours is the Monk's Cell. Can you imagine?" At her door, he had said, "Miss Chadwick, I think you have more injuries than you are letting on. I am going to ask our landlady, Mistress Sudden, if she has some lotion to ease the bruises and scrapes. No need to mention it to Dr. Chadwick if you don't want to."

He had headed back downstairs, looking for their landlady.

Frederica had opened the door to the Dunstan Room, remembering how Mistress Sudden had specifically mentioned yesterday that the rooms on this floor were all named after old abbots. She had smiled, thinking of Dering and Mr. Grant in a monk's cell. Inside, she found Mary. The little housemaid had brought up hot water for washing and was now making up the fire. They were shortly joined by Mistress Sudden.

By then, Frederica's bruises had become particularly painful and she hurt in places she didn't think possible. Her knees were especially stiff and the left one, the one that had hit the slate when she had fallen, had a nasty scrape on it. She took the time to take Mr. Dering's cravat pin out and place it carefully on the bureau. That was the last thing she had wanted to lose.

"Now, miss, let me see what the problem is," Mistress Sudden asked.

Frederica lifted her skirts to show the damage.

"Oh my, that does look nasty, miss. How did you do this?"

Frederica replied, "I fell on the Tor. One of the stepping stones came loose and I slipped."

"Well, these stockings are ruined for sure. Mary, go bring more hot water, some cloths, and my jar of balm. The one in the pantry we keep for burns. It will feel good on those scrapes." As Mary rushed off, she asked, "How did you not get blood all over your dress?"

Frederica had blushed, remembering how her dress had rucked up. "I am afraid while I was falling down the hill, I showed more leg than I should have," she said ruefully.

Mistress Sudden's formidable expression had softened to a smile. "I expect that sort of accident happened so fast no one had time to see anything they should not have," she offered comfortingly. "Best let me have that dress, though. The sleeves look like they need a good washing with those grass stains and all. You can mend the rip when you get to your next stop."

"Oh thank you. I do not have that many dresses. We had a carriage accident a while back and Dr. Chadwick bled all over my other dress. It had to be re-cut and the whole front taken out." Frederica took the muslin out of the cupboard and showed the interested landlady where the dress had been redesigned.

* * *

Uncle Festus had arranged for them to stay at a friend's house in Queen Square. He explained that Lady Charlotte Aislabie was out of town, visiting a new grandchild, he thought. She had invited him and his companions to stay at her Bath home and make themselves comfortable. But Frederica wondered how anyone could be comfortable in such a perfect house and with some of the most snobbish servants Frederica had ever met.

It was immediately apparent from the look on the face of Mrs. Smithson, the housekeeper, that Frederica's arrival without a maid was a major affront. The room assigned her was adequate, but certainly not of the quality she had expected from viewing the rest of the house. Her case stood in the middle of the floor. No one had unpacked it.

After a day in the carriage, Frederica was exhausted and her bumps and bruises were again causing her pain. She wanted desperately to take off her dress and fall into bed, but the housekeeper didn't seem to want to leave.

"Lady Charlotte has taken with her the only lady's maid on staff, miss," Mrs. Smithson said stiffly. "I see you did not bring one of your own…or will she be coming later?" The housekeeper seemed to be suggesting something, but Frederica was too tired to understand what it was.

"No, I don't have a maid," Frederica responded. "But I am used to seeing about myself, so I don't think the lack of a maid will be a problem." To change the subject, she continued, "Mrs. Smithson, may I have a cup of tea? It has been a very long day."

"Of course, miss," the housekeeper sniffed. Frederica looked at her in amazement. She had heard about people who sniffed their disapproval, but she had never actually seen anyone do it before. "I'll send the kitchen skivvy up with it if the cook can part with her. Dinner is at seven." The housekeeper went off rather briskly.

"Oh, that didn't go well and I am not even sure why." Frederica positioned her half boots by the small chair, thought briefly about taking off her dress, then crawled under the blanket without bothering and immediately fell asleep.

Sometime later an insistent tap on the door brought Frederica groggily awake.

"Come in," she called, as she struggled with her skirts and the blanket. The housekeeper entered the room without ado and without tea.

"Dinner is served, miss. The gentlemen are wondering where you are." She placed a candle on the fireplace mantle.

Frederica jumped up. "Oh, I fell asleep. I'll be right along; just let me brush my hair." She began to rustle around in her valise.

Mrs. Smithson didn't leave. "Are you changing your dress, miss?" she asked pointedly.

As Frederica looked at the wrinkled and travel-stained dress, a quiet cough sounded from the doorway. She realized Mr. Grant was standing there. From the way the housekeeper jumped, she must not have realized he had followed her to Frederica's room.

"You look fine, Miss Chadwick. I do not blame you for falling asleep; it has been a long travel day. Just tidy your hair and join us. I will wait here to escort you to the dining room." His quiet voice seemed to take all the starch out of Mrs. Smithson, as she quickly left without a word.

"I am sorry to keep you waiting," she said as she took the fourth seat. "I fell asleep."

Uncle Festus smiled at Frederica. "I thought that might happen. You looked exhausted when we finally got here. How is your room? Mrs. Smithson told me several times they were not prepared for a 'young lady.'"

"Yes, she told me that, too. But I don't understand why she is so concerned," Frederica answered. "I can take care of myself; I don't mean to cause her any extra work."

Clive cleared his throat. "Bath is somewhat old-fashioned. I think she finds a young woman travelling with three men and no maid to be…" He paused, searching for words.

Mr. Grant filled in, "Not in her experience? Unusual? Inappropriate?" He turned to Uncle Festus. "You did tell her Miss Chadwick is your niece, did you not, Festus?"

Uncle Festus frowned. "You know, Tommy, I may have forgotten that bit of information. I wonder if she thinks Frederica is a – what do you call 'em, Clive – a light slip?" He started to laugh.

"A light skirt," Clive corrected, also laughing.

Mrs. Smithson came into the dining room with the footman and a maid. They were loaded with steaming platters that made up the second course. Clive drummed his fingers on the tablecloth. He waited while the house-keeper arranged dishes: chicken surrounded by roasted potatoes, fish in wine sauce, and lamb chops, all in the center of the table. Vegetables, including cucumbers, beets, and cabbage with apples were placed in the spaces between the diners. The staff left before he continued.

"Dr. Chadwick, this may be a problem. Bath is a rather small town and everyone knows everyone. We do not want Miss Chadwick to be seen as a 'curiosity.' Do you have some proper female friend in Bath who might introduce her around?"

"Clive, do you think that is necessary? We are only staying a couple of days," Uncle Festus protested.

Dering and Mr. Grant exchanged looks.

"Festus, we were hoping to stay at least a week, if your friend will let us. My arm is bothering me a bit and I think Miss Chadwick was more bruised yesterday than she is letting on."

Before Frederica could protest that she was fine, she felt pressure being exerted on her foot. She glanced at Clive, who gave a quick shake of the head. As her mouth was already open, she felt she needed to say something.

"I would not mind a bit of a rest," she said cautiously. It must have been the right thing to say, as Mr. Grant was smiling. She struggled for something to add. "If it is not too much trouble, I have never been to Bath and I hear there are wonderful bookstores."

Uncle Festus frowned. "I didn't realize how knocked up you were, my dear. Of course we can extend our stay. Our hostess begged me to linger as long as we wanted; she will not be back from Scotland for three months. How does a week sound?"

Clive nodded enthusiastically. "Sounds terrific. I see in the Gazette there are several acquaintances of mine in town. In fact, after dinner, I think I will stop around and see if I can find them."

Frederica began to wonder about Clive's motives in wanting to stay longer in Bath. Maybe he was getting tired of spending all his time with her and two older men.

Uncle Festus broke in, "Clive, do you still have the Gazette? I want to see if I know anyone in Bath to whom I may introduce Frederica. I think the idea of asking a lady friend to take her around is a good one. I wonder if Flo Nesfield is at home right now…" he mused out loud. "She flits about so much among her children, it is hard to keep track of her. Her husband and I were good friends from the time we were at Oxford together. He died a few years back."

True to his word, after dinner Clive took himself off while Uncle Festus, Mr. Grant, and Frederica sat in the drawing room. Uncle Festus perused the Gazette closely, while Mr. Grant read one of his studious tomes. Frederica took out her pencil and made some quick character studies of Mr. Grant reading. The nap and a full meal had refreshed her wonderfully.

"Aha!" Dr. Chadwick exclaimed jubilantly. "The Gazette says Florence is in town. She is staying in Laura Place as usual. That is good news; I shall call on her in the morning."

"Do you actually think it is necessary? I am quite comfortable going on just as we are."

"No, Clive is right. You mustn't have a hint of scandal about you, especially if you are coming out in society next year. The other thing Florence can help us with is some shopping. Jeffrey said you might not have enough clothes for a trip of this kind and he gave me money for just that eventuality. You certainly need to replace the dress that went down the Tor yesterday," Uncle Festus grinned at Frederica. "I do not think even Polly and Mistress Chettle could fix the gown with those tears."

"I expect I can fix the splits," Frederica responded. "And I doubt very much if anyone can make a dress in the time that we will be here. However, I should very much like to get a short jacket, a spencer. The maid from Wolverton, Polly, suggested it. It would be much more practical to wear than my cloak when walking about. I am now convinced the cloak is what tripped me up on the Tor. Do you think Jeffrey gave you enough to pay for a spencer?" she asked anxiously.

"I am sure there is enough to cover a spencer if that is what you want. But we'll ask Flo Nesfield. I am sure she knows all the best places to shop."

Mr. Grant suddenly looked up from his book and cleared his throat. "Ahem, Festus. Clive's sisters always had some pin money to spend on their own," he said quietly.

"Oh my, of course, Tommy! I must be getting old, the way I keep forgetting things. Jeffrey also gave me pin money for you, Frederica, but I forgot all about it. Please forgive me. He thought you might need more drawing paper and such." He brought out his pocketbook and handed Frederica five guineas.

Frederica, who had blushed in shame at the discussion of her poverty, now sat back in shock. Her father had always paid for any of her purchases. She had never had so much money in her possession before. "All this is for me?" she asked.

"Is it enough? I have more," he said anxiously. "Just not in small coins. I can get them changed tomorrow." Uncle Festus seemed oblivious to her surprise.

"Enough!? Of course it is enough. This is so generous!"

"Well, I am sure it is not as much as you deserve, so say no more. I am sorry I forgot to give it to you before. But then we were not truly in a place where there were any stores. I understand besides bookstores, there are some excellent art supply stores in Bath. Do let me know when you need more money. I think I will turn in now. Tomorrow, we go visiting, Frederica." Uncle Festus rose and moved slowly from the room. "See you at breakfast. Good night, Tommy. Good night, Frederica...try to get some rest, m'dear." They heard his voice from the hall, "Ah, Mrs. Smithson, if you please, a moment of your time."

Frederica had meant to go to bed when her uncle did, but Mr. Grant signaled her to stay back with a raised hand. He waited until they could no longer hear Dr. Chadwick's voice.

"Thank you so much for agreeing to stay in Bath, Miss Chadwick. That was pretty quick thinking at dinner. I am afraid we rather sprang it on you. You see, I am concerned your uncle is still not well from the carriage mishap and is trying to do too much."

"Of course, Mr. Grant. It is an excellent idea. I just hope I wasn't too obvious. Mr. Dering practically had to kick me under the table to get my attention."

Grant smiled. "Actually, staying was Clive's idea. He's the one who noticed Festus is not quite his energetic self. Once he brought it to my attention, I agreed."

"You are sure Uncle Festus is still not well, and it is not just Mr. Dering wanting to stay in Bath to be social?"

Grant shrugged rather complacently. "Clive's suggestion may be somewhat self-serving, but I do think Dr. Chadwick would benefit from some further rest." He paused as if in thought. "Ah, Miss Chadwick, I don't know much about women's clothes and such, but I suspect that five guineas will not go far in buying a spencer and a new dress. When Mrs. Nesfield takes you to the modieste, just tell them Dr. Chadwick will be paying and to send the bill to him. Use the cash to pay for sundries. I know your brother can well afford a few dresses for you. I expect that is what Festus means for you to do, but he sometimes forgets little details like pin money."

"Thank you, Mr. Grant, for all your help. You have been very kind to all of us. You are a good friend to my uncle and to me. You know, I am exhausted. I think I will say good night, as well. Sleep well." With a brief curtsy, Frederica, too, went off to bed.

To her surprise, however, a maid waiting for her in the hallway directed her to a new room, one much more opulently appointed. Frederica gave a small smile as she realized Uncle Festus must have had a few words with the housekeeper. He did not forget that!

There was a crackling fire in the room and her clothes had been moved and hung. Her brush had been placed on the dressing table. A quiet knock signaled the arrival of another maid with a cup of chocolate.

"Mrs. Smithson thought you might like this before you retire, miss."

Frederica reflected how being thought ill by the servants really could make your life miserable.

* * *

Grant disappeared into the crowd, leaving Frederica alone on the couch. They were seated in the second row surrounding the dance floor in the Bath Assembly rooms. Nothing Frederica had seen in Tunbridge Wells had prepared her for the glitter of these rooms – wide swaths of walls painted brilliant shades of blue with gilt accents and thousands of candles in huge chandeliers lighting the festivities. And this happened every week, not just a few times a year. A small orchestra was tuning up in the loft to one side. As soon as the music started, throngs of people started to fill the area set aside for dancing. However, only a handful of people moved about the dance floor.

Clive Dering was one of them, of course. He and his red-haired partner were now at the opposite end of the constantly moving columns, as each couple took their turn parading down the gauntlet between two rows of dancers. Frederica admired how gracefully Clive handled his companion through the steps of the dance. She sighed enviously. They did look like they were having a lot of fun. She was beginning to regret refusing the dance lessons her father had suggested. The Bath Assembly was a world apart from the bookish life she had been living. And yet, as Uncle Festus and Mr. Grant were quick to point out, there were also many opportunities for intellectual enrichment in Bath.

Frederica looked with satisfaction at the lovely white beaded dress she was wearing. When Dering had raised the subject of attending an assembly, she had to admit she had not brought anything appropriate to wear. Mrs. Nesfield proved herself to be a premier shopper, though. She knew everyone and every store in town. To Frederica's surprise, Mrs. Nesfield introduced her to a store specializing in renting dresses appropriate for the Assembly gatherings. There, visitors who found themselves without the correct attire could get fitted out quickly. The dress they finally settled on seemed to her to exemplify the glamour and sophistication of Bath. It had a low neckline with cap sleeves and a short train that had perplexed Frederica until the shop assistant showed her how to thread her fingers into the hooks on the train. This allowed the dress to drape gracefully and not impede dancing. She lightly touched the froth of curls that covered her head. The bulk of her hair was pulled away from her face and secured with glittery combs behind her ears. A few wispy pieces of hair were allowed to frame her face; the rest had been tortured with heat and tongs into long curls that hung down her back. It was a much more elaborate style than anything she was capable of doing herself. In fact, it had been Dering who had suggested a hairdresser be brought to the house to help Frederica get ready for the ball, an idea with which Uncle Festus readily agreed. All in all, she felt she was looking her best.

By the time Mr. Grant came back carrying two cups of lemonade, the dance floor had filled with elegantly clad couples walking through a very stately quadrille.

"Here you are, Miss Chadwick," he said, waking Frederica from her reverie. He handed her one of the cups and retook his seat on the couch. "My, Clive is quite the dancing wonder," he said admiringly.

Another tune had started and couples were now forming into squares. While Clive was partnering with another young woman, his previous partner, also part of the square, was trading bows with a young man sporting similarly vivid red hair.

Mr. Grant continued, "It is a shame the Pump Room is undergoing repairs. That is where you would have been introduced around."

"What do you mean?" Frederica asked curiously.

"Most of the fashionable folks spend the morning at the Pump Room to the Baths, drinking the water and visiting. If it was open, Festus would have taken you there and introduced you to everyone he knew. Between him and Mrs. Nesfield, they seem to know everyone who is anyone in Bath. But it would be the place to introduce you around."

"Oh do not worry, Mr. Grant. I am quite happy sitting here talking to you." Frederica tried to put him at ease. "And I actually do not know these dances anyway."

"You are very kind to say you don't mind sitting with me, Miss Chadwick, but in my experience, it is a rare young lady indeed who would not be happier out on the dance floor with some admirers hanging about," Mr. Grant replied, smiling genially at her. "Ah, here comes Clive now, and good, he has brought some friends."

Frederica finished her lemonade when Dering arrived.

"Mr. Grant and Miss Chadwick," he said, "may I introduce my friends? This is Robert Padgett and his sister, Miss Rachel Padgett. Robert and I know each other from Oxford." Dering finished the introductions with ease, explaining that the young Padgetts were staying with their grandparents in Bath and that it had been Robert's name he had identified in the arrivals section of the paper. Frederica shook hands with the newcomers, who proved to be charming and quickly put her at ease. Rachel admired Frederica's dress and remarked that being with others their age in Bath was a very welcome change.

"I love Grandmama dearly, but you and Mr. Dering are the only young people we have met. I am dying for conversation that does not discuss illness and aches and pains, or what I call 'the organ recital,' " she laughed.

He brother smilingly agreed and added, "Say, now that there are four of us, we can be partners for the next set. Look, it is starting soon! Miss Chadwick, will you honor me?"

They laughed cheerfully at her protestations that she didn't know the dance.

"Don't worry, I'll help you," Miss Padgett promised. "Between the three of us, we'll keep you in step." Without much more ado, Frederica found herself pulled onto the floor and into the set.

Frederica was breathless by the time Dering announced it was intermission. Part of it was from the liveliness of the country dances. The orchestra, seemingly recognizing some younger dancers, had changed to more energetic music. But part of her breathlessness was from Clive Dering. When they partnered in the last set, he had turned his gaze on her intently.

"You are looking particularly well this evening, Miss Chadwick," he murmured.

Frederica looked at him in surprise. His tone was far from the mirthful manner he had previously used. She missed a step but his warm clasp pulled her back into place. Dering's manner confused her, but there was little time to mull over his words.

"I think we are a little unruly for this crowd," Miss Padgett remarked smugly as they joined Mr. Grant and Uncle Festus making their way to the refreshment room.

The two young women left the men to find a table and snacks and made their way to the ladies' retiring room. Once there, Frederica re-pinned a few straggling curls and used a little rice powder on her nose.

"I had no idea dances could be so much fun, Miss Padgett," she admitted to her companion.

"Oh, please call me Rachel. I know we are going to be friends. Have you not been to many assemblies?" she asked curiously. "I know Grandmama will have something to say about it, but Robert is such a cut-up, I cannot keep from laughing."

"He is quite comfortable to be with, as is Mr. Dering." She paused to think how to phrase her question. "Are we not supposed to dance with other men?"

"If we were in London, of course everyone would be horrified if we danced more than once with the same person. But this is Bath in the off-season; things are not as strict, and Robert is my brother."

"Neither one is *my* brother," Frederica said, sadly thinking of her own brother Jeffrey, transferred so far away.

"Well, I certainly do not see anyone else I want to dance with," Rachel pronounced stoutly. "I am dancing with Robert and Mr. Dering until Grandmama says otherwise."

Thinking that was as good a plan as any, Frederica left the retiring room, following her new friend up the stairs to the Tea Room. But out of the corner of her eye, she glimpsed a man that seemed familiar.

I am sure I know him from somewhere, but I cannot imagine where.

The man was hard not to notice. He was handsome, with dark hair and flashing brown eyes. She leaned over the railing and tried to peer into the crowd to see if another glimpse would jog her memory but he had faded into the crowds. Rachel looked at her curiously but made no comment.

The men had pushed together two small tables in the Tea Room. There were plates of delicacies scattered about with a large number of glasses. The size of the table was explained by the addition of Mrs. Nesfield and a man and woman Frederica did not recognize.

"Grandmama," Rachel exclaimed and bent to kiss the woman on her cheek. "This is Frederica Chadwick."

Frederica had to admire the confidence Rachel exhibited as she smoothly introduced her to the older couple. Rachel's grandparents looked to be contemporaries of her uncle. Mrs. Padgett wore an impressive turquoise silk gown with a matching turban covering most of her hair. What hair Frederica could see was a distinctive white. Her husband was equally well-dressed and when he stood to bow, he seemed almost as tall as Robert. He smiled and she thought his eyes seemed kind.

"Oh my dear, how lovely you look!" Mrs. Nesfield clasped Frederica's hands and gave her cheek a kiss. "That dress looks such a treat on you! Very nicely done." She nodded approvingly, taking in the simple combs and ear bobs that complemented the gown.

Taking her seat next to Uncle Festus, Frederica noticed a buffet had been laid out along one wall. Chairs and tables of various sizes filled the rest of the space. Mr. Grant offered her a dish with a couple of small sandwiches and several confections.

"I hope these are satisfactory, Miss Chadwick," he said.

Dering handed her another glass of lemonade. "Sorry it is not wine, but Dr. Chadwick said no spirits this evening."

Assuring them everything was perfect, Frederica took in the details of the room. It was as large as the ballroom and featured many of the same lovely architectural details.

"I say, Miss Chadwick, does that man over there by the wall know you?" Dering asked suddenly. "He has been staring quite rudely for some time."

But when Frederica turned to look, no one was there.

Chapter Eight: Stones of Avebury

Clive

The carriage ride from Bath to Avebury was a repeat of their previous rides, with Dr. Chadwick and Mr. Grant debating the history of the place they were about to visit and why they found it interesting. Clive was not particularly engaged in the conversation, so he pretended to doze in his corner, leaving Frederica to listen avidly to the scholars. Clive had to admire her interest in almost any topic. She would have done much better at Oxford than he had ever done.

"Excuse me, Mr. Grant," she interrupted, "but I don't understand. Why are the stones of Avebury considered important? There are lots of other places with stone rings."

"True, Miss Chadwick," Grant answered. "The most famous one is on the Salisbury Plain. Stonehenge, it is called. No one knows quite what any of them were intended for, but Avebury seems to be older than most of the other stone rings."

The older scholar interposed, "Aubrey has some interesting theories about Avebury. He believes the stones went up during the time of Druids."

"They were pre-Christian?" Frederica asked.

"Yes, the Druids supposedly worshiped trees. He also theorizes that Merlin is buried here and that the Druids made human sacrifices."

"Well, Stukeley has a totally different opinion," Grant responded. "He thinks the stones are a landscaped model of the Trinity."

Clive tried to keep from laughing and when he opened his eyes, he found Frederica looking at him quizzically. He grinned back and rolled his eyes. She shook her head slightly in reproof, but he noticed her lips gave a small twitch upwards.

Evidently, she was not satisfied with Grant's answer. "Why are we visiting this place? Why is it important to you?"

Both older men paused to consider the question. Clive had to appreciate that neither man ever ignored any of Frederica's questions, no matter how naive or basic. But then, he remembered, Grant had always had a lot of patience with him. Both Grant and the professor gave this question their full consideration.

Finally, Mr. Grant said, "No one is sure of the original purpose of the place, but I think we can safely assume it was some spiritual matter. I know this sounds a little silly, but Festus and I wanted to compare its atmosphere to that of Glastonbury. That has been a place of great spirituality for at least 1,500 years. This place is much older but in some ways is similar. Use of stone to worship the gods and so forth."

Frederica seemed fascinated and Clive found even his interest was piqued. "You say this Avebury is a ring of giant stones?" he asked.

"Yes, but not smooth ones like those at Stonehenge. Rough, giant stones that were set in a great circle. Over the years, there has been a lot of damage. A village has been built in the center. We shall have to see if there is any peacefulness left."

The discussion continued between Chadwick and Grant. After a while, Frederica took out her sketchbook. Although the road was not at all smooth, she looked at Clive as though she wanted to start another portrait of him.

"Let me see what you've done so far. Every time I've watched you this past week, you have been working furiously in that sketchpad. And don't you start with 'these aren't any good.' I do not know why people always say that. You've got a lot of natural talent."

She grinned with pleasure at the compliment. "That is so kind of you to say, but I have been working furiously this week because Rachel was kind enough to give me some instruction. She has had real lessons in watercolors and oils, as well as sketching. She knows a lot about faces, so I wanted to practice as much as possible while she was with me." Frederica flipped back to the front of the pad. "I know these first ones are not very good, but that was before I met Rachel. This page is of some impressions of the Assembly I made last week after she helped me." She opened to a collage of faces and figures in various attitudes.

Clive studied the pictures, intrigued. Unlike her earlier work, this time he could identify people. "That is Robert and there is Rachel. I think her nose is a little shorter than that, Miss Chadwick. Oh, and there's Mrs. Nesfield and Robert's grandparents. You know, I think you are getting pretty good at this portrait thing. I certainly can recognize these people."

"Technically," Mr. Grant interrupted, "I think these might be called caricatures rather than portraits."

"Why do you say that, Tommy?" Clive asked his former tutor.

"Not to take away from Miss Chadwick's efforts, but what she is doing is taking a particular feature of the person and forming a picture around it. Take, for example, Mrs. Nesfield's headdress. We recognize the headdress, so we expect the features below to be recognizable. But don't worry, soon she will get the hang of replicating the rest of the features and it will turn into a real portrait."

Frederica nodded in agreement. "Well, how about this one?" Frederica made to turn the page, but Clive stopped her.

"That's the oily person I saw staring at you that night, isn't it?" He pointed to a figure in the corner of the page standing by himself. "Did he ever try to talk to you?"

"No, not at all. I still cannot place him. I suppose I must have seen him in Tunbridge Wells somewhere. I am sure we were never properly introduced."

"Did you ever see him again?" Clive asked.

"Several times. After all, Bath is not such a large place."

"Where did you see him?" Uncle Festus asked.

"On the day after the Assembly, when Mrs. Nesfield took me 'round the shops.'" Frederica laughed as she described how she was exhausted by trying to see the city and keep up with the highly energetic woman, who had been on a mission to find Frederica the perfect short jacket.

"When we finally stopped for tea, he came into the tea shop. He bowed, wished Mrs. Nesfield good day. He evidently already knew Mrs. Nesfield."

Dr. Chadwick asked, "What did Mrs. Nesfield say?"

Clive saw Frederica frown and tried to remember the exchange.

"Do you know that man?" she had demanded after he had left their table for his own.

"No, but he looks familiar, like I have seen him somewhere. I assume I must have seen in Tunbridge Wells. But I cannot say for sure."

"He hasn't been here long, just the past week or so," Mrs. Nesfield answered. "I was

introduced to him at Lady Millicent's card party. Claims to be a captain in the military."
She gave an unlady-like snort to show what she thought of the man. "He is a bit too
smooth, if you ask me. I would not introduce my daughters to him. And that is why I did
not introduce you. He seemed to be quite lucky at cards last night, if you ask me. I am
pretty sure he is not perfectly acceptable, especially for a young girl, if you know what I
mean? Now, are you done? The stores are going to close soon, and we still haven't found
you that spencer."

Following up on Mrs. Nesfield's question, Dering asked, "Have you seen
this man, Dr. Chadwick?"

Chadwick leaned forward to look again at the sketch in Frederica's book.
"No, I've not been introduced, but I have seen him around. He was playing
cards, I think, the night of the Assembly." He looked intently at Clive. "Why
are you bringing this up?"

"I am not sure, sir. Robert seemed to hint that he was not all acceptable
to have as an acquaintance. He did not go into detail as the man didn't seem
to intend to make a pest of himself. But then, I thought you only saw him on
the night of the Assembly," Clive responded.

"Well, I think the issue has now resolved itself, since we have left Bath,"
Dr. Chadwick said calmly. "Now, Frederica, please show us the rest of your
artwork. I agree with Clive – you are definitely showing some improved skill
here."

The next hour passed agreeably as they used Frederica's sketchbook to
relive the events of the previous week, which Clive and Frederica agreed had
been absolutely top-notch.

The Padgetts had proven to be wonderful guides to Bath. The brother
and sister had spent all their school holidays visiting their grandparents, as
their father worked for the Foreign Office and was often posted abroad. He
and his wife were currently in St. Kitts. Consequently, the young Padgetts
knew Bath better than their native Somerset.

Uncle Festus and the senior Mrs. Padgett gave the young people an unusual
amount of leave to enjoy Bath without supervision or chaperones. Frederica
had never known such freedom, but Rachel had taken it as a matter of course.
The four young people spent hours wandering the shops in Milvern. They
crossed the Poltney Bridge to take picnics to the park. They went riding into

the countryside. Frederica filled her books with sketches of the siblings and of Clive. She worked on landscapes of the area surrounding Bath. She tried her hand at figures in motion while Robert and Clive practiced their fencing. Rachel, whose own drawing efforts were stiff, turned out not only to have a natural bent for instruction but to actually enjoy helping Frederica improve her skill.

"Most of the conversation I heard this past week between Miss Chadwick and Miss Padgett seemed to consist of instructions," Clive teased. He raised his voice to imitate Rachel. "'Balance the proportions…start with the nose and ears…' But she seems to have made quite a difference, don't you think, Dr. Chadwick?" he asked.

Late in the afternoon, as the carriage started down Kennett Avenue, the main approach to Avebury, a storm hit. It came complete with lighting and loud bursts of thunder that roared nearby, causing them all to jump. In between the thunder, Frederica could hear the driver yelling at the horses, trying to keep them from bolting. The travelers breathed a collective sigh of relief when they finally arrived at The Catherine Wheel, the one inn in the tiny village owned and run, as Dr. Chadwick said, by a Mr. Stephens.

"Jeffrey recommended this place, but it does seem small," he said doubtfully as he surveyed the inn. "We shall see."

Clive emerged first from the carriage and helped the two older men down and through the downpour to the inn's door. He returned to the carriage to find Frederica had already pulled her cloak on and put up her hood, bundling her drawing satchel under the cloak to keep it dry. Before she had a chance to step down, Clive allowed himself to do what he had been wanting to do since the dance at the Assembly. He reached up, grasped her about the waist, and lifted her down. Before he let her feet touch the ground, he held her close enough to feel her body against him. He was right – she had some lovely curves.

"Mr. Dering!" came a shocked gasp. She tipped her head back to look at his face, and her hood slipped a bit. He peered down to see with relief that yes, her cheeks were flushed. But she did not appear as angry as she might have. He was about to lean in to steal a kiss when a renewed downpour drenched both their faces. He grabbed her hand and together they dashed to the entry.

In the hallway, the landlord received Frederica's presence with dismay.

"But, sir, I wasn't knowing you were to have a young lady in your party. The letter only mentioned four gentlemen." Mr. Stephens sounded very unhappy. "I just don't have an extra room."

"Well, sir," Dr. Chadwick replied in a consolatory manner, "I am sorry. We had a last-minute change to our group. We have traveled a long way today, so please let us sit in the lounge, have a glass of wine, and discuss what is to be done."

"Of course, sir. This way, please." The landlord opened a door off the hallway leading to a cozy room with a welcome fire burning briskly in the hearth. Comfortable chairs formed a half-circle around the hearth. Dr. Chadwick and Grant sank into them gratefully. Dering watched as Frederica gracefully put her art satchel on the table. She smiled at him shyly.

The landlord came in shortly thereafter with a tray filled with glasses, a bottle of port, and some bread and cheese. He put them on the table and served the gentlemen their wine.

"Missus will be bringing the tea tray shortly," he said to Frederica. "Will you be needing anything else at the moment?"

With the tea tray came both the landlord and the "missus." The owner and his wife had obviously been discussing the problem of what do to with their unexpected guest. Good innkeepers that they were, they had found a solution, just as Uncle Festus thought they might. It seemed the nearest inn was several miles off.

"But I have a sister here in Avebury. She has some rooms she rents out, but she doesn't provide food. If you would like, I could send Jimmy over to see if the room with the two beds is free and have her make up beds. I was thinking that would suit two of the gentlemen very well. It is not a far walk, just down the path a bit."

They would, of course, take all their meals at the inn and receive a discount for the inconvenience. With their agreement, Mistress Stephens sent the lad off to speak for the room. The travelers decided to have dinner before Clive and Mr. Grant moved onto their lodgings.

Frederica was wearing a white dress that day. Clive remembered she had worn it at Corfe Castle on the first day of the trip. He had wondered about a white dress on such a trip, but if she was just coming out of mourning, white was a choice many made. He noticed now the dress was pristine, even after a day in the carriage. He waited for her at the bottom of the stairs and when she appeared from tidying her hair, Mr. Stephens, the landlord, announced the meal was ready.

"The missus has a lovely hare soup to start," he was saying as they came into the room. A table had been laid before the window, but the drapes had been drawn so they could no longer see out to the dripping wet street. The thunder now seemed much farther away.

"After the soup, we will have a nice beef joint with some poached quail. The missus also fixed a salamagundi. Young people usually like that," he nodded at Dering and Frederica as he spoke. "To finish, the pudding is a trifle, fixed with our own raspberries and cream from our own cows. You won't get better anywhere else." He finished the menu with a proud flourish.

"Sounds magnificent, Mr. Stephens. I can't wait. The ride today has certainly improved my appetite." Dr. Chadwick rose from his chair by the fire and took a seat at the table.

Dering held Frederica's chair and then seated himself opposite Dr. Chadwick. "So, Mr. Stephens, what do you propose serving to drink with this heavenly smelling feast?" Clive found himself still studying Frederica.

The landlord had been helping Grant get settled. With his arm still in the sling, moving a chair close to the table was a challenge. Stephens bustled to the sideboard, where several bottles had been placed.

"I thought this white Rhenish would go very nicely with the soup, sir. Shall I pour you some?" The last was addressed to Dr. Chadwick.

"Oh, let the young man try it, Mr. Stephens. He needs to learn about wine."

While the landlord was opening the bottle and pouring Clive a taste, he continued to describe his beverage recommendations for dinner.

"I have a red wine from Burgundy to go with the beef, sir, and a nice port for after the pudding. For you, miss, we have some lemonade or ratafia. Which would you like?" After opening several bottles and making sure all the glasses were filled, he retired to let them serve themselves dinner.

"Well, I must say the service here is as good as one would get in London," Dr. Chadwick said. "But then, when Jeffrey and I were laying out the plans, he did say Stephens had been in service and knew his way about. The Catherine Wheel comes well-recommended by some friends of his who say the fellow keeps a good wine cellar for a place so far from London."

"This is the direct route to Bristol, so he probably hosts a fair number of London businessmen going back and forth on business," Clive offered. "This wine is actually quite acceptable. I am impressed at finding it here."

"Well, I am impressed with this soup. It is wonderful," Frederica said. "I did not realize how hungry I was. I am sure you are right, Uncle Festus; the long carriage trip made us all ravenous." She paused to eat more soup and then continued, "Where do you suppose the name Catherine Wheel comes from? I've never heard of a name like that."

Grant, always the schoolmaster, couldn't resist an opportunity for instruction. "I bet there is a mine around here somewhere. Wheel is an old name for mines, you know."

"We shall have to ask Mr. Stephens about the name before we leave, but Tommy is probably right. It is an unusual name for a pub," Dr. Chadwick commented.

"I hope the rain will end before we have to venture out, Clive," Mr. Grant opined. "Else it's going to be a real muddy walk around here."

"Do you think we could accompany you when you go to the landlord's sister's house?" Frederica asked. "I think the storm is moving away and I am eager to see one of these giant mysterious stones you have been talking about."

"If the rain stops, I certainly don't see why not," Uncle Festus agreed. "I could use a little perambulation before bed after being in the carriage all day. What do you think, Tommy? Want some company on your trek to the other side of Avebury?"

They all agreed that an after-dinner walk would be good for all of them. Mr. Stephens, when asked about the route to his sister's, assured them it was a clear path, even in the dark. He would send the potboy, Jimmy, with a lantern to guide them and to see that Uncle Festus and Frederica got back safely. Because of the lateness of the hour, the gentlemen cut their repast a bit short by drinking only one glass of port.

By the time they had organized themselves at the front door with their young guide, the rain had stopped and the clouds were drifting off. A faint moon and some stars were trying to break through. Clive helped Frederica don her cloak. He could not seem to keep his hands from her.

"I fear the wind is still sending sharp breezes our way," he commented as he took her arm. The air, however, was refreshing and it felt good to be moving about instead of sitting cooped up in a carriage.

Almost immediately, Jimmy, who took his role of guide seriously, was pointing out a stone by the side of the path. "Here's one, sir!" he called.

The stone was indeed huge. With Jimmy standing next to it with the lantern, they could see it was at least twice the height of an average man. The travelers all gazed in amazement.

"Did you say, Tommy, that these stones are not from around here?" Clive asked.

"That's right. They are not the kind of stone one finds in this area. They probably were brought here from around the border of Wales and then, once here, they were somehow stood on their ends."

Both Frederica and Clive reached out to touch it. The surface was reasonably smooth. "They must have dressed it somewhat. This is not the way rocks come out of the earth," he said.

"It is so wonderful, considering how old these stones must be," Frederica said in wonder. "What kind of tools do you think they had for working with stone back then? How did they move them?"

She peered around the stone in the dusk to see if she could spot another. She could make out several large dark masses marching off into the distance. When she looked over her shoulder in the other direction, she could see nothing in the gloom.

"That there is the 'tingling stone,' miss," Jimmy announced.

"Tingling? Whatever do you mean?" she asked.

"You are supposed to put your arms around it and if you feel tingling…it cures you of something." Jimmy ran out of explanation.

"Probably an old cure for arthritic aches and pains," Grant added. "I have heard about such curing stones in other places."

"Do you feel any tingling?" Dering asked intently. His put his hand swiftly over hers and pressed it against the stone. "I do," he whispered.

Before she could respond, Jimmy called back, "There's a dip in the path, sir."

Dr. Chadwick went to study the dip intently. "This looks like a moat. Say, Jimmy, how far around does it continue?" he asked.

"All around the village, sir."

"So, it *is* like a moat. Amazing. Not all that different from Maiden Castle, eh, Tommy?"

Dering pulled Frederica ahead of their companions.

"Can you hear all the sheep?" she asked in amusement.

Clive gave a low chuckle. "How could I not hear them? Somehow, I don't think our companions are going to find the peace and spirituality they are looking for here. I think the stones are rather scary, although maybe they will be less so in the daylight. With the sheep and the village, I bet there is never any real quiet, either."

"I can't wait to see them in the daylight. The ring of stones must be miles across if the village is in the middle." Frederica sounded intrigued.

Mr. Stephens proved correct in his directions. His sister's house was not far and the path was reasonably straight. Soon they were walking up to the front door.

"Do you want us to wait while you check to see if the room is adequate, Tommy?" Dr. Chadwick asked.

"No, Festus. I am sure the room will be perfectly fine. I don't think you and Miss Chadwick should be kept on the doorstep while Clive and I decide if the room has been aired enough. We shall be fine. After all, Mr. Stephens has a reputation to uphold. He can hardly send us to a dump and expect us to be happy with him in the morning."

Then there was a discussion about whether Dering and Mr. Grant should escort Frederica and her uncle back to The Catherine Wheel.

"Don't be silly," Uncle Festus protested. "It is a short walk, and we have Jimmy and his lantern. We shall see you in the morning for breakfast."

Dering turned to Frederica to wish her a good night. He could not try to kiss her as he wished, not with the audience of the two older scholars. As she offered soft wishes for good dreams, he lifted her hand and kissed the palm. He wondered if she felt anything from the intimate gesture. Maybe, because she smiled widely at him. "Until tomorrow, Mr. Dering."

* * *

When the pounding on the door started, Dering was removing his pants and preparing to don his nightshirt. Grant was already in bed, dozing over his book. Clive glanced at him with concern as he started to the door.

"This doesn't bode well," he remarked as he swung open the door.

"Sirs, there's been a 'orrible accident."

To Clive's astonishment, Stephens from The Catherine Wheel stood in the hallway. He was surrounded by people. The commotion woke Grant from his snooze.

"The old gent that was travelling with you has been set upon! You'd best come quickly!" Clive caught the landlord by the arm as he started to turn away.

"Set upon? Where and how?" he demanded as he fumbled with his boots.

"My Jimmy came a short time ago, blood pouring down his face, saying some robbers had attacked them. We never had this around here before," he exclaimed.

"Wait, Stephens!" he ordered when the landlord made to leave. "I need to put some clothes on. Tell us everything while we dress."

What at first had seemed like a crowd, Clive now saw was only Stephens, his sister, and a couple of the sister's children, all crushed into the small hall way. Disregarding modesty, he left the door open so he could hear the land-lord's response. Out of the corner of his eye, he noticed Tommy's awkward efforts to pull on trousers with one hand.

"Tell me again what you know!" Clive pulled on his pants, then flung on his shirt and waistcoat without tucking anything in. Jacket and overcoat followed. He thrust his cravat into his pocket. After pulling on his boots, he moved over to help Grant with buttons and jackets.

When the landlord didn't respond quickly enough, Dering barked, "Well! Come on, man, talk!"

"It was the lad, Jimmy, sir. He came running in saying they had been set upon. Whoever done it hit him on the head, too. Savage blow it was, lot of blood on him. Probably knocked what little sense he had right out, but he did think enough to come straight back to the inn. We set out immediately. Such a thing!" he said disapprovingly.

"Stephens, you are not making sense!" Dering snapped as he struggled with Grant's coat. "Who got hit on the head?"

"Jimmy, the boy..."

"Yes," Dering cut in, "I got that part. Who else? The young lady and the old man, where are they?" He inwardly flinched when he thought about Dr. Chadwick's concussion from the carriage accident and hoped with a sinking heart that he had not been badly hurt. Clive practically shoved Tommy's good arm into his coat, pulled the empty sleeve around his sling, and buttoned it in front. To him, Tommy and the landlord looked equally rattled.

"Well, sir, the old gent is still lying on the path where they was attacked. I left my good wife and son with him until we could get help." He paused and continued, "We didn't get a chance to search everywhere – we came straight here to get you – but we didn't see the young lady at all."

Chapter Nine: Calamity

Frederica

Frederica's head twisted back and forth trying to find precious air. She could not breathe! Her whole body arched as she tried to take a deep breath. She tried screaming, but everything was wrong. She couldn't take a deep breath. She couldn't open her mouth; it was full of some foul-tasting rag. She couldn't open her eyes...or were they already open? Everything was black. She continued to struggle for air, but she was quickly exhausted.

"Take that cloth off her head!" a male voice commanded. "If we are not careful, she will be smothered. Look at her twisting about."

The smelly blanket that had bound her head was roughly pulled back from her face. The rest of her body was still securely wrapped in that blanket, preventing her from making any movement. Frederica lay in shocked silence, trying to draw air in through her nose, which by now was badly congested with the dust from the dirty cloth. Her head throbbed. She tried to move her hands and realized ropes wound around her body, tying the blanket securely around her chest and keeping her from being able to so much as twitch. She seemed to be in a cart of some kind, but she only knew that from the rocking of the vehicle that tossed her from side to side.

"If you promise not to make any noise, girl, I'll take the gag out."

Frederica nodded vigorously, not even wondering if the speaker could see her in the dark. As the gag was removed, her stomach gave several uncertain lurches, but she managed not to vomit, swallowing the vile matter so she wouldn't choke, which, as she was laying on her back and unable to move, she felt she was sure to do. The cold night air had never seemed so sweet.

Then suddenly it wasn't so sweet. She became aware of a noxious odor, a mixture of manure, human sweat, and dirt. A man knelt over her, holding a torch up as he surveyed her. Frederica stared back at him, speechless with terror.

116

"Well, well, well, looky here. This is a real pretty one."

Frederica could barely see his lips through his beard as he grimaced at her. His foul breath almost set her stomach off again. From where she lay, he looked enormous, dirty, threatening, and much too close.

The cart rocked as they made a turn and the man and the torch jerked back a bit. The movement caused embers to fly off. Frederica could see sparks from the torch that wafted down; several landed on her. The man, almost gleefully, noticed them, too. He started to pat and stroke the spots where the embers had landed. Frederica tried to squirm away from his wandering hand. His groping became more familiar and he casually reached under the blanket to feel her breast. No one had ever touched her breast before. Frederica felt defiled and tried to squirm away. But the ropes and the tight folds of the blanket kept her from any productive movement.

"No, no…don't touch me!" Frederica stammered.

"What's the matter, bitch? Don't you like a real man, better than that boy you been goin' around with?" He shoved his hand down her neckline and grabbed her right breast. He squeezed it until tears came to her eyes. Frederica shrieked, unable to hide how much he had hurt her.

"Alright, leave her alone. He told us no damaged goods."

"Jus' a little feel… I ain't goin' to hurt nothing."

"We got a ways to go yet and I ain't goin' to spend it listenin' to you trying to pop that virgin, with her screaming and waking the dead. Just leave it be, alright? Now get out front with the torch and light the way."

"Shit." The man climbed off the cart, leaving Frederica in the dark again. At least now she could breathe. The cart started to rock as it hit more ruts and potholes. Frederica tried to brace herself to keep from being thrown around, but the jolting only got worse. They must be on some track not used very often. Waves of despair washed over Frederica as she realized no one would be able to find her. And she still had no idea why she had been taken and what they wanted! Dering and Mr. Grant would not even realize until morning she was missing. And Uncle Festus…the attack had happened so quickly she had no idea what had happened to him.

Eventually the cart came to a stop. Frederica could not estimate how long they had been travelling. Her arms were now numb and her back and legs felt bruised from having been tossed around the cart. One of the men grabbed her and slung her over his shoulder, carrying her into a building. From her upside-down position and in her panicked state of mind, she couldn't get a good view of either the building or the kidnapper. She could see even less when he dumped her on a bundle of smelly straw in the corner and left her facing the wall.

She grunted in pain as she hit the floor. Such straw as there was, proved to be very thin and the floor quite hard. With her arms still tied, she was unable to break her fall.

"What do you want with me? Money?" The words tumbled out in spite of his previous warning about talking. "I don't have any money on me, but I am sure my uncle will give you some if you return me."

"Bah! You don't know anything. Just shut up! You better retie the gag. I don't want to listen to her while we are waiting." The speaker, the man who had carried her in, seemed to be in charge. From his voice, Frederica realized he was the driver. He busied himself starting a fire.

"No, please don't gag me," Frederica pleaded. "It is so hard to breathe. I promise I won't talk."

"Ah, shut yer' gob!" The man who had grabbed her in the cart shoved a rag into her mouth, but he didn't tie it very tightly. Frederica started to feel grateful for even this small kindness until he reached a hand under the blanket and began to grope her breasts again. Aghast, she stared up at him helplessly while he grinned wolfishly back. She could see broken yellow teeth through his beard.

"Just you wait. You'll get your chance to show me how grateful you are when the captain gets his. Then I'll show you what a real man is!" With a last vicious pinch of her nipple, he went over to the fire. "Hey, save some of that drink for me!"

Frederica could hear the two men settle in front of the fire. She heard a jug being unplugged and then passed back and forth. She tried to put thoughts of her own thirst and discomfort aside. She strained to hear their whispers by the fire. What was happening?

"When's he showing up?"

"He said about dawn. Had some society gathering he had to go to first."

"He didn't tell us the girl was such a looker."

"What difference does it make?"

"Well, I'd like to have a go at her. She's quite a morsel."

"Forget it until he gets here. He said no damage until then, but he didn't say about after."

"Did he ever tell you what he wants her for?"

"No, we only talked money. Seems we ain't the first blokes he hired."

"What happened to the others?"

"One of the idiots got himself killed in a carriage accident without killing anyone else. The next time they tried, they didn't get the job done."

"What'd they do?"

"Loosened some stones so she would fall down and break her neck, but it didn't work out that way. Stupid idiots didn't know what they was doin.'"

"Well, them fools weren't as smart as us. Got what we wanted on the first try!" His self-congratulatory comments were only greeted with a snort.

Although Frederica could hear the words of the bandits as they sat drinking, what they were saying made little impression on her. They were waiting for someone who evidently had tried to kill her before and now may get his chance. Hopeless, Frederica lay on the straw facing the wall. She could see little more than a few shadows thrown up by the fire. She closed her eyes and began to pray with more fervor than she had felt in years, even as she kept rubbing her wrists together trying to loosen her bonds. She had never felt so cold and alone in all her life.

* * *

Clive

Clive draped the cloak around Mr. Grant's shoulders and headed for the door. "All right then, let's go!"

"How many lanterns do you have?" Grant asked as they thundered down the stairs.

"Just the one; left the other with the wife."

"Wait, brother, take these." Their landlady dashed off to the kitchen and returned carrying two lanterns and two torches. "I'll go around the village and round up some others to help search." Taking one lantern for herself, she hurried off in a different direction from the men.

Clive frowned at Stephens. "Should she be by herself? We don't know who did the attacking."

"She'll be alright. Only a step that way until she reaches the miller's house."

The men hurried along the same path they had so recently trod. Clive could see a light low on the track ahead of them. "Where is Jimmy? I want to talk to him."

"I left him at the inn getting his head wrapped. I told him to follow us as soon as he could. I didn't even wait to hear the whole story."

"Good man," Clive said approvingly.

Shortly, they came upon the landlady, sitting in the path with Festus's head in her lap, her son kneeling beside her. Clive noticed the son cradled a rifle in his arms.

"Oh William, I am that worried about him. He is breathing, but he hasn't shown a bit of life at all," the landlady said anxiously to her husband.

"Clive, I'll see about Festus, you start looking for Frederica. Hurry, man, hurry! She must be about here somewhere!" Tommy Grant fell to his knees on the path and with his one good hand started to feel about Dr. Chadwick for broken bones.

Clive surveyed the area, trying to determine the best way to cover as much ground as possible in his search. He lit one of the torches to see if it was brighter than the lantern. It was, so he kept it.

"Stephens, since you came down the path and didn't see her, we will assume she is not lying there. You start on the far side of the path where the stones are, and I will search on this side. We must try to cover as much ground as possible, as we don't know when others will get here to help us. We can each make half-circles using the path as the starting and ending points and get progressively bigger with each arc."

The landlord nodded his agreement and immediately set off up the path. As he worked his half-circle away from the track, his torch threw a light that Clive could see. On his own side, the young man patterned his route on the landlord's model. However, there was so much high grass and so many low bushes he despaired of finding anything in the dark. And the big stones weren't helpful, either. Several times, he bumped unexpectedly against one in the night. They definitely made good hiding places. After several unproductive swings, Clive could hear voices coming from the direction of the village.

"William, what's amiss? Sally says two of your guests have been set upon?"

Clive could hear no more, as what sounded like a mob around the landlady drowned each other out. It looked like a good number of villagers had come to help search. He headed back to the group to help organize the volunteers into parties to search more effectively.

"Clive, come quick and hear this lad!" Mr. Grant's voice was unusually forceful. "Start from the beginning," he commanded the lad when Dering arrived. Clive recognized the potboy Jimmy from the inn. Their previous guide now sat next to the landlady, head clothed in bandages and looking dazed.

"What happened here, lad?" Clive asked gently. The villagers were immediately quiet as they strained to hear the boy's whispered response.

"We was walking back, me in the lead, the old gent and the lady together behind me, so I didn't see what happened right off. But I heard it as the lady started screaming."

Dering and Grant exchanged glances of dismay. "Go on!"

"A couple of men jumped out of the bushes. See, where they are kinda' thick?" The boy pointed to some bushes that were close to where Dr. Chadwick lay. Even as he tried to tell his story, more men arrived, hauling a door. They transferred Dr. Chadwick to the door and then carefully carried him in the direction of the inn. Mistress Stephens walked at his side swinging a lantern. Noting the gentleness with which they were treating his fallen friend, Clive turned back to Jimmy.

Jimmy continued, "I turned to see what was happening when one of the men hit me hard on the head with something, maybe a stick. It knocked me to the ground, but it didn't completely put out my lights. I laid in the dirt, and when it seemed like the men weren't paying me no mind, I crawled into the bushes and watched. They were busy with the young lady, who sure was putting up a fight! Finally, one of them hit her and she got all quiet. Last I saw, one of them had her over his shoulder and they were heading off that way." The boy pointed in the dark. The direction led away from the village. "I ran for help," he said simply.

"And a good thing you did," Mr. Grant said encouragingly. "You did well to get help so quickly." He turned to Clive, who was starting to walk in the direction the boy had indicated, his eyes focused on the ground. Several villagers followed him and fanned out looking for signs of Frederica.

"Clive, wait, we should have a plan."

"I agree and here is my plan," Dering responded. "You go with Chadwick to the inn. Pray God he is alright, but such a blow after the last one might be mortal. Send that coachman to me with a horse – no, make that two horses – and some food. I am going to try to follow those bastards. And have him bring that road guide, too – *Paterson's*. I don't know this area and will need the maps. I have a bad feeling about this, and I don't dare wait too long. Got all that, Tommy?"

If Mr. Grant was astonished at the authoritative tone in Clive's voice, he made no complaint. "By yourself, Clive?" was his only comment.

"Yes, who is there to help?" He gestured to the villagers. "These fellows are willing to search here, but I doubt they are ready to leave the town for long. And Tommy, I am sorry, but you are in no shape to come with me. Besides, Dr. Chadwick needs you." Grant had to agree he would not be much help in a search and rescue. He was not much of a horseman to begin with, and with a broken arm, riding would be very difficult, if not impossible. He did, however, offer some ideas for Clive to mull over.

"Too many accidents on this trip to my liking, Clive. Someone evil is behind this. As soon as I get Festus settled, I will go myself as quickly as possible to London for help. I know Jeffrey has a friend in his office who is skilled at such tracking and fighting. I am sure he would be willing to help. How shall we find you?"

"Yes, that's a good idea. Try to be as fast as you can. I can follow them, but I am less sure about facing armed kidnappers alone." Clive tried to think, even as his eyes roamed the ground looking for footprints. "This direction is northwest. At each town I come to, I will pick the main inn described in *Paterson's* to leave messages for you. If I get Frederica…" his stomach gave a bit of a lurch at the qualifier, "…*when* I get Frederica back, we will head home to Ripon. Father will keep her safe until Jeffrey or his friend can resolve this madness. Now go, Tommy, and send me those horses! Oh, and any money you have, too, if you don't mind."

Brandishing his torch, Clive headed off, hoping against hope he would find some clue as to the direction of the kidnappers. The why of it all, he couldn't even begin to fathom. Later, he would think about the why…later.

"Sir, over here!" one of the villagers called out sharply. Clive hurried over to him. "Look there!" Several others joined them holding their torches high.

A ribbon from Frederica's hair lay on a bush.

"Oh good girl!" Clive bent and retrieved the ribbon. "This is in too good a condition to have been snagged by the bush. I believe she put it there. That means she is conscious. Now at least we know what direction to go in!"

The men around him nodded approvingly at his reasoning.

"Fan out into a line, with an arm's length between you," Clive ordered. "Let's see what else we can find."

Almost immediately a voice called, "Sir, over here!" Off to the right, Clive could see a torch waving to get his attention. "Look at this!"

Thanks to the recent rain, older markings in the soil had been washed away, leaving only one new set of tracks clear for all to see. The searchers had passed beyond the rim of the stones and were standing on the edge of a field that was ready for planting. The wheels had sunk fairly deeply into the soft soil of what appeared to be a seldom-used footpath joining two fields.

"Sir, with that amount of dung, I figure the carriage was here some time."

"I agree. I'm amazed the carriage fit in here at all!"

"Not a real carriage, sir. One of them governess-type carts, I should think."

One of the older men was studying the ground thoughtfully. "The dung also tells us what direction they were pointed in."

"What is in that direction?" Clive asked.

The same villager answered. "If you follow this path for a maybe a mile, you come to a fork, and if you goes to the left, you will get to Chippenham. If these men that took the young lady went that way, they aren't too stupid. Not much out there. Couple of farms, but they are set back from the road and probably can't see or hear anything."

"How long to make Chippenham?"

Another voice chimed in, "It's not long, sir, if you go by the main road. This way will be a bit longer. When Bill there says there is not much that way, he speaks true. Lots of woods and marshland. If you stick to the track, you should be fine, but I wouldn't go wandering off the track."

"Aye, some of them folks out there are downright unfriendly. They like their privacy."

Even as they spoke, Clive could hear the sound of horses' hooves. Good old Tommy hadn't wasted any time. The coachman had arrived. However, he only had one horse with him.

"My horses are not trained to the saddle, sir," he said when he reached the search party. "But the gentleman hired this nag from the inn. He said to tell you everything you wanted is in the saddlebags."

"Did he say anything about the old gent?" Dering asked as he checked the girth. The horse wasn't the youngest nag he had ever seen, but neither was she the worst. She should at least get him to a town where he could hire a better one.

"Sorry, sir, the old gent hasn't come around yet. He is still breathing, though."

"Well. I guess that is something."

"Oh and sir, the other gentleman sent this." From under his coat, the coachman drew a pistol, which he handed to Dering. "I guess you know how to use it?"

"Yes, to be sure. My father has had me shooting for many years now." Clive weighed the weapon in his hand. The gun looked old but still service-able. There was not a bit of rust about it. It had obviously been well cared-for. He wondered from where Tommy had produced such an item. The coachman handed him a small pouch with powder and shot in it.

"You'll be wanting this, I am sure. And this, too." He handed Clive an-other pouch, which clinked with coins.

Clive put the coins in his coat pocket and thought about where best to keep the pistol. If he put the weapon and powder in his saddlebags, they would not be readily accessible. However, he would have his hands full with his horse and the lantern. He decided to load the gun and keep it in his inner pocket, even though carrying a loaded pistol made him nervous. Clive quickly rearranged his belong-ings. He felt an urgency to get moving. The longer it took to get started, the far-ther the kidnappers would get and the less chance he would be able to catch them.

"Gentlemen," Clive mounted the horse and turned to speak to the towns-people, "thank you for your help. I hope I am back soon with good news, but a few prayers would not go amiss."

He directed the horse onto the track the local had previously pointed out. With only a dim lantern to light it, the track looked like a road into fathomless hell. Trees hung over the path and cut off any moonlight that might have been available. As he kicked the horse into a walk, he could hear various voices en-couraging him: "Amen, lad!" "You got 'em!" "Good luck, sir."

* * *

The night seemed endless. It was impossible for Clive to see anything with only the dim light of his lantern. He certainly could not make any time, as he needed to keep stopping to make sure he had not lost the tracks made by the cart.

His frustration with his lack of progress almost made him miss the shadow of a trail going off to the right. Only a second look at the deepened wheel tracks and some broken weeds saved him from riding past it.

"They must have turned suddenly. Too bad the wheels didn't get stuck in this soft dirt," he murmured to himself. He dismounted so he could follow the faint markings better, hoping the trees would shelter his lantern's light from any suspicious eyes. He was getting tired. A glance at his pocket watch told him it was past three in the morning.

The trail seemed to broaden. Assuming the kidnappers must have headed for some nearby shelter or meeting place, Clive led his horse into the trees and tied it to a bush so he could approach more quietly on foot.

"Poor old thing, you look done in, too." The horse gave a deep sigh as Dering absently patted it on the neck while surveying the area. Was that a glimmer of light he could see through the trees? Leaving the nag and his now-dark lantern behind, Clive started to walk cautiously down the overgrown path.

He sensed rather than saw when the trees gave way to a small clearing. The first he knew of the cart was when he ran into it, barking his shins and almost causing him to swear aloud.

Two wheels. Just like the farmer said. Must be what they used to take her away.

Clive crouched behind the cart so he could study the shack carefully. He guessed the glimmer of light he was following was from a fireplace inside the cabin. The building was in such poor condition that slivers of light came through the cracks in the walls and the shutters covering the small window. Just as he was working his nerve up to go closer and peer through one of the cracks, the door opened and a man stepped out. Whoever he was stood just outside the door and relieved himself.

To Dering, the man seemed totally unconcerned that he might have been followed. *What insolence! To think they can just snatch anyone and no one will notice or come after her.* He took several deep breaths to calm his anger and continued to study the shack.

Through the open door, the firelight cast everything else into such darkness that the scene in the room was perfectly clear. In front of the smoky fireplace there was a stool, empty, and a wooden chair, occupied. To the right, he could see a pile of rags or blankets. His crouching position behind the cart limited his line of sight and he couldn't see if there was anyone else in the room.

The door slammed shut as the man reentered the shack, cutting off the bright light and leaving Dering in the dark.

Clive sat back on his heels to think. Where was she? He carefully replayed the small room in his mind. Was there a loft? Was she somewhere behind the door? He reached into the cart and felt the bed to see if he had overlooked anything there. No, nothing had been left in the cart.

He circled the shack to see if he could see in from another angle. He could hear a horse snorting and moving about towards the back of the building. He approached the animal and when he patted its shoulder, he could feel its coat was damp with sweat.

"You poor thing. You haven't been standing here resting all night, have you?" He untied it, hoping the beast would wander off on its own without him needing to make a lot of noise to encourage it. Maybe he would find Frederica and they would be lucky enough to escape. Without a horse, it would be harder for the kidnappers to follow them.

He saw another chink in the shack wall and crept forward. Suddenly, he was staring right into Frederica's terrified eyes. He could see she was gagged and that probably kept her from giving a startled outcry. Clive could see her relax as she recognized him. He put his finger to his lips to signify silence, knowing she could not make any noise but wanting her to understand he couldn't talk because her captors were too close. At least from this angle, he could see that there were only two men in the room. Now he understood that what he had seen as a rag pile to the right of the fireplace was actually Frederica.

Two men. He only had one pistol with one shot, and it was a pistol he had never fired. Would it even work? What could he do? The men seemed relaxed, unconcerned, but seemingly waiting for something or someone. As he peered over Frederica's head, Clive could see one dozing and the other sipping from a jug. Probably rum, he guessed. Would they drink themselves into a stupor? Could he be that lucky?

Clive needed a plan. He tried to gauge the strength of the two felons from their size. Although both were older than he and fairly ragged, they looked like fighters, judging by the scars on their faces. Both, too, were bigger than him and he didn't think he could take either one physically, in spite of the boxing lessons his father had provided. So whatever he did would have to be done quickly while he had the element of surprise. Incapacitating both at once would be ideal, but how? Desperately, he tried to come up with a plan that had some possibility of success.

If I shoot one and not the other, the one I don't shoot might get to Frederica and use her as a hostage against me. Clive chewed his lips as he weighed his options. *On the other hand, they have not hurt Frederica yet, so they must be holding her for ransom.* The possibility of killing men didn't bother him. After all, they had probably murdered Dr. Chadwick and had kidnapped Frederica. Remembering their brutality against the old scholar also convinced him that he wouldn't get a second chance at freeing Frederica. These men looked like serious villains.

A slight change in the sky warned Dering that the false dawn was not far off. *These bastards must be waiting for someone. If they weren't, they would be sleeping. I bet he is due soon.* He took a deep breath. *So I better not put this off.* He pulled the pistol from his pocket and tried to check the powder pan by the light of one of the chinks in the wall of the shack. It was impossible to see well enough to check the gun accurately. He crept to the front of the shack. Taking another deep breath, he charged the door.

Chapter Ten: Flight

Clive

The door swung open so easily that he staggered as he went through it. *That was an impressive entry. The latch must be broken and the scum were so cocky they didn't do anything about keeping the door shut.* The kidnappers' initial reaction saved him from having to think of anything intimidating to say.

"Jesus! You don't need to take the door off."

"Took you long enough."

Both men talked and stood at the same time. It took them a while to either wake up or sober up enough to realize Clive was not the man for whom they were waiting. The one on Clive's left blinked owlishly at the pistol in Dering's hand. "What's the smoker for?" he asked.

"You ain't the captain!" The other man, shorter and less brutish-looking, seemed more awake. He started to reach into his pocket. "None of that! Just get your hands up and keep them where I can see them!" Clive ordered as he waved the pistol between them in what he hoped was an impressive manner.

Both men responded slowly, but to his relief they at least kept their hands raised. He could sense, rather than see, Frederica straining to turn her body so she could see what was going on. He didn't want to take his eyes off the kidnappers. "Take your clothes off!"

"What?"

"No!"

"How are you goin' to make us?" the more awake scoundrel demanded. "Your pistol has only one shot and there are two of us."

"Which means one of you is going to die," Clive shot back. "Want to choose which one?" That seemed to shut them up, at least for the moment.

"Now take off your clothes," he ordered. "Now, before I put a bullet in your head." He kept his pistol moving to and from each man. "Come on, I do not have all night."

It took longer than he wanted, but eventually both were naked and obviously quite angry.

"You," he pointed to the one who seemed a tad smarter. "You, untie her." The other man just seemed too rough to touch Frederica. The kidnapper sidled towards her slowly. Clive could feel sweat breaking out on his body. This was going to be the very tricky part.

"Wait!" He had another idea. "Tie him up first," he demanded.

"With what?" the man replied sullenly.

"Rip up his shirt."

This was taking much longer than Clive wanted, but he couldn't think of a way to free Frederica while keeping his eyes on the brigands. He knew if he dropped his guard for even one instant, they would both jump him.

The older man started to slowly tear up the shirt. He was taking so long, Clive felt sure he was stalling. "Faster!" They were expecting someone. Someone called Captain. Then he noticed Frederica had somehow rolled off the straw and was struggling to her feet. Still raveled in the blanket, she was not making much progress with the ropes, but she had gotten to her feet. He needed her untied; he couldn't both carry her and fend off the men at the same time. She looked to him for instruction. He hoped he could do this one-handed.

"Hold still," he directed her. He moved to her right so he could use his left hand and keep his pistol aimed with his right. "Are your feet tied?"

She shook her head. Finally, something in their favor. He changed his plan.

"Move to the door, but go behind me and walk very slowly. Don't go anywhere near them. Don't let them grab you." Nodding her understanding, Frederica started to inch to the door, hobbled as she was by the blanket.

She got to the door before the one villain had started to tie the other's hands. Obviously he was going to drag this out as long as possible.

"Frederica, go outside and walk down the track. I will catch up. If you need, hide in the bushes. I think there is someone coming to meet this *scum* and we need to get away as quickly as possible. I will be along as soon as I secure them." He was not at all sure how he was going to accomplish that.

Suddenly, the untied man charged. Dering pulled the trigger, causing a small explosion and a lot of smoke. The villain dropped like a stone to the floor, where he lay moaning in a growing pool of blood. The other man, even with half untied hands, didn't move. He just stood staring in shock at his dying accomplice.

"Come on, Frederica, move!" Realizing she could not walk any faster, he pocketed his pistol and threw her over his shoulder. They would not get far, but at least they would be in the dark. "Let's get out of here!"

Even when they reached the horse, Dering did not take the time to untie her. A sense of urgency drove him. If the man coming to meet the brigands did not show up, the surviving kidnapper might get himself together and follow Clive and Frederica on foot. He probably had a pistol in his coat and whoever he was working for certainly would be armed. He might also not be alone when he did show up. Dering draped Frederica over the horse's back, but instead of heading back the way he had come, he led them straight into the woods, hoping the darkness would hide them. Then he reversed to try and parallel the path leading back to the main road.

"Sorry you are so uncomfortable, but I want to get off this track. I think the man who hired those two has to come this way and I don't want to meet him. I'll untie you as soon as possible," he promised.

Frederica grunted. When Clive decided they had gone deep enough to lose any followers, he stopped and lifted Frederica off the horse. He untied the gag first and then went to work on the ropes. She took deep breaths while he finally got the knots undone and freed her arms. She started to rub her wrists where the rope had cut in, but he turned her to face him, pulled her into his arms, and gave her a fierce hug.

"Are you all right? Are you hurt? Did they hurt you?" he asked in a rush. Then without another thought, he leaned in and kissed her. Maybe it was the relief at being freed, but she did not stiffen or reject him. In fact, she seemed to lean into him.

"Oh Clive, I was never so thankful to see anyone. I know you saved my life!"

"Are you all right?" he asked again anxiously. He took her hands and began to massage her fingers, helping her get the feeling back.

"My legs are like rubber and my shoulders hurt, but so what? I am alive and I owe that to you."

"We'll talk later about what they were up to. Damn, I should have taken the time to run off their horse. Too late now."

"Are we far enough off the road?"

"I don't think so, but in the dark who can tell?" he asked her. "Unfortunately for us, it is going to be light soon. Here, let me give you a boost back up. I'll walk. We need to get out of here. I think someone named the captain is supposed to arrive and I don't want to be here when it happens. We may not be so lucky a second time." With that, he cupped his hands and gave Frederica a boost up to the saddle. Frederica ended up astride the horse. "Can you hold on?" he asked.

"Don't worry about me. I'll manage."

Bold words, but to him she did not sound so bold. She had said her legs felt unsteady and he could see her hands were trembling. He hoped they didn't have to go far. And that brought up another thought: Where exactly were they going? Staying here was dangerous, but retracing his steps from Avebury would probably lead them straight to the captain. That left the road in the other direction. He had forgotten where it led to. Hopefully, though, it had more trees for hiding places than did the open fields towards Avebury. "I think I had better take the reins. Just hold on to the pommel."

"They kept talking about 'the captain,'" she murmured. "I think they expected him around dawn."

After he had Frederica situated in the saddle, Clive took the time to reload the pistol and stash it in his pocket. His father had taught him about firearms, but he had never loaded one in the dark. He had also never loaded one with his hands shaking. As much as he was appalled that he had shot someone, he hoped he got the pistol right in case he needed to shoot another bandit. He was determined not to let Frederica be grabbed again without a fight. He started leading them through the woods. "Can you see anyone following us from up there, Frederica?" he asked quietly.

"I don't see any lights in any direction," she responded, also keeping her voice low.

"Excellent. But this captain could be travelling without a light."

"I don't hear anyone or anything, either. That was brilliant, making them take their clothes off."

"I am worried that little idea delayed us too much, and in the end, I still had to shoot one of them."

In what seemed a very short time, they came out of the woods onto a track. "This should be the road between Avebury and some other village whose name I forget. If it is, it is the way I came to find you. Yes, it is! Here is the turn to the shack. I almost missed this cutoff in the dark," Clive said. He pointed to ruts in the dirt where the cart had turned into the lane. "Lucky for us, the cart left some deep marks."

Frederica looked down to where he was pointing. "I can see the tracks," she said. "It's getting light. It must be almost dawn," she added worriedly. "Shouldn't we be going back the way we came if we want to get to Avebury?" She glanced over her shoulder.

"We can't. We are going to head in the other direction," he responded. "I'm guessing this captain person is probably coming through Avebury and we certainly don't want to meet him on the road. I did not see much cover as I rode here."

It wasn't long, however, before both could hear faint hoof-beats breaking the silence of the predawn air. Dering quickly pulled the horse into the woods again, not stopping until the trees and branches and undergrowth were deep enough to make them invisible.

He lifted Frederica from the horse. "I am exhausted, Frederica, as I am sure you are. We can rest here and hopefully let them pass us by," he murmured.

"Can you tell what direction they are coming from?" she asked.

"No, I can't." Clive was discouraged. "Could be either. Maybe the daylight will help us out."

The hoof-beats sounded like claps of thunder in the forest quiet.

"Remember, they can't see us." Clive tried to sound more confident than he actually felt.

* * *

Clive could tell when Frederica woke. She tried to sit up and finding him draped over her, she began to struggle. He was so stiff, he could not stifle a groan as he tried to move.

"Stop, stop, I'm moving," he sounded groggy, even to himself. They were in a small area between some low bushes surrounded by trees. He could hear the horse snorting and stomping behind them. He scrubbed his face with his hands, trying to wake up.

"I am sorry, Miss Chadwick. I must have gotten cold and tried to get close to you for warmth. I didn't mean to be rude."

He could see the attractive flush in her cheeks as she no doubt remembered how close they had gotten last night. The early morning air had been quite chilly and when they stopped running, both had been thoroughly chilled. They had Frederica's cloak and the ratty blanket the kidnappers had used to wrap her in. Clive had his jacket, but no overcoat. After they tied up the horse, he had used the ratty blanket as ground cover. They had pulled Frederica's cloak over themselves. Dering had fallen instantly and deeply asleep, but he must have moved closer to her when he got chilled. At least, that was the story he told her.

"You've nothing to apologize for. I was so cold, it took me quite a while to doze off. Do you think we could start a fire?" she responded stoutly. And then, more shyly, "Please call me Frederica. I think we have been through enough to be on a first-name basis, don't you?"

"Yes, thank you, I would like that very much." He took her hand and squeezed it. "It is a very pretty name, you know. But I am sorry about the fire. I don't think it's a good idea. It might be noticed. We still don't know if we are being followed. I assume the captain has arrived by now and found you gone. He could be anywhere."

Clive got to his feet. He started pulling bread and cheese out of the saddlebags. He passed the food to Frederica. "Here, break this up between us while I check out the *Paterson's Guide*. I want to see where this road goes and how far it is to the next town. Maybe there is an inn nearby."

"Do you have anything to drink?"

"No, I'm sorry. I didn't have a lot of time to pack. I have a cup, but no water. I feel bad we have no way to give that poor horse anything."

Frederica broke off a chunk of bread. "Well, at least we didn't take his blanket last night."

"I thought about it, but it did seem too mean, especially after the night we put him through."

"Speaking of last night, have you got any idea why I was kidnapped? I also want to know how you found me. What has happened to Uncle Festus and Mr. Grant?"

"Sounds like you have a few questions." He found to his surprise that he could actually chuckle. But he became serious again quickly. "I hate to disappoint you, but I can only answer one of those questions right now and that is where we are. That road there, over behind those trees," he gestured to the road they had been on the night before, "leads to Chippenham. The guidebook says there is an inn and a hostelry there. We should be able to get some decent food and find out about the stage to Shrewsbury." He took a large bite of cheese.

"Shrewsbury? Why there? Why can't we go back to Avebury and meet up with Uncle Festus? Do horses eat bread or cheese?"

Clive chose to answer the last question first. "Can't say as I have ever seen them eat bread or cheese, but they eat grass and grains. How different can bread be?"

Frederica got to her feet with a great deal of difficulty. Obviously, being tied up and immobile for some hours had left her stiff. The cold last night probably had not helped.

"The more you walk around, the easier it will become," he told her. But she was still moving uncomfortably even after she finished feeding the horse. Clive finished packing up the saddlebags while he studied her stride.

"Do you want to walk or ride?"

"How far is it?" she asked.

"Five, maybe six, miles."

"I think I had better walk a bit," she responded. "I feel so stiff, I know I need to work out the pain. If we have to run for it, I don't want you to have to carry me. We wouldn't get too far. Before we leave, though, let me rub my feet a bit to get some feeling back." Frederica sat on the ground and began to untie her boots.

"I should have thought of that before." Clive knelt beside her and before she could protest, he took one stockinged foot in his hand. "Let me help."

He started to massage her arch, working his way to her heel. He was rather pleased to see an attractive blush was creeping up her cheeks. Maybe she wasn't too repelled by him. She did not stop him when he reached for the other foot.

"Oh thank you. I was feeling that someone was sticking hundreds of pins into the soles of my feet. Now I feel like I can walk a bit. But turn around, will you? I want to tie my stockings up again." She was ready by the time he finished saddling the horse. "I am going to walk a bit now."

"Seems like a good idea to me. I'll walk, too, but if you start to have trouble, up you go," Clive answered. "This may help a bit. You keep to the left side of the horse and put your right hand on the stirrup and sort of hold on. It will help steady you."

Frederica nodded and did as Clive suggested. Clive kept the reins in his left hand and slowly urged the horse forward. He kept his right hand in his pocket.

"Yes, I do feel steadier," she said. "Do you have the pistol in your pocket?"

"Yes, I'm afraid I do not think we are at all safe yet. I wish I understood what was going on here."

"You never answered my question as to why Shrewsbury?"

"Right. The easy answer is that Dr. Chadwick and Tommy should be headed to London by now. No reason to return to Avebury." Clive offered up a sincere hope that what he was saying was true and that Dr. Chadwick was riding in a carriage, not a coffin. However, as he did not know the depth of Dr. Chadwick's injuries, he kept quiet, certain that Frederica had enough to worry about.

"Why can't we follow them?"

"Why Shrewsbury?" Clive was following his own thoughts and did not answer her directly. "Tommy and I had no time to plan anything. The best I could come up with is that if I found you, we would head to my father in Ripon. Shrewsbury has a direct stage to Ripon. My father would certainly protect you." He did not want Frederica to think him a sissy wanting to run home to his father, but with all that had happened—the kidnapping and especially the fact that he had probably killed a man last night—he welcomed being able to put their troubles in his father's capable hands.

At the edge of the woods, he went ahead to check to see if anyone was about who might be waiting to ambush them. To his relief, nothing. No visible travelers, no sounds except birdsong. He continued his train of thought. "I am not saying we cannot follow them to London, and maybe going to Shrewsbury isn't necessary, but we need to know more about what is going on than we do now. We could be walking right into the kidnappers' hands again. So let's be careful and keep an eye open for anything suspicious. We know those villains were waiting for someone else last night."

"This is so frustrating," Frederica said despondently. "All this horrid stuff is happening and we have no idea why!"

The hopelessness in her voice made Clive look at Frederica with concern. "How are you feeling? Are we going too fast? You will let me know if you are having any trouble, please."

"No, I am fine. Thirsty, but fine."

"I could use some water, too. Maybe we will cross a creek. I am sure this poor horse could use some, as well."

"Who do you think this captain might be?" Frederica asked.

Dering shook his head. "I am at as much of a loss as you are," he said. "While we're walking, let's compare what we know. Maybe something will come to light. You go first. Start when you left Tommy and me and began walking back to the inn."

"I am afraid my story won't take long. I wasn't awake for most of it."

"Did they knock you out?" Clive asked, shocked.

"With their fists, no. They had some drug that made me sleepy. I remember saying 'good night' to you and Mr. Grant and starting to walk back with Uncle Festus and that young lad from the inn. We were on the part of the path that dips – do you remember it?"

"Yes, we spent some time there looking for clues to find you," Clive answered with a nod.

"We were walking along and I was holding Uncle Festus by the arm. Suddenly, someone grabbed my arm and jerked me away from him. They came out of the dark; I had no warning. They put a cloth over my face, and I don't remember anything else until I woke up in a cart. It was so dark, it was impossible to see at all. The only light was from a torch one of them held." From the flush in her cheeks, Clive thought there was more to the story, but if she did not want to tell him, he decided he would not badger her.

"What then?" he prodded her memory along.

"I was feeling pretty bruised. It was hard to keep from rolling about the cart. The road was just ruts. When we got to the shack, one of them carried me inside and put me on the pile of rags. The rags smelled, the man smelled… it was awful. They had taken my gag off in the cart but they put it back on in the shack. It was hard to breathe."

Clive cringed sympathetically. He could only imagine what she had gone through. "What did they talk about? Did they ever say why?"

"I'm sorry, Mr. Dering." At his glance, she said, "I mean, Clive. I just don't remember. The driver did tell the other man not to hurt me, mentioning something about the captain saying 'no damaged goods.'"

"Why did he have to say that? Was the scoundrel doing something to you?" Clive demanded.

"No, he didn't hurt me, but he seemed to want to."

Clive gave an inarticulate growl of rage.

"Anyway, the other fellow promised he couldn't hurt me." She took a deep breath and continued, "As you saw, they laid me on the pile facing the wall so I couldn't see them. But it sounded like they were drinking at first, and then maybe sleeping. The one who was in charge did say they were not the first fellows the captain had hired. He said that one of the first men had been killed in a coach crash. So, whatever they are trying to do, they have been at it a while and that coachman must have been in on it."

Frederica was becoming agitated as she filled him in on what she had learned and pieced together key points of information. Clive felt anger and a sense of dismay as he realized how organized the kidnappers were and how long they had been following them.

"He also said the first men were not very smart, as they had loosened some stones but no one was hurt. I think that must have been when we were on the Tor in Glastonbury. That's all I can remember of their conversation. They seemed to stop talking after that, except to say the captain was due around dawn. When I think about it, it was probably a good thing I had a gag on, as your popping up outside the shack really gave me a fright."

To Clive's astonishment, Frederica put her head back and gave a crow of laughter. "Oh my, that was startling," she continued to chuckle. "I so wish I could have seen their faces when you charged in the door. They thought you were their lousy captain!" she crowed. Soon, she calmed. But, still smiling, she offered, "You were wonderful! So now it's your turn. Tell me your story."

"In a minute. Look, we're crossing a creek. Let's see if we can get a drink." Without their noticing, the woods had thinned and now, bordered by the stream, had given way to cultivated fields. They could see land that looked ready for planting, each field neatly bordered by hedges or stonewalls.

Dering brought their tired mount to a stop by the side of the road. He rustled in the saddlebags until he emerged with a drinking cup. "Wait here; I'll go down." He scrambled down the slight embankment and quickly filled the cup. He brought it back to Frederica. He handed it to her to drink first.

"Thank you…Clive. I guess we are definitely on a first-name basis now. That water tastes wonderful." She handed the cup back. "How are we going to water the horse?"

"It's not too steep; he should be able to get down there himself." Clive led the horse to the edge of the water with relative ease. "I bet he smells the water and that is what is making him so agreeable." When Clive and the horse rejoined Frederica on the road, both were dripping water from their faces.

Clive studied Frederica's face while wiping his own on his sleeve. "Want to ride for a while? You look a bit tired."

"Right now, I think I want to get down to that water and wash, too. Can you help me?"

After she rubbed her face and hands with icy cold water and dried them with Clive's handkerchief, he helped her back up the bank to the road.

"I think I had better ride for a while. I am a bit tired." Clive clasped his hands to give her a leg up.

In the saddle, she repeated her request. "Now, your turn!" she commanded. "Tell me your part of the story."

Dering took the reins and continued their trek to the village they could now see in the distance.

"Tommy was already in bed and I was about to join him when Stephens came pounding on the door. The lad managed to make it to the inn after the attack and was able to raise the alarm. If he had not, I do not know when we would have realized you were missing."

"Why didn't Uncle Festus raise the alarm?"

Clive sighed and said, "Frederica, both Dr. Chadwick and the lad were laid out with blows to the head. The lad, at least, never lost consciousness, but he did have to leave your uncle lying in the road."

Frederica's cry of distress interrupted his story. "Oh no! How is he now?"

"I am sorry, I do not know. He was still unconscious when I left." Clive stopped himself from saying more. He actually did not know how Dr. Chadwick was. He looked up at Frederica and could see tears on her cheeks. She looked so sad. He thought about all she had gone through in the last twenty-four hours. Yet, this was the first time he had seen tears and they were not for herself. Instinctively, he wanted to comfort her. He reached up and covered her hand where it rested on her leg with his.

"But he was still alive when I left, Frederica. He is a tough old fellow. I feel sure he will pull through." He tried to sound encouraging.

Frederica covered his hand with her other hand and squeezed it before releasing it and wiping her tears away. "Thank you. You are very kind. I am sorry to be so teary. It is just that Uncle Festus has gone through so much on my account." She took a deep breath. "I am sure you are right; he will be fine. Please continue."

Clive retrieved his hand and then checked over his shoulder to see if they were being followed. No one was there. "Do you think it is unusually quiet today? I would have thought we would have seen someone by now."

Frederica surveyed the area from her perch. The road was now framed by the usual hedge, but over it she could see alternating fields of crops and sheep. It seemed so peaceful. In the quiet, a church bell could be heard tolling in the far distance reminding her of the day of the week. "It's Sunday, Clive. I guess most folk are at church. It is still very early, too." She leaned down and poked him in the shoulder. "Talk!" she commanded. "Tell me how you found me."

"We thought at first that you might have been bashed in the head and left in the bushes, but then we heard the lad's story and realized it was not a robbery but a kidnapping and that you had been taken away. I wish we knew why. Anyway, Tommy's not a particularly accomplished horseman, even if he had the use of both arms. We decided he would stay with Dr. Chadwick and I would search for you. He is to send immediately to London for Jeffrey's friend Nathan. Like your brother, Nathan works with the Alien Office. Jeffrey told me once Nathan was a great one to have if you found yourself in trouble. He is smart and can hold his own in a fight. Tommy knows him better than I do, of course. We were so rushed and it was hard to make plans. We just decided I would try to find you and if possible head for home in Ripon. I am to try to leave messages at inns so whoever follows us knows where we are and can catch up."

"What would you have done if you could not find me?"

Clive chewed his lip, an old habit when he was embarrassed or at a loss for words. "I am afraid we had no other plan. Not particularly well thought out, was it?" he said ruefully.

"I think the fact you found that shack in the dark and managed to free me was just amazing."

"You know, finding the shack was the easy part. As the cart they used only had two wheels, it made very distinctive ruts. I am not sure I would have known that, but one of the villagers at Avebury pointed it out to me. He is the one who actually figured out the direction they took you in. The villagers were very helpful. They know the area well and gave me good advice about what to expect. The first part was pretty scary. The track the villains took was an old lane that went through some trees. I had the strange feeling of being in a cellar, so closed off. It was hard to see anything with only a lantern and I was sort of worried your captors would be in the bushes ready to jump out at anyone following them. But that part of the track wasn't long and I was able to make better time once we hit a bigger road. This road, in fact. You know, those men were so cocky they didn't even try to hide where they turned off. I would never have found that shack if I had missed that turn, but the ruts were deep and fresh and the hot manure made it easy to see."

"I still think it was very clever of you to find me, and extremely brave to barge in like that." She paused as she stared ahead of them. "Oh Clive, I think we are coming to the village. I must stop and try to tidy myself. I must look a fright, all night bound in a dirty blanket and then sleeping in the woods. People will think you kidnapped me or worse."

Clive could not laugh as she probably intended. She definitely had a point.

"We certainly want to avoid attention. Let's see what we can do about making ourselves presentable." He stopped the horse and helped her down. "Your face is clean, but your hair could use some attention. Let me see if I can find a comb. I do not know what Tommy put in these bags," he muttered as he started to rummage through the saddlebags again.

"Ah, here's a comb." He produced the implement and Frederica promptly fell to trying to unsnarl her hair.

"Here, let me help or we will be here all day." He took over the comb and made short work of the mass of tangles. "Let me braid it down the back; it will look more proper."

"It might make me appear proper, but I will look like a child. Though I guess that's better than anything I can do without a mirror. Where did you ever learn to braid hair?"

"Sisters," was his short reply. "No hat? Oh, well you can use the hood from your cloak. I didn't think much of the head gear you've been wearing anyway." Clive's fingers itched to smooth the soft skin on the back of her neck. He forced himself to concentrate and worked her hair into three sections.

"My hat got lost at Avebury," Frederica replied dolefully. "I didn't think much of it, either. I hope Mr. Stephens stores my belongings until we get back to Avebury. Or do you think Mr. Grant will take them to London? All my art supplies are in my luggage." She could feel he was getting to the end of the braid.

"What shall we tie the braid with?"

"Got any lace on your petticoat?"

"Yes, as a matter of fact I do." She leaned over and quickly ripped a bit off. As she handed the lace to Clive, Frederica thought about how her petticoats had taken a lot of abuse on this trip. With her hair somewhat decent, Frederica surveyed her white dress. It might have been a good choice for the carriage ride from Bath to Avebury, but it had not been a good choice for kidnapping and sleeping rough in the woods. She tried to rub out some of the more egregious patterns of dirt and straw. "Not much I can do here," she moaned.

Clive tried to smarten up, too, retying his cravat and brushing off his coat. "Too bad it is Sunday. The market and stores will be closed. Well, let us see what else this village has to offer."

"At least the hostelry will have food and maybe some coffee or tea," Frederica responded.

"Amen to that!" Clive agreed wholeheartedly.

Chapter Eleven: Legging It!

Frederica

The small village had two main streets with a very unusual building at the intersection. It appeared to be built on stone stilts that were at least the height of a full-grown man.

"What *is* that?" Frederica asked. "Surely they don't get floods that high here?"

"No, I don't think it floods at all. That is the wool exchange. All these Cotswold villages have open-sided buildings where farmers bring their wool. It is then sold to middlemen who take it to London to be resold overseas, usually to merchants in Holland." As Clive filled Frederica in on the details, he paused their horse near the exchange to survey the village and search for an inn. "This place is so different from what I am used to in Kent. Of course we have villages, with high streets for shops and the markets, but we use a lot more wood in our buildings. This town is all made of stone, which gives it a very different look." She paused as Clive lifted her down from the horse.

"How do you know about wool and where it is bought and sold?"

"I went about a lot with my father when I was younger. He often travels through this region looking for prime horses. That's what we do, you know, besides farming: we raise horses."

"Have you ever been here before?" Frederica asked, looking about.

"No, but most of these Cotswold villages are set up in the same way and I have seen others with similar exchanges. Oh, look, down there is an inn." He pulled at the reins and they moved off. As they got closer, Frederica could see the sign naming the inn as the Ram's Head. A picture of a large, almost fat, sheep adorned the placard.

The landlord looked at them somewhat questioningly until Dering's money encouraged him to put aside his doubts about their propriety. Soon, the couple was in a private parlor with plates of ham, cheese, and bread in front of them, and their tired beast was waiting in the stable to be retrieved by the innkeeper from Avebury, where Grant had originally rented him.

While they ate, they discussed their next steps. Clive consulted his guide-book and laid out the map for Frederica to follow. "We are here." An index finger indicated a spot on the map. "And here is where we want to go." The index finger indicated a dot about eight inches to the right of the original spot. "That is Ripon, about two hundred miles from here. That is where I live."

"Why do we have to go there? Why can't we just go to London ourselves?"

"To do that, we would have to go back to Bath and take a coach to London."

"Well, let's do that then. Surely being in Bath, where we know at least a few people like Robert and Rachel, would be safer than wandering about England. I am sure even Mrs. Nesfield would take us in. And then once we are there, we can send a message to London and just sit and wait for help."

Clive had to admit her plan sounded reasonable. At least in a stagecoach, they would be unlikely to have to face the kidnappers. "You know, Frederica that is brilliant! I have been so focused on evading your kidnappers that I couldn't come up with a simple, straightforward plan. And I've been worried about money. I only have what little I had on me and whatever Tommy gave me. It will cost less for us to take a coach to Bath than to Ripon, so that will help. I would hope we could borrow something for the fare if we need to. Let me go consult with the landlord about when the coach to Bath is due."

Clive went to find the landlord to discuss stage prices. He found him in an intense discussion with a man Clive had seen before. He made his way back to Frederica, grabbing his saddlebags and barking, "Grab the food."

"Clive, what is going on?" Frederica demanded.

"That man from the Assembly is in the hallway asking about his 'daugh-ter' who has run away. He must mean you."

"Oh my God! Yes, I just saw him ride up out front."

"We have to get out of here. I don't know why he is asking about you as his daughter, but they'll never believe we are not running away together."

"How?"

"How what?"

"How do we get out of here?"

Clive surveyed the room quickly. They both spoke at the same time. "The windows!"

Clive threw open the window and leaned out. They could hear pounding on the door. "Hurry, Clive. It sounds like they are going to knock down the door."

Clive jumped the short distance to the ground and reached up for Frederica. Holding her cloak and some bread wrapped in a napkin, Frederica jumped into his arms. Clive settled his saddlebags over one shoulder and grabbed her by the other hand.

"Look, Frederica, over there." He pointed at a stagecoach that was starting to move down the street.

"Driver, wait!" he yelled.

"Luckily for you, lad, I am not full today. There's room inside. We'll settle up when we get there." The carriage never came to a complete stop but continued at a walking pace as Clive pulled open the door and practically threw Frederica into the compartment. The saddlebags followed and then Clive tumbled in. As soon as the door shut, the driver urged his horse on.

* * *

"Davy, the driver that is, is already a bit late, so he wouldn't want to be coming to a total halt. It would take that much extra time to get the horses stopped and then up to speed again," a voice explained.

Dering threw his bags on a seat first, then leaned down to help Frederica haul herself off the floor and scramble onto an empty, worn leather seat facing the rear of the coach. He slouched beside her. The only other occupant of the coach, and the speaker, took up most of the seat facing them. Frederica's first impression was of a woman swathed in many yards of black drapery. She kept talking as if they were old acquaintances.

"We were just getting underway when some gent, ex-military is my guess – he stood real straight and tall-like – come up. Anyway, this military gent starts talking to Davy, that's the driver. The guard is Pete. Likeable lads; I've known them from the time they were little tykes. Anyway, this gent comes up and starts asking questions. Excuse me a moment."

The wall of words stopped at this point, and to Frederica's consternation, the woman took a snuffbox out of a large bag parked on the seat beside her and helped herself to a healthy pinch. While the ensuing sneezes kept her busy, Frederica and Clive exchanged bemused looks. They tried to make themselves comfortable on the slick seat. Frederica held onto the hand grip by her window as the carriage picked up speed and began to rock side to side.

"Now, that's better." When the woman took a breath of air and seemed about to continue with her monologue, Dering reached forward and offered her his hand.

"Good afternoon. You must think us without any manners. Please forgive our sudden entry to the coach. Obviously, we were late. I am Clive Dering and this is Miss Frederica Chadwick. Miss Chadwick is travelling to Bath to stay with friends and her parents asked me to accompany her." He smiled charmingly at the woman.

The woman reached forward and shook his hand warmly. Then she shook Frederica's. "Oh my dear, you are going to need a better story than that!"

"Excuse me?" Clive asked sharply.

"That military chap I was trying to tell you about, the one that made the coach late, he was asking questions about whether Davy had seen a young woman travelling, maybe with a young man. Then he said his daughter had eloped, but he had traced her to Chippenham. That is the village we were just in. He described Miss Chadwick here perfectly. Said she was blonde and tall and thin. Said she was wearing a white dress with a black cloak. Davy wasn't half happy about his start time being late. He could get docked for it. My guess is he, the other man that is, was looking for you two."

"I'm not his daughter!" Frederica cut in suddenly. Just the thought that someone could announce they were related and have others believe it, made her cringe in horror.

"Can you prove it?"

"Prove it? Why should I have to? The man is no relation of mine!"

Clive spoke quietly, "Miss Chadwick, think about it. This fellow has the perfect cover story. He claims you have run away and elicits sympathy from people who will help him save you from a disastrous marriage. I bet he is describing me as a black-hearted villain chasing after a young innocent heiress." He looked questioningly at the woman.

She nodded in agreement and said, "Sounds pretty much like what I heard. But you have another problem."

"What's that?" Clive asked.

"This coach isn't going to Bath."

"What?!" he yelped in dismay.

"No, this coach is going in the other direction. It's going to Cirencester. That's what I meant when I said you needed a better story. Obviously, if you were going to Bath you would know what coach to take."

Clive slumped back into his corner while Frederica looked at him in distress.

"Oh, Mr. Dering! What are we going to do?"

The woman continued talking, "Well, you have two hours to think about it."

Both Frederica and Clive looked at her questioningly.

"Davy here is not going to stop the coach for any reason. He is already late and as I said, he could get docked. So he is going to try to make up time and you won't be getting off before he stops at the square in Malmesbury. That is the only stop before we get to Cirencester, and trust me, there is not much there."

The carriage's increased rocking supported the woman's assessment of Davy and his desire to keep to the schedule.

"How do you know so much about Davy and this coach?" Frederica asked politely.

"You mean besides the fact I've known the lad since he was just running wild and stealing apples from my orchard?" She chuckled reminiscently. "Oh, I ride the coach a lot. My daughter lives over in Cirencester and I go about once a month or so to see her and my grandchildren. Her husband is a lawyer and the sessions are held there, so it is easier for them to live near where he works. I love my daughter, mind you, but I can only stand that husband of hers for a few days, so then I come home. Lovely children, but while the husband is too stiff, the little darlings are too rambunctious for my taste."

"Well, mistress, does this coach go back and forth every day?" Clive asked.

"Oh, I did forget to tell you my name, now didn't I? I am Mistress

Pontypool, relick of Henry Pontypool. Poor man passed from this life over ten years ago. Good man, but not what I would call exciting."

Frederica hid a smile from Mistress Pontypool. She did seem to have an opinion on everyone.

"Now, here's what I think." Both Frederica and Clive looked at her attentively. "Whether you are running away or eloping is your business." Deep sighs of relief greeted this announcement. "But that fellow after you is a very serious man. People are going to take him at his word. You two, on the other hand…" She shook her head. "You two don't look like you could go anywhere on your own, much less elope to Gretna Green in Scotland. Look at yourselves," she commanded.

Frederica looked at Dering. Mistress Pontypool was right about one thing. After riding a horse all night and napping in the woods, he didn't look very respectable.

"Do I look as ratty as you do?" she asked him.

"I am afraid so," he answered. "That frock has certainly seen better days."

Frederica sighed, studying the stains marking her white skirt. They seemed to be a mixture of grass, straw, and other disgusting stuff from the rotting pile in the cottage. The dress certainly did not look as clean and crisp as it had two weeks ago.

"We are going to have to get some better clothes and clean up a bit. I was hoping we could do that in Bath, but I'm guessing we will have to stay over in Cirencester before we can get the coach to Bath."

"Lad, you worry me. If I wasn't such a romantic myself, I would be thinking someone should turn you in to save you from yourself."

"Why? What do you mean?"

"First, you won't be able to get married in Bath without a special license. You need to go to Scotland for that."

"Oh, I know that. I told you, we are not eloping."

"Well, then, just what *are* you doing?" she demanded.

"We are trying to save our lives," Frederica interjected. "I was kidnapped last night—or was it the night before? I'm afraid I am getting confused about the dates. Anyway, Mr. Dering here, saved me from two horrid men. And I have reason to think that man following us is in on it, too."

"Oh, my." Mistress Pontypool's eyes got wide as saucers. "Go on, tell me the whole story. This is ever so much better than one of them novels I get from the lending library. This is for real."

So between them, Mistress Pontypool offering interruptions—requests for embellishments and sighs of appreciation for Clive's bravery—they retold the events leading up to their sudden arrival on the floor of the Bath-to-Cirencester coach.

"So what are you going to do now?" the chatty old widow asked at the end of the tale.

Clive answered, "I guess we will stay in Cirencester until we can get a coach to Bath."

"Mr. Dering, what do you suppose that villain is up to?" Frederica asked.

"I don't know. It would help if we had a clue as to why he wants to kidnap you. We have no idea what he wants or how far he is willing to go to get it."

"Mistress, did you see where he was headed as the coach took off?" Frederica asked.

"Last I saw, he was talking to a couple of rather uncouth types standing in front of the market column."

Clive and Frederica exchanged glances as they both remembered the man Clive had shot and who they had both assumed to be dead.

He spoke first. "Looks like he has some other chaps working with him. We should probably refer to him as a captain, as we do not even know his name." He shook his head in dismay as he continued, "There were two at the cottage and we heard more than one horse—maybe two or three—on the road last night. That could total about four to five men. That seems a pretty serious threat to me – we had better take all the precautions we can."

Frederica nodded in agreement. "If he gets hold of me way out here, it will take you ages to find help to rescue me. I am afraid, Clive, it might be too late to get help. In fact, right now I am just afraid."

Mistress Pontypool leaned over and took Frederica's hands and patted them comfortingly. "Now don't you worry, dear. I will help you. We have some time to plan what you should do if that man finds you." She turned to Dering. "Do you know anyone in Cirencester?" she asked.

"No, mistress, we don't. As I said, I thought we were going back to Bath, where we do have friends."

"Well, you can't stay with my daughter and her husband. He is just the type to help that captain. We will have to figure out another place for you to wait. You see the coach-run ends in Gloucester. It only passes through Cirencester. If you want to go on, say to Edinburgh or any place north, you have to go to Gloucester to change coaches."

Clive gave a groan. "When this captain realizes we haven't gone back to Bath and follows us to Cirencester, he will likely look for us. And we'll be vulnerable as long as we are in Cirencester waiting for a coach." He pulled his trusty guidebook out of his saddlebags and began perusing the map of the surrounding area.

"Does the coach go back to Bath immediately?" Frederica asked Mistress Pontypool.

"No, not until tomorrow. As I said, the run starts in Wells and goes through Bath, Chippenham, and a few other places, including Cirencester, and then on to Gloucester. They do the same route tomorrow, only backwards, and then the day after, they go from Wells to Gloucester. So it is every other day. I'm afraid you will need to keep out of sight at least overnight."

"We can do that, can't we?" Frederica turned to Clive and asked desperately.

"Yes, it sounds like we can do that." He squeezed her clenched hand and answered calmly, "Do you have any suggestions where we can stay? The guidebook mentions King's Head and the Ram. We want a respectable place, but not one where the landlord is going to ask a lot of questions."

"Those are both posting inns. My son-in-law spends a good deal of time at the King's Head, so I think you would be best off somewhere more out of the way. I think you would be better off at the White Hart. That's a respectable place but smaller, and it seems mostly locals go there."

Clive nodded in agreement. "We arrive in Cirencester in the early afternoon. It's Sunday, so the market and probably everything else will be closed. Our best option seems to be to hole up at the White Hart and wait until the coach leaves for Bath tomorrow." He looked at Frederica inquiringly.

"We can spend our time indoors resting and cleaning up," she answered. "It's not like we are here to see the sights anyway. That miserable cottage was as 'picturesque' as I want to get for a long time to come, I can tell you that. And I certainly could use a long sleep. I bet you could, too."

"I should be able to get messages off to Tommy and maybe my father. It makes it a lot easier that Cirencester is a post town. There should be a coach going to London. No, don't get your hopes up. I don't have enough money for tickets."

"I think you should send a message to Bath, too, and tell Robert and his grandfather, what has happened."

"Why do that – won't we be on the same coach?"

"Just in case. I have this bad feeling we haven't seen the last of this captain."

"Look, chicks." Mistress Pontypool pointed, "We must be on the out-skirts of Malmesbury. That means we are halfway there. This stop is usually very quick."

And, in fact, it was. The horses were changed, the mail offloaded, and they were back on the road with all speed possible. Unfortunately for Frederica and Clive, two other passengers joined the coach. One, a thin gentleman with a priest's collar and an unhappy way of looking down his nose at the world around him – and Frederica in particular, it seemed – sat with Mistress Pontypool. A much larger man seated himself on their side, squeezing Frederica into the middle. From the smell, he had prepared himself for the trip with liberal quantities of ale. Not surprisingly, he fell asleep immediately. Without a grip to hang onto, Frederica was forced to hold onto Dering's arm to keep from being thrown about. It seemed the coachman was still trying to make up for lost time.

The second half of the trip was much quieter. The presence of the dis-approving minister seemed to quell even Mistress Pontypool and she soon fell asleep. Frederica would have liked to nap, but the rocking of the coach prevented her from finding a comfortable spot. At first, she pulled her cloak closer around her, trying to hide the disreputable condition of the dress from the minister's critical eyes, but eventually she resolutely ignored him. Dering did not speak much, either, instead spending his time staring out the window. She could not tell what he was thinking but assumed he was worried about the same things she was: Were they being followed, and what could they do to stay safe?

Frederica sighed with relief when the coach pulled into the Cirencester market square and rolled to a stop in front of a church. Without a word, the minister opened the door on his side and swiftly departed up the street.

The other gentleman, having slept off his liquor, proved to have much better manners. He got the steps out for Mistress Pontypool, held the door, and helped her and Frederica out of the coach. Then with a bow, he got back on the coach. Frederica assumed he was going on to Gloucester. Dering gave her a conspiratorial wink when he joined her on the ground.

As soon as Mistress Pontypool was on firm ground, she found herself surrounded by several children, all vying loudly for her attention. A young woman who Frederica thought must be the image of Mistress Pontypool thirty years ago was standing on the steps of the church with a stiff-looking man in a high cravat. He could only be the much-despised son-in-law. Obviously, they were there to meet the coach. Almost immediately, Mistress Pontypool was being handed into their curricle and driven off with only a nod in Clive and Frederica's direction.

Frederica surveyed her dress sorrowfully. "I can understand why she wouldn't want to introduce us to her daughter. We hardly look respectable."

Clive just smiled and shrugged. Before Davy could drive off, Dering asked him for the way to the White Hart. It seemed to be somewhere towards the town through which the coach had just come. "At least that is what I think he said. Rather thick accent."

Slinging the saddlebags over his shoulder, he took Frederica's arm and they started back up the street. Frederica studied the area with interest. They were on a small street that opened onto what looked to be a market square. Yet it was not actually a square, but a sort of bulge where the street widened to the width of several and then squeezed back to a single lane near its end where the church stood. When the coach moved on, Frederica could read the name, St. John the Baptist, over the main portal. Shops lined both sides of the bulge but were, of course, closed.

"What's that pillar in the street? There was one in Bath, but I forgot to ask about it then."

"That's the market obelisk. It is in the center of the town and it identifies Cirencester as a market town. Don't the towns in Kent have them?" Clive asked. "This area will be the focal point of the market. All the sellers will put their stalls in this area. *Paterson*'s says Monday and Friday are market days, so I imagine tomorrow this place will be crowded with townspeople and vendors. Once I find out when the coach leaves, we might have some time for a look around. But I have to warn you, we won't be able to buy much."

"You seem to be worried about money, Clive. You've mentioned it a few times."

"As your uncle was paying the bills for the trip, I didn't have much cash on me. Frankly, I never have much cash, and Tommy only had a few pounds. Still, I can't imagine why I ever thought we would be able to get home to Ripon on what I have."

"Maybe you could by yourself, but with me along, I guess things are more expensive. What are we going to do at this inn? Do you have enough money for two rooms?" Frederica was beginning to understand how easy travelling with Uncle Festus had been.

"Yes, I am sure I have enough for two rooms and something decent to eat. But it's probably best if I find out first how much it is going to cost us to get back to Bath."

They sauntered along, getting the kinks out of their legs and window-shopping until the square turned into a narrow street. Dering stopped a prosperous-looking man who kindly gave them directions to the inn. While they were headed in the general direction of The White Hart, the inn was on a side street they would certainly have overlooked without his help.

Compared with their lodging in Glastonbury and even in Avebury, the White Hart was a decidedly poorer choice. The outside needed paint and the inside opened immediately into the taproom. The floors were bare and the furniture basic. But the bored-looking innkeeper greeted them without any questions, remarking that he had only one room available. Did they or did they not want it?

When Clive hesitated, Frederica spoke up, "Yes, we want it."

The innkeeper pointed to the stairs at the back of the room. "Last room at the end of the hall." He turned away to serve beer to some customers.

Frederica whispered to Clive as they started up the stairs, "We have to hide *somewhere*; wandering about the streets can't be safe. I can sleep on the floor. We'll manage somehow. After all, we just spent the night in the woods and survived."

He nodded in agreement. "You are right. We don't have so many options that we can be too choosy. I was thinking of your reputation. But actually, we do not know anyone here, so it should be fine."

The hall was dreadfully dark with no light except from the pub below. As there were only two doors, it was fairly easy to find the room. It proved to be small but surprisingly clean. A tiny window looked out over the backyard and gave a dim, rather watery light to the room. The bed was big enough for two people. The rest of the furnishings consisted of a lone table, a washbasin, and a chair. Frederica slumped into the chair in exhaustion.

Before they could come to any resolution about their next step, the two were startled by a knock on the door. It proved to be the inn's maid-of-all-work with hot water for washing.

"You use the water first. I'll go downstairs and talk to the landlord about dinner, writing materials, and the coach to Bath."

"Will we have time for a rest before dinner?"

"Yes, I am sure we will. It is still only the middle of the afternoon."

"Good, because I am very tired. The ground was not conducive to sleeping."

* * *

It was dusk by the time Clive returned. Frederica was drowsing and not in the mood for conversation, so she pretended to be asleep. But when she heard him remove clothing, she could not help but peek. He had removed his shirt and stood with his back to her by the washbasin. Her life had been fairly sheltered and she had never seen a man without his shirt before, but she was pretty sure Dering was a good specimen.

He wasn't exceptionally tall; when they stood face to face, she only had to tip her face up slightly to meet his eyes. And she knew he was strong. After all, he had carried her over his shoulder while running through the woods. Right now, he was obviously trying to be very quiet and not wake her. But she could hear water as he washed his face, arms, and shoulders. She studied his figure with interest – no rolls of fat, just taut muscles that glistened in the dim light. She wished she could see his chest to see if the muscles there matched.

She dozed off, thinking of Clive's shoulders and how good it felt when he braided her hair. The way he had massaged her scalp as he had worked had sent shivers down her body. Who would have imagined when she met him kicking stones that he was such an Adonis?

* * *

Frederica woke in the morning to a knocking on the door. Dering was already awake and answering it. It seemed obvious from the saddle bags and blanket on the floor that he had slept in front of the door. Trying to sleep rough two nights in a row, she assumed, could not be good. While the maid brought in the hot water, Clive handed Frederica several letters to read. He must have written them before lying down.

"Please read these. I want to post them as soon as possible," he said.

In each letter – one to Robert in Bath, one to Mr. Grant care of the inn in Avebury, and two to his father – he tried to explain the predicament in which they had found themselves, emphasizing the danger they believed their follower posed. He also added that they intended to take the coach back to Bath the next day, but if this proved impossible, they would try to leave information with the landlord at the White Hart in Cirencester. In the letter to Bath, he added a sentence: "Robert, this is no joke. If we don't show up on the Monday coach, please come and find us as soon as possible. Bring your grandfather. Dr. Chadwick has been seriously injured and I fear this is a desperate situation."

Upon rereading the last sentence, Frederica felt a rush of panic. Up until now, she had been facing practical issues such as where to stay and the condition of her dress. Facing the real threat and admitting that evil men were hot on their trail and seemed to mean her harm caused her to catch her breath. Her stomach heaved in anxiety.

"Two letters to your father?"

"I am not sure where he is at the moment," he responded. "He could be at home or in London. So I am hedging my bets by writing to his London club, as well." He walked to the window, where he stood chewing at his lips again. "I am beginning to question the amount of information we gave Mistress Pontypool," Clive said.

"Now that you mention it, it was odd, the way she stopped talking as soon as the other passengers boarded," Fredericka mused. "Obviously part of her story was true, as her daughter and her husband had come to meet her. But she was so chatty that I guess we have to assume she might tell her son-in-law."

"And now we are actually staying in the inn she suggested," Clive moaned. "I feel so stupid."

Frederica threw off the blanket. "I think we need to get out of here," she said. "Where is my dress?" she asked in surprise.

Chapter Twelve: Cirencester

Frederica

As if in answer to her statement, there was another knock at the door. Dering was already opening the door. His blanket and saddlebags still lay on the floor, but Frederica saw to her astonishment that he held a pistol behind his back, well-hidden from whomever was standing at the door.

"Sorry to be bothering you, sir." The inn's maid-of-all-work was back. "Mister Crumb says you should be getting up if you wants to make the Bath coach, sir."

"Oh right, thank you." Clive sounded groggy to Frederica. "We'll be down in a few minutes. Any hope of coffee before we leave?" he asked.

"There is some tea, sir. And I have your shirt and the mistress's dress. Couldn't give it a real wash as you were needing them today, but I did the best I could." She held out her arm and Frederica could see white material draped over it. Clive backed up to open the door and let the maid into the room. He quickly hid the pistol under his saddlebags.

"Just put them over the chair there." He gestured with his right hand.

The maid returned to the doorway, where she stooped to pick up a tray she had placed on the floor. "Here's the tea, sir, and some bread and butter."

"Thank you very much." Dering started to fumble in his pocket for some coins. "What time is it?" he asked.

"Jest goin' on six or so, sir." The maid reentered the room and placed the tray on the table against the wall. "Good morning, mum." She glanced at Frederica and then at the blanket and saddlebags on the floor in front of the door. She gave a slight shrug and turned back to Clive.

"Landlord says seeing as how you folks didn't make it to dinner last night, I was to pack up what I could so you can take it with you for the coach ride. I'll have it waiting by the door when you leave."

Dering slipped her a few precious coins. "Thank you. The food will be most welcome on the stage. I didn't realize how tired we were to sleep right through dinner."

"Thank you, sir. That's real nice of you." With a bob of her head and a sketchy curtsy, the maid left, closing the door behind her.

Clive locked the door.

"What do you think of the letters?" he asked. He sounded weary. Frederica nodded her approval and handed them back. He gave her a rather embarrassed grimace. "Forgive the intimacy, but I need to shave. I don't know when I will get another chance." Turning his back to his companion, he proceeded to lather up his face.

Frederica surveyed her dress. It still had several stains—no white dress could go through the events of yesterday and still look pristine—but it did look a whole lot better than it had when she had taken it off yesterday. Again, she wished she had brought something more serviceable for travelling, but she knew the state of her wardrobe was the least of their problems. She scrambled into the dress and finished tying her stockings before Clive finished shaving. She was trying to get the snarls out of her tresses when Dering, now fully dressed, handed her a cup of tea.

"Are you able to braid your hair, or do you want some help?"

"I would love some help. I am embarrassed to admit it, but you braid better than I do. Your sisters trained you well."

It was another twenty minutes before they were both satisfied with her hair and ready to venture out. At the bottom of the stairs, they found the landlord sweeping up the taproom from the night before.

"Off, are ye'?" he asked.

"Yes, thank you. If was very kind of you to send the maid up this morning. I am afraid we might have overslept if you had not," Clive answered.

"Not at all. When you didn't get down for dinner last night, I figured you was that knackered. Oh, speaking of dinner, Mary wrapped up some of the food for you to take with you. It is over there." He pointed to a paper parcel on the table near the door.

Frederica went over and picked it up. "That was kind of you, sir."

"Can you give us directions to the coaching office?" Clive asked.

With the package and directions in tow, they were soon on their way back to the market square. Today, it looked like a different place: awnings had been rigged, tables and stalls set up, and, early as it was, the market was in full swing. Frederica was fascinated. Neither her father nor Hermione had ever taken her to an open-air market like this one. She noted that the nearest stalls were filled with vegetables and farm produce. On the other side of the street, people seemed mainly to be selling clothes and shoes. Soon, the two travelers were looking at housewares, tools, and just about anything else anyone could imagine a household might need.

"Oh Mr. Dering—Clive, look! A stationery stall. Please, please, could we stop a moment? Do you have enough money to buy me some paper and a pencil? There is so much I would love to get on paper here." Frederica clasped his arm imploringly.

Clive smiled down at her pleading face. He could not resist. He mentally recounted the diminishing coins in his pocket. "Yes, I think we can afford a few sheets. Not too many, though. I don't want to have to sit on the top of the coach where we can easily be seen."

Frederica eagerly studied the display and selected a few large sheets she could fold into quartos. Her enthusiasm and obvious pleasure in the paper laid out in the stall so pleased the old man selling the goods that he gave her a stub of a pencil for free. Clutching her treasures and the food parcel, Frederica followed Clive to the bottom of the square to look for the coaching office.

"Over there by the post office." Clive pointed out the small office allotted to selling tickets to travelers. "Why don't you wait in the church while I go get the tickets? Even if the captain is about, he doesn't know what I look like."

"You cannot be sure he won't recognize you. He might have noticed you in Bath, if not at the Assembly, then maybe around town. Finding you in Cirencester would be a remarkable coincidence. Besides, that horrible character we left in the cottage might be with him, and he might recognize you. So I think it would be a good idea for you to be careful, too."

"All good points," he agreed.

Frederica glanced about anxiously. "I do feel so conspicuous. I have never felt this way before. Even with my hood up, I feel like everyone is staring at me. I know they could not possibly be; it's just a feeling, but I can't help it."

Clive patted her arm encouragingly. "I rather feel that way, too," he said. "Hopefully, once we get to Bath, we will lose those feelings. In the church, keep to the right side so it will be easier for me to find you."

Frederica nodded and they separated, Dering going to the coaching office and Frederica heading to the church of St John the Baptist. Its porch was entered from steps that rose right from the market square. She had to dodge several coaches and piles of hot dung to get to the church steps. Inside the nave, though, it was as if the bustle of the market was another world. She was taken back to the Middle Ages as she wandered down the right aisle admiring the clean, simple lines of the interior. Although it was smaller than the abbey in Bath, it somehow looked brighter and more welcoming. Then she looked closely at the windows, entranced by the stories of early Cirencester and the wool trade that artisans had worked into the stained glass. The sheep were particularly charming. Her fingers itched to sit and sketch the scenes, but she didn't know how long it would take Clive to get their tickets and she wanted to be ready when he returned.

Some twenty minutes later, Dering found her in the depths of the church studying the window behind the altar whose seven colors so captivated her that she jumped when he touched her arm. "Frederica, there is a problem."

"What? Is he here?"

"No, but almost as bad. The coach to Bath is full; even the spots on the roof are taken. It seems there is a horse race at the track in Bath tomorrow that everyone is trying to get to."

Clive took her hand and pulled her to one of the pews at the side of the church so they could talk quietly. They sat sideways in the pew, facing each other. "I did mail the letters. I am glad you suggested it. I was so sure we would be on that coach," he said apologetically.

Frederica studied Clive's face. She hadn't seen him look so concerned before. "Is that all that is worrying you? Anything else I should know?" she asked.

"I am not sure how serious this other bit is. I saw that son-in-law of Mistress Pontypool's. He did not talk to me, but he certainly was watching closely." Clive started to rub Frederica's hand absently. "Remember what you said about feeling watched? It just started me thinking, and then I saw him across the street, sort of studying me."

"Is he still there?"

"Once I recognized him, I walked down the street and came in the church from the yard on the other side. I don't think he followed me."

"We may have told Mistress Pontypool more than we should have, but it won't do us any good to worry about it now. What do you think we should do?"

Frederica was aware of several sensations all going on at once. First, there was the hollow pit in her stomach caused by the idea that someone was too interested in their activities. The other was the warm feeling caused by Dering's handclasp. He was proving to be someone she could rely on and trust. At least she didn't have that hopelessly alone feeling she had had when she had been in the shack with the roughs. "Clive, were you able to find tickets to anywhere?"

"Money is going to be a real problem. I have enough money to get us to Bath but certainly not enough to get us to London."

"Should we consider throwing ourselves on the mercy of the local magistrate?"

"Isn't Mistress Pontypool's son-in-law one of the magistrates?" Clive asked.

"I'm not sure. But he's a lawyer, so I assume he knows the magistrates. You're right, though – we can't really trust him. If he was on our side, why didn't he just walk over and talk to you? Do you think he was showing too much interest in you because he is going to set the watch on us?"

Dering nodded but didn't answer immediately. When he did, he spoke slowly. "I do not want to sound overly suspicious, but I don't think we should trust *anyone*. Even if this thug just wants to kidnap you for a ransom, everyone seems too willing to believe him." Here he paused and Frederica filled in the unspoken thought.

"Do you actually think he wants to kill me?" she whispered incredulously.

"No, of course not. I am beginning to think, though, that he wants to force you into marriage. And last night, a possible reason occurred to me. Isn't the middle of the night a great time for worrying?" He took a deep breath. "How much do you know about your father's will, Frederica?" he asked.

"I don't know all the details, but I believe Father divided the estate between Jeffrey and me. Jeffrey, of course, is the executor and in charge of my half until I gain my majority or marry."

"Didn't he leave your step-mother anything?"

"Oh yes, of course. She has use of the house during her lifetime and an allowance from the estate."

"Ah, I see. So it is unlikely she is behind this. It sounds like your father planned for her welfare generously. But perhaps she was not careful who she told about the contents of the will and it is this captain is behind all of this. If you get your inheritance when you marry, that might be what he is planning here. Marry you and he gets a nice income." Clive's hands tightened on hers. "But we are not going to let that happen.

"Clive," Frederica said hesitantly, "we are not even sure he is in Cirencester. Maybe he went back to Bath thinking we went there."

"I do not believe we can take that chance, Frederica. Once he finds we are not in Chippenham, he will figure out that there was only one coach out of town and which way it was going. We need to plan as if he has followed us and perhaps is even talking about a reward. That would explain Pontypool's son-in-law's interest."

"You certainly are taking the grimmest view of things. But what you say makes some awful sense." She paused and just enjoyed the warmth of his hold on her hands. Again, she felt relief that she did not have to face this misfortune alone. "You did get those letters off to Bath and London, didn't you? Do you think we could stay at the inn and wait for Robert and his grandfather and maybe even Mr. Grant to come for us?"

"Not if this unnamed captain walks in and announces you are his daughter or whatever his story is now. He probably has a letter from Hermione saying you have run away. Who is going to believe us? You are underage."

Frederica sighed. "So much for the easy route. How are we going to leave a trail for our friends if we have to leave Cirencester?"

Clive dropped one of her hands to run his own hand through his hair and over his face. Then he reached over to tuck a lock of Frederica's hair that had escaped her braid behind her ear.

"I missed a piece," he said softly. His hand stroked her cheek gently. "Frederica, I really do not know what to do right now. I have never been in such a situation. But I can promise you this – we are in this together!"

Frederica gripped his hand with both of hers. "Clive, I am frightened but not as scared as when I thought I was alone. Having you with me makes all the difference in the world. I am sure we can come up with something together," she said stoutly.

The low murmuring of real worshipers reminded them that they were not alone. Clive looked around, trying to judge the safety of their surroundings. It didn't take him long to realize any number of people could approach them from behind and block them from the doors. "Let's see if we can find somewhere safer. How about the choir loft?"

Frederica was also scanning the church. "No, let's try the bell tower. Maybe we can find a window that we can use to check out the crowds and see if our followers are down there."

"That's brilliant!" Dering was all admiration.

Clive with his saddlebags and Frederica with her food parcel and precious paper walked sedately down the aisle, ignoring other visitors to the church, and towards the back where the entrance to the bell tower should be. As they admired the baptismal font, they looked around for a door. There were three.

"Which one of those do you think it is?" Frederica asked.

"The one straight back. The others look like they would lead to offices or rooms off to the side. If you think of the outside of the building, there was no bump out that would signify a room." Clive indicated the door with his chin. Then he glanced about the nave to see who might be watching them. Several middle-aged women were working on flower displays and some other older folks were on their knees praying. The porch might be full of shoppers, but few had found their way inside. "Let me see if the door opens."

The door opened easily and Frederica and Clive slipped through. They were immediately faced with a dark, narrow staircase that seemed to coil endlessly upward. They started climbing.

"Where is the bell pull?" Frederica asked.

"The stairs must lead to a platform or room soon," he answered. "We should get past that point so that when they come to ring the bell no one will notice us."

"It will get very loud up there when they do ring the bell, won't it?" Frederica asked. "Did you notice if they chime the bell on each hour?"

"No, I haven't heard it since we got to the marketplace this morning, so I assume they probably only ring at noon. Yes, I imagine it will be loud. Maybe we'll be out by then."

"Look, this must be the place." Frederica paused when the stair opened onto a small windowless room with a single rope coming through the ceiling. But the room was empty, and more stairs led further up. "Do we keep going?"

They soon reached the top of the tower, where the bell hung. There, they could peek over the low walls to see the market below.

"Good, I am getting bushed."

Frederica nodded her head in agreement. "Me, too!" she panted. "I'm on the wrong side; this window looks over another part of town."

Clive moved to the next side. "Here we go. Nice view. We can see the whole square, including the street where the White Hart is. Now we have to try to spot that captain or his henchmen in that milieu."

"I suppose we can just stay here until we either see them, or better yet don't, or we devise another plan. I feel pretty safe here. What do you think?" Frederica asked.

"I think we are fine unless someone comes along and throws us out. Nature calls might be a bit rough." Embarrassed, Clive did not look Frederica in the face but gazed fixedly over the market place.

"There was a bucket in the rope room," Frederica said quietly, sincerely hoping she would not need it in the near future.

Clive was impressed. Again, Frederica's ability to face a difficult situation without the usual female hysterics impressed him. "Good! All right then. We are set for a bit. Let's see what we can see."

For the next few hours they watched the crowd, trying to identify any familiar faces. They did see a few they recognized: Mistress Pontypool, with the small tyrants from yesterday in tow, and the maid from the White Hart, running errands. But, with relief, they did not spot anyone else they knew.

Their vigil was broken by the ringing of the bell at noon. The sound was incredible. They huddled on the floor, with their hands clasped firmly over their ears, but Frederica felt the vibration through the walls and by the twelfth ring, even in her bones. When it finally ended, they looked at each other in amazement.

Frederica gasped, "It feels like there are hundreds of bells up here instead of just one."

Clive took his hands from his ears. "That was an experience I hope not to repeat. I can still hear it!"

Frederica had to chuckle at the look on his face. "Hopefully we won't be trapped in a bell tower too often." She grinned at him.

"As long as I am trapped with you..." Suddenly Clive reached forward and placed a hand on the side of her face. His thumb stroked her jaw line, gently pressing his lips to hers. His arms circled her waist and he pulled her into his lap. He settled back against the wall, holding her close. To her surprise, Frederica found that leaning against him was extremely comfortable. The kiss in the forest had rather surprised her but now that she had time to enjoy the process, she was even more amazed to find how soft his lips were. She had just assumed men's lips were hard. Clive's were anything but. Now he pulled her even tighter against him. She stroked his shoulder through his jacket, and she imagined she could still feel the taut muscle beneath.

But he did not presume any more. Just held her tightly. She felt his lips on her neck as he nuzzled her. He seemed to be taking deep breaths, inhaling her scent. She put her hands on his chest and tried to pull away in order to look at his face and see what was happening. His arms imprisoned her so she could only tilt her head back.

"Clive? This is new to me," she said hesitantly. "What am I supposed to do?"

"Hmmm, you are not supposed to know what to do." He sighed deeply and continued, "I am the one taking advantage of you. I should not be doing this, but I can't stop myself. You smell unbelievably wonderful," he murmured. His lips moved back to her mouth. This time, they were not quite as soft as before but became more demanding.

Leaning against his body, Frederica was happier and more excited than she could ever remember. Unbelievable darts of pleasure shot through her. She put her arms around his neck and tried to press closer. She wasn't quite sure what she should be doing, but getting closer felt right so that was what she tried to do.

Clive's hand stroked her neck, gently outlined her ear, and moved slowly down to her shoulder. He raised his head and looked down into her eyes.

"You know you are amazing. Any other girl caught in this situation would probably had dissolved into hysterics. You are brave, funny, and very beautiful. I am also becoming very, very fond of you."

Frederica let her hands frame his face as she looked into his eyes. She started to outline his mouth with her thumb. "You have a terrific mouth, Clive. Strong but…oh, I don't know what to say. I just know I love to sketch you." They smiled into each other's eyes.

Oh, don't let this end. But even as the thought came to her, she felt him stiffen. "What is it?" she asked.

"Look," Clive said as he turned her to look below. This view overlooked the post office end of the square and even from that height she could see what had disturbed Clive. The captain was coming out of the coach's office, accompanied by Mistress Pontypool's son-in-law and followed by some incredibly grubby individuals. The two men were involved in an intense discussion. Frederica was aghast; she had to take a deep breath before she could speak.

"Oh my God, Clive! What are we going to do?" she whispered, as if they could hear her in the tower.

Dering wrapped his arms around her and kept her pressed against his body as he stared out.

"Oh shit!" he groaned. "Sorry, but that is just what we didn't want. Proof!"

Pressed together, they watched as the two men talked for some time. Then the captain went off to one side of the market and the son-in-law went towards the other. The two roughs ambled self-importantly down the center aisles of the market.

"At least we know they are still looking for us, but they can't have any idea where we are," Frederica said.

"I think we are stuck here at least until dark," Clive sighed. "Let's see if we can get comfortable." He sat down with his back to the corner and held out his arms. "See if you can nap a bit. I have this feeling that when we leave here, we are going to be travelling rough for quite a while."

"You mean by foot?" Frederica settled down with her head on his shoulder. The intense physical attraction of the previous moments had faded, but it was obvious Clive stilled wanted her near him. She was more than fine with that.

"Yes, I can see where travelling by night would be better. Do coaches move by night?"

"Let me get my *Paterson*'s out of the saddlebags and see if there are any coaches going through here any time soon. You try to rest."

* * *

"Wake up, Frederica!" She felt pressure on her arm. She recognized Clive's voice, low but insistent. "Come on, Frederica. Time for us to make our move if we are ever going to get out of here."

She sat up, rubbing her eyes and pushing her hair out of her face. "I must have dozed off." She looked around to see if she could tell how long she had been asleep. From the pain in her leg where she had lain on it, it must have been quite a while. She rubbed that part gingerly. "How long?"

"Not all that long. About an hour." Clive was repacking his saddlebags, obviously preparing to leave. "I have a plan."

"Good." She turned and gave him all her attention. Before she dozed off, she had lain awake thinking about their predicament and not seeing any easy way out. "Because *I* don't have any useful ideas," she admitted.

"I have read every page in the guide that has any information about Cirencester. There aren't any other large towns in the area, only a few smaller villages. I think we should go to the nearest big city or town, try to lose ourselves among the crowd, and stay lost until someone arrives with help."

Frederica nodded in agreement. "All right. Which one?"

"As we cannot get the coach to Bath, I think we should go west to Gloucester. It is about ten to fifteen miles away."

"Ten miles is a long way to walk, Clive."

"Look down into the marketplace. See that coach unloading at the market obelisk?" Frederica nodded. "That's going to Gloucester."

"How do you know that?"

"Wish I could convince you I was clever, but I heard the coachman yell it out when they arrived," he admitted.

"How are we going to get on it?" she asked.

"I saw the driver go off to that pub on the corner. Last time I saw the thugs, they were headed to the other end of the market. It looks like most of the merchants are beginning to pack up. While there is still some crowd wandering about, I am going to slip over there and see if we can get on the coach. While I am doing that, you should wait here. I will wave to you when it is safe to come down. Now, I have to hurry; they don't stop long."

"Oh, please let this work!" Frederica hated being left alone, but she could see that they would be much more noticeable if they tried to talk to the driver together. She continued to peer anxiously over the wall, searching for their enemies. Soon she could see Dering walk casually across the street from the church and then disappear into an alley. He must be using the back entrance to the pub. She envied his ability to appear calm and collected when she knew he didn't feel that way.

She passed the time remembering Clive's kisses and how excited they made her feel. But even with such pleasant thoughts, it still seemed an eternity before she saw him slip back out the alley and head to the church. Something was wrong – he didn't wave! No, he was waving. She put on her cloak and pulled up the hood, grabbed the small packet of food, checked her pockets for her paper and pencil, and headed down the stairs.

As soon as she emerged from the church door, he grabbed her arm and sped her around the corner. They hurried down the street, away from the market square and the coach to Gloucester.

"Clive, what is wrong? Why are we going this way? Is there no room on that coach, either?"

"Hold on. We need to get a bit of the way first and quickly. Then we can talk." Holding her hand, he continued at a rapid pace, practically running. Clive came to a stop at an alley branching off to the right.

"Please, madam, what's the name of this alley?" he asked a woman standing on the corner.

"Eh?"

"The alley, missus, what's it called?"

"Oh, that'd be Spitalgate. Will take ye' out to the Gloucester road, that."

"Thank you, missus." Clive smiled affably at the woman and then, grabbing Frederica's hand, started running down the lane. Frederica was becoming more and more confused. To her, their direction seemed to be away from the coach. The alleyway was close and littered with garbage and other nameless debris. Her breath started to come in gasps, and she could feel her hair coming out of its braid and falling down her back. She must look like a hoyden or something worse.

"Clive, please slow down. I can't keep up," she panted. Her stays pressed uncomfortably into her ribs, keeping her from drawing a deep breath.

"Just a little farther." They had come to the end of the alley where, exactly as the woman had said, it opened onto a broader avenue that looked well-traveled.

"We just need to cross the street and then we can catch our breath." Clive led her across the street and then leaned against the wall of a building that might have been a store of some kind. Frederica bent over, gasping for air but still holding onto his hand, her anchor in a storm of confusion.

Clive took several deep breaths. "Here's the plan." He took more deep breaths. "Remember I went to see the coachman at the pub, not at the coaching office?"

"Yes, the pub. I saw you go down the side alley."

"Right, I went in the back door. Anyway, I found the driver at the bar. For a price, he'll take us to Gloucester, but we are going on what he called 'the shoulder.' We get out of the main part of town, and he will pick us up as the coach goes by. We won't be on the official tally so he can pocket the fare. But it is better for us, as we don't have to stand around and risk being recognized. I dragged us down this street because the coach should be along soon and will catch us up at the edge of town."

"But are we going in the right direction? The coach looked like it was headed towards the other side of town."

"He goes out that way as the road is wider but then makes a turn. It will be coming along this road shortly. He told me the names of the lanes to follow to meet him at the corner of Spitalgate Lane and Abbey Road."

"This is Abbey Road?" Frederica straightened up and started to look around for a street sign.

"Up there." Dering pointed to the side of the corner building, at about the level of two men. "See the sign?"

"Yes, Abbey Road. Now we wait."

"Don't worry, it shouldn't be long. He was finishing up his drink when I left."

Frederica's breath was no longer coming in loud gasps. She started to comb out her hair with her fingers, trying to bring some control to it.

"Clive, did you see any of the men? I was looking from the tower and I didn't see anyone."

"No, I didn't see anyone, either. Hopefully, they are at the other end of town and in some pub getting drunk, far away from us." He paused and looked over his shoulder. "Here comes the coach now. You are going to ride inside, I will be on top."

"We won't be together?" Frederica started to protest being separated.

"Sorry, Frederica, it was all the space they had. It won't be long. It is only ten miles or so to Gloucester. It should not be more than a couple of hours."

She gave up trying to braid her hair but smoothed it back from her face as best she could and pulled her hood back up. Frederica could see that they were in luck. The coach hadn't picked up speed yet, as the driver was still negotiating the town streets. He came to a stop just past the corner they were standing on.

"Hurry up, lad, I don't have all night. Room for the lassie inside. You get yourself up here with me."

Clive opened the door. Rather than take the time to pull down the steps, he bodily lifted Frederica in. She took the only seat left, the dreaded middle seat between a man sitting with his arms folded across his chest and a large woman holding a live chicken. The coach tipped a bit. She assumed it was caused by Clive climbing to the driver's box. Almost immediately, the coach was in motion.

Chapter Thirteen: To Gloucester

Frederica

Frederica sat stiffly in the middle seat. No one made eye contact. No one smiled or welcomed her. She felt their resentment like a thick miasma. *They probably hoped to have the seat to themselves and now they have to share with me, someone who obviously does not have a proper ticket.* Feeling very self-conscious and clutching her food parcel, Frederica tried to make herself as small as possible so she did not bump against her seat companions. She pushed her hood back a bit and tried to glance around surreptitiously at her fellow travelers. Without turning her head, all she could see of the man next to her was his totally black clothing. She guessed he was a minister of some sort. The woman to her other side wore a cloak of good quality but not in the latest fashion. Frederica judged her to be a farmer's wife. Who else would travel with a live chicken in a cage on a public stage? As both people purposefully ignored her, she lifted her eyes to study the people on the opposite seat.

Three pairs of eyes looked back curiously. A man and a woman, married, she supposed, and parents to the little girl seated between them. The parents were dressed in rather boring shades of black and gray. The mother did not even have a lace or any speck of color to break the monotony. Next to them, the little girl was a ray of life in a dark green dress with a navy blue mantle. She also wore a straw bonnet but it was only decorated with a navy blue ribbon. The woman's hat was also simple; her ribbon was gray. The man and woman gave guilty starts when Frederica caught them staring at her. They immediately looked back out the window and ignored her, but the little girl smiled, causing Frederica to smile back. The mother must have noticed the little interchange because she leaned down and whispered to the little girl, "We don't talk to strangers, Lucy. Now be a good girl and mind thy own business. Quietly."

The coach started to pick up speed. Frederica could feel the now-familiar rocking as the horses hit their stride. They must have left Cirencester behind.

She was miserable without Clive to talk to and keep her from dwelling on their problems. Breakfast, such as it had been, was far in the past. *Oh, I hope this ride is not long. I am so hungry. But Clive must be, too, and I need to share with him. If I pull out anything, I will be tempted to eat it all. Better not to start. Can I sleep and make this endless ride go faster?* She leaned her head back against the seat and closed her eyes. However, sleep would not come. She had already had a nap today and could not relax.

Her mind would not quiet itself, instead mulling whether the men would continue to follow them. Of course he would – the question was when, not if. Even though Frederica could not sleep, her companions did not seem to have any problems doing so, as evidenced by the snores. The little girl, Lucy, was staring at her fixedly for some reason.

Frederica studied the coach, comparing it with the one to Cirencester. This coach was not as clean and had a definite smell about it. The chicken did not help. After she had studied the worn leather seats, the broken strap by the window, and the unspeakable floor, she looked back at Lucy. The child was still staring at her. She stared back, studying Lucy's little round face surrounded by fat curls, topped by that straw bonnet.

After a few cautious glances at her seat companions to be sure she was not disturbing them, Frederica pulled a precious sheet of paper out of her pocket. Then she had to worm around to remove her pencil stub from her skirt pocket without bumping and waking either the preacher or the farmer's wife. Frederica folded one of her sheets into quarters and, with a secret grin at Lucy, started to make a small sketch of Lucy's head.

So intent upon her work was she that at first she did not notice the coach slowing. With a jerk, the coachman pulled the horses to a stop, waking the farmer's wife. Her head swiveled around as she checked out her surroundings. Frederica's little sketch caught her eye. "That's a right pretty picture. Did you do that?" she asked.

"Just a moment, mistress. I'll have the steps down for ye'!" the coachman called.

Frederica was leaning forward to see where they were. She couldn't see any buildings, only fields of grain. "Where are we?" she asked.

The farm woman gave a chuckle. "Not much to see, is there? My son works this land; it's called High Gate Farm. My daughter-in-law is about to have another little one and I am come to help out. Ah, Jacob, thank ye' kindly."

As the door opened and the coachman helped the woman out, Frederica chuckled to herself. Once that woman got started talking, she probably could have gone on as long as Mistress Pontypool. Then she stopped smiling, thinking of Mistress Pontypool's treachery. Then she smiled again. At least that smelly chicken was gone with the farmer's wife. No one got in to take her seat, so Frederica could slide over and put some room between her and the man in black. Shortly, they were underway again.

This coachman seems to make a lot of unorthodox stops, Frederica mused. She drew big dangling curls to frame Lucy's little pointed face. "Balance" was what Uncle Festus said. At least she would not have to worry about Lucy's ears as the thick curls and the straw hat hid them.

"Are thou drawing me?" Lucy's piping voice cut into Frederica's reverie and woke her father. Her mother's attention now focused on Frederica. Before anyone else could speak, Lucy slid over to the empty seat next to Frederica. "Can I see?"

Frederica turned her drawing so Lucy could see her work.

"Ohhhh Mummy, look!" she said delightedly. "She's got my hat just so and my curls and everything. It is ever so nice."

"It's not finished, mistress, and it is just a sketch, but would you like to see it?" Frederica asked the mother.

The woman nodded, even while the husband was frowning, and leaned forward to take the proffered paper. She smiled as she recognized her daughter.

"Look, husband. It does look like our Lucy. How clever thou are to be able to do that!" She handed the paper to Lucy's father. He studied the paper but made no comment. He held onto the little picture so long Frederica was beginning to think he would not return it.

"It is not finished, sir," Frederica repeated. "I am not very good with mouths yet. I still need a lot of practice. But if you like, once we get to Gloucester, you can have the sketch. I would like to finish the mouth and chin first." She reached out a hand for it.

The father started to hand it back but the "preacher" intercepted it before it got back to Frederica.

"This is not bad at all," he said grudgingly. He had a superior accent in direct contrast to his clothes, which she could now see were pretty worn. "I have seen a great many portraits in the halls of your betters, and I can tell you this would not look totally amiss among them." He seemed set to continue in what Frederica found to be a snobby and off-putting manner.

She interrupted him. "Thank you, sir, for your kind compliments. If you could just hand it back, I would like to finish it before the light goes. It is getting dark." She took the paper out of his hand even as she spoke to the woman.

"Do you know how long it will be before we reach Gloucester? When I start to sketch, I lose all track of time." She smiled at the wife, thinking she was the least intimidating of the adult company.

Lucy cut in before her mother could answer, "Do you think thee will have time to finish my picture?"

Surprisingly, it was the father who answered. "We are at least halfway there. Lucy, sit back over here so the artist can see thee before it gets too dark. You have some skill, miss. It is not often that folks of our station can have our likeness down on paper. The wife and I would very much like to have the picture when thou are finished." Both his women beamed at him and Lucy obediently took her original seat.

Frederica went back to work. But the problem now was that her pencil stub was just that: a stub, with almost no point. And with the growing dimness in the carriage, it was getting harder to work. She decided to shade areas rather than draw clear lines, especially around the jaw and neck. By the time the light was gone, she had captured a reasonable likeness of a little girl. *Truth be told, it could be any of hundreds of little girls, but Lucy and her parents don't seem to mind too much.*

"Do you have a knife, sir, to cut the picture out of the paper?" she asked the father.

He produced a knife, neatly folded the sheet in fourths, and then sliced the folds, giving the little portrait clean lines. He handed Frederica the unused pieces. "Very kind of thee, miss. Thank you."

"You are welcome, sir." She peered closer at him in the gloom of the carriage. He didn't look like any tradesman she had ever seen. And, in spite of his stern demeanor, he was better spoken than she would have guessed. Now that she had looked both men over, she had to think the "preacher" was no such thing, but rather an empty-pocketed snob with little or no income, though he certainly had a high opinion of himself.

Shortly after the brief interaction, Frederica turned her attention back to the windows, where she could see lights revealing more houses and buildings lining the road. It would appear the coach had entered a town.

The mother noticed Frederica looking out the window. "We are almost to Gloucester."

Without warning, the coach started to descend a very steep hill. In order to keep her seat, Frederica had to grab the broken window strap and use her feet to steady herself.

"This is Birdlip Hill," Lucy's mother continued. "It is an awful piece of road. There are many accidents coming down this hill in winter. We should be fine, it hasn't rained recently, but I do hate this part of the trip. However, we should be getting to the center of town shortly. The carriage stops about a block from the cathedral."

Frederica breathed a sigh of relief when the coach was level again. "Do you live here, mistress?" Frederica asked politely.

"No, we live near Cirencester, but my husband has business here. Lucy and I are going to visit friends. It is not a long trip, as you may have noticed. The Mail is so prompt in its timetable that travelling back and forth has become very simple." Her accent was a bit more cultured than her husband's, although she seemed to defer to him in all things.

"Could you perhaps recommend a respectable inn where my brother and I could stay?"

But as soon as Frederica mentioned Clive, the mother became distant.

"I am very sorry, I couldn't say. We never stay at inns or hostelries."

"Oh, thank you anyway." Conversation, such as it was, dried up.

Shortly, the coach stopped. With great speed, the stairs were dropped and the passengers exited. The man, dressed all in black, used the far door to depart rapidly without a word. It looked like other people traveled with little or no luggage, too. Frederica found herself on the sidewalk, waiting for Clive to get down from the box. He seemed to be getting directions from one of the other passengers who had ridden with him on top of the coach. Frederica hoped he had more luck than she in getting suggestions for a place to stay.

"Thank you for my picture, miss. It is ever so lovely. I am going to have mother put it in a frame over the fireplace."

"Lucy, you are very welcome! You have such a pretty face, it is easy to draw. Good luck to you, now." Frederica and Lucy shook hands before the parents turned to leave. The father paused and then handed Frederica a coin.

"Thank you, miss. We are glad to have Lucy's picture. As Friends, we don't usually hold with such frivolities, but it is a sweet rendering. In fact, for a leader in my community, it is probably not such a proper thing. But Lucy is our only child and we sometimes spoil her." He shook his head ruefully. "A couple of blocks behind Gloucester Cathedral, there is an inn called the Coach and Horses. It is on St. Catherine Street. I hear they are fair and honest. Thee and thy brother should be able to find clean lodging there." And with a brief bow, he hurried off before Frederica could thank him for the information and whatever it was he handed her.

Almost immediately, Clive joined her on the street. "Everything all right?" he asked.

Frederica nodded. "Yes, the trip wasn't too bad. The other passengers were pretty stuffy to start with, but they turned out to be fine."

"What did that chap give you?"

"Well, I can't see in the dark. I think it is money."

"Money!" Clive exclaimed. "Whatever for?" Even as he spoke, he took Frederica's arm and guided her in the direction of a lamp the beadle was just lighting.

"Well, to pass the time, I did a rough sketch of their little girl. Nothing very special, as you know I am not very good with faces. But they seemed to like it, so I gave it to them!" Frederica was inordinately pleased with the reception of her artistic efforts. With the exception of the maid Polly in Dorset, it was the first time someone outside of her immediate circle had ever shown any positive interest in her efforts. They reached the lamplight.

"Look, he gave me a whole shilling! Clive, that is my first real sale!" Frederica was delighted.

Clive seemed struck by the coin in Frederica's hand. Then he got a thoughtful look. He covered her hand with his, closing the coin in both their clasps.

"Frederica, this is amazing stroke of good fortune." Frederica looked at him questioningly. "The trip here took the last of my ready cash. Honestly, I don't even have the money to get us a bed at the inn tonight. I was so worried about getting out of Cirencester, I just paid what the coachman demanded."

Frederica felt her stomach tightening up again. All her worries came back in a flood. "Oh Clive, what are we going to do?" Suddenly she held up her small package of food. "We still have some bread and cheese left. But where are we going to stay the night?"

"Well, now, I have a couple of ideas. I was going to see if an innkeeper would take my cravat pin for room and board, at least for tonight. If that chap gave you a shilling for a rough sketch, maybe there are others who would pay for a portrait, too."

"Oh no, I don't think so," Frederica interrupted. "I am not good enough. I am sure it was just a fluke. Most people aren't going to pay me to draw anything."

"Wait! Wait before you say no. You don't have to decide anything now. I doubt we would be able to drum up any business tonight anyway. First, though, we should probably eat. I am starving and I bet you are, too."

"Yes, let's eat. Do you have any idea where we can get a drink of water?"

"Are you willing to part with some of that shilling?"

Frederica nodded.

"We can get some beer at a pub for a penny. That, along with what is in your package, will do us for the night."

"But where will we sleep?" Suddenly bells began tolling out the time, nine strokes.

"The cathedral!" The answer burst from both of them simultaneously.

"Right." Clive turned them in the direction of the bells. "We will just have to sneak in before they lock the doors for the night."

"The pews might be hard, but they will be better and hopefully safer than the streets," Frederica agreed.

"Good, we have a plan." Some of the worried lines softened from Clive's face as he smiled down at Frederica. "Let's get the beer and eat in the churchyard. Just like a picnic. I think there will be enough light from the combination of the cathedral and the moon. I hope there will be, anyway. And then we can discuss my next idea while we wait until we can sneak into the church."

"I am just grateful that you *have* a next idea. I am lost right now and really scared. We are in a strange town with no money and no friends and there are horrid men chasing us!"

Clive cupped her face with his hand and kissed her lips softly. He whispered, "I am scared, too, but I am more scared of losing you than facing those ruffians." He kissed her again. "Now pull your hood up; you will have to go with me into the pub and I don't want anyone staring at you. You are entirely too young and pretty."

* * *

"I bought a couple of pasties," Clive announced as he emerged from the tavern. "However, I am not sure how old they are."

"What are pasties?"

"Never heard of them before either? What a quiet life you have led up to now," he teased as he took her arm with his empty hand and turned her to walk back up the street. Dusk had long since cast its shadows and fewer people seemed to be about. "They're usually some kind of meat and potatoes cooked in a pastry that you can eat with your hands – no need for spoons and dishes."

"Well, that is convenient as we have neither," Frederica responded. "Did it take all our money?"

"Most of it. But I did get that bottle of beer, too." Clive gestured to the bottle Frederica was carrying. "Mind you, don't spill it; there is no cork. I would carry it but I don't want both hands full, as I am sure you understand."

"Both hands full? Of course I don't mind carrying it…Oh, you mean getting at the pistol. Sorry, I am not thinking quickly. Odd how riding in a carriage can be so exhausting. Do you think the churchyard is much further?"

Clive stopped and looked around, trying to get his bearings. "Look, there is the market cross where we got off the coach. That means the cathedral is only a couple of blocks on our right. There are not a lot of people around here, are there?"

Frederica considered what he was saying. "Is that good, not a lot of people about? They won't be asking us questions."

"Yes and no. Yes, it is a good thing for just that reason, but it also means there wouldn't be a lot of help for us if those villains showed up. We don't have a lot to show we are respectable people."

"Fine time to be having doubts," Frederica grumbled. "It is not as if we have a lot of paths open to us."

"I am not having doubts." To her relief, he was firm and reassuring. "I am trying to look at all the possibilities. And one possibility is that they are following us from Cirencester and will get here before we are ready for them. Ah, here is the cathedral!"

They came to the end of a block and a quick right placed them at the bottom of the stairs leading to the front doors of the church. "Let's see if we can get inside and find a hiding place before it is all locked up."

Frederica gave a deep sigh. She was hungry and tired and would like nothing better than to sit on the cathedral steps and rest. However, their followers had an unpleasant way of showing up at the most inopportune moments. She felt Dering as he prodded her up the steps.

"Wait, not these doors. Let's see if the side-door is still unlocked."

"Side door?"

"Yes, over here." Clive directed her to the right side of the cathedral, where an imposing stone porch covered a much smaller door. He pulled the door open and they slipped into the gloom of the church. Frederica put the beer bottle under her cloak and noticed that Clive had stashed the pasties under his jacket. They certainly did not want anyone to think they were being disrespectful by bringing food into the church. But they were in luck, as no one was at the door. Inside, they stood at the side of the door to find their bearings.

"Remember, we are visitors to this town and we have every right to be here!" Clive spoke softly. "If anyone questions us, just be as nonchalant as you can."

"I don't think I have ever been in a building so huge," she whispered as she gazed about in awe. "I thought the church in Cirencester was charming, but it was nothing compared to this." The nave was lit by only a few candles. The wide spaces between those few only accentuated the fact that the interior many times larger than any entire church Frederica had ever been in. They couldn't even see the altar.

"It is more like St. Paul's in London. You should see these windows in the daylight." Clive took her arm again and they proceeded down the right side of the church. The sound of their footsteps was swallowed up by the cavernous spaces.

The dark aisle was intimidating and seemed to go on endlessly. "Do you see anyone?" she asked quietly.

Instead of answering her, Clive pulled gently on her arm, turning her at an angle so she could see the dark figure that was moving down the left side of the church in the opposite direction of them. He appeared to be extinguishing the candles. If he had seen them, he gave no sign, so they quietly moved deeper into the cathedral. The shadows were becoming so dark that Frederica could no longer see Clive's face clearly. His hand on her arm was a secure anchor and at least twice, it was the only reason she did not stumble and fall on the uneven slabs that were the floor.

After some time of creeping forward, the right-hand wall gave way to a wide open space. It was less gloomy there, as windows let in some light from outside. Frederica noticed that the church was darker inside than the night sky. Dering gave her little time to peer around, propelling her at a right angle to their previous direction. Then, shortly, he pulled on her arm to signal her to stop.

"Step up," he voiced close to her ear. "It's a side chapel with a tomb we can hide behind. Give me your hand." Taking her hand, he led her up the one step. "There is a low railing. Can you get over it?"

"Hold this a minute." Frederica handed Clive the beer bottle and felt the railing with both hands. "Yes, I can get over."

As no one was around to see, she hoisted up her skirts in one hand while she swung a leg over the rail. Soon she was standing on the inside and Clive was handing her the beer and pasties so he could climb over to join her.

The tomb stood in the middle of the small chapel, lit by one small votive candle. Dering blew out the flame before leading them to the far side of the chapel, where they crouched down behind the tomb on the slab floor.

"I don't want him to feel he needs to blow out the candle before going home."

"I thought we were going to picnic in the graveyard," Frederica said quietly.

"Seemed like a good idea to take advantage of getting into the church while we could. Let's sit here quietly for a while and make sure that other person has gone."

This turned out to be a good idea, as shortly they could see a candle—or maybe a lantern's glow—coming around the corner.

"I could have sworn I seen someone walking up this side, Father. I was darkening the lights on the other side. These tramps always sneaking in here like it was an inn or something," a voice grumbled.

"I have no doubt you did. But there doesn't seem to be anyone here now," an older, more cultured voice answered. "Old Sir Potters seems to be sleeping alone tonight. But could you just shine that light on the other side?"

Realizing that the light was coming closer and the men would check down both sides of the tomb, Frederica and Clive crawled to the short end of the sarcophagus, the point farthest away from the caretaker and the priest. While they crouched there anxiously, Frederica held her breath and squeezed her eyes shut. *I am just like a rabbit hoping that if I do not see the hunters, they won't see me.*

Suddenly one of the men gave a shout, "Hey there, you over there! Stop! Told you, sir."

Frederica and Clive both gasped with delight when they realized the light had moved off in another direction, leaving them in the thickening murkiness. There must have been another soul looking for a dry place to sleep. They could not hear if the other person was caught and summarily dispatched, but they did hear the big door clang shut and the bolt being thrown. The sound of iron on iron resonated down the nave. They soon heard the voices of the two men as they came back down the aisle, but to their relief, the two turned into the north transept, where they exited through a door in the far wall.

Clive sighed and relaxed against the tomb. Frederica followed suit, and they were soon sitting shoulder to shoulder, arm to arm. When their thighs touched, she gave a slight jerk at the intimacy. She felt his hand on her arm.

"Please don't move," he murmured. "It is just more reassuring to feel you beside me," he said. To her surprise, he sounded embarrassed. Surely, he was so much more experienced.

At his words, she stopped inching away and moved back. It did feel more reassuring.

"That was close, I don't mind telling you," Clive was still whispering. "I guess we are not the only ones with the bright idea of sleeping in the cathedral. Sounds like a pretty normal occurrence from what the caretaker was saying. I wonder if there are any others still around." There was a pause as he considered. "I think I will take a quiet look around just to make sure we are the only ones hiding out tonight."

"Why?"

"I do not want anyone sneaking up on us," he replied.

"I would feel more comfortable if you waited a bit before you started moving around. If there are other folks here, they may be doing the same thing we are. Let them get confident and comfortable. It might be easier to spot them if they think they are alone."

"Yes, good idea," he responded. "Let's eat the pasties while we are waiting. Do you think you can eat in the dark? I had intended to borrow a candle, but maybe I can do that later."

"I'll manage. I am so hungry. Can you give a bit of the paper it is wrapped in? I don't want to drip down my frock."

Clive brought out their dinner and carefully handed Frederica hers with the paper already folded back. "Take small bites; it probably has gravy in it."

Sitting with their backs to Sir Potter's tomb, Frederica and Clive polished off the pasties, the rest of the cheese and bread from Frederica's pocket, and the beer. They ate as quietly as possible and did not speak again for some time. Finally, Clive thought they had waited long enough. There was a rustling as he took off his boots so he could walk in his stocking feet.

He started to move around, getting ready to see if there were other intruders when he felt her hand on his arm. "What about a privy?"

"If I remember rightly, the transept on the other side leads to where the monks used to live, a beautiful cloister. If the door is unlocked, there should be a privy over there. I'll check and let you know. But I may be gone some time, so please be patient and wait here." He stroked her cheek as he stood.

To his surprise, she turned her face and kissed his fingers. That was all it took for him to take her in his arms and kiss her lips. They were so soft. He broke the kiss and moved off before he couldn't.

Chapter Fourteen: Street Life

Clive

He took his time creeping from column to column along the walls, listening intently for something to tell him they were not alone. It seemed to take an eternity to walk the aisles of the cathedral. Finally, he turned back to the sarcophagus where she waited.

"Frederica?" the young man whispered.

"Oh thank God it is you, Clive!"

"Yes. I am sorry if you were worried, but I wanted to be very careful and it took some time to search the whole church." He reached out his hands to find her, then gathered her completely into his arms. He held her tightly against him while whispering into her ear.

"I am not sure we need to be so quiet, but I rather like your ears and definitely like being so close to you. Do you mind?"

Frederica found she liked being held by him, too, but she was too shy to find the words to say so. She nodded, sure this time he could feel her nod.

"Come, sit down," he said. "Let me tell you what I have found." They settled again with their backs to the tomb. This time Clive kept his arm around Frederica's shoulders and held her snugly against him. "The cathedral is laid out like a giant cross. We are in the right arm of the cross, and I followed it around. There are three side chapels, as well as the choir in the middle. I couldn't search them all, but I did listen carefully and all I heard were some birds, maybe bats."

"Bats?" Frederica shuddered.

"I heard something flying about in the—you know, the part with the very high ceiling. Anyway, I am pretty sure we are alone, but we should be quiet and not wander about too much, just in case the caretaker makes rounds at night."

"How did you find your way around without a light?"

"It is lighter in the center than it is here. There is some skylight coming through the windows and there were a few candles about, particularly around the other side where the tomb of Edward II is."

"Clive, how do you know all this?"

"As I said, I have been here before. Couple of years ago, when my father was taking me to Oxford, we stopped here to look at some horses. I spent a lot of time in the cathedral looking around. It is a marvelous place and the architecture is fantastic. Our ancestors did amazing things with stone. That is why I remembered this chapel has a tomb in it."

Frederica's mind was on more practical circumstances. "Do you remember where the privy is?"

"Right. I did forget to look, I got so excited about looking around. But I think I remember a door on this side that goes to a sacristy."

"Can we check?"

"I'll check. You stay here." Clive got to his feet and she could see his shadow step over the railing again. Shortly she heard a door being open. It was just the barest creak, she realized, but in the quiet of the church it seemed extraordinarily loud. Luck still seemed to be with them, as the sound of the door opening brought no response. Clive was back almost instantly.

"Your lucky day," he whispered. "It is a sacristy and there is a necessary right inside the door. Come on."

He investigated the sacristy while he waited for her. When she emerged, he showed his find. "There is a pitcher of water over on the side board. I assume it is for the priest to wash up before services."

"That feels wonderful after all we have been through today," she said, as she vigorously applied the towel to her face and hands. "Oh, it feels so good to wash!"

"Can you find your way back to our tomb? I'll be along in just a few moments."

"Of course! You keep the candle." He watched as she cautiously went to the door and peered out. She must not have seen anything as she stepped out and the door quietly closed.

"I could do with another beer." She jumped as he came up next to her. "Sorry, I did not mean to startle you." He blew out the small candle he was carrying.

"What, no wine in the sacristy?"

"I forgot to look." He made as if to rise but Frederica held him down.

"Enough running about. We've been lucky so far. Listen." A church bell was ringing.

"Curfew bell," Clive offered. He settled down with his back to the tomb. "Here, let's try this. Sit between my legs and lean back against me." He was tired, but not enough to go to sleep. He found it surprisingly comfortable to have his arms around her. He wondered if she felt the same. He was pleased when she accepted his suggestion and nestled against his chest. Maybe the darkness gave her a self-confidence she had not had in the church tower earlier. He did not actually care; he just wanted her close. He felt her head tip back as if she was trying to see his face. Unerringly, his lips found hers in the dark. This time there were no interruptions.

After a while, Clive broke the kiss. By then, Frederica had turned in his arms to face him. Her arms were locked around his neck. But his hands were not so motionless. One was deep in her hair, holding her head and lips close to his. The other hand found its way down the side of her face. There was no way in the dark he could figure out how to unfasten her dress. Anyway, he tried to warn himself, he was probably moving too fast for her. She did not stop him, as his fingers moved to fondle her breast through the fabric. Even with the layers of cloth, they were full and perfect. Frederica's breath came more rapidly. "You are so beautiful!" he said hoarsely.

"You can't even see me," Frederica teased.

"I have spent the past days doing little but looking at you. I know you are beautiful. I also know you have a beautiful and brave spirit."

"You are quite brave yourself. I could not believe how you charged into the shack and faced down those men," she said admiringly.

He could feel her relax against him, but not too relaxed. Obviously such intimacies were new to her. And then she tried to press closer. She probably had no idea what she was doing to him.

"Ah, Frederica." He sighed deeply and tried to get himself under control. "I actually want to be with you in every way. But you deserve better than a stone floor in a church, even if it is a cathedral. Also, if we don't stop now,

I can't be accountable later." He kissed her again, then pressed light kisses across her cheeks and forehead.

"I'm not sure I understand." Frederica was confused. "I thought…

"Oh Frederica, I do love you, but I don't think we should be together that way tonight," he said softly. "But later, I do so want to be with you. In a proper bed, and after the banns have been called." He continued to run his hand up and down her back. "Now, however, I think we need to lay plans and try to rest up for tomorrow."

Frederica was still confused by Clive's attitude. She sat up and started to retie her neckline. Had she done something wrong?

Clive seemed to sense her confusion. "Frederica, darling, please don't be angry. I love you. You are very special to me, but the first time we are together as man and wife, I want it to be special for you. Not on the floor of a church. Please say you understand."

"Yes, yes, I think I do," she said, sounding shy. He took her hand and pulled her against him again. She came willingly.

"Plans?" she asked, obviously trying to change the subject. "What plans do you have in mind?"

"I don't have any more cash, but I do have my cravat pin and first thing tomorrow we are going to find a place to pawn it. I don't want to sleep in a church again tomorrow." Clive rolled over and put his head on Frederica's stomach.

Frederica's fingers began to play with his hair. It was unbelievable how such a small gesture could feel so good. "How much money do you think it will get us?"

"I'm not sure, but this is what I have been thinking. Suppose my letter to Tommy gets to him tomorrow in Avebury and he sets out the same day. Remember, I said we were going to Bath. That means he will have to make a detour only to find out we are not in Bath. I am not sure how many hours it will take, but I think the earliest he could get here would be Wednesday or Thursday. Alternatively, say Tommy is actually in London and my letter does not get to him for three days. *Paterson* says it is about one hundred miles to London from here and I saw a poster in Cirencester saying it takes two days by coach. Bath, of course, is much closer and Robert will know when he gets my letter that we are not in Bath. Possibly, he and General Padgett would get here sooner, as they will be on horseback. But I am not sure. I think we need enough money to last at least three days, minimum."

Frederica took some time to think over Clive's reasoning. She said thoughtfully, "All that assumes the landlord forwards the letter to Mr. Grant in London."

"Even if he does, I am worried we cannot count on Tommy Grant. We know he would stay with your uncle, and that means we don't know where he is. If Dr. Chadwick couldn't be moved, they will still be in Avebury. Otherwise, Tommy should be on his way to London, probably by a slow coach. Of course, he will contact my father as soon as he can, but I don't think we should put our hopes on anyone showing up too soon."

"Where does that leave us?"

"Needing money for food and a place to hide for at least three days."

"Counting from when?"

"From today. My letter went to Bath this afternoon. If it is delivered immediately, I suppose the general and Robert could be here tomorrow, but again that assumes they are currently in Bath."

"Did they have any plans to leave? I do not remember Rachel saying anything about travelling."

"Frankly, I have this horrible fear of my letter sitting on the mantle waiting for Robert to get back from some horse race somewhere."

"Is there anyone else we can write to?" Frederica wondered. "I can't say as I have a lot of friends about. If I did, I probably would not be in this mess."

"Remember, I did send letters to my father," Clive offered.

"Would he come?"

"Of course, and I shall certainly write him again as soon as we have some more cash to pay for the postage."

"Do you know anyone around here?"

"No. Father and I were travelling through looking at horses. I don't actually remember everywhere we stopped, but I do remember this church. It was just so beautiful."

"So you think your cravat pin will bring us enough money to hide for three days and send letters to London?"

"No, not really. It isn't an expensive pin to begin with. To be honest, I have pawned it before, so I sort of know what it is worth and it won't be enough. Here's the other part of my idea." He paused long enough for Frederica to wonder if he had fallen asleep.

"What?" she prodded suspiciously.

"You sell some sketches. Those people on the coach liked the one you did of their daughter. Several of those could make the difference between our being vulnerable on the streets for the next couple of days and finding some safety."

"Well, of course I want to help as much as possible. If you actually think people will pay money, I am willing to try. But how would I find customers?"

"First, we need to get you some supplies. Then you do a few sketches and we show them to people and see if anyone wants their portrait done. The cathedral gets lots of visitors. Maybe we could start there."

"You make it sound so simple," Frederica complained. "You know it won't be that easy."

"It should be pretty easy for you," Clive responded. "I am thinking you will be sitting on a little stool with your art supplies around you, looking all pretty and talented, while I go about drumming up clients."

Frederica stretched. "You are dreaming, but it certainly is worth a try." Another thought occurred to her. "What about our thugs following us?"

"This is a city. They can follow us here, but if they do, they will have to find us." Clive's voice sounded overly brave to Frederica.

"Right, Clive. And we will be sitting at the cathedral in full view of everyone drawing sketches."

"Well, let me think. Maybe we should consider someplace else. But first things first – let's get some sleep and make a plan for getting out of here tomorrow. One challenge at a time."

But Frederica still had another issue to discuss. She started nervously. "Clive, about earlier…"

"Oh, too right." Clive said, his arms tightening and pulling her to him as hard as he could, "Frederica Chadwick, will you marry me?"

* * *

Frederica woke with a jerk. Something was wrong. *Of course something is wrong. I am lying on the floor of an enormous cathedral with a man that I allowed, even enjoyed, to touch me as if we were married! We are being chased, we have no money, and it is almost dawn!* She sat up with a start, or at least tried to. Clive's arms kept her firmly in place against his chest.

"What?" he murmured into her hair.

"It is getting light," she said. "I can see the outlines of the statues around the altar."

Clive gave an un-loverlike grunt. "I suppose you wouldn't consider..." Instead of releasing her, his arms tightened around her and he started nuzzling her neck.

"Clive, let me up." The stubble on his cheeks tickled her and she started to wiggle.

Faced with her determined squirming, Clive gave up the attempt to go back to sleep and relaxed his tight hold. "What time do you think it is?"

"It seems early enough that I doubt anyone is up and about yet." He yawned hugely.

The sight of him sitting there looking tousled and vulnerable made her smile. He smiled back. "Say, you haven't forgotten your promise to marry me, have you?"

"No, I have not forgotten. However, if this is going to be our usual bed, I may have to rethink my decision," Frederica teased. "At least I won't need a candle to find the privy in the sanctuary."

When she returned, Clive was dressed and had pulled out the comb, which he handed her. "I figure if your hair looks good, no one will notice your dress is not pristine. No one expects young-bloods like myself to be immaculate. Which is a good thing, as I cannot tie this cravat without a mirror," he grumbled as he headed off to the closet in the sacristy and Frederica started putting her hair in order.

They did not have to wait long for the first signs of activity. From their hiding place behind the sarcophagus, they could hear the bolts being pulled back and the main doors opening. "We should split up."

"Why? I feel better when I can see you."

"How many couples do you see strolling around a church at this time of morning? We do not want anything to bring attention to ourselves. I will go first and slip around the corner," Clive decided. "Why don't you kneel at the chapel's altar rail, pray, and then join the people coming in for the service?"

"Where are we going to meet? And when?"

"Just outside at the bottom of the front steps. I am going there now; meet me as soon as you can. Ready?" At her nod, he peered around the corner of the tomb and quickly went over the railing.

"Frederica, it's clear," he whispered urgently.

Frederica held her skirts tightly in one hand. She chose the part of the railing farthest from the main part of the church and least likely to be visible as a result. She stepped over quickly and practically threw herself onto her knees at the railing, pulling the hood of her cloak over her head and trying to assume the devoted attitude of a regular worshiper. And a good thing she was quick. Almost immediately, she could hear footsteps and whispered voices as early congregants wandered in. After a few minutes, when she had exhausted all the prayers her father had taught her and her knees were burning from kneeling on marble, she rose and moved with bowed head to the nave. Keeping close to the sidewall, she headed to the main doors at the west end. At the doors, she turned back to gaze at the cathedral to see what it looked like in daylight. She was standing at one end of a huge cavernous hall with many large columns, evenly spaced, dividing the main section of the cathedral. What looked like a large wooden wall crossed the center, cutting off the altar. She could only see to the area where she supposed the worshipers were to stand. That alone was breathtaking.

Outside, she easily found Clive at the bottom of the steps. "I want to come back sometime and explore this cathedral. Maybe when we have all this behind us." She gestured widely with one hand to indicate the world at large. "It is so beautiful and I want to see so much more of it."

"I agree. There is an amazing tomb on the other side. The stonework looks like lace."

They started down the steps together. "Whose tomb? Do you have any idea?"

"Maybe Edward II. I think I remember he is buried here. Let's go this way." He nodded to an alley angling off to the right of the cathedral.

"Don't you think it is too early for pawnshops to be open?" she asked.

"It probably is, but I do not think they would be in this part of town anyway. We shall probably have to walk a bit." He sighed deeply and confessed, "I could really use a cup of coffee or even tea right now."

"Which way are we going? And didn't you say you had a few pennies left from yesterday?"

"Very few," he agreed. "Probably enough to buy some coffee if you don't mind standing in the street to drink it."

"Last week, I probably would have objected. Today, I am a woman open to experience. Lead me to it!"

For her show of bravado, she earned a hug and a kiss on the cheek. Soon they found a street vendor who sold them two mugs of reasonably tepid tea for a penny. They both agreed the weak liquid was the best tea they had ever had. As they stood on the sidewalk and sipped their morning beverage, Clive explained where he thought they would find a pawnshop.

"This is a port of some size. I assume the harbor frontage will have a lot of places where sailors can hawk their effects. At least I hope so." He settled up with the vendor and then asked her for directions to the harbor. As it turned out, she also knew a few pawnshops or, as she called them, "dolly shops." It was still early, so they took their time winding their way through the maze of streets. "This reminds me of the shambles in York. Probably these streets were also laid down during the Middle Ages," Clive observed.

"Shambles?"

"It is a small lane in York where all the butchers had their shops in medieval times. I have no idea why it is called Shambles. But it is very old and some of the buildings sort of lean sideways. One wonders why they never fall down." Clive was holding her hand, but she noticed he still kept his other hand in his coat pocket. Obviously, this wasn't the most savory part of town.

"Why are you smiling? What are you finding funny?"

"Funny? No," she said. "Happy? Yes."

"And why is that? Wouldn't be the company, would it?" He raised her hand and kissed her palm. Frederica thought the gesture lovely, but some street urchins didn't agree and they showed it with whistles and disgusting noises. Clive waved at them and kept going down the street.

"Why?" he prodded.

Frederica pulled Clive to a stop. "I am happy because I am with you. I am happy with you in a way I have never been happy before."

"I feel the same way," he responded. "I know this. I want to spend the rest of my life with you. Sure, I want to make love with you. Last night, as hard as that floor was, was the best night of my life and I know it is going to get better, especially if we have a real bed. But even more, I love just being with you. So maybe this is love. If it is not, I think it is an especially good start. Except, of course, for the fellows chasing us."

Frederica immediately looked over her shoulder to see if the "fellows" were there. She shook her head. "Yes, let's be practical for a bit. Besides, I am hungry again." She started to look up and down the streets. "How far to that pawnshop the vendor told us about?"

Clive seemed to consult an internal map. "A couple of blocks to the right. At least I think that was what she said. We were on Westgate when we talked to her and she said to start looking around Ladytalegate Street." They walked to the end of the lane and suddenly found themselves in the middle of a working harbor.

"This must be the Quay," he said.

In front of them, the harbor opened up with a veritable forest of masts from the ships docked there. They turned left and followed the sidewalk in front of the warehouses lining the Quay. The street was dirt with small rocks mixed in for drainage, but Frederica could see it probably was mostly mud in the winter. There were a lot of men about, but not a lot of activity.

Dering must have noticed the lack of purposeful bustle, too. "Last time I spoke with my father, before our fight that is, he mentioned that commerce was down." At Frederica's lack of comprehension, he went on. "It's the war, you see. We can't trade with Europe, so a lot of goods have no place to go. Take a good look at the ships; most of them are just floating there, idle."

Uncomfortable with so many stares, Frederica pulled her hood up and kept her eyes down. "Do you actually know where we are going?"

Dering did not answer directly but stopped a man dressed slightly better than most to ask directions.

"Turn left at the main intersection and it should be on the left several blocks down." The man walked off before he could be thanked.

At the snub, Clive commented with a shrug, "Guess we are part of the riffraff now."

"As long as we are part of the living riffraff," Frederica answered stoutly.

Finally, a sign for Ladytalegate appeared on a large building that seemed to be part tavern and part inn.

"Look, Clive, at all the women in the windows. What are they doing?" But Dering had started walking faster down the street, practically dragging Frederica behind him.

"They are not women you should be concerned about, Frederica. Jeffrey would kill me if he knew you had seen that house."

"Prostitutes?" Frederica asked.

"How do you know about prostitutes?" he asked astonished.

"Well, I have never seen them before, but I do read a lot. When my father was alive he always answered any question I asked him. I read *Moll Flanders* last year and he was pretty uncomfortable about it, but he didn't stop me. Very enlightening." Frederica glanced once more over her shoulder at the building on the corner.

"Ah, here we are!"

Mr. Miller's Used Goods was in the middle of a block of worn and sagging buildings. The sign over the door was barely readable and the window so dingy it was difficult to see in. Clive pointed out the three balls hanging by the side of the door.

"There is the sign for a pawnshop, same as in Oxford."

But Frederica had been peering in the dirty front window.

"Oh look Clive, he has some artists' pencils. Maybe he has some paper you can talk him out of."

Quite a number of household goods were stashed on rickety shelves. Nothing looked particularly clean or even useable by Hermione's standards.

"I do not see any jewelry anywhere."

"He probably has it behind the counter."

"Of course." Frederica followed Clive into the shop. The morning sun turned instantly to gloom. An aged, bent figure sat on a tall stool behind the counter. Long yellow fingernails tapped out a rhythm on the counter.

"Buying or selling?" The voice was old but imperious.

Even Dering seemed a bit cowed. But he gathered himself and spoke up bravely, "Selling."

"What?" While Mr. Miller was cheap with words, Frederica could only hope his prices were not.

Dering pulled his cravat pin out and laid it on the counter.

Mr. Miller picked it up greedily and held it close to his eyes. "One pound."

Clive reached out his hand. "Sorry, not enough."

"One-five."

"Sorry I wasted your time. I want five pounds." Now Clive sounded very firm. His hand was still extended.

The negotiations went on for some time, the old man raising his offer incredibly slowly, Clive standing with his hand outstretched. Finally they settled on three pounds five, and the pencils were thrown in for good measure.

On the street, Clive was livid.

"That horror! That slimy, money-grubbing..." He seemed to run out of words. "That pin is worth three times that! He knew we were desperate." He looked around and, grabbing her hand, started to walk furiously down the street. Finally he calmed down. "Oh well, let's find a stationery shop and get some paper so we can write those letters. Then perhaps you can draw some pictures."

Back in front of the cathedral, an open-air market was in full swing.

"This is just like Cirencester." Frederica eyed the various booths with delight. "Can we walk around and look for drawing paper?"

"Yes, let's do that for a while. We can stay in a decent inn for a couple of days on the three pounds, but we will need money for food and whatnot."

"You know, if I were home, I would never be allowed to do any of these things."

"Things?" Clive asked.

"Yes, like visiting the market, sketching strangers, drinking tea from a street vendor. Those things."

"Oh, I thought you meant sleeping in a church with a young handsome git like me." Clive was grinning. "They kept you pretty well under wraps down in Kent, didn't they?"

"Oh rather! Since my father died, it is always 'don't do this,' 'don't do that.' She would not even let me buy any new books."

"Well, things are going to change," Clive said encouragingly. "I want my wife to be well-read and I certainly want my wife to exercise her artistic talents, especially if she can make some money at it. Look over there; is that a bookstall?"

It was indeed a bookstall, although the proprietor did not have any paper suitable for sketching portraits. He was able to suggest several shops along the eastern part of Westgate that specialized in stationery, though. While Clive had been discussing directions with the proprietor, Frederica had been poking through a basket of old books. She brought one to Clive.

"Buy this for me, please?"

"What do you want an old book on theology for?"

"Well, I don't really, but it has a lot of blank pages, front and back, I can use in case the real art paper is too expensive. The price is just a few pennies."

"Good thinking." With their one purchase, they headed through the market to the obelisk where the coach had dropped them off the previous evening. They stopped to buy hot pasties from one vendor and real coffee from another. The stationery store was several blocks past the market in a quieter section of town. Their luck was holding, as it did have sketchpads similar to the ones Frederica had left in Avebury, although the price was higher than they had anticipated.

"Good thing you thought to buy that book for extra paper," Clive said after he discussed prices with the clerk.

Frederica was more at home in the store and briskly asked the clerk if he had some large unbound sheets. These proved to be more reasonable in price, so they purchased those instead of a full pad.

"With the paper I have left over from Cirencester and the old book, this should give us a good start."

Clive was amused to note how she used the word "us." They were definitely a team now.

The clerk took pity on them. Seeing that they were buying letter stationery as well as the sketching sheets, he let Clive borrow his quill and ink to write follow-up notes to his father, Robert, and Mr. Grant. He even gave them directions to the coaching office, advising that their letters should make the afternoon coach to Bath and hopefully even London if they hurried.

The coaching office proved to be near the market obelisk and not at all out of their way as they headed to the cathedral.

"Frederica, I was thinking." They were strolling among the booths of the marketplace with the intention of sitting on the steps of the cathedral so Frederica could sketch in the sunlight. She was carrying all the art supplies and trying to keep her skirts out of the street dirt, hardly paying attention to Clive as she was admiring the architecture of the buildings, watching the many people rushing about and the commerce and activity of the market.

"Frederica? Are you hearing me?" Clive seemed to realize she was distracted.

"Yes, yes. What?"

"When we get a room for tonight at the inn – at least we can afford that – I was thinking…" Clive seemed at a loss for words.

"What? Clive, oh look! Strawberries! Aren't they just the most beautiful things?"

"Frederica," Clive gave a burst of words, "it would be cheaper if we shared a room."

Frederica turned from admiring the strawberries and laughed out loud. "What are you worried about? Did you honestly think I would want my own room?" She took his free hand and squeezed it. "You asked me to marry you last night, remember? And I said yes. Besides, we have already spent one night together in an inn and one in a church." She laughed as she said, "We are practically married already."

"Oh my God, Frederica!" Now it was Clive's turn to be distracted. Frederica was still gazing at Clive's face, though he was no longer looking at her face but over her shoulder. She turned around with a jerk to see what he was looking at. Horrified, they watched an open brochette drive into the market place with the captain at the reins and his two bullies with him. "Quick! Put your hood up!"

Breakfast Room: Chelsea

Marion Donnay was eating alone; her husband Nathan was on an unusually long assignment. Long and also self-inflicted. To the best of her knowledge, but without her approval, he was in France, trying to track down their friend, Jeffrey Chadwick.

The polite knock on the breakfast room door heralded her butler's arrival. Thornton had already brought the mail and newspapers. This interruption was uncommon.

"Come in," she called immediately.

"There is a message for Mr. Donnay," Thornton announced as he entered the room. "Brought by special messenger. From Avebury, Mistress, not from France."

If it is for Nathan, it cannot be from him. But it could be about him. She grabbed the missive and broke the seal. Scanning the note quickly, she told Thornton, "I was hoping this was news about my husband, but it is not. It is from someone who needs his help." She drummed her fingers on the table and tried to think quickly. "Thornton, have John Coachman go around to Miss Ferguson's and ask her to come over quickly. I need her advice."

Thornton left immediately to do as directed.

* * *

"Who is Thomas Grant and why is he asking for help?" Charlotte Ferguson asked. She was standing in the parlor of her good friend Marion's house in Chelsea. Charlotte had not even had a chance to remove her bonnet or sit down before her friend had shoved a letter into her hands with the order to "read this."

"He is acquainted with Jeffrey Chadwick and it is Jeffrey's sister who had been kidnapped. She was on a sightseeing trip with Mr. Grant and her uncle,

Festus Chadwick. As Grant says in the letter, both he and Chadwick were injured in a carriage accident earlier on the trip. Now the uncle is again incapacitated and Grant is in no shape to mount a rescue. The young person he mentions, Clive Dering, appears to be his former student. I know nothing about him at all."

"Is there no one closer they can call on?" Charlotte asked incredulously. "That seems improbable."

"Apparently not. Grant enclosed a copy of Dering's note. It is here if you want to read it. He says he found Miss Chadwick—Frederica—and they are being tailed by someone claiming to be her father. He, this kidnapper, is telling everyone he meets that Frederica and Clive are attempting to elope and he is trying to bring her home. It seems they are both frightened and almost penniless at the moment."

"What does Grant expect you to do?"

"The letter is for Nathan. I suppose he hopes Nathan will show up and save the day."

"That is not going to happen," Charlotte exclaimed. "Do you even know when he will be back to get this message? He's been gone some time, hasn't he?"

"Yes, I am beginning to start to worry. I know he would not want to leave me too long in this condition." Her hand settled on the bump in her stomach that each day seemed to get bigger.

"Where is General Coxe? Surely he would be glad to assist."

"I know he would. But Grenville just sent him on a mission to interview some informer along the Kent coast. My father couldn't tell me for sure when he would be back," Marion replied.

"Is there no one else you can contact at the Alien Office?"

"Not actually."

Charlotte sat quietly for a few moments trying to come up with options. Finally her friend gave a frustrated groan.

"Another kidnapping!" Marion exclaimed. "This is the third one affecting someone I know in less than two years!" She stood by the fireplace, drumming her fingers on the mantle. Charlotte thought the habit to be less than lady-like but it was better than swearing or throwing things. Both activities she had seen Marion engage in during their long friendship.

Finally her friend announced firmly, "We will have to go ourselves."

"Marion!" Charlotte exclaimed. "Not in your condition."

"Oh stuff and nonsense. I am pregnant, not ill. A carriage ride to the country might be quite nice. And I will have you along for company, after all."

Charlotte shook her head. For all the years she had known Marion, she knew her friend always took control of the situation and charged in. Charlotte thought herself the voice of reason in their friendship. But this time, it was a real emergency with little or no time to waste.

"I am with you," she said sturdily. "I will write a note to my mother to pack me a bag while I go upstairs and pack yours. You probably have letters to write before we leave?"

"Yes, to my father, first, and then to Nathan, of course."

"I am sure your father will follow us as soon as he learns what is happening," Charlotte said, blushing slightly. She and Ambrose, as he insisted she call him, had decided to keep quiet about this new feeling that was growing between them. He was her father's peer, some thirty years her senior, but his kindness and integrity impressed her. She felt she knew him well enough to be sure he would not willingly leave his daughter—or her—in any danger.

"Thornton!" Marion called. He usually could be found in the hall, listening to conversations or, as he liked to say, waiting for orders.

As expected, he appeared immediately.

"Miss Ferguson and I are taking a sudden trip," his mistress announced. "I have some directions for you."

* * *

By midafternoon, the two friends were standing in the hall waiting for John Coachman to give them the signal that he was ready. He had brought the travel coach around and was loading the hastily packed bags. This included a hurriedly prepared picnic basket because, of course, Marion's cook did not believe a pregnant person could sustain a trip without something to snack on constantly.

"More pillows?" Marion cried watching the downstairs maid scurry by with an armload. Thornton followed with blankets folded over his arms. "Anything else, Charlotte?" she asked shaking her head.

"Thornton has all the letters, I believe," her friend answered. "It looks like the carriage has been properly organized to maximize your comfort. Do you have ready money?"

Before Marion could answer, a tap sounded on the frame of the open door. Turning, she saw a slight man in the doorway. He was probably the same age as he father, well dressed and bearing himself well. He carried a letter in one hand and a walking stick in the other.

"Mistress Donnay?" he asked.

Marion nodded in reply waiting for the man to introduce himself.

"I am Clifford Dering of Ripon, Yorkshire. I believe we have a common concern. May I enter so we can discuss it?"

Chapter Fifteen: Waiting

Clive

"I don't see how he could! The carriage came from the opposite direction."

"Is it too early to find an inn to hide in?"

"That is the best idea! Walk, don't run! Go with the flow of the crowd." With their heads down, Frederica and Clive headed up the nearest alley.

"I think it is time to see if we can find the inn that Lucy's father recommended."

"That is the name of the inn you mentioned in the letter to Robert, isn't it?"

"Yes, The Coaches and Horses. I did think we would have more time to look for it and to spruce up so we could arrive looking respectable, even though we'll be arriving without any luggage and on foot. Alas, that was not to be." Clive sighed as he stopped at a corner to check signs. "Northgate. Lad, how do we get to St. Catherine Street?"

The grimy urchin he was addressing held up his hand. After Clive tossed him a penny, he gestured with his left hand. "Go up Hare Street. It crosses St Catherine after a bit. Can't miss it, mister."

"Which way to The Coaches and Horses?" Again, the child gestured to the left.

"Thanks," Clive called and, taking Frederica's arm, hurried her up the street. After about four blocks of rather tidy houses and shops, the street did indeed come to a large cross street where they turned left. Clive periodically checked over his shoulder.

"Doesn't look like they are following us. So what story are we going to tell them?"

"Tell who?"

"The innkeeper. He is not going to be happy taking us in off the street. They like it when folks arrive in coaches with lots of servants and luggage. People who spend money and are respectable."

"I see what you mean," Frederica responded. "I am thinking aloud so this may not work. Why don't we say we are victims of an assault who are waiting for our friends to arrive to help us out?"

Clive considered the story and asked, "Where would we say the assault happened?"

"On the road from Avebury. Just like it really did. I guess we should stick as close to the truth as possible but say our coach was stolen and we have been taking the mail coach."

Clive pointed up the street. "Look, there's our destination. Quick, what is the rest of the story? Are we married or brother and sister?"

"Married, of course. On our honeymoon. And we lost everything and had to pawn your watch. Our marriage lines were in my luggage. Those miserable thieves even took my wedding ring and the new earrings you bought me as a wedding gift."

"Oh those earrings, were they the ones with the pearls?" Clive quickly got into the story. "You know, Frederica, this just may work. Especially as we have some cash. It certainly is as good as anything as I can come up with."

And surprisingly, it did work. In the beginning, the innkeeper looked a bit askance, but once Clive produced enough coin and asked for three nights instead of one, he agreed that the roads were a real hazard at times and assured them that they would be safe at The Coaches and Horses for a few days until their friends showed up. He showed them to a small room at the back of the house. Clive thought it was probably the meanest room the inn had, but it had a lock on the door and a sense of safety. Three days of safety.

"Who would have known you were such a good spinner of tales?" Clive wrapped Frederica in his arms as soon as the door closed behind the landlord. "Ah, Frederica, they got here so fast! We have to last at least three days. I don't think Robert can get here before then, and I am certain Tommy can't. So far I have not even been able to mail my father's letter."

Frederica leaned into Clive's embrace, welcoming the security it offered.

"We don't have enough money for food for the next three days, do we?" She started to trace his jaw with her fingertips. "I still have the paper and pencils," she offered.

Clive started to untie the strings on Frederica's cloak. "At least we have already eaten today," he said. "We will not have to go down to the dining room until later. We have time for you to make some practice drawings."

"Don't you think we might get more interest in the portraits if people saw me drawing you? They might come over to watch and decide they just have to have one of their own."

While they were talking, Dering noticed Frederica seemed to be increasingly nervous. Her eyes fluttered around the room, her hands clenched and unclenched. She wasn't making any effort to climb into bed although he knew she was exhausted. The stone floor at the cathedral had not been at all comfortable. He wondered if she was afraid he was going to grab her and take her immediately now that they had a bed. Regretfully, he realized all he wanted to do was sleep – with her, but still just sleep.

"I need to ask the landlord something," he said quickly. "Claim your side of the bed. I am sure you and I both need sleep." Her grateful look did not help his ego, but he understood her anxiety.

When he returned, he found her snuggled in bed and seemingly dozing off. He reached out to touch her hand and felt her tense. She did not jerk away, though. He slipped an arm around her and pulled her close, whispering, "Sleep, Frederica, everything is better when you have enough sleep."

When Frederica woke, it was quite dark. She tried to sit up and found Clive was lying on his side with his arms circling her waist, keeping her in place.

"Where are you going?" he asked quietly.

"Nowhere," she answered, just as softly. "I just did not realize where I was." Through the curtain-less window, she could see dusk had settled outside. She was only in her shift and could feel him warm and smooth along her back. He had no shirt on.

As she turned to face him, he drew closer for a kiss. He was right: a bed was much better than a stone floor. Was he going to make love to her? Butterflies erupted in her stomach. "Clive, I have never…" she gasped.

"I know," he answered. "I am not exactly all that experienced myself. We will take it slow and learn together. How about that?" His hand was on her neck, with a thumb stroking her lips and cheek. She could hardly breathe.

"You need to tell me what to do," she murmured. She so did not want to disappoint him, but what did he expect her to do?

"We tell each other. If you like something I do, like this," his hand smoothed down her front and stopped to softly cup her breast, "you tell me. If I do something you do not like, tell me and we will try something else."

"But what do I do while you are 'trying' things?" she asked. Silence.

Whatever he was doing felt very good, as her body heated up. His hands were back up in her hair, while he massaged her scalp. She almost moaned out loud with pleasure.

"Do you like that?" he asked.

"Yes," she ground out.

"See, not so hard. Now you try something."

"Like this?" she whispered.

"Yes, oh my God, yes!"

* * *

When she woke again, the room was empty. No Clive. She stretched, feeling aches in the usual places. Her shift, just out of reach, lay on the floor. Rolling over, she pushed back the blanket, trying to reach the garment without getting out of bed. She was hanging half out of bed when the door opened and Clive entered carrying a steaming can of something.

"I thought you might like some hot water. We don't exactly get the best service at this end of the inn, so I went for it myself."

"Oh Clive, you are too good to me!" she gasped, wiggling into her shift. Even after their recent activities, she thought it seemed improper for him to see her nude.

"Here you go, m'lady. Soap and towels and me to help with your hair." He watched her squirming under the covers for a few seconds and then said, "It would be easier, Frederica, if you came out. Putting on your stays under the sheets will be almost impossible." She could hear the laughter in his voice.

She popped her head out, cheeks flushed. "I am not used to dressing in front of a man. Even if we just…"

Clive sat on the bed, giving her a hug and kissing her cheek.

"Of course you are not comfortable. I should have thought of that before I barged in." He gave her another squeeze and stood. "I will go to the bar and have a pint while you dress. Come down when you are finished and we will have dinner. I am sorry, but we will have to eat in the common room. Our funds won't allow us to eat in the private rooms. By the way, what you said about people seeing you draw me makes sense."

"So that is another reason to eat in the common room; we could not make any money if we ate alone." Standing up in her shift, Frederica picked up her stockings. "These stockings have seen better days," she commented sorrowfully.

"Ah, Frederica." Clive turned back from the door to hug and kiss her. "You are so brave. Any other young woman I know would have fallen into fainting fits any number of times over the past few days. I do love that strength about you."

He had reason to admire her strength later when, even as they were eating, she calmly pulled her pencils and paper out and started to outline his face.

"You know, Clive, one of the best things about this trip," she confided, "is the lack of ceremony. At home, I would never think of sketching during a meal, but around here no one cares what I do. I absolutely do *not* want to go home."

"Do not worry about going back to Kent. Remember, we are engaged. You are going home with me," he said firmly.

* * *

Frederica flopped onto the bed. "I am tired! And my hands are cramped," she complained. "Drawing so quickly and with the customer waiting is harder than I thought it was going to be."

Clive sat next to her. He took her left hand and started to massage it. "I don't know why you are upset. I thought the sketches you did tonight were very good."

"Well, that merchant, the big gentleman with the red nose, was actually hard to do. He wouldn't sit still for very long." She rolled over on her side and gave him her right hand to rub.

"Yes, I noticed. I think he was a bit worse for the amount of drink he had taken."

"Yes, I was thankful you did not go far away when he was around. However, if he hadn't been drunk, he might not have given me so much money." Frederica reached into the pocket hidden in her dress and handed a handful of coins to Clive.

Clive's eyes widened when he noticed the gold guinea in the collection. "You know this is worth about twenty shillings?" He asked. "We can eat for several days on this guinea alone."

"I am rather hoping we will not have to. We've been here two days now. Surely Robert will get here tomorrow?"

He gave her hand a final squeeze, then stood and wandered over to the window. It was dark outside and they were at the back of the building. Dering could only see the occasional glimmer of light in various windows and from the lanterns carried by folks making their way home. "I wish we had some idea what that captain is doing. I bet he is combing the city, checking any place we could be staying. It must be pretty easy to realize we did not leave yet."

"Why do you say that? How could he be sure?"

"If it was me, I would station one of my beastie boys at the coaching office near the market obelisk and watch to see who actually gets on the coach. He must suspect we don't have the money to hire a private chase." Clive sighed. "This waiting is really getting to me. At least thanks to you we are not completely without funds. You have been amazing."

"We're a team."

A raised voice interrupted them.

"Where is she?" A loud drawling voice sounded as if right outside their door. Startled, Clive turned to look at Frederica. Frederica sat up sharply.

"Where is my daughter? I know she is hiding here with that *predator*. Where are they?" The voices got louder and closer. Obviously there was more than one person in the hallway.

"Captain Piercy, please. Lower your voice. I have other guests here," the landlord was responding just as loudly as the person he was talking to.

Panic-stricken, Frederica gasped, "It's that captain!"

Dering cracked the door and peeked out. He shut it quickly, throwing the bolt. "You are right. They are coming up the stairs. Frederica, get your stuff together! We have to get out of here!" He grabbed his coat and shoved combs, pencils, and other gear into his saddlebags. Frederica tumbled off the bed, glad she hadn't taken off her shoes, and grabbed her cloak.

"How are we getting out of here?"

Already there was pounding on the door.

"We can't just go down the hall."

"The window!" Clive threw up the sash and scrambled out onto the low roof of the shed that leaned against the building. "Blow out the candle!" He steadied Frederica by the hand as she joined him on the roof. He tossed the saddlebags onto the street and then peered over the edge.

"Here, lad," A voice with a thick Gloucester accent spoke out of the darkness. "Hang by the edge and I'll catch ya.'" Sure enough, when Clive hung over the edge, arms grasped his legs and eased him to the pavement.

"Come on, Frederica, I'll get you!" Shortly, Frederica joined him in the alley, even as they could hear the door to their room being smashed open.

Dering turned to thank their helper, but the man silently handed him his saddlebags and pointed up the alley.

"Go on, lad, get your lassie out of here. That man don't mean you any good."

They could hear yells and curses from the inn as they headed up the alley. In the darkness they followed narrow, twisting streets, one dark lane after another until they were pretty sure no one was following them. Unfortunately, by then they were also lost.

Clive came to a stop and pulled Frederica into a dark doorway to some closed shop. "No warning, yet he seemed to know we were there."

Frederica nodded, gasping for breath. "How do you think he found out?" she panted.

"Here, wrap up in your cloak. That dress is still too white, even in this darkness." He took her cloak and held it so she could drape it around her shoulders, covering as much of the dress as possible. "To answer your questions, I suppose he must have had help going to all the taverns and inns. I guess his spy noticed us in the taproom and turned us in. We were lucky the innkeeper seemed to like us. He could have let him up to our room quietly. I think he caused the fuss in the hallway just to give us time to get away and now we know his name is Piercy."

Frederica finally got her breath under control. "Maybe Piercy didn't tip him enough to sneak up quietly." She took several deep breaths. "Anyway, who was the fellow in the alley? Did you know him?"

"You mean our guardian angel?" Clive chuckled. "Didn't you recognize the tapster? He must have been going to the jakes. We were just lucky he took a dislike to Piercy."

"I'd rather think it is because he liked us. After all, I did do a lovely picture of his wife for him and she was no prize." Frederica leaned against Clive, put her arms around his waist, and rested her head against his shoulder. "I suppose the cathedral is already shut up. I guess this time we are going to have to spend the night on the streets."

"What is very annoying is that we are not getting our last night at the inn. We already paid for it," Clive grumbled. "I wonder if I can get a refund tomorrow."

Frederica chuckled, "You are being silly. We are being chased through the streets of a town we don't know by some very evil men and you're worried about getting your money back. You are something."

Dering rested his chin on top of her head. "Does the name Piercy mean anything to you?"

"No, although I still believe I have seen him before. I guess it does not really matter."

"We should plan what we are going to do next. Have you got any suggestions?"

"I am awfully tired of running," Frederica said softly.

"You're not giving up, are you?"

"No, of course I am not giving up. After all, if we get caught, I may end up married to a monster," she returned tartly.

"I understand. I also understand that you must be tired." Clive rubbed his hands up and down her arms. "I am confident that when Robert gets my letter he will come as fast as he is able."

"When we were with them in Bath, did he talk about going anywhere?" Frederica knew she was returning to a topic they had already hashed over several times, but she needed to hear Clive repeat his belief that help was coming soon.

"No, his plans were to stay in Bath for the rest of the month. He intended to stay until it was time for him to go back to Oxford. I am sure of this. Robert and I talked about it several times."

Frederica wondered if Clive was speaking so emphatically to comfort her or to comfort himself. "So you calculate tomorrow morning would be the earliest he could get here?"

"Yes, Frederica. I believe if we can hang on until tomorrow morning, Robert and Mr. Padgett will show up and get us out of here." He sighed and said more softly, "I have to believe it."

"Clive, what else could we be doing? How else could we get out of here?"

Clive shifted their positions until they were sitting on the stoop. He draped his arm over her shoulder. Frederica reached up and threaded her fingers though his. They were in a part of Gloucester that seemed to be mainly shops and warehouses, all closed for the night. They could see very few people moving about.

"You are right, Frederica. We need a way to escape if no one shows up to help us." His shoulders sagged in defeat. "We have little money and no friends. Our situation hasn't changed much, has it?"

"We still have each other." Frederica reached up and smoothed his cheek. "And we do have friends. They will get here. It just might take some time." She paused, thinking. "Where can we hide? Obviously this Piercy can find us in any public place. Can you think of anywhere he can't get into?"

"Frederica, remember the family from the coach...do you remember their names?"

"I don't think they ever told us their family name. I only remember the little girl's name, Lucy. The father said they were Quakers. Do Quakers have churches? Do you think we could we find them through their church?"

"Not churches, but meetinghouses."

"So we go back to the inn tomorrow to see if Robert shows up. If he doesn't, then we look up Lucy's father and throw ourselves on his mercy and ask for help. He did seem like a nice man." Dering nodded in agreement but Frederica sensed he wasn't totally listening to her. She felt his head turning to look up and down the street. "What?"

"Sssh!" He barely breathed the admonition. "Over there," he whispered.

Following his gaze, Frederica could see the outline of a figure slowly making its way down the opposite side of the street. Carrying a lantern and stopping in alleys and doorways, the shadow moved relentlessly in their direction. Clive stood and carefully picked up his saddlebags. He took Frederica's hand and pulled her into the shadows of a nearby alley. "We have to go…" Their movement must have caught the attention of the man with the lantern, as his steps grew more rapid and drew closer. Clive picked up their pace, fairly flying down the alley with Frederica in tow.

After a short time, Frederica was gasping, "Clive, please slow down! I can't run anymore!" Her heart thudded painfully, her breath was coming in gasps, and her half boots and skirt were now covered in mud and who knew what else.

Clive did not respond in words, but he did slow his pace somewhat, putting his arm around her waist to help move her along. They had not been able to lose their pursuers this time, no matter how many twists and turns they took. In fact, the shadow with the lantern looked to be gaining on them. How was it possible that no matter how much they ran, their pursuers only got closer?

"I have an idea. Please, Frederica, hold on a little longer. I just need to find the right alley." Now even Clive's breath was coming in gasps.

At the next corner, he pulled her into a passage even darker than the streets they had stumbled through. This alley continued to twist and turn, but Frederica could also feel an incline. At least they were no longer running but walking quickly. Frederica struggled to control her breathing. Clive was obviously seeking something. He kept looking in corners and over his shoulder. In the gloom, Frederica could not imagine what he was searching for. She kept quiet, though, and tried to save her breath for running.

Frederica saw more people in this alleyway than she had noticed in most of the streets they had run through, but the dark made them faceless. She was so tired she was beginning to doubt her own eyes. As no one seemed to be paying them any attention, she started to hope they, too, might find anonymity in this dark, dank alley.

Finally, Clive stopped altogether. He pushed Frederica into a corner where the alley took another turn and sharply inclined upwards. She leaned against the wall in relief.

"Here's what I want you to do," he whispered. "You have to trust me, Frederica. We can't run anymore; they are too close." Clive's words tumbled over one another. He dropped his saddlebags at their feet but close to the wall, hopefully out of sight.

Frederica realized he had placed his body directly against hers, forcing her into the corner and against the wall. His left forearm rested on the wall above her head, turning his coat into a sort of cocoon tent against the world. His right hand now gripped her bottom tightly.

"Clive, what are you doing?" This did not seem to be the time or place for such physical displays. Clive held her tightly. His voice was heavy as he whispered urgently in her ear. "Frederica, be quiet. Listen to me! This is the lane where the whores work. In York, it is called Grope Alley. They will not be looking for a nice girl like you in this alley. I hope if we act like all the other couples here, they will just pass us by. I'm sorry, but can you do this? Just put your arms around my neck and I'll do the rest. Frederica, please, I don't know what else to do." Clive sounded exhausted and maybe a little scared.

Frederica pushed his coat aside so she could peer around him and down the alley. "Oh my God! I can see some men turning the corner. Quick, tell me what to do. I am so ignorant. Standing up? Can you do that? What do I do?" Frederica whispered desperately.

Clive whispered back, "I keep my back to them. I will lift you up and you wrap your legs around me…well, maybe one leg. Pull your skirts up enough so that…"

Frederica's shocked imagination blanked out the danger approaching. Clive put one arm around her and the other under her buttocks and lifted her so her legs could encircle his waist. It was immediately apparent to them both that her cloak would be in the way and they flayed around a bit.

"Wait, let me keep one foot on the ground and wrap the other leg around you, over the cloak so they can see it."

At least the mud-soaked boot and filthy sagging stocking would help her fulfill her new role as streetwalker. With a vengeance, she pulled her skirt up to her hips as he lifted her again so that his hand connected with bare skin.

"Damn, I left the pistol in the room," Clive said dispiritedly.

But it was too late to worry now.

The lantern moved closer as their pursuers crept along, peering at the other couples in the alley. Clive had her so tightly pressed against him she could hardly breathe. The wall felt dank and slimy where her cloak had been pushed aside and her thin dress was even more abused. The leg clinched around Clive was cold from the night air and from fear.

His mouth came down on hers and his tongue invaded her mouth. She jerked with surprise as he bumped against her. *Is it possible to make love standing up? It must be, as he is pretending we are.* The lantern came closer, but Clive continued to cover her with his body. The light came even with them and she heard one of the men speak, but she couldn't understand what he said. Clive growled at the men without turning or letting his mouth leave hers. He kept bumping and grinding against Frederica, even while he shielded her face with his arm and head. Finally, he yelled at the men using language Frederica had never heard before in an accent she did not recognize.

The men laughed rudely but kept moving up the alley. As they continued, Clive loosened his hold a bit and she could now hear them discussing whether they would have time to get themselves a whore, once they found the "little bitch" or maybe they would just use "her." Frederica realized with a jolt they were talking about her. She started to shake when reality set in that these people did mean her harm. This nightmare was not going to end easily. She dropped back to two feet.

Dering kept both his arms around her. Frederica leaned against him, reeling from the close call and the beating her emotions had been subjected to. She felt safe with Clive, but even he could not protect her from Piercy forever.

"So," she whispered, "do you think I would have passed as a *whore?*"

Clive's chuckle seemed to come from deep in his throat. His arms tightened spasmodically. "No," he mumbled, "not without a lot more practice. With me!" He might have continued with the thought, but then their lips connected. Frederica searched back in her memory for their first kiss at Corfe Castle and then to more recent ones. This kiss was nothing like any of them. Then, his lips had been warm and laughing. Now, they were hot and demanding. These kisses were more...something? She stopped trying to compare them.

"Well," he teased, "maybe you could learn." And he bent to kiss her again.

Clive's hand moved down to her shoulder and arm as his lips moved to her neck. He nibbled her ear and nuzzled her neck, sending little lightning strikes up and down her body. She responded by kissing him again, this time moving deeper into his mouth with her tongue. Clive's hand had moved down from her shoulder and he pushed aside her shift so that his cool hand could cup her breast. With a groan, Clive stepped back a small pace. He put his hands on either side of her face and kissed her again, only now gently and tenderly.

"We have to move on. I can't think clearly when you are near me." He chuckled as he shook his head.

Frederica tried to rearrange her clothes and adjusted her hood. Clive retrieved his saddlebags and they walked back down the alley to its entrance. They both carefully glanced in each direction, on the lookout for the hunters.

"What do we do now?" Frederica asked softly.

"We need to find some shelter for the rest of the night, someplace where we will be somewhat safe. I think it must be near midnight by now. I am not sure…"

"It should be light in a few hours, so let us not waste the money. Can't we just sit in a doorway somewhere?"

"Yes, I think it will be easier than trying to find an inn at this hour. Since they already searched this area, maybe we should find a doorway around here. We can take turns keeping watch." In the end, though, neither slept very much.

Chapter Sixteen: Carriage Yard

Clive

As soon as the pitch blackness of the night transitioned to the heavy grayness of predawn, Clive and Frederica started to make their way back to The Coaches and Horses Inn. That was where he had told Robert to meet them and this morning was the earliest he estimated his friend could arrive. He sincerely hoped he had judged correctly and that Robert would arrive, as the events of the previous night had shown Piercy to be closing in.

He tried to lighten Frederica's spirits by commenting on how many more dawns he had seen recently than in his whole time at Oxford. Her forced smile gave him some idea as to how much anxiety she was feeling. As usual, she was trying to present a brave front. He could not admire her more.

Near the inn, he tucked her into a doorway down the street while he approached the coaching yard alone.

"This way, if by some obscene run of bad luck Piercy recognizes me, you at least will still be able to escape." Neither of them discussed where she would go.

He glanced around anxiously to see if, by some miracle, Robert had arrived. Failing Robert's immediate appearance, he hoped to give the tapster a message for when his friend did show up.

"Oh thank God, my prayers are answered," he murmured to himself as he spotted a bright carrot top across the yard.

"Clive!" Robert's most welcome voice called to Dering from across the yard. Clive reached him with a few quick strides. He did not think he had ever been so happy to see anyone before.

"Robert, I cannot tell you how glad I am that you came!"

"Clive, what is happening? Your letter was so strange. I came as fast as I could. Spent hours on horseback. I would not do that for just anyone!" He paused and looked carefully at Clive. "Are you all right? You look…maybe drawn. Whatever it is, you don't look yourself. Where is Miss Chadwick?"

"She's down the street. As I said in the letter, it appears this Captain Piercy fellow arranged to kidnap Miss Chadwick, and when that didn't work, he began chasing us. It started in Avebury; now he is here in Gloucester, still trying to get his hands on her. We are out of money and just exhausted. I really need your help to get Frederica out of here and back to Bath."

"That is a rare story, Clive!" Robert exclaimed. "But why? She's just a girl. She's a pretty girl, but why would he want to harm her?"

"We think from something the kidnappers said that Piercy hopes to get his hands on Frederica's inheritance. Probably by forcing her to marry him."

"But Clive, you are accusing this fellow of kidnapping and I don't know what else. Is forcing someone to marry a crime? Are you talking about rape? Those are serious charges. And you are basing all this on the words of some criminals?"

"I realize I am making serious accusations, Robert, but the kidnapping was dreadfully real. Frederica disappeared from Avebury and Dr. Chadwick was hit so hard on the head he could possibly have been killed. I don't know for sure that he survived, as I had to leave Avebury before he regained consciousness. I did rescue Frederica from some awful men who had her tied up in a shed and were waiting for Piercy to show up. If I had not, at the very least her reputation would be ruined and her future questionable. Those thugs seemed to think he was going to put an end to her." Clive paused as he shook his head. "I was up most of last night, Robert. Truly, I have been up a lot the last few days. I feel very mutton-headed." He paused and took a few calming breathes. "Where's your grandfather?"

"He's off to some horse races in Somerset. I did not want to wait for him to come back. Your letter seemed a little desperate."

"Desperate is right. These men are serious and dangerous."

The innkeeper stepped forward. "I am sorry, sir, about yesterday. That man seemed so sure of himself. He even had a letter from her mother saying the young lady had run away. But this gentleman…" he gestured to Robert, "has explained to me the terribleness of the situation."

"Let's go find Miss Chadwick, my dear fellow, and then let's get out of here. I brought enough money to get a chase back to Bath and I brought the clean clothes you asked for. However, Rachel wasn't sure her dress would fit Miss Chadwick."

"Oh good! We need them and I am sure Frederica won't care a fig about the fit. Let me find Frederica while you take care of getting the coach ready."

Robert and the innkeeper were watching the harnessing of two horses to an open barouche when Clive returned empty handed.

Before Robert could inquire about the absence of Miss Chadwick, the gates to the street were pushed open and several men strode arrogantly into the stable yard. To Dering's horror, it was the captain, accompanied by two huge burly men. Piercy was gripping Frederica tightly by the arm.

"Clive, help!" she pleaded, trying frantically to get out of Piercy's hold.

"You," he commanded, giving her a rough shake, "are coming home with me, young lady! You have caused your mother and me more trouble than you are worth!" He viciously twisted her arm and started to drag Frederica to a closed coach waiting across the yard.

Frederica immediately started screaming, "No! Clive! Help!"

Both Clive and Robert rushed Piercy.

"She is not going anywhere with you!" Clive yelled. He started to attack Piercy with his fists, just as Piercy's henchmen charged into the melee, attacking both Clive and Robert with fists and cudgels. All the yelling and commotion in the yard caused the horses to become anxious and difficult to handle. Several were pulling at their reins, refusing to be put in traces. The innkeeper, appalled at what was fast becoming a riot in his yard, tried to intervene and separate the fighters.

Over the shoulder of his attacker, Clive could see all the activity in the yard had attracted the attention of a crowd of early-morning gawkers. Among them was a young couple with their daughter, dressed in the simple gray clothing of the Quakers.

"There's the lady who drew my picture!" Clive could hear a light young voice carrying over the sound of the struggle.

Even as his attacker raised his stick to beat him around the head, Dering managed to get under the man's reach and land a telling blow against his throat. To Clive's amazement, the bully dropped his cudgel and clutched his throat. His eyes rolled up and he dropped to his knees and finally laid motionless. Clive quickly scanned the coaching yard to see where Frederica was. To his dismay, he was separated from her by the yard, several carriages, milling horses, and the crowd of gawkers.

Dering could see that even as Piercy tried to drag her away, Frederica was still struggling. Then a small figure emerged from the crowd and started towards her. The child was followed by a tall, stern figure who Dering recognized as Lucy's father.

"Help me, please!" Frederica was screaming. "He is not my father! He wants to kill me!"

Before anyone could stop her, brave little Lucy charged Piercy and grabbed him by the coat sleeve. With his free hand, Piercy shoved Lucy out of the way. She fell dangerously near the hooves of the horses pulling the carriage hired by Robert.

To Clive, everything was happening in slow motion. As he struggled against the milling tide of horses and people, he saw Piercy reach into his pocket and pull out a pistol. Frederica, still in the bully's grip, continued to resist fiercely, digging in her heels and pulling against Piercy, trying to land the occasional kick. The captain seemed to lose patience and began to wave his pistol about. "Stop fighting and get into the carriage before someone gets shot," he yelled. To Clive's horror, Piercy waved the revolver alternately at Frederica and the little girl with the blonde curls who was still lying on the ground.

As Clive neared Piercy, Frederica lunged towards the arm holding the gun, trying to force his aim away from Lucy. With a frustrated growl, Piercy turned on her. Using his pistol butt, he struck her on the head, then kept hitting her until Clive finally reached him. As Dering propelled himself forward to tackle the former captain, a pistol shot rang out.

* * *

Frederica

The pain in her head required all the attention she could muster. It would not let her think of anything besides the throbbing; it made her feel like her skull had been crushed on one side. Frederica kept her eyes closed, knowing that if she opened them the pain would only get worse. Her head throbbed so violently it caused a sympathy revolt in her stomach. Suddenly, she needed to vomit and struggled to sit up to do so. As she gagged, hands helped her into a sitting position, pushed a basin into position, and held her hair out of her face. When the stomach revolt was over and she lay back down, a cool cloth was placed over her forehead. She knew she had heard the voice before, but it seemed too much effort to remember from where.

"Frederica?"

She moaned in response, keeping her eyes shut, "Oh my head."

"That ass actually *walloped* you good with his pistol. I imagine your head hurts so much because of that. But you are going to be fine. Drink this." An arm went around her shoulders and helped lift her so she could drink the bitter brew.

"What is it?"

"Laudanum. The doctor left it to give to you when you woke up."

"I heard a pistol shot," Frederica whispered, her eyes still closed.

"You did?" the calm voice continued. "Do not worry about it. Everything is fine. Piercy will not be bothering you again. Now you rest. Everything is in hand."

"Clive?"

"Mr. Dering is fine. He has a few bruises. As soon as you are feeling a bit better, I want to hear the whole story. You two have had some adventures."

"Yes, yes, we have," Frederica concurred softly before she went back to sleep.

* * *

The next time she regained consciousness, there were low voices talking in the room.

"You need to rest also. I will sit with her," a gentle female voice she had not heard before said. "There are more rescuers arriving and they will all want to know how she is."

"I will go down and talk to them and then go rest." Frederica recognized the same voice she had heard previously. "I think she should be waking soon. I will send up some broth."

Frederica tried to open her eyes, but they seemed glued shut. Who were these people?

* * *

The third time she surfaced, she managed to open her eyes and study her surroundings. It looked similar to the room she and Clive had stayed in at The Coaches and Horses, but it was bigger and better appointed. There were curtains at the windows, mostly drawn shut, which was good as the light hurt her eyes. A young woman, a lady by her dress, was reading in the chair by her bed. Frederica did not recognize her.

"Ah, you are awake," she said cheerfully. "I am Charlotte Ferguson, a good friend of Marion Donnay. Marion and her husband Nathan are friends of your brother Jeffrey. How are you feeling?"

Frederica struggled to sit up. Miss Ferguson leaned forward to help her, saying, "Are you sure you want to sit up? You took a bad blow to the head." But even as she asked, she helped Frederica settle against the pillows and then offered her a sip of water.

"Laudanum?" she asked.

"No," her nurse answered. "Just water right now. Laudanum is only if the pain gets too bad." Miss Ferguson put her hand to Frederica's forehead. "Good, no fever," she said. "Rest here while I get Marion. She asked me to call her as soon as you woke."

"Wait," Frederica gasped. "How is Clive?"

"Mr. Dering is bruised and battered. I think there are some cracked ribs involved, but he will be fine in a few days." Miss Ferguson clasped Frederica's ankle comfortingly as she left the room on her errand.

Left alone, Frederica could only wonder what circumstances had brought Marion Donnay to her bedside. She knew exactly who Marion was. Frederica had met her once when her brother had brought her to tea to meet Frederica and her father. She understood that Jeffrey had hoped to marry her. But shortly after, their father had died and Jeffrey had never mentioned Marion again. The next thing Frederica heard was that Marion had married Jeffrey's best friend, Nathan Donnay. But why was she here? Did Clive write to Marion? She did not think so; it was not a name Clive had ever mentioned. She doubted he even knew her.

Clive. Yes. Miss Ferguson had assured Frederica he only had some bruises, but she wanted to see him for herself.

She started to swing her legs over the side of the bed, intending to stand up in spite of the fact that the room was starting to spin. There was a brief knock at the door before it swung open.

"No, not yet." Marion herself was crossing the room and putting an arm around Frederica. "Back to bed with you until the doctor says otherwise."

For a tiny woman, either she was strong or Frederica was very weak. The young woman was pushed back into bed, although Marion allowed her to recline instead of forcing her to lay flat.

"I have a tray with some food coming up," Marion explained. "After that, we will see about some visitors."

"Clive," Frederica insisted. "I want to see him for myself."

Marion laughed, a warm, relaxing sound. "The feeling is mutual, for sure. I left him pacing the parlor or the inn or the streets or somewhere. He has been like a caged lion. He feels so responsible for you and wants to see for himself that you have not died. Eat something and I will let him come up for a few minutes."

"I remember a pistol shot," Frederica said. "I have been so afraid he was killed."

A tap at the door signaled the arrival of the food tray. As Marion rose to arrange the dishes on a nearby table, Frederica realized for the first time that Mistress Donnay was obviously with child.

"You are *enceinte*!" she blabbed.

Marion laughed again, not at all offended. "How observant of you. Yes, this little one is expected in a couple of months."

"You should not be waiting on me," Frederica gasped.

"Frederica," Marion said disapprovingly, "I am pregnant, not ill. Spooning some soup into your mouth is not going to hurt me. Now be good and open your mouth. Or," she threatened, "no visit from Mr. Dering."

That threat was all it took for Frederica to be compliant. Marion helped her wash and change her shift and nightgown into cleaner garments belonging to Miss Ferguson. When Frederica was finally settled with her hair braided and a shawl over her shoulders, Clive was let into the room.

He crossed the room in a few strides, while she admired his graceful movements. He stopped by the bed, taking her hands and gazing at her keenly.

"How are you feeling?" he asked anxiously. "He hit you so hard."

"My head hurts," she answered. "But every time I wake up, I feel better."

Marion leaned forward from where she was standing by the other side of the bed and smoothed some of Frederica's hair away from her face.

"The doctor said it may take some time for all the headaches to recede, but he expects you to make a full recovery. He was very clear you were not to be moved for at least a week, if not longer."

"You are going to stay right here until you are totally recovered," Clive said firmly.

"I do not feel like going anywhere right now anyway. But tell me what has happened? I am so confused," Frederica admitted faintly.

Marion chuckled and then said, "I am not surprised. I think we all are." She started towards the door. "I will give Mr. Dering a few minutes to try to catch you up. Do not overtire her; she is far from recovered. Also, don't be alarmed if she falls asleep on you, Mr. Dering. I understand drowsiness is a common side effect." The door closed quietly after her.

Clive, not letting go of one hand, used the other to snag a chair and pull it closer. "I assume sitting on the bed is not good form right now." He paused and gripped her hands tightly. "Oh Frederica, I thought he had killed you. You were stock-still."

"Clive, please start at the beginning and tell me everything. The last I remember is Piercy waving the pistol around and I thought he was going to shoot Lucy."

"I am not sure I can do justice to everything that came next. So much happened at once and I was partially deafened when the pistol went off so close to my ears. I am still not sure how or why Mistress Donnay and Miss Ferguson showed up when they did. They will have to fill you in on their side of the story."

"Just start somewhere, Clive. Please tell me what you know," she pleaded.

Clive bent over their hands until his forehead rested on their fingers. "I killed a man," he whispered.

"Piercy?" she asked. Frederica wiggled her fingers until she got one hand free. She smoothed his hair away from his forehead and then continued to run her fingers through his hair.

"No, that was not me. I was still too far away when the pistol went off. That shot came from the carriage that just arrived."

"Then who *did* you kill?"

"The brute from the shack. The one who kidnapped you. He was here with Piercy."

"Clive," she said softly, "start from when you left me. Just tell me the events as they happened to you." She tried to soothe him by stroking his knuckles with her thumb.

Clive was nodding his head as he struggled to speak. She had never seen him so speechless. Then she realized he was trying to control his emotions and keep from crying. Finally, the dam broke and he gave a great sob. His shoulders heaved as his emotions gained the upper hand. She stroked his head, but that was not enough. For all his swagger, killing a man obviously had upset him deeply, even if it was a man who had kidnapped her and threatened to rape her.

Trying to ignore the pain in her head, she scooted down the bed until she was even with his face. She stretched her arms as far as possible around his shoulders and crooned softly. "Oh Clive," she murmured, "talk to me. Tell me why you are upset. Tell me how I can help."

The past few weeks had affected him as mightily as they had affected her.

"I thought he had killed you," he gasped finally. He pulled a handkerchief from his pocket and sat up to wipe his face. He still would not look at her.

"Clive, look at me," she murmured.

"Oh Frederica, I have upset you, too," he said softly. His thumbs wiped the tears from her cheeks.

"Oh Clive," she choked, "I know I am not very experienced, but even I can tell that the past week—has it been only a week?—has been...hard. Of course you should be upset. How often do people face kidnapping and all the other horrid things that happened to us? Killing a man and shooting the one in the shack, even ones as evil as those monsters…" Words eluded her as Clive pulled her into his arms and buried his face in her neck.

"I almost lost you," he gasped.

"Yes, Piercy almost won," she agreed. "But he did not. And I still do not know how the miracle happened. I stayed where you left me, in the doorway. I stayed as far back as I could after you left. I could hear footsteps and men talking to each other, but I couldn't make out what they were saying. I just knew they were searching for me, but there was nowhere to go. I was in front of a business, not a residence, and it was far too early for anyone to be about." She paused to get her breath. "So it is obvious what happened. They found me and dragged me to the carriage yard at the inn. I saw you with Robert. Now you," she demanded.

He settled at the head of the bed with his back against the headboard. He pulled her closer, until she was tucked up against him with her head on his shoulder.

"Comfortable?" he asked. After she nodded, he continued.

"Robert did not let us down. He was there as soon as I walked into the yard. I cannot remember when I was so glad to see anyone. His grandfather was away when my letter arrived, so he came alone rather than waiting. Then everything seemed to go bad extremely quickly."

"Did you get a chance to talk to him before Piercy arrived?" she asked.

"Not for very long. But he understood the urgency. He was getting the carriage ready while I went for you. Somehow, Piercy saw me and realized you would be in the area. They must have sprinted down the street looking for you and then come back a different route. First I saw of that fiend was when he dragged you into the yard."

"Yes, that was bad," she murmured. "I could see you and Robert but could not get free of Piercy. Then I could see you and Robert fighting those horrid men. Were you hurt?"

"Just some bruises and scraped knuckles, that sort of thing. You should have seen the black eye Robert received. Mostly gone now. He was pretty proud of that shiner." Clive almost seemed back to his old self as he discussed his friend's battle scars. Then he sobered. "Those bullies came with batons that I think had some metal in them. They meant to do real damage."

"Clive," she interrupted. "If they were so well-armed, how did you manage to get the best of them?" She did not want to upset him again by discussing the death of his adversary, but she knew he had been armed only with his fists. He had left his pistol in the saddlebags back in the doorway where she had been hiding.

"When I saw Piercy holding you and trying to force you into the carriage, I sort of lost myself."

Curious as to his meaning, Frederica leaned forward to look at his face. He was still flushed, but she thought the flush was probably a result from his emotional outburst. The color extended to his neck. Then she saw the look in his eyes. Not embarrassment, but rage.

She dredged up a word from a book on the Norsemen she had read once. "Berserker?" she asked in wonder. "How related to the Vikings are you?"

He looked at her in amazement. "You are not appalled? I killed a man with my bare hands!"

She grinned at him. "You got that angry defending me. How can I be upset?" She laid her aching head back on his shoulder. "You love me," she said smugly. "You would never get that angry with me. Tell me the rest," she urged. "I saw little Lucy."

"Yes, wasn't that a surprise? Her father told me later they were waiting for the coach to go back to Cirencester."

"Was she hurt? I saw Piercy shove her and then wave his pistol at her."

"No, just bruised a little. What a brave little girl she is. She barely missed being stepped on by the horses, but her father got her out from under them very quickly. I did not realize it at the time, of course. I was focused on you. But she held up Piercy just enough for help to arrive. When he struck you with the pistol, it felt like everything was happening so slowly. I could not reach you, there were so many people and horses in the way. I have never felt so hopeless…unless it was the night I realized you had been kidnapped."

Frederica reached up and cupped his cheek with her hand. "I was pretty terrified, too." Clive kissed the hand framing his face, then bent to gently kiss her lips.

"You had better hurry up with the story," she said softly. "I am falling asleep again."

"Not a whole lot more to tell," he responded.

"Yes, there is. I have been out of it for some days. You have to fill me in on all my missed time."

"I don't think you will stay awake for long," he chuckled. "I can tell you about the rest of the carriage yard. Piercy knocked you out and then the idiot realized he had to lift you into the carriage. It takes two hands. You can't wave a pistol about while you are lifting an unconscious body. I found that out at the shack when I needed to untie you. Piercy stood there frozen when he realized his bully boys were not going to help him. Robert and a couple of the ostlers had put paid to the other chap. As I said, I was focused on getting to you. The yard was absolute chaos – horses stomping and milling about, fighting and yelling going on, and Piercy and that damn pistol. But that's when Piercy realized he needed to get you into the carriage. I didn't even notice because of all the bedlam that another carriage had pulled in. And here is the amazing part of the story…" He paused. "Are you still awake?"

Frederica stared at him. "Clive, who shot him?"

He kissed her briefly. "I cannot seem to stop doing that. Now, where was I? Right. As soon as this new carriage comes to a halt, the door pops open and someone shoots Piercy in the head!"

"Who?!" she demanded a little more forcefully. How many times did she have to ask him the same question?

"Mistress Donnay!"

Frederica sat up so fast her vision swam. And then the pain struck. "Oh my head," she moaned. Dering immediately helped her lay flat and got a cool cloth for her head. He held it to her forehead and stroked her hair gently.

"Yes, Mistress Donnay! It seems her husband Nathan has been giving her target lessons with pistols."

"But why is she even here?" Frederica asked. "I am so confused."

"And you are going to stay confused. Close your eyes and go to sleep. I have told you enough for now. The rest will wait until tomorrow. Downstairs we have more rescuers than I believed possible."

Chapter Seventeen: Coaches and Horses Inn

T he innkeeper was waiting as Clive and Frederica came down the stairs. "Everyone is in the parlor," he said, gesturing to the closed door and the end of the hall. "There is food and drink, but just give a tug on the bell pull if you need anything else." With a nod, he took himself off to the kitchen.

From where they stood, Frederica and Clive could hear a lively argument.

"I am not sure I want to go in there," she said slowly. "They sound angry."

"I would not worry too much. That discussion has been going on for some time. Actually, I think since they got here, in fact. Come on, you know almost everyone in there." He paused and listened again. "No, wait that is one voice I don't recognize."

He thought Frederica was still too pale, even after several days in bed. She seemed thinner, too, and more somber than he was used to. As he studied her features, he tucked a stray wisp behind an ear. He leaned in and kissed her gently. Yes, the events of the last few weeks had caught up with both of them; the last week had also brought an overabundance of rescuers.

He pulled her hand through his arm and knitted their fingers together.

"Come on. There are people in there who have been waiting quite some time to see you."

The conversation abruptly stopped as all eyes came to rest on the couple.

"I don't know these people!" Frederica gasped as Clive pulled her into the parlor.

Dering had come to know this room well while waiting for Frederica to recover from Piercy's blow. It fronted the street and today, sun was streaming through its windows. That was a good sign, right? There was a large table in the middle of the room and several comfortable chairs were scattered about. True to the landlord's word, a buffet along one wall had been laid out with a selection of platters of food and, he saw with relief, bottles of wine and other more potent beverages. He was pretty sure the discussion this afternoon was going to be a long one.

The occupants formed small conversational groups. Mistress Donnay and her husband Nathan were standing at the table closest to the door. It had been their voices coming through the door. He studied the others to see who Frederica would not know. *Oh, maybe she is right. I have been with these people for the past week. She has been laid up.* Then his eyes landed on a figure who had not been there earlier.

"Father!" he gasped.

An older gentleman, thin like Clive and of the same height, rose from his seat at the table. Gray liberally threaded his hair, which, like Clive's, had been very dark at one time. Young Dering imagined that in thirty years he would look exactly like his sire. At least he would not go to fat as he aged.

Clive did not drop Frederica's hand, but held tightly as he pulled her to meet the elder Mr. Dering. He stretched out his hand to his father, only to be enveloped in a hug. The hug surprised Clive, as his father was not given to public displays of affection, but he returned it with warmth. His father had come to his rescue, albeit a bit late.

"Son," Mr. Dering murmured, "I am so proud of you. By all accounts, you have handled yourself well."

"I am very glad to see you, Father," the younger Dering replied. "It has all been a bit much. How is Mother?"

"Fine, fine, everyone is fine."

Dering finally relaxed and stepped back slightly from his father's embrace. He had returned it with one arm, never releasing Frederica's hand. Finally, he had a chance to pull her forward.

"Father, may I introduce Miss Frederica Chadwick?"

The elder Dering reached out both hands in welcome. "I am pleased to make your acquaintance finally." As Frederica was not releasing Clive's hand any more than he was releasing hers, his father simply took her free hand in both of his and held it tightly. "I cannot tell you how happy I am that this misadventure has had a satisfactory resolution. I have been hearing such good things about you from your friends here," he said earnestly.

Clive looked at him closely to make sure he was serious. He appeared to be deadly serious.

"You had better introduce Miss Chadwick to your friends. I believe she has not met all of them."

"We are no longer strangers," Marion Donnay declared. She was the first to come forward to grasp Frederica's hand. "I think there are only two people here you have not met." Marion slipped her arm around Frederica's waist and turned her to face the rest of the room. Clive did not let go of his betrothed's hand. She who had faced down kidnappers and danger now looked decidedly apprehensive at meeting friendly strangers.

Marion was still talking. "Look. See? You know me and Charlotte Ferguson, of course." Frederica and Charlotte exchanged smiles and bows. "There is Robert, although from the bruises you might not recognize him, and his grandfather, Mr. Padgett." Both men bowed deeply from their place near the window.

Dering studied his friend's face. Yes, he still had a lot of bruises, but the swelling had gone down and the black eye was now yellow. *She must be making a joke to make Frederica more comfortable. That red hair would identify him anywhere.*

"And, of course, you know Mr. Grant," Mistress Donnay was saying.

"Mr. Grant, how glad I am to see you!" Frederica responded warmly. Tommy smiled in return, but as he was across the table, he could not reach her for a hug or even a handshake. His arm was still in a sling, but Clive thought Tommy looked much better than when he had last seen him in Avebury. He had more color and seemed to move with a lot less pain.

Mr. Grant stood and said with obvious pleasure, "I am most happy to see you, Miss Chadwick. I have been quite concerned about your welfare. I should have realized you and my former student would be able to handle yourselves."

Clive felt one of his eyebrows raise in astonishment at Tommy's words. He remembered the sheer terror of the previous weeks. He glanced at Frederica to see her looking at him with eyes filled with mirth.

"Handle ourselves?" she murmured. "Does he have any idea...?"

"The only two you do not know are my gentlemen," Marion was continuing. "This is my father, General Ambrose Coxe, and my husband, Nathan Donnay. My father caught up with Charlotte and me as we were driving from London. My husband arrived later. He is a very good friend of your brother Jeffrey. Well, both of us consider Jeffrey a friend."

The older gentleman was standing near the window, where he had been conversing with Mr. Padgett. At Marion's introduction, he bowed. "It is good to see you up and about. Getting hit with the butt of a pistol is no laughing matter."

"Miss Chadwick," the younger man said, "we have met, although it has been some time. I came with Jeffrey to visit you and your father in Kent, before your father had married again. I doubt if you remember me."

Clive thought that if anyone could be the antithesis of Jeffrey Chadwick, it would be Nathan Donnay. Nathan was shorter than Frederica's brother, dark where Jeffrey was blonde. Clive had seen him box once and knew that although the man was thin, solid muscle lay under his coat. Jeffrey's manners were those of a perfect gentleman. Donnay, on the other hand, seemed less cultured. His conduct in public was without fault, but there was an air of menace about him. When he looked at you with those cold gray eyes, Dering thought, one did well to observe one's manners.

"I am sorry I do not remember you, but I do remember your name. Jeffrey has spoken of you often. I am pleased to meet all of you," Frederica was saying.

Then she turned to him. "But Clive, I am still very confused. Why are all these people here and where is Uncle Festus?" She gazed at him with questioning eyes. "Surely you only wrote to Robert and your father?"

Clive's father intervened, "Let us all sit and avail ourselves of the refreshments the landlord has laid out. Then I suggest we chronologically tell our stories. That way, everyone will have the same information and we can fill Miss Chadwick in on what she has missed."

Everyone agreed that this seemed like a good way to proceed. For the next few minutes, the room bustled with people filling plates, pouring drinks, and finding seats. Clive tucked Frederica next to Mr. Grant at the table and went off to fill a plate for her. "Do not worry, Tommy," he called over his shoulder, "I will get some food for you, too."

When Clive returned with two plates of bread and sliced meat, he overheard Mr. Grant saying to Frederica, "I see you received your trunk from Avebury. Isn't that the dress Clive redesigned for you in Wolverton?"

"Yes, it is," she answered. "I am so glad the trunk arrived. I have presumed on Mistress Donnay's charity too much."

Voices quieted as wine and tea were poured. Dering took this as his cue.

"Yesterday, as I said to most of you, I had the chance to fill Miss Chadwick in on what happened in the carriage yard, at least from my perspective. I took her up to the moment that Mistress Donnay shot Piercy. I did not get a chance to share with her any of your stories, other than Robert's ride to Gloucester. I thought it best if you all were able to tell your own tales." He saw heads nodding around the table. "Who shall we start with?"

"Before you start, I want to know," Frederica's voice was not as strong as usual, but it was clear she was determined, "where is Uncle Festus and why is he not here?"

"I can start the tale-telling and answer your question in one," Mr. Grant offered. After various comments of "of course" and "go ahead," he continued.

"Dr. Chadwick will eventually be fine. However, he did sustain another severe head wound. Honestly, at times we feared for his life. However, he seems to have taken a turn for the better. He is still at the inn in Avebury under the care of the landlord's sister. The doctor did not want him moved for several weeks. Festus gave me a hard time when he realized I was coming here. I had to promise to write him immediately and often to fill him in. He was especially concerned about your well-being. Since I arrived, I have already written him several letters because, of course when I left Avebury, we had no idea what had happened to you both. I have some other things I need to contribute."

The scholar poured himself more tea and refilled Frederica's before continuing. "Before Jeffrey left for Dublin, he took me aside and instructed me to write Nathan Donnay in Chelsea if we had any problems. Jeffrey felt badly about leaving us in the lurch at the last minute, and as he had asked Festus to take Frederica, he wanted to make sure there would be help available if anything happened. I do not understand why he thought there might be problems, but there it is.

"Early on in the trip, after the carriage crash in Dorset, I wrote to Mr. Donnay. I was not convinced that the crash had been an accident, but with a broken arm, there was little I could do. I thought I would at least warn them that something seemed off. After Avebury, I sent a plea for assistance by special messenger to London. As both Mistress and Mr. Donnay are here, I see my letter got through. Now, Clive, if you would be so good, I would like a bit of that brandy."

Nathan stood and retrieved the brandy bottle from the sideboard. As he refilled glasses, he said "I think, my love, that this is our cue to add our bits. I do not have much to say, as I was on an assignment at the time." Nathan was deliberately vague about his whereabouts. He had not been in Dublin, but rather in France. There, his mission was to find Jeffrey Chadwick, who had disappeared in France while searching for the kidnapped daughter of an Irish politician. Nathan had retained faith that Jeffrey would pop up eventually, but Marion was less sanguine. Neither wanted to add to Frederica's woes at this point by revealing that her brother was overdue from his mission.

"Nathan, would you ask the landlord for some lemonade for me? I have had enough tea, but I would like something cool to drink."

Donnay grinned at Clive. "That is how a lady gets you out of the room when she is going to talk about events in a way that will get you riled up." He dropped a quick kiss on his wife's cheek as he left the room.

"Nathan is still irritated with me," Marion said smugly, "but Mr. Grant's letter was no laughing matter. The situation was very worrying. He explained that Clive and Frederica were in Gloucester and some stranger was going around looking for his runaway 'daughter.' Also, that they were out of funds and practically on the streets." She leaned over and squeezed Frederica's hand. "As disturbing as it was to us, I cannot imagine what it was like for you two. I knew immediately that with Nathan away, I had to do something."

"You know, Marion, doing something did not necessarily mean jumping into a carriage and dashing off to Gloucester. Especially in your condition." General Coxe sounded peeved at his daughter. "I certainly could have come alone."

"I am sure you could have, Father," Marion replied, "but we are talking about a gently reared girl alone with Clive on the streets with that villain searching for them. As Piercy managed to give her a nice concussion, it was a good thing Charlotte and I were along to take care of her."

Donnay, returning with his wife's lemonade, heard the last part of her statement. He set the glass in front of Marion, then put his hand on her shoulder. "I think you have to admit, Marion, you miss adventure. You did not give your actions serious thought; you just jumped into the carriage and dragged Charlotte along. I count it a good thing the general caught up with you along the way."

Clive had listened to this argument in various forms over the past few days. This time, though, it seemed Mistress Donnay was not going to listen quietly to the men in her life. He could see the flush start at her neck and rise up to her cheeks. She put her hand over her husband's.

"Jeffrey is my friend too, Nathan. When the letter came, you were off and Father was tied up in the Home Office. Who else was I supposed to send? Was I supposed to write Mr. Grant and say, 'Sorry, but we are too busy to try to find a young couple that have gone missing and might be in trouble?'" she snapped. "You both are treating me like I am an invalid. I am only pregnant. Enough of this. Someone had to help and I was there to be that someone."

"Well, did you have to have a loaded pistol in the carriage?" the general demanded. "It could have gone off at any time and killed someone."

"I did not load it until we were close to Gloucester," his daughter retorted, "and it is a good thing I did. When we got to the yard, Piercy was already trying to drag Frederica into his carriage."

Frederica, still holding Marion's hand, had been following the argument closely. Then she interrupted, "Thank you, Mistress Donnay, for coming as quickly as you did. Thank you, Miss Ferguson, for coming with her. From what I remember of the scene in the carriage yard, Piercy might very well have ridden off with me. I think his pistol was still loaded. He could have killed Clive or little Lucy." The young artist took a deep breath while everyone waited to see if she would go on. She had been quiet until then. Clive thought she might find the company overwhelming. He loved that she was standing up to Donnay, who rather intimidated him.

"Mr. Dering told me it was you who made the shot that killed Piercy."

"Yes, it was me."

"That was an amazing shot."

"Nathan has been giving me lessons."

Clive decided he, too, wanted to praise Mistress Donnay's actions. "It was not just an amazing shot, mistress, it was astounding. Your carriage had not even come to a stop. Without your pistol, I fear Piercy would indeed have taken Frederica off to who knows what end. I simply could not have reached her in time. I am deeply grateful to you," he said with a little bow. He decided to give the company another thing to think about. "Miss Chadwick has agreed to become my wife and the thought of her in that bastard's hands makes me physically ill."

Frederica's head jerked back to him in surprise. "I thought we were going to wait," she murmured.

Clive shrugged. He raised her knuckles and kissed them while the conversation swirled around them. He glanced at his father who, to his surprise, was standing. The elder Dering moved rapidly around the table and grabbed Clive's hand.

"Congratulations, son," he said, much to Clive's astonishment. "I think you are a lucky man." He turned to Frederica and gathered her into his arms. "Welcome to the family," he said warmly.

The other occupants of the room surrounded the happy couple to offer their felicitations. Finally, Clive got everyone's attention long enough to say, "I have not, obviously, had a chance to ask Jeffrey for Frederica's hand, but I will as soon as I can. Father, should I speak to her step-mother?"

"Ah, that is a question I can answer," his father said. "However, it is a bit complicated, so everyone please sit. I will offer information that I think you all need to hear." With that tantalizing statement, he filled his glass with wine and then offered the bottle around.

Following his father's directions, Clive helped his betrothed to her seat and asked if she wanted anything more to eat or drink. Frederica assured him she was fine. Everyone waited to hear what the older Dering would say.

"I found my letter from Clive at my London club the same day Mistress Donnay received theirs. Clive did mention that he was also writing Mr. Grant in Avebury and Nathan Donnay in Chelsea. After I read his message, and I admit had a glass of brandy while I mulled over the situation, I decided to contact the Donnays. I ascertained their address in Chelsea and went there as quickly as possible. Mistress Donnay welcomed me warmly, even as she was packing and planning to set off immediately. I must say, General Coxe, your daughter has excellent organizational skills. She was managing household questions, packing for an unexpected trip, and holding a conversation with me. It was an impressive performance. Our talk was quite enlightening. I had never met Miss Chadwick, but Mistress Donnay had. She had a lot of good things to say about my future daughter-in-law, but little good to say about the step-mother. Up to now, there has been no evidence of collusion between Piercy and anyone else. But, Mistress Donnay was very sure that Piercy and Miss Chadwick's step-mother were acquainted. It seemed one of us should head to Kent to see what she knew about Piercy and his activities."

"How could you be so sure Piercy and Hermione were connected?" Frederica asked.

Marion's brow furrowed as she mulled over her response. "First, and foremost, was the fact Jeffrey was wary enough to warn Mr. Grant to contact Nathan about any trouble. He must have felt anxiety about Frederica's situation. Also, he had made arrangements with me for Frederica to live with us during her season. I personally have seen Hermione in action, surrounding herself with young men and spending lavishly. It just seemed obvious, that any trouble probably started with her."

The men around the table looked at her with bemused expressions. Finally her husband spoke, "You sent Mr. Dering to Kent on what is essentially a gut feeling?"

"Mistress Donnay made a simple case here," Clive's father responded. "We talked about the step-mother's possible involvement in some detail and she convinced me that of her thinking. Mistress Donnay also mentioned that General Coxe would be accompanying his daughter and Miss Ferguson, so I volunteered to head south."

"How did you know I would be joining you?" General Coxe interrupted the older Dering to ask his daughter.

Marion just returned a serene smile. "I know you."

Dering continued, "I arrived at the Chadwick estate and I was certainly surprised by my reception. Mistress Chadwick had me shown right in and started demanding information even before I introduced myself. She was in quite a state of dishabille and was pacing the floor. For some reason, she just assumed I was a messenger from this Piercy and had information about the whole affair. Honestly, I was just gob-smacked as I stood there while she spewed out the whole sordid tale."

"What tale, Father? Did she know anything?"

"I should say she did!" his father declaimed. "Unbelievably, she planned it."

The room broke out in an uproar. "The devil she did," "That witch," and various other comments flew about. Finally, Mr. Padgett's voice rose above the tumult. "Mr. Dering, what did she hope to gain by having her paramour marry Miss Chadwick?" he demanded.

"I am sorry to say marriage was never part of the scheme."

"But Father," Clive asked, "why else was Piercy trying to kidnap Frederica? Oh…" Dering turned to look at the woman he loved with dismay. "It was even worse than we imagined."

"What could be worse?" she wondered. Then the truth hit her. "She was trying to have me killed?" Her voice cracked over the final word and tears welled up in her eyes. "What did I ever do to her?"

Clive was in deep trouble if, for the rest of his life, he was going to fight dragons every time she cried. Thankfully, judging by the past few weeks, it did not seem she cried often. Ignoring the interested audience, Dering tried to comfort his fiancé by putting his arms around her and drawing her into an embrace. "Nothing, of course. You did nothing," he said softly. "It must have been your father's will. She simply wanted your money."

A feminine hand dangled a handkerchief in front of him. Miss Ferguson proved to belong to the hand. He smiled gratefully and helped Frederica mop her face. When she was composed, they sat down and faced the table. He noticed that Miss Ferguson had moved to a chair next to the general, who reached out and clasped her hand. Mistress Donnay also noticed the gesture. She leaned over to squeeze her friend's other hand and smiled.

Dering Senior cleared his throat. "Clive is absolutely right; this has all been about money. Mistress Hermione Chadwick was attracted to Piercy. She is a handsome woman, has a reasonable income, and your father was generous, too. His will does not take away her income if she remarries. But evidently, Piercy wanted more. He has – had – a bad gambling habit. She was not very clear whose idea it was originally to do away with Miss Chadwick, but they both agreed on the plan. He was to marry Miss Chadwick and then murder my future daughter-in-law. All the rock throwing and carriage accident was to separate her from her travel companions. They figured that if Piercy kidnapped Miss Chadwick away from Kent, it would be less likely that suspicion would fall on Hermione. The fact that everyone except the driver walked away from the carriage accident threw their plans into a tizzy. The next attempt on the Tor was really just a chance opportunity. After that, Piercy hired real thugs and gave up trying to make it look like an accident. But they were still amateurs. Clive was the loose cannon in the mix. They had not counted on a young, competent man being part of the company." Dering Senior toasted his son.

"If Clive had not been along, things might have turned out differently," Grant agreed.

"So, it was a good thing I got sent down from Oxford?" Clive asked impishly.

"Do not go there, son," his father returned sternly. "Let us just put that episode aside and not discuss it again."

"Agreed!" Clive raised his glass to his father in return.

"Mr. Dering," Nathan Donnay spoke up thoughtfully, "I think there is more to your story. Is the step-mother still in Kent?" At this point, no one but Dering Senior seemed to want to call her by name.

"No, not actually," the elder Dering's pitch got deeper. Clive recognized it as the voice his father used when he was extremely angry. "By the time I identified myself, she had said too much to pass as an innocent in this sordid mess. When she realized who I was, she tried fainting. She is not a good actress. I let her fall to the floor while I sent the footman for a magistrate."

"You had her arrested?" Frederica gasped.

"No; irritatingly, the damn man was not available. I sat myself down to the writing table and wrote a confession for her. I made her sign it. Then I told her to run to the continent, Italy or Malta, as France is not open. I let her take her clothes and nothing else. The footman could not be bribed to take her to Dover, but the stableman said he would be glad to see the back of her. He will return with the horses. The butler will send word. Your step-mother has no friends among the staff and when they heard what she had countenanced, they almost hanged her themselves. Whether your brother continues her allowance is up to him. You may find the house is missing a few trinkets, but I thought the faster she left the country and the less gossip, the better, as long as she is away from you. It was a calculated risk, as I did not know what was happening with her. But I thought it prudent to separate her from Piercy and get her out of your sphere."

"It will be some time before she knows Piercy will not be joining her," Donnay observed dryly.

"Where does that leave us?" Marion asked the room in general.

Before anyone could answer, Frederica asked, "Speaking of magistrates, did anyone show any interest in the carriage yard fight, especially in two dead men?"

Robert's grandfather laughed out loud at the question. "Oh they tried, Miss Chadwick," he crowed. "Oh they tried. I got here later in the day of the 'carriage yard brawl,' as it is being called in the taproom. Piercy and his thug were laid out in the barn. Everywhere else, were people milling about. Participants like Robert and Clive and the last thug that couldn't talk because Robert broke his jaw, as well as observers like the Quaker gentleman and his young daughter. All sorts who had seen the fight and a lot who wished they had seen it, as well as the two magistrates in here asking questions."

"The only question they kept coming back to was, 'Who really shot Piercy?'" Charlotte Ferguson was just as amused as Mr. Padgett. "I had to sit here for a couple of hours trying to keep Marion calm as they went on and on. They just could not believe a woman had killed him. Ambrose had to go through the same grilling." She patted the general on his knee with an air of familiarity...or was it possessiveness? Clive was not sure, but he thought the general looked quite comfortable with it. "I thought Marion would start yelling at them, she was so mad."

"They thought I wanted to take the credit away from my father," Marion huffed. "It got to be very tedious very quickly. I am sorry, Frederica, that you were hurt so badly, but it saved me from listening to them as I insisted on nursing you. They never once said anything about arrest; they just wouldn't believe I was the one holding the gun."

"The loaded gun that *you* brought into a carriage," Nathan pointed out.

"Stop!" she exclaimed. "We are putting that away with Oxford exploits and not talking about it again." She leaned forward and kissed him before he could say anything else.

Clive leaned forward to address Nathan. "Mr. Donnay?" he asked.

"Nathan – please call me Nathan."

"How do I get hold of Jeffrey? I have urgent business with him."

"Isn't he in Dublin?" Frederica asked curiously.

"I seem to remember getting a note that he was going on an assignment. I expect he will return anytime now. Why don't you write him a letter and I will see it gets into the next diplomatic pouch to Dublin? That way, you can take Miss Chadwick to Ripon to meet your family and not have to chase all over looking for him."

"I would like to add a note if I may," the elder Dering said. "I want Mr. Chadwick to know that his sister is more than welcome to our family."

After that, everyone started to drift away, some to leave Gloucester altogether. Robert and his grandfather were off to Bath. "My sister will do me bodily harm if I don't get back and tell her what has happened."

After saying goodbye to the Padgetts and assuring the others they would be back for dinner, Clive and Frederica strolled off to see the cathedral in daylight.

"Are you sure you feel up to this?"

"It is only a couple of streets, and it feels so good to be outside instead of cooped up indoors. We can pay our respects to whomever is in the tomb we hid behind the other night. And," she said smiling at him, "I have you to lean on if I get tired."

They sat in the cathedral for some time, enjoying the peace and each other. Finally, they lighted candles by the knight's tomb and strolled by the Lady Chapel and the cloisters where they admired the delicate stonework.

Arms locked together, they made their way back to the inn. "Where are we going now?" she asked.

"Right now, we are headed back to the inn so you can rest before dinner."

Frederica gave him a slight push in exaggeration. "No, silly, I mean when we leave the Inn."

"We have two options," he replied, kissing her wrist. "We can go straight to Ripon to meet my mama or we can go to Avebury to see Dr. Chadwick and then on to Ripon. After you meet my mother, we can have the banns called and get married."

"I like your plan. Unlike some of your others, it is simple and seemingly straightforward."

"I am sensing a problem," he replied. "What is it?"

"You do know, I only have the dress I am standing in?"

Clive laughed out loud, startling a number of passersby as he grabbed Frederica by the waist and swung her around. Several matrons were scandalized when he finally pulled her close and kissed her decisively.

Epilogue:

Ripon Cathedral: Boxing Day

Ripon Cathedral was smaller than the one in Gloucester, but in Clive's opinion, no less beautiful. Maybe it was its manageable size that he found more pleasing. As he and Robert waited in the front row of the sanctuary, he could not help but admire the greenery and candles used by his sisters to decorate the altar. This time of year, few flowers were available and he had been informed that whatever could be found would be in Frederica's bouquet.

He certainly could not have imagined this time last year, he would be happy, even eager, to tie the knot. Frederica was late. That was unlike her and it was enough to make him very nervous. He sat back and tried to relax. He knew she would not change her mind. Would she? He had proposed after only knowing her a week.

But what a week it had been. Their ill-fated trip through the southwest had only been the beginning. Once Frederica had fully recovered they had traveled to Ripon to meet his female relatives. They had taken her under their wings and collectively bought her a new and much more attractive wardrobe. Frederica had blossomed under the attention. She went from pretty to striking. Clive was certain that in the coming years she would be one of the most beautiful women in Yorkshire. His mother had also found her future daughter-in-law, an art teacher. Frederica's nascent talent was blossoming.

Clive was still surprised by the enthusiasm that his family showed toward him and his unexpected betrothed. His father had been especially welcoming. There was no further mention of Oxford. Instead the elder Dering had begun to include Clive in the management of his properties and encouraged him to visit various farms and estates to study new husbandry methods. Dering found he liked the challenge of solving the real, every-day problems facing the farming community in a way that academic studies at Oxford had never appealed to him.

Yet his father's change of attitude perplexed him. One day, Clive had approached his mother about it, as she sat at her dressing table.

"Ah, yes dear. Your father is sometimes very stubborn," she said in that calm voice she always used. "In your case, I think he knew he had overreacted but did not know how to make peace." She took his hand and patted it even as she smiled at him. "You do know, you are very like him. No, do not talk." Clive's mouth had hung open as he started to protest this slander. "You will not admit it, but you will recognize the similarities when you are older. Especially when you have your own sons. However, that does not answer your question. I believe several things happened.

"I talked to him and pointed out that he was driving you away, always being critical but not giving you any authority or training. That on its own might not have changed his mind, but how you conducted yourself on this whole misadventure with Frederica, impressed him. Also, while he was in Gloucester, he had some long chats with General Coxe and Mr. Padgett about raising sons.

"They both have quite successful sons, in the diplomatic service, I believe. Honestly, I thought only women gossiped about their children, but I am proved wrong. Your father came back from Gloucester with some new thoughts and thankfully a different attitude." She smiled at him warmly. "I was a bit perplexed also. It is good to know he can still surprise me after all these years."

Clive thought about what she said. "I am still a bit confused about why you both are willing for us to marry by the end of the year. I actually thought you would argue we are too young."

"I do think you are young, but your father was only a year or two older when we married. You are not the same boy who got sent down from university. Frederica could use some stability in her life and there just doesn't seem to be a good reason to force you to wait. I am quite fond of her, Clive. I believe she will make you a good wife."

Unfortunately, although everyone was in agreement that Clive and Frederica should marry, they had to wait until the Christmas season, the earliest her brother could get away from his duties to travel to Ripon to give her away.

Even though she had spent only three nights in his bed, Clive missed her presence. Very much.

Finally, Captain Jeffrey Chadwick, retired, arrived with his new wife and his Irish assistant. Dering did not get his name. Frederica was transcendent with happiness until she found out that after her wedding, the three would be travelling to Boston where they hoped to settle. That news was met with dismay and tears.

And yet, both he and Frederica could understand the motivation for what seemed like a drastic move. It was common knowledge in Dublin that Jeffrey's new wife, Georgina, had been kidnapped, held for several weeks, and spirited away to France by dubious characters. Even though she was now married to the very respectable Captain, her reputation was in tatters and she was not accepted into polite society. Rather than face the ostracism, they determined to make a new start in a new country.

"What about your position in the government here?" Frederica had asked.

"It is possible I can still have some duties if I want them," Chadwick explained. "It depends on what kind of work I find there." He interlaced his fingers with Georgina's. "Say, Frederica, did you know we have relatives on the other side of the ocean? I am certainly going to look them up."

* * *

Robert's elbow cut into his musings.

He and Dering both stood and faced the rear of the church waiting for Frederica to appear. The congregation lining both sides of the Presbytery stood. Dering was surprised to see how full it was. So many guests had arrived while he had been lost in thought.

And then, suddenly, there she was. Standing in the opening leading to the high altar, with Captain Chadwick at her side. When her eyes found his, she broke into a smile that lit up the cathedral. The blue of her dress emphasized her delicate coloring, her blonde hair bound in a bun on top of her head with lots of loose curls. He would enjoy pulling the pins out and brushing her hair for her.

There were a lot of things he just knew, he was going to enjoy.

Mary Ann Trail is an author, traveler, mother and lover of history. She is a lifelong resident of southern New Jersey, where she spent most of her professional life as a college librarian. She loves living equidistant from the Philadelphia and Newark International airports—both jumping off points for travel that allows her to explore, first hand, the settings for her stories. Frequent trips to England with her sister fanned her interest in English history as they strolled through Bath, followed Roman roads in Wales, and wandered prehistoric mounds in Dorset.

The early nineteenth century (1800 – 1815) remains her favorite era because of its similarities to today, especially comparisons in the social and political arenas.

She is currently researching and writing her next novel which will take Jeffrey and Georgina Chadwick to the New World. With their friend Patrick Cavanaugh to face the physical hardships of the Americas well as danger from unknown enemies.

She can be reached through her webpage Maryanntrail.com or her Facebook page, Mary Ann Trail, Writer.

* * *

Dear Reader

If you enjoyed reading *Facing Enemies* and spending some time in 1803, I hope you will spend a moment and leave a review on Amazon. Even a few sentences would be much appreciated. Review here: *Facing Enemies.*

As an author, I can only improve with your feedback. Reviews also have a major impact on how books are sold. They affect the way books are displayed on Amazon. They affect readers' choices, as some 85% of us read the reviews before making a purchase on Amazon. I know I do. Other sites—places like the Fussy Librarian and Bookbub—require a certain number of reviews before an author is even allowed to advertise.

Your willingness to write a review can make a huge difference.

I can be reached through my webpage Maryanntrail.com or at my Facebook page, Mary Ann Trail, Writer.

Thank you,
Mary Ann

What to read next?

The Enemies Collection

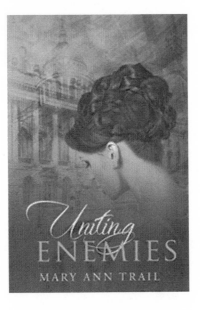

A determined woman. An angry man. London is dangerous but so is love.

England, 1801, as negotiations for the unification of England and Ireland grow heated, Marion Coxe and her family are the focus of a militant anti-unification group.

Fleeing to her father's home in London, she soon finds her heart in peril: caught between a fresh, new love and her old. With her soul pulled in two directions, a terrorist attack could destroy both her life and her love.

Will fighting for a happier future put her entire family in grave danger?

Each title in the Enemies series can be read as a standalone but *Uniting Enemies* is the first chronologically.

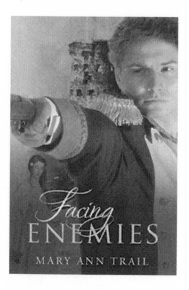

A first-time spy. An abducted gentlewoman. Can he pull off a daring rescue right under Napoleon's nose?

Dublin, 1803. Soldier-turned-translator Jeffrey Chadwick is behind a desk by his own request. But the expert linguist must become a field agent when he's ordered to retrieve a high-ranking local official's kidnapped daughter. With the clues taking him beyond the English Channel, Chadwick quickly finds himself in dangerously hostile territory…

Disguising himself as an American wine merchant, the inexperienced operative follows the kidnapper's trail across France. But when he discovers Napoleon's men assembling a vast army on the shores, he's duty-bound to warn his unsuspecting homeland of the impending invasion.

Can the reluctant agent track down the lady and prevent a military massacre?

Each title in the Enemies series can be read as a stand-alone novel. Facing Enemies is chronologically the second book in the suspenseful historical fiction series. If you like authentic settings, pivotal real events, and a dash of romance, then you'll love Mary Ann Trail's enthralling story.

Made in the USA
Middletown, DE
11 February 2023

24561375R00154